The Devil's Bastard

A Novel

Charlsie Russell

Loblolly Writer's House
Gulfport, Mississippi

Loblolly Writer's House
P.O. Box 7438
Gulfport, MS 39506-7438
Visit our website at www.loblollywritershouse.com

First Edition: September 2006

This book is a work of fiction. Names, characters, and incidents are products of the
author's imagination. Any resemblance to actual events or persons is coincidental.
Any scenes depicting actual historical persons are fictitious.

Library of Congress Catalogue Number: 2005904850
Russell, Charlsie.
    The devil's bastard: a novel

ISBN 0-9769824-0-4
     978-0-9769824-0-1
    1. Gothic – Fiction

Book design by Lucretia Gibson
Copy editor, Nancy McDowell

Printed and bound in the United States of America.

For my poor neglected family

Family Tree

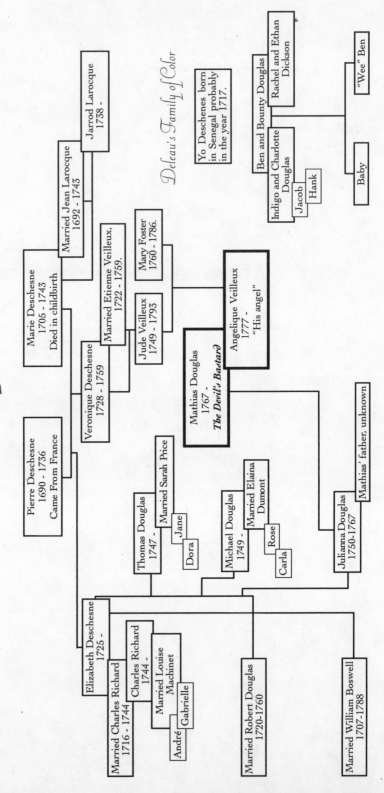

Pierre Deschesne
1690 - 1736
Came From France

Marie Deschesne
1705 - 1743
Died in childbirth

Married Jean Larocque
1692 - 1743

Jarrod Larocque
1738 -

Veronique Deschesne
1728 - 1759

Married Etienne Veilleux,
1722 - 1759.

Jude Veilleux
1749 - 1793

Mary Foster
1760 - 1786.

Angelique Veilleux
1777 -
"His angel"

Mathias Douglas
1767 -
The Devil's Bastard

Elizabeth Deschesne
1725 -

Married Charles Richard
1716 - 1744

Charles Richard
1744 -

Married Louise Machinet

André   Gabrielle

Married Robert Douglas
1720-1760

Married William Boswell
1707-1788

Thomas Douglas
1747 -

Married Sarah Price

Jane

Dora

Michael Douglas
1749 -

Married Elaina Dumont

Rose

Carla

Julianna Douglas
1750-1767

Mathias' father, unknown

Deleau's Family of Color

Yo Deschenes born
in Senegal probably
in the year 1717.

Ben and Bounty Douglas

Indigo and Charlotte
Douglas

Jacob

Hank

Rachel and Ethan
Dickson

Baby

"Wee" Ben

Historical Note

In 1716, Jean-Baptiste Le Moyne de Bienville, lieutenant governor of French Louisiana, induced the Natchez Indians to build a fort for him on the bluffs overlooking the Mississippi River. Bienville called the bastion Fort Rosalie. Today it is the site of Natchez, Mississippi.

French presence in the heart of the Natchez Nation secured for France a lucrative fur trade in the lower Mississippi Valley. During the 1720s, however, French interest in the area shifted from pelts to planting tobacco in the area's rich silt loam soil. The Natchez resented the increasing encroachment onto their land, and in 1729, tensions erupted into open warfare. Under truce, the Natchez gained access to Fort Rosalie, then slaughtered its inhabitants.

France's military response from its provincial capital in New Orleans proved a deathblow to the Natchez. By 1731, what remained of the Natchez Nation had been absorbed into other local tribes. Though the French had avenged the slaughter of Fort Rosalie and established tentative control over the region, colonization in and around the fort had ended. For the purpose of my story, the Deschesnes survived the slaughter and held on to their small farm. In reality, the existence of isolated farms in the decades following the massacre of Rosalie would have been rare. Still, the presence of French colonists in the area, living off the land and trading extensively with the Indians, is not outside the realm of possibility.

Between 1730 and 1763, Indian wars marred life in French Louisiana. These conflicts, driven by the interests of European powers in the New World, ultimately boiled down to one between France and her Choctaw Indian allies and Britain, aligned with the Chickasaw. The conflict was an extension of what in 1756 exploded into the French and Indian War. When the smoke settled, in 1763, Britain possessed all France's New World colonies east of the Mississippi (except New Orleans). Spain had everything else, including New Orleans.

Schoolbooks give the period of British dominion over the Old Southwest little more than a footnote. Though educators might ignore the period, historical scholars do not. This period played a key role in making the South southern.

As she had with her Atlantic seaboard colonies, Great Britain planned for the newly acquired "British West Florida" not only to produce, but also to thrive. That meant successfully dealing with the Indian problem and the increase of slaves in the region. Like the British system of indentured service, slavery in the South (and this is true even during the French era) was a means of increasing laborers for settlement and for safety in the face of Indian attack. Farmers and their slaves, freemen and those of mixed blood, as well as Indians, lived and worked, fought and died side by side.

The brief British period between 1763 and 1783 remained rife with Indian wars and short-lived treaties. Land speculation, the result of massive land grants awarded by the crown to encourage settlement, ran rampant. A significant timber and naval stores trade existed between British West Florida and the West Indies. Additionally, legal and illegal trade thrived between British merchants and their counterparts living inside Spanish territory to the west. Although Spanish military might cast its shadow over British West Florida, Spain's Louisiana subjects were not Spaniards. The occupants of New Orleans were primarily French, with a fair smattering of British merchants who moved into New Orleans after 1763 to gain access to Spanish and other European markets.

Outnumbering the wealthy merchants and land speculators were frontiersmen, vagabonds, displaced (and disgraced) soldiers, cutthroats, thieves, gamblers, and whores. More significantly, hardworking men and women came and carved out a place to raise their children. On the brink of the American Revolution, British West Florida teemed with British subjects whose interests tied them to Great Britain. With the outbreak of war in 1776, more Tories poured into the region. These people were openly hostile to the American cause, which at worst had disenfranchised them and at best drained British military assets from the region. To the west, Spanish governors wined and dined American traitors and marauders.

In the autumn of 1779, Spanish forces under the military governor, Bernardo de Galvez, moved north into British Manchac and Baton Rouge. Natchez fell to Galvez on October 5, 1779, and Mobile in March 1780. The British territorial capital at Pensacola fell a year later. By separate treaties establishing peace in 1783, Britain ceded the Natchez District to both the United States and Spain. Britain also granted the Americans full navigation of the Mississippi River. This proviso, missing from the Anglo-Spanish treaty, was significant in that Spain controlled the river and, as a matter of policy, intended to deny Americans use of it.

Neither Spain nor the United States were aware of the discrepancies in the treaties when they signed them. Britain's joke on her enemies created headaches for both Washington and Madrid and resulted in a period of Spanish-American intrigue that makes rich story fodder to this day.

With the fall of Natchez to Spain, a number of influential Britons left the area. Some eventually returned. Many less prominent Britons, however, stayed to see what life under the Spanish Dons would bring.

Galvez brought Natchez under the governorship of Spanish Louisiana in New Orleans. Several years later, the Natchez District became its own government, headed by the brilliant and personable Manuel Gayoso de Lemos. Galvez' conquest had ushered in a fifteen-year period that was truly a golden age, long before the cotton kingdom made Natchez a household name. The Spanish ruled their British subjects with a patient hand, and, to tell the truth, the British Tories gave them little concern. The immigrants Spain invited in from the American frontier proved a greater menace.

For Madrid, the Natchez District represented a buffer protecting its more valuable New World holdings in Mexico and California. Spain encouraged disgruntled Americans to move into the Natchez District and swear allegiance to Spain. Many Americans today are unaware of the growing pains the young United States suffered at its beginning. Observers, beyond its borders and within, speculated the infant nation would not survive, and Spain gambled heavily on its inevitable demise.

In defiance of their own central government, Americans on the frontier itched to expand westward. Claims made by eastern states on the newly acquired federal lands west to the Mississippi exacerbated Washington's problems. Additionally, Spain, as I suspect the British knew she would, closed the Mississippi River to American commerce. Angry farmers in Kentucky and Ohio, having lost the lucrative markets along the Mississippi to its mouth, demanded war with Spain.

In the end, Spain's gamble failed. Under threat of war, but mostly, I think, tired of dealing with the problem, Spain quietly relinquished Natchez to the United States in 1798.

It is in the midst of Spanish hegemony over Natchez that my main story opens; however, the tale actually begins with the French Dominion in the early eighteenth century. But *The Devil's Bastard* is less a historical novel than it is a romance set in a historical period—a sensual love story woven within a family saga—and a dark mystery. A Southern Gothic, if you will.

Enjoy!

Prologue

Sweet Jesus, her wrists burned. Struggling for support, Julianna ground her toes into the prickly carpet of cypress needles and wrapped weak fingers around the hemp rope eating her skin like acid. Relief, if only for a moment, from the agony gnawing her hands. A high-pitched whine buzzed in her ear. She groaned, then twitched helplessly, unable to slap away the vermin stinging her neck. The mosquito stayed to feed as its kind had fed on her periodically for weeks, feasting on her as he feasted on her, cruel and bloodthirsty, unlike the gentle nourishing of her lover. Sweat dripped into her eyes. She closed them and waited.

A sickening stench overwhelmed the now familiar scent of swamp rot, and with it, a feverish shudder wracked her body. Damn his dark soul, he'd come up behind her. She squeezed her eyes tighter and braced.

Behind her closed lids, pain exploded into light, and she opened her eyes. Stifling a hiss, she brought her throbbing foot against her good leg, and enduring the pain searing the bloody wrists over her head, she fought to retain her precarious balance on one twisted toe. For sure, his well-placed kick had shattered her ankle this time. He tapped the back of the leg supporting her, and she fell against the ropes. Wrists on fire, she sought her footing, biting the insides of her mouth all the while to throttle the scream surging up her throat. He liked her to show pain, and she fought with all her remaining strength to deny him that pleasure.

He yanked her back against him. Immediately his arms imprisoned her, pressing her naked buttocks against his hardness. Brutal fingers found her breasts, and he pinched them, using his sharp nails to cut her flesh. She

1

loathed any form of surrender to this foul thing, but despite the bitterness filling her throat, she begged him to stop.

He did not.

With a start, she blinked, then licked at the sweat beading above her upper lip. Salty. At the small of her back, a dull cramp tugged at her. Terror constricted her chest as a new pain, different, gripped her tortured body, stretching and stiffening her taut belly before climaxing deep inside her pelvis. Writhing violently, she cursed the devil inside her and strained to push him out. She failed, and the spasm exploded between her legs, ripping her....

This time, the scream escaped her lips.

Elizabeth Douglas's heart seized with her daughter's shriek. Julianna, her body arched unnaturally upward, opened her eyes.

"Shh, my sweet," Elizabeth said. "It will be over soon."

Julianna moaned as the contraction abated, then stared up at Elizabeth, who gently pushed her into the pillows.

"Water, Mama..."

Elizabeth glanced at Yo, standing on the other side of the bed watching her. The Negress shrugged. "It will make no difference. Let her drink."

Elizabeth inhaled—damn the woman's dark soul—and reached for the pewter tumbler on the mahogany table next to the bed. Sitting, she cradled Julianna's head in her arms, lifting slightly to help....

Another contraction ripped through Julianna's contorted body, and Elizabeth dropped the vessel and grasped her daughter to her.

"Yo?"

Yo had already moved to the foot of the bed and parted Julianna's legs.

"Nothing. The baby will not fit." Yo bent her cloth-covered head closer to the birth canal. "Pains come fast and hard. She wants to push. The baby's head should be here. She's too weak from fever." The woman stepped back. "Eight months, Elizabeth, a bad sign. Both will die. It is God's will."

Hate-fed heat washed over Elizabeth. The malevolence passed, leaving only a simmering anger in its wake.

"Mama?"

Elizabeth closed her eyes and hugged her daughter tighter.

"The baby—"

"Do not talk," she said, kissing the top of Julianna's head and rocking her. "Neither of you will die."

Julianna shook her head, and her sweat-matted curls brushed Elizabeth's chin. "The baby, Mama...."

Elizabeth pushed damp hair from the girl's face. "I know, my love, I know everything. Do not worry."

Stiffening once more, Julianna fell back, then reached out and grasped Elizabeth's hand. Her hold tightened. Elizabeth winced, but did not try to free herself, suffering the contraction as Julianna suffered. God, she'd take all her pain, if she could.

The crushing agony in Elizabeth's fingers eased.

"You will care for it?" Julianna asked.

With a gentle pressure, Elizabeth squeezed in return. In front of her, Julianna's face blurred, and she felt a tear trickle down her cheek. She swiped at it before Julianna could see. "You will care for it yourself."

"Please, Mama, promise me."

Elizabeth leaned forward. "I promise. I will care for it as though it were my own."

Julianna closed her eyes and whined through clenched teeth while another contraction tore through her swollen body. The violent twist of her torso forced Elizabeth to rise from where she sat. Julianna opened her eyes and stared at her mother, then let out a breath.

In peace she stilled, her eyes open. Beautiful hazel eyes. Once so bright, full of love and hope.

That hadn't been so long ago.

Those eyes were glazed now. No love. No hope. Nothing ever again. The emptiness flowed through Elizabeth, swelling her chest and squeezing her heart. She knew grief, but never had the pain been greater.

Robert's precious little darling was dead.

Yo bent over Julianna and closed her lifeless eyes. "She is gone. It is over."

The words seared Elizabeth like a brand, and she straightened.

"Indigo!"

Instantly the door to the cramped death room opened, and the boy entered. So small and thin. With large, soulful eyes, his dark face tear-streaked, he looked at the bed where Julianna lay.

"Fetch your daddy! Hurry, for Julianna's babe!" He pivoted quickly and disappeared. Bless him, he'd been outside that door the whole day. For all his ten years, he'd loved Julianna so.

Benjamin was outside the cabin. She'd sent for him hours ago. Everyone was near, family and slave. Elizabeth watched him bow his head to enter the room. He was tall and strong and skilled with the plough, in hunting, and with the care of domestic animals, and Elizabeth didn't know how she would have survived out here without him following Robert's death.

She didn't speak to him. She didn't have to. He was a contingency put in place during the late morning when Julianna's labor pains began and when Yo repeated to Elizabeth once again what she had stated for months, Julianna's hips were too narrow. She would die in childbirth. Elizabeth refused to accept the woman's prediction. Still, she listened.

For a lifetime, she'd listened to Yo. If only she'd heeded her better.

Yo watched her now. Damn the witch, she could read her thoughts. Briefly, Elizabeth returned her gaze, then looked to the bed.

Benjamin touched Julianna's taut stomach, deftly feeling for the baby. Indigo had followed him in and now held out his father's large knife, boiled and sterile in a clean cloth. Benjamin's left hand steadied, and with his right, he took the knife and cut, freeing the baby from its prison within seconds.

Silence screamed against the cabin walls.

With an unspoken prayer, Elizabeth watched Benjamin take

4

the infant by its slimy feet, hold it upside down, and strike its buttocks.

The accompanying wail drowned the echoing silence of the crowded room, and Elizabeth bowed her head in thanks. When she opened her eyes, she saw Indigo, his sweet, tear-stained face brightened by a smile. Yo took the crying baby and began to wipe it dry.

Elizabeth reached for a sheet and gazed on Julianna. Her gut twisted. With a shaking hand, she pulled the sheet over her daughter, then stretched across Julianna's shrouded body and touched Benjamin's arm.

"Thank you," she said, choking on the words.

Benjamin nodded, then taking her hand in his, he gently squeezed her fingers. "I'll send Bounty to nurse the babe, Miss Elizabeth." His voice cracked, and placing his hand on Indigo's back, he ushered himself and his son from the room.

Yo held out the squalling baby. Elizabeth looked at it a moment before taking it, then she touched its satin cheek.

"It is a boy," Yo volunteered, cool disdain in her voice.

A boy, Elizabeth thought, fighting to quell her quivering chin. Another to love and lose.

"Devil's seed," Yo said. "The Maker willed the child dead.

"You brought this evil upon De Leau, Elizabeth. You played God, then dared to appease Satan. Today you play God again. Your devil is out of your control, and you've allowed his spawn within our home."

Memory as bitter as a pecan's hull swept over her. Yes, once she bartered with a devil. She paid the price now. But the demon would be paid in full.

"Play God, Yo? Though not nearly as effective as you, I am merely His instrument." She looked down at the whimpering baby. "If God had willed Julianna's son dead, he'd be dead. Weave your lies, old witch. I welcome them. They will keep him safe with me where he belongs."

Chapter One

"There was a girl with this party?" Mathias asked.

A bareheaded man, trapper by dress, straightened from his grim labor and looked at him.

"Young." Mathias tightened the hold on his mount's reins. "Sixteen. Angelique Veilleux?"

"And who are you to her to be askin'?"

Mathias spun the prancing stallion, the impact of its hooves soft and hollow on the autumn leaves and underlying humus of a thousand summers past. His gaze locked on unflinching, pale-blue eyes.

"I'm her kinsman, Mathias Douglas."

She was a large woman with a ruddy complexion and tawny, gray-streaked hair pushed beneath the ruffles of a mobcap. Feet spread, hands fisted on broad hips, she looked mean. Female not withstanding, this woman was a bully.

From the corner of his eye, Mathias saw André draw his mount closer.

Behind the woman, a tall, dark-haired man, horse-faced but relatively young, averted his eyes, and Mathias' heartbeat quickened. He turned to the six bodies laid out along the trail. All but one was covered.

He swung his leg over the saddle, and his boots hit the ground, jolting him.

One of the dead was female.

Clenching his jaw, he stepped to the corpse. He felt André's eyes on his back...and the eyes of the others.

A breeze blew through the canopy of trees that cloaked the Trace, rustling the foliage and stirring fallen leaves at his feet. Death hovered beneath him and around him. He could feel it, smell it, even taste it.

Mathias knelt on one knee, and with a shaking hand, he pulled back the coat covering the woman's face. Fair-haired and frail. Pretty once, but worn now with hard work and time. Middle-aged. A musket ball had pierced her chest. She was not Angelique, and he swallowed the lump in his throat.

Apprehension filled the air, so thick he might choke on it, and he pushed up from where he knelt beside the dead woman.

He turned to the trapper he'd first spoken to. "Where is she?"

The man gave his companions a furtive glance, then looked away.

Mathias balled his hands into fists. He looked to the blue-eyed termagant, then beyond, to the dark-haired man behind her.

Shame stared back at him.

"Where is Angelique Veilleux?" he asked again, taking a step toward the man.

"Perhaps she's not with this group, Cousin."

Mathias didn't look at André, still mounted. "No, she's not. But she was."

He'd locked his gaze on the big cow in front of the dark-haired man. This time the woman lowered her eyes, and he stepped around her, after the man she protected.

The woman moved to block him. "No!"

Mathias raised an arm to push her out of the way.

"Let him be," the woman cried. "We've suffered enough."

Mathias' lips tightened, and his gaze passed over the group of men and women. Mute, impassive faces watched him.

"I only want to know where she is, damn you, and if you people don't tell me now, I will beat it out of you one at a time."

"Tell him, so he can go for her."

Mathias pivoted, searching the group for the owner of the

voice. She was young and thin with brown hair, which she wore uncovered. Her gray eyes welled tears.

"They took her," she said.

Gnarled fingers, felt but unseen, seized Mathias' gut and twisted. He knew it. From the moment he realized Angelique wasn't dead, he knew the thieves had taken her.

"They thought she was pretty." The brown-haired woman took a step toward him, her lips trembling. "One of them yanked her head back and kissed her." She sucked in a breath and narrowed her eyes. "He touched her. There were seven of them, and they took her."

A young man moved up behind the woman and placed a hand on her shoulder. She shrugged it off.

"They said they couldn't take her to their camp"—her voice contorted—"they feared what their women would do if they brought someone who looked like Angelique back there."

"How long ago?" Mathias asked, reaching for his stallion's reins.

"Not a quarter hour passed before you came," the young man with the brown-haired woman said.

"You couldn't expect us to stop them," the cow of a woman screeched at his back. "There was nothing we could do. Mr. Tucker tried, and they killed—"

Mathias silenced her with his eyes. Guilt. He saw it. For something she'd failed to do?

The woman glared, then snorted in defiance.

No, not for something she hadn't done, but for something she did.

And the others had let her.

Slowly Mathias' gaze moved past the woman to the black-haired man behind her. The man averted his eyes. Mathias met the eyes of the other four living men in the party. This motley group had traveled long and far, and now, almost at the end of their journey, they'd met disaster. He returned to the hateful beast of a woman.

"As long as one man lived, something could have been done."

Mathias turned from them and forced himself calm. He had no right to judge. They'd have to live with themselves.

Resolve permeated his senses and left them acute. He hungered. An animal on the hunt, the butchers its prey. Refocused, he mounted. The leather of the fine Spanish saddle squeaked, strained by his weight. He breathed in the cool autumn air and with it the smell of summer's fading and the underlying scent of fall's decay.

His eyes found the brown-haired woman. "Which way?"

She pointed across the Trace to the thick woods.

Indigo was already there, and as if he'd heard the woman's silent directive, he looked up and called Mathias' name.

"That's Will Hossman's gang out there," André cautioned.

Mathias didn't look at him. "Indigo has the trail."

"There's seven of them, dammit. We are but three."

"I'll come," the man with the brown-haired woman said.

Mathias urged his horse forward. "You've no mount. You'll slow our pace." He kicked the stallion to a lope; André followed. In unison, the two bowed their heads in deference to low limbs guarding the virgin forest, then weaved their way toward Indigo, visible amid the towering walnut and oak.

"Listen to me," André said, his voice rife with irritation. "We need to go back to Natchez for help."

Mathias drew up beside Indigo, and the man pointed. "They've made no effort to conceal their trail. Tracks are fresh. They're mounted. Moving fast here. They'll slow."

"We need to catch them. They have the girl."

"We'll do her no good dead," André called, hesitating when Mathias and Indigo moved out.

"We'll do her no good even an hour from now, and you're talking many hours to drum up a hunting party."

Mathias increased his pace. He didn't know if André followed. Perhaps he would return to Natchez for help, but help would come too late. The militia was in New Orleans, a precaution against a feared French Jacobin uprising against the Spanish. That was one reason William Hossman had become so bold.

9

Mathias would depend on stealth and the likelihood his prey would be so preoccupied with the girl they would not notice his and Indigo's approach.

He thought of André and shook his head. The man was proud and had already balked at Mathias' leadership. But despite André's arrogance, Mathias needed him. The extra man could prove pivotal if Angelique's rescue was to be successful.

But with or without André, if Mathias could not free the girl before forfeiting his own life, he would end her degradation by taking hers.

"Git her down," the one called Hoss ordered. He left his mulish-looking horse untethered and strode toward her and the man who held her. Her heart throbbed in her throat.

One by one the others dismounted. "We should go farther," a man said, looking around.

Hoss laughed. "Why? You thinkin' one of them gutless pilgrims gonna come after 'er?"

Hoss' fingers bit into her arm. "Gonna come save her pretty, tight ass?" He yanked her from the horse. Her head jarred with the rough landing, but she stayed afoot.

They were in a clearing, not so far, she sensed, from where they'd taken her. If she screamed, would the others in her party hear? Would it matter?

She looked up. Filthy, leering men had surrounded her.

She knew, in general, what they had in mind, but until this moment had refused to believe seven men would share one woman. She didn't realize such a thing was done. Despite what the one had said, she'd clung to the hope they would take her to their camp with their other women and share her one at a time.

No matter how horrible, there would be other women there. Women to sympathize. Women to help.

But women hadn't helped her a short while ago.

She wrapped her arms tightly around herself. Purposely, she did not blink. Her captors' features blurred.

10

"You," the man they called Hoss said.

Her eyes were stinging now, and loath for these men to see her tears, she looked to the ground.

"That old sow, she called ya a whore."

Angelique stiffened and looked up. Take the whore and be done with this, Mrs. Scruggs had said. Enough men have died because of her already.

That had been after Hoss killed Mr. Tucker, but before the thieves' leader had forced a foul kiss on her and pinched her breast.

An ugly grin spread over Hoss' pockmarked face. Angelique started to shake and tightened the grip on her body. One knee knocked against the other, and she almost lost her balance and collapsed at their feet.

"And are ya a good whore or a bad 'un?" Hoss asked.

"To be one, she's gotta be the other," another said, then laughed. Others laughed with him.

Her bottom lip trembled, but she was determined not to cry. "I am not a whore," she said with a quaking voice, and she was sure they considered her lack of conviction to mean a lie.

"You will be," one of them called.

"A good whore. All of us to teach ya."

A shudder coursed through her body. A whore. She would be once they tainted her. Her father would spit on her.

She smelled the stench of the foul men and cringed. She could not live if this happened to her.

A horse neighed. Normality intruding in a nightmare. She whirled, determined to bolt, but found herself face to chest with a human animal blocking her retreat. She spun back into the circle, tighter now, and her gaze moved quickly over each hardened face. From the corner of her eye, she caught movement. A resounding pop filled her ears, light blinded her eyes, and pain burned her cheek at the instant her head jolted sideways with the impact of Hoss' slap. She covered her stinging face.

"You too good for us?"

Hoss' words came from beside her, and quickly she shook her

head. Despite her protest, he raised his hand again, and she covered her head with her arms. It didn't matter what she said or did. They were going to force her, one after the other, while the remainder watched.

The defilement would be unbearable…and the disgrace her behavior would levy on her father. He would curse her from heaven.

"Please," she said, the word muffled by her arms.

"In a hurry?"

A different voice, and she dared peek. A fat, sweating man stood naked to the waist before her. "Hoss got a kiss," he said, his lips curling into a sneer. "That's what I'm wantin', honey, before anythin' else, gimme a kiss."

He had no right. Hoss had no right. She didn't want to kiss this pig. Uncovering her head, she parried away from him, but he held his arms out wide and pursed his lips. She backed up, until someone struck her hard between the shoulder blades and thrust her into the fat man's belly. She braced her hands against his hairy paunch, then she pushed with all her strength. He grunted in response, but had already managed to close his arms around her. He bent his bulging body for his kiss, but she freed one arm and raked her nails across his jowl. The disgusting person cried out and stepped back before touching his jaw. He narrowed his eyes at the blood sticking to his fingertips.

Several of the men laughed, and her tormentor shoved her roughly backwards into the arms of another.

"You're a foul, reeking pig," she said, twisting in the new man's grasp.

Hoss stepped forward.

"You're all pigs," she snarled at the leader. "Even if I were a whore, I'd spit on the likes of you."

"Hold 'er tight."

The man behind her wrenched her shoulders. Hoss drew back his fist, then struck with brutal accuracy, knocking the air from her lungs. Her knees buckled, and she hung in breathless agony.

"Best keep yer thinkin' to ye'self and yer men happy till we be done with ya."

Hoss yanked her head back and brought his face close to hers. His image blurred. "Now," he said, his foul breath permeating her nostrils and turning her stomach. "Time for you to git ye'-self undressed."

"Everything, Hoss, I want 'er stark naked," one shouted. "Ain't never seen no woman with no clothes on at all."

Through a splotchy veil of dark spots, she made out Hoss' grin.

"Yes, siree," he said, "ev'ry damn stitch. Then you lay yer ass down, and us men'll give ya whatcha be wantin'." She watched him turn to the others, then closed her eyes and tried to draw a breath. Pain sliced her side.

"The rest of us'll cheer yer man on." His voice sounded far away. "We'll jest see which of us can pleasure you most tonight, right lads?"

Despite her darkening world, she noted the guffaws and the mumbled replies of her captors.

Hoss reached for the top of her bodice and gave it a vicious yank, jerking her body forward. Pain surged through her shoulders and chest. Angelique dumbly noted her chemise remained intact but, focused on dealing with the pain, she didn't care.

"I've helped you git started"—Hoss' words penetrated her tortured senses—"now you do the rest."

The man holding her let her go, and she slid down his length to the ground and vomited.

With a curse, Hoss kicked her injured side. Fire and light, then darkness. She couldn't see or breathe or even cry out, and she curled into a ball, trying to make herself very, very small. Twigs and vines and cool dirt touched her cheek. Hands grabbed her ankles.

"No," Hoss bellowed, "I'm wantin' to watch her do it."

"She ain't gittin' up. You done hurt her bad, damn yer hide."

She breathed in, but only half a breath. Fire seared her side, and panic muted her pain. They were moving around her. Dark shadows. Scurrying, speaking. She didn't know what they were saying. They had her on her back. Overhead, the towering trees spun. Grief eclipsed her physical suffering.

13

Her body numbed, and the darkness passed, but not the hopelessness. She watched the fat pig of a man, the one who had wanted a kiss, drop his pants and expose his stiff manhood. He loomed closer. She smelled his musky scent, foreign to her, and she closed her eyes in disgust.

"Git my whip," Hoss called. "She'll git up, or I'm gonna beat her to death."

Death. She prayed for it, before they violated her. But had there been a better choice, she would not have chosen to die.

"You can beat her when we're done," the fat man said, bending toward her feet. He pulled at her skirt. She felt other hands reach to help.

"Stay back," Hoss warned, but movement around her didn't stop. The leader no longer had control. Angelique watched a man remove a hunting knife from his boot and lean over her. She reached out and pushed at the armed hand, then her wrists were immobile, pinned above her head. The man with the knife seized her chemise and slit it, then laid the cloth aside to expose her breasts. On the damp ground, Angelique rolled her head from side to side. Soon she wouldn't know what was happening. Above her, the now quiet countenance of Hoss swam in and out of view.

"Git 'er skirts up," the fat man rasped. "I'm ready, dammit. Spread them legs."

"You ain't the only one," another said. "Hurry up, Boggs."

Boggs, filthy, disgusting Boggs, squatted between her legs. Her body tensed. She breathed through her nostrils. Whoever held her, wasn't doing so tightly. Garnering her failing strength, Angelique twisted. The pain in her side stabbed through her, but she pulled her ankle free and kicked out. Boggs cursed...

Then fell on top of her. A distant pop echoed his collapse.

Her hands were free, and the small clearing was alive with repeated pops, shouts, and pounding hooves. Through a growing haze, Angelique vaguely noted her attackers scrambling for their mangy horses, but most of those were bolting, frightened by the cracks of gunshot and, she realized, the sweeping attack

14

of her rescuers. One abductor fell while trying to prime his weapon.

Violence and death swirled around her, but touched only the periphery of her pain-numbed mind. She tried to move, but Boggs' lifeless body trapped her naked thighs beneath him. Bile swelled her stomach, and she gagged. Lord save her, she had to get this thing off her.

She pulled on her legs. Cutting pain halted her efforts. Boggs' hadn't budged. She sobbed once, then wiped sweat from her eyes. Clenching her jaw to endure the pain, she reached out and touched his greasy skin, then pushed against his shoulders. With excruciating slowness, she pulled her battered body from beneath his.

Exhausted, she closed her chemise and tugged her bodice over it. Holding both with one shaking hand, she drew her knees to her chest and smoothed the skirt over her legs with the other. She laid her head on her knees and watched a man fall near the refuge of the trees, then watched another plow face-first into the ground. She stared at the prone body, unmoved by the man's fate.

A moan intruded on the sudden stillness. A pistol cracked. The moaning stopped. Cheek still lying on her knee, Angelique blinked. The threatening presence of her would-be defilers had dissipated like smoke.

Beneath her, the ground began to vibrate. Stomach tensing, she raised her head. The shaking earth expanded to a terrifying roar. Heart in her throat, she looked over her shoulder, and the nightmare of the last hour climaxed into raw power, soaring through the mist on a fast steed, hell-bent to plough her under the earth.

But the rider looked beyond her.

He drew the thundering horse close and dismounted in a flash of golden color and light, an avenging angel sent in answer to her prayer. He rounded his horse, and she saw him then in the form of a magnificent man, beautiful to look upon, a misty glow in the haze of gun smoke, highlighted by the setting sun. His golden hair hung loose around broad shoulders, which flexed with corded tension each time he moved his hands. He held a formidable hunting knife.

Following his gaze, Angelique realized the object of his attention was not she, but Hoss, standing a short distance beyond. The leader of the thieves parried in reaction to the man before him. Then he went completely still. The hateful grin Hoss wore disappeared from his face, and his visage sobered. "Douglas," he said, and he cursed. Hoss crouched slightly at the knees, passing his own knife from hand to hand.

Her rescuer didn't acknowledge Hoss' challenge. Moving with predatory grace, he stepped away from her and, in one fluid movement, flipped the knife in his hand and forcibly tossed it, end over end, into Hoss' chest. The man's mouth dropped open in apparent surprise, and he fell to the ground, his head an arm's length from Angelique.

She jerked away. The movement hurt. Hoss' killer stepped closer to his victim. Perhaps it was the play of light from the waning sun, but Angelique swore his face darkened while he hovered like death over the corpse. She must be dead, also. That was why she could see this celestial warrior prepare to cast Hoss into hell. She sucked in a breath. Hot agony shot through her side, a cruel reminder she wasn't dead, but very much alive.

Her savior dragged Hoss' body a short distance from her. Turning the corpse over, he fell to one knee and pulled his knife from the dead man's chest. Fiercely, he pushed it back in. His back was to her, but she watched each strained movement, heard each hollow thrust when he forced the knife in, then out of the lifeless Hoss.

The movement stopped, and with bloody hands, he reached for a leather pouch at his waist. His body shielding the sight, the golden god stuffed something inside that pouch, then relaxed his shoulders and raised his face to heaven. He drew in a breath before returning his gaze to the corpse. In what seemed to her an afterthought, her warrior wiped his hands on Hoss' trousers, then rose, straight and tall, and retrieved a wooden canteen hanging from his saddle. Pouring water into his palm, he washed his hands, ridding himself of the contamination without seeming overly offended by it. He plugged the canteen, then turned and looked at her.

Her body convulsed with a massive shudder. Painfully she caught her breath. He stepped toward her. Helpless, she watched him come, her face tilting up with each step he took until her head bent over her shoulders, and he towered above her. Immediately, he crouched to her eye level. Taking off his buckskin jacket, he wrapped it around her shoulders. "It's all right," he said.

At the sound of his voice, Angelique breathed again. Her side twinged, and for a moment, her sight dimmed. Despite its ill effects, she was strangely oblivious of the pain racking her body.

"What manner of being are you?" she said, then bit her bottom lip to still its quivering.

She saw his jaw tense. Then the hint of a smile played at the corners of his finely sculpted mouth.

"Despite popular opinion, sweet Angelique," he said wryly, "I am but a man."

Narrowing her eyes, she studied his beautiful face, his clear, green eyes watching her with like intensity. Tentatively, she reached out to touch him, but balled her hand into a fist a scant inch from his cheek. She would have withdrawn, but he caught her wrist. Slowly he brought her hand to his face and laid it against his skin. Opening her fist, she touched him. His grip relaxed, and he moved his hand so that his thumb stroked her palm. He smelled of sandalwood and leather, sweet tobacco and soap.

"Mathias?" she whispered.

"Yes."

"Papa spoke of you."

Holding her hand, he meshed his fingers with hers, and they intertwined. He squeezed gently. Warmth flooded her.

"Did he?"

But the person Papa had spoken of was not like this. She leaned into him, hiding her face against his neck, and he wrapped his arms around her shoulders and pulled her close. She felt his breath whisper against her ear. He told her to cry, and she did.

17

Chapter Two

"**D**oes she sleep?" the dark-haired one asked. The one Mathias introduced as André. Angelique could not see his face, but she knew he was the one speaking. "I hope for her sake."

Ah, Mathias, whose name evoked darkness and sin, but whose voice warmed her body and seduced her soul.

Evil seduced, Papa always said so. Papa found fault with anything that brought happiness.

Her rescuers were kinsmen, grandsons of her grandaunt, Elizabeth Boswell, who had sent them to escort her home.

She and they were on the Trace, camped some distance from the remainder of her brutalized party. The mixed-blood tracker, the one they called Indigo, had returned to Natchez with news.

She had seen her fellow travelers' campfire to the north, before Mathias gave her something foul to drink and laid her on a bed of straw and dead leaves covered with blankets. The brew would relieve her suffering, he said, and bring sleep. The potion had numbed her body and trapped her mind in a netherworld.

But her cousins thought she slept.

"Did you feed her Hossman's minced liver?"

Angelique struggled to open her eyes. Subtle pain tickled her side.

"I gave her Yo's brew from the Choctaw Lily. She told me she has blood in her urine. The drug will stem the bleeding. The liver is for Yo."

"She looks nothing like...."

Sense and sound ceased as fiery pain seared her side and

18

wrenched her from a precarious peace. She heard herself groan, but she remained cloistered in darkness.

Mathias cursed. "I barely touched her. I fear her rib is broken."

He touched her again, and she struck out, trying to tell him to leave her be. Suddenly she was spinning, and her stomach reeled.

A cool palm covered her forehead, and the spinning stopped. "Shh," Mathias said. His breath caressed her cheek. Now, she wanted sleep.

"She does not favor the mother."

André again, drawing her from the peace she sought.

"Do you remember her? Plain little thing."

"Vaguely."

"I always wondered what Jude saw in her."

"His father-in-law."

André's laugh rippled through her. "And that son of a whore saw De Leau."

De Leau is an evil place. Angelique tried to open her eyes, but could not.

"As if there weren't enough free land for the taking," Mathias said.

"Not improved. Grandmama would have seen them both in hell first."

Angelique drifted now, but hoped they'd say more.

"...big risk today. She could have been killed."

"Had she been with them a moment longer," Mathias said, "she would not have wanted to live."

"Was she soiled?"

"No."

"It will make no difference. She looks sorely used, and you may be sure the pilgrims she traveled with believe her ruined."

"Angelique knows the truth. That's what matters."

"She's not you, Mathias. To a woman like this, appearance is important. She'll not easily live with the shame."

Her father's words from a stranger's mouth. Papa would have never forgiven this disgrace, even the appearance of disgrace, no matter how unjustified. She had caused the lust in those men. Now they were dead.

"Better Hossman's gang had known her and no one knew she survived than to be saved and people believe her violated."

A calloused finger touched her bruised jaw. "I think this girl can deal more favorably with a lie than a violation."

"But can Grandmama?"

"Her concern will be for Angelique."

"I cannot believe Grandmama has graciously taken her in. What are her plans for this girl?"

"To provide her a home."

André snorted. "There's more."

Angelique fought the oblivion she'd coveted.

"She might be Jude's daughter, but she's also Véronique Veilleux's granddaughter." Mathias stopped his probing, and she felt a blanket tucked around her. "Her breathing is unsteady, and she's not sleeping well."

She tried to tell him she wasn't sleeping at all, but only senseless mumbles escaped her lips.

"Your drug is not effective."

A hand touched her cheek. Instinctively, she knew it was Mathias' and knew, too, that he would check her through the night.

"She would have made a fine match," André said.

Angelique sensed Mathias rise.

"Or does Elizabeth Boswell have some other plan for Jude Veilleux's daughter?" Even drugged, Angelique did not miss the sarcasm in André's voice. "Something for the devil's bastard himself?"

"Keep silent! I fear she can hear you."

A contemptuous laugh defied the warning implicit in Mathias' voice. "What sweet vengeance Grandmama would find in that, eh, Mathias?"

"Old Bess," Mathias called.

Angelique watched him disappear through the door of an impressive wood-frame house, two-storied and built high off the

20

ground. They were in a residential section of Natchez, Mathias told her, but the lot was so large, the house seemed, to her, isolated in the country.

"We have brought Angelique home."

Angelique crossed the wide front porch, leaning heavily on André, who'd helped her from Mathias' horse. He seemed determined to maintain his hold on her, and Mathias offered no objection. She'd heard no more of their discussion last night and was not certain, in the light of day, what had been real and what she'd dreamed. During the arduous trip to town, the relationship between the two men simmered scarcely short of open hostility and, she sensed, their mutual dislike was long running.

André wanted to carry her into the house, but she had too much pride. She was dirty and beaten, felt awful and looked, she was sure, worse. For weeks, anxiety over this meeting twisted her stomach. She could not think of worse circumstances under which to meet her grandaunt.

André ushered her into a foyer, which divided the house into two sections. The faint scent of cypress and wood dust clung to the air. This house was not old. Angelique gazed over the white paneled entry. A pewter chandelier and a stairwell boasting spindles and intricately carved newel posts greeted her. At the front of the room, glazed windows glittered in the sun. This was a fine, new home, richly furnished.

A handsome woman hurried into the entry. She slowed, studying Angelique, who now pulled away from André and stood on her own. She knew this woman, though she'd never seen her.

Tall, her hair elegantly coiffed, Elizabeth Douglas Boswell displayed dignity, refinement, and the pretext, Angelique's father had emphasized, of propriety. Under the woman's scrutiny, Angelique wanted to crawl out the door, and in her condition, that was the only way she could have escaped.

Aunt Elizabeth's unreadable expression passed, replaced by the cool demeanor Angelique's father had spoken of when describing the woman who raised him. "I hear your journey was eventful, my dear Angelique." The words were gently spoken, despite their irony, and held the scarcely discernable hint of a French accent. Elizabeth Boswell's voice was as beautiful as she was.

A lump formed in Angelique's throat. "I fear it was, Aunt Elizabeth."

Her aunt smiled, in relief it seemed, and she leaned forward to kiss Angelique's forehead.

"Welcome home, little angel."

Tears filled Angelique's eyes and clogged her throat. *Home.* The softness in her aunt's voice told Angelique she meant her words. For weeks she'd dreaded this moment, this anti-climactic end to her odyssey. Angelique blinked away the tears.

"Thank you. I..."

She had wanted to say she was glad to be here, but her voice caught, and she dropped her gaze. Aunt Elizabeth immediately enclosed her in a gentle embrace, then surprised her again when she stepped back and caught her chin. The woman's features hardened as she studied Angelique's jaw.

"Her other injuries?"

"I sent Wee Ben to fetch Doctor Frey," Mathias answered. "I think three ribs are cracked, or if not, badly bruised."

Her aunt pursed her lips. "Baby," she called over her shoulder. A young woman, exotic in appearance and most assuredly of mixed blood, appeared suddenly, and Angelique suspected she'd been listening out of sight in the room beyond. "Our Angelique is home," Aunt Elizabeth said. "She is my nephew Jude's daughter. Your mother and father remember."

Baby responded with a curtsey.

"She's hurt. Can you help her upstairs?"

At Angelique's side, André moved, and he lifted her in his arms. He hurt her. Dismayed, she sought Mathias. Briefly, he returned her gaze, then looked away and crossed the foyer into another room, and André carried her up the stairs.

The whiskey burned Mathias' throat, then his chest, mollifying him. Angelique would have preferred him to carry her up the stairs, as she had insisted riding double with him today. He'd accommodated her, and André seethed.

Bess entered the parlor, and from his position by the fireplace, he looked her way. André stepped in behind her and closed the door.

"Those jackals at the gates of Natchez," his grandmother blurted out. She watched André make his way to the console. "I feared Indians."

Mathias nodded. "She told me on the way here a hunting party stopped them three days out of the Cumberland. A fur trader with the group had a Spanish license, or they might have made it no farther. As it was, they still felt compelled to barter with them."

"Who were they?"

"The trader, his name was Tucker, told her they were Creek."

"Far north for the Creek. Carondelet is playing a dangerous game using the Indians and their British keepers. That group must have bartered well." Bess pursed her lips. "You say *was*. This Tucker is dead?"

He looked his grandmother in the eye. "Killed trying to protect Angelique."

"Indigo was not sure," she said. "Was she violated?"

"You should be thankful you sent for us when you did."

Bess closed her eyes. "But for the missive Angelique sent by that post rider two days ago, I would not have done so. I had no idea she was on the Trace."

André sucked in an audible breath with the downing of his whiskey. "I myself didn't see. You would not lie to protect Angelique's reputation, would you, Cousin?"

Mathias' heart thumped at André's artifice, and he set his empty glass on the console with a thud.

"I would, but in this case I don't have to."

Bess shifted her gaze from André to him. "They are all dead?"

"All," André answered. "Not one is left to contradict Mathias' tale, except the travelers who saw Angelique after we recovered her. She looked worse than what you just witnessed."

Damn André's selfish soul, she did not. Her bruises were darker this morning, her body slower.

"Mathias removed Hossman's liver in front of the girl. Perhaps he should have killed the rest of her party as well and shut their mouths for good."

Perhaps he should kill André. Mathias met his grandmother's cool appraisal. She would never allow that, no matter how much she agreed with his solution.

"Mathias and I dispatched Hossman's gang in short order," André continued. The bastard winked at her when Bess turned his way. "Worthy of a land grant or a legislative posting would you not think?"

She frowned. "How many others were killed?"

"Five in the party and one thief during the robbery."

"A bloody day. Angelique must be impressed with us."

"Her most pressing concern was meeting you," Mathias said.

His grandmother shook her head. "Her flatboat arrived this morning. Apparently the captain waited almost two weeks in the Cumberland before he found the rumors of Spain's closing of the Mississippi were unfounded." She sat down on the settee. "If only she had waited."

"Why didn't she?" André asked.

"Money, no doubt," Bess answered. "No one knew the rumors were false, and the captain didn't know how long he'd be stranded. Angelique undoubtedly feared using up whatever money she had. I'm sure she didn't have much."

"She should have sent word to you."

Mathias sighed. "She didn't want to be an inconvenience. She was doubtful of her welcome, given the things her father told her about Bess."

"She told you that?" his grandmother asked.

"In more words."

"Goodness only knows what venom Jude placed in the child's head." Old Bess was twisting her fingers together so hard Mathias winced. "The ungrateful, self-righteous...." Her lips thinned. "It was the fever."

24

The hell it was. She always cited the malaria, which had almost taken Jude Veilleux's life and had orphaned him at age ten, to excuse his treachery in later years.

André shook his head. "He wasn't given to fits of ill temper, Grandmama. He was the foolish dupe of a conniving opportunist who shielded himself behind the monster of a god he created. Thank sweet heaven you held more influence with Pensacola than that rabid dog or you'd have lost everything you suffered for, and Véronique's son would have helped him steal it."

"Jude's betrayal could have cost you your life," Mathias said softly. He glanced at André. Some things they did agree on.

Bess rose and pulled a man's timepiece from the pocket of her skirt. "I have no desire to reminisce over Jude Veilleux's change of loyalties. And as far as Angelique's tactical error in braving the Trace, we can do nothing about that now. I'm thankful the damage is no worse than it is." She opened the enameled piece and studied its face. "Monsieur and Madame Delacroix await you at Stephen Minor's home," she said to André. "Clarice is with them."

"Ah, Clarice, how she pales in comparison to the beauty I carried upstairs."

"Go."

"Considering her parentage," André said, reaching for the door, "her beauty is more astounding still. Are you sure she is Jude and Mary Foster's daughter?"

"I have no doubt. And," she called to him over her shoulder, "Benjamin killed a buck yesterday. We'll have fresh venison tonight in honor of Angelique's homecoming. Be here, if the Delacroix have no plans for you."

"I'll be here, though I doubt your most recent ward"—he smirked at Mathias—"will make it to the dining room table."

André closed the door, and Bess turned to Mathias, as he knew she would. He averted his eyes and poured himself another drink. "There were seven of them, Bess. *Seven* of them. They had already beaten her beyond resistance before even one had tried to mount her. Rape would have been bad enough, but they could

25

have easily held her down without beating her. She is little more than a child, not yet seventeen, and you've seen how small she is."

"Yes, I saw."

"They would have continued to rape and beat her. She would not have survived the night."

"And what do you intend to do with the liver?"

He downed the whiskey. "Yo will ensure the bastard's soul remains in perpetual agony."

"Yo be damned." Bess waved a hand. "And you, too, pandering to her heathen ways. If that bastard is in agony, God will keep him there. Yo's interference will do nothing more than keep her fiendish lies of your sire circulating."

"You've made use of the lies."

"She created the legend to hurt me. I confounded the witch by embracing it, but I never liked it. She feeds the lie and poisons minds, yours included. Her lurid stories do nothing to hurt me and serve no purpose now but to isolate you from society."

"Whether my father is a demon or not, he isn't here. I have no place in society."

"You have no use for society, and," she said, pointing a finger at him, "your father was a man, flesh and blood."

"If you know that for certain, you could tell me who he was."

She rolled her eyes. "A demon stimulates sexual pleasure, Mathias, not pain. Therein lies possession of the soul. Only a man would be so cruel as to do what was done to your mother."

"Who?"

She walked to the console table and poured herself a shot. "Let's not have this conversation again." She downed her whiskey and looked at him. "Remember, Mathias, you are still no match for me."

"That's because you are the witch who controls the demon."

She shook her head, resignation etched across her face. "I should have sold Yo years ago."

"Life would have been so much duller then."

His grandmother snorted.

"Why didn't you?"

"I wanted to keep her where I could control her."

He chuckled. "But you don't control her."

Bess poured herself another shot.

"Truth is, Bess, she's part of the family."

"Yes," she agreed dryly, "on your father's side."

Mathias laughed.

"Did you have to remove the liver in front of Angelique?" she asked abruptly.

"When one is in a killing frenzy, one doesn't always think rationally."

His grandmother released a sibilant sound, then looked toward the ceiling. Willing herself, he surmised, to see the girl upstairs.

"You're glad she came."

Bess turned to him. "I always wanted her home."

And she had, for reasons he could guess. "When you looked at her, it wasn't Jude's daughter you saw, was it, Bess?"

She stiffened to granite, revealing not even a hint of the tears he suspected locked away behind that veil of fortitude she wore like a second skin. He set his glass down.

"I know who you saw when you looked at her, *Grand-mère.*"

"So wise for your twenty-six years. Whom did I see?"

He came to her and cupped her aging face in his hands, then kissed her forehead. This time, he told himself, her rigid stance was not the result of coldness, but of a monumental effort to retain her composure. "You saw Véronique Deschesne Veilleux, right down to the brown eyes."

"And why would you think such a thing? Véronique was dead before you were born. I cannot even recall her face."

"You recalled your sister's face when you looked at Angelique. Who else could it have been? You said so with your eyes."

She gazed at him, her expression non-committal. He pursed his lips, then wrapped her in his arms as he often did when he said good-bye. Her body did not yield, but Mathias had already steeled himself for her response. His grandmother's unspoken

27

rejection of his affection was expected, if not completely understood. Given her resentment, he wondered that she allowed him
to touch her at all.

"Go from me now," she said after a moment. "You've worn me
out. Go to your wicked widow and forget the havoc you wrought
these past two days."

"I love you, Grandmother."

She squeezed his arm, but did not reciprocate his words.

He released her, but before he opened the door, he turned.
"Who do you remember when you look at me, Old Bess?"

Her eyes met his.

"Someone you hated, *Grand-mère*...or someone you loved?"

Her gray eyes pierced him, but her voice remained soft. "Tell
me, Grandson, which would be worse?"

Mathias came and went from this place at will, but he was
always careful not to barge in when she was with another. And
he knew there were others. Not many though. Kate was discrim-
inating, as well as imaginative, in her tastes. Money no longer
mattered to her. She had enough to last a lifetime. Men and the
sex they provided were what concerned her now.

Wealthy, attractive, experienced, and perverse, Kate Mallory,
with her red hair and rich body, was everything a man could ask
for in a lover, and she wanted Mathias anytime and every time.

The bed linens would be clean; the silk scarves she found and
purchased in New Orleans still tied to the bedposts from their
last time. He wished he'd washed before leaving his grandmother's house, but he'd gotten out while the getting was good.
Kate would not want to wait, and she would like the smell of
blood, sweat, and yes, even death. It would be so much more like
real rape that way.

He sneaked in the rear of the dogtrot. It was daylight, but the
house her husband had built for her was on the outskirts of town.
Kate didn't mind her reputation, but she was discreet.

The doors leading from the dogtrot into the house proper
were open to take advantage of the cool fall air. Her hair pulled

up, Kate sat on the settee in the parlor, dressed in an elegantly proper dark green silk skirt and bodice. The ruffled neck of her chemise was fastened with a pearl button. Maddy, the youthful daughter of Kate's free hand Jim, stooped to remove a tea service. Mathias placed a booted foot inside the parlor. A floorboard groaned, and Maddy looked up at the same time Kate turned her head and saw him. Her eyes darkened. Pretentiously, she raised a hand to her breast, masking anticipation with feigned nervousness. Her mouth opened slightly, and she whispered out a captured breath. She didn't take her eyes off him. "Maddy, you're done for today. Close the door on your way out."

The girl nodded.

The door closed with a click. Mathias stepped inside and shut his door. He started across the room, and Kate rose as he came around the fine upholstered sofa. Grasping her, he crushed her full lips against his, then pulled back and placed his hands at the neck of her silk bodice and yanked. She gasped, but the garment only partly opened. He yanked again, harder, and the cloth gave. The chemise lay beneath. She begged him to wait, but charged with day-old violence and death, his body screamed for release, and he forced her to the floor and tore the delicate garment. She struggled beneath him, her protests dissolving into cries of pleasure, then demands he hurry. His mouth found a waiting nipple.

"O God, Mathias," she cried, arching toward him, "you are a devil. No man can make love like you!"

At times like these, when he held a woman possessed in his arms, he almost believed it himself.

Chapter Three

"Mathias?"

The hail came from outside the window, and Angelique stretched across the feather mattress to look on the shade-mottled yard below.

The last of summer's searing heat had passed, giving way to the cooler mornings and warm, pleasant days of early October. A hint of color touched the trees, and the sky, its blue off hue, was crystal clear. For two weeks Angelique rested, confined at first almost entirely to her room, but today she'd gotten out of bed and dressed with the help of the servant, Baby.

The doctor's visits were stretching farther and farther apart. Angelique welcomed that. He'd confirmed her cracked ribs, but the blood in her urine had cleared on its own. He gave her powders for the pain and for sleeping. They might have been more sophisticated than what Mathias gave her that awful first night, but they hadn't tasted any better, and they hadn't been as effective.

André stopped by routinely to check her welfare, but she had not seen Mathias since the day they brought her home. Heart racing, she spied him now beneath the branches of the huge water oak that grew outside her window.

"Mathias!"

From her spot on the bed, Angelique watched him stop and turn at the harried approach of yet another cousin, Jane Douglas. Angelique's skin tingled with apprehension when the willowy young woman flattened her hands against his chest. Their faces were close, and Angelique's stomach soured. But instead of the kiss Angelique expected, Mathias took Jane's hands in his and pushed her to arm's length.

The bedroom window was partly open, and Angelique, watching Jane's head bob up and down in cadence with her speech, picked up bits and pieces of what sounded like an argument. Abruptly, Mathias dropped her hands and turned toward the back of the house. Jane hurried after him a few steps before the commanding voice of Sarah Douglas called to her daughter from the direction of the front porch. In obvious frustration, Jane aborted her pursuit, lifted her skirt, and scurried to join her mother.

A knock sounded on the bedroom door, and Angelique looked around from where she hovered on all fours in the middle of the bed. The door opened with a soft squeak, and Aunt Elizabeth peeked in. Angelique's cheeks heated.

"I heard Mathias' name—"

"I know. Jane's infatuation with him is a persistent worry for Sarah and Thomas."

Angelique squelched the urge to ask more and maneuvered to sit properly. Aunt Elizabeth partially closed the door and sat at the foot of the bed. Situating herself, she smoothed her wine-colored skirt over her lap, drawing a pleasant hum from the satin.

"Parents wish many things for their children. Those are not necessarily the same things the child desires."

"And Jane wants Mathias?"

Aunt Elizabeth chuckled. "Jane wants Mathias to want her."

And he doesn't. Angelique stifled a relieved smile.

"Mathias represents something dangerous and forbidden to Jane, as he does to any number of young women in these parts." Aunt Elizabeth frowned. "Or people in general for that matter."

Not to Angelique. To her he was strong and warm and wonderful. "But to Jane in a man-woman way?" she asked.

"Most assuredly, Jane's interest is sexual." Her aunt studied her momentarily. "Mathias can, and does, have any number of willing women."

Angelique felt her skin prick as the blood drained from her

face, and she wondered at Aunt Elizabeth's purpose for telling her this.

"But he hasn't had Jane," her aunt continued. "Jane is lovely and rich. Many men, young and old, have indicated an interest in her, yet the most handsome and exciting man in the area shows her no interest. That offends her."

"Why does he—"

"Mathias has plans of his own."

Heart-rending disappointment washed over Angelique. "Do you know—"

"I know Mathias better than he knows himself."

Down the stairs and outside the open front door, Cousin Sarah could be heard admonishing Jane. Aunt Elizabeth tilted her head to listen, then said, "Thomas and Sarah worry over Jane's willfulness, but they have nothing to fear from Mathias. Still, the sooner they've made a good match for her, the easier they will rest." Her aunt's gaze found hers. "I'm sure your father worried...and wished...similarly for you. I'm surprised you came to me, child."

So, Aunt Elizabeth finally wanted answers, and she hadn't tarried long getting to the point. Angelique bowed her head and studied her hands twisted in her lap. Elizabeth Boswell reached over and covered those hands.

"I am glad you've come, sweet angel, but I cannot believe your father encouraged you to come here."

"Papa died suddenly. He fell down in a fit at church, and he was gone."

"A failure of the heart, you said in your missive."

"Yes." Angelique swallowed, then glanced at her aunt, who watched her, waiting.

"I had little choice but to come here." Her aunt's visage blurred, and Angelique looked away to hide her tears. "There was a man. He was much older, much older than Papa even. Oh, Aunt Elizabeth, he had a granddaughter only five years my junior. He was fat and bearded and when he ate, his food got caught in his mustache." She shook her head and looked at her aunt, hoping the woman could understand. "He disgusted me."

"And he wished to marry you?"

"Yes, Papa had agreed to the betrothal."

"Jude had arranged your marriage before he died?"

"Three days before."

"Did he know how you felt?"

Angelique nodded vigorously. "And I argued with him. I rarely argued with him over anything, choosing to bide my time until I could leave his house."

Her aunt's eyes widened.

"It did no good to try to talk to him. He discussed nothing with me, ever. In truth, he discussed little with Mama before she died. He felt wives were a necessary liability suited for serving their husbands and raising children. Daughters he regarded much the same. Papa wanted a son, and Mama died trying to give him one. I kept his house after, but hoped to grow up and marry a more agreeable man and keep his house."

"And who would have kept your papa's house after he'd married you off?"

Angelique shrugged. "I don't know. Perhaps he'd have remarried.

"Jonas Buckworth was wealthy, and he contributed a great deal to the church. Papa saw an advantage in my marrying him."

Lord, but her aunt's expression had darkened. "And this Buckworth insisted on honoring the betrothal, am I right?"

"Yes. And he wanted us wed immediately."

"So you ran?"

"I didn't have access to Papa's money, nor did I have any idea how to get it. Jonas Buckworth took control of everything."

"What did you do?"

"Mr. Buckworth's son-in-law is Peter Rothbottom, a solicitor in Baltimore. He and Buckworth's daughter had no more desire to see me wed her father than I did. They feared I would bear him a son, and they'd lose everything. Mr. Rothbottom helped me acquire Papa's cash, then arranged my trip to Natchez. I don't know what I'd have done otherwise, but I'd have died before I married that man."

Her aunt patted her hands. "So, I am the lesser of two evils?"

Angelique started to protest, but decided against it. Her father despised and feared his aunt, and there was no use trying to deny it. Still, seeing where she'd come to and comparing it to what she'd left behind, Angelique could not help thinking her father had overstated Natchez' flaws.

"Papa considered Jonas Buckworth a comfortable older man and a good Christian. He felt the match was good for me."

"The match was good for him, but had you been able to stomach the man's disagreeableness, you could have ended up a wealthy young widow."

Angelique's eyes widened. No wonder her father had regarded Aunt Elizabeth as greedy and lascivious.

"He could have lived another twenty years, filling my belly with children I didn't want and wearing me out before I passed thirty."

Aunt Elizabeth laughed, to Angelique's ears, a surprisingly happy laugh. "Oh, child, you are nothing like your mother, and I agree with you. I've lived long enough to know old men belong with old women. Your father's reasoning was that of a man."

A man who considered his daughter a liability to be bartered for personal gain. Perhaps Aunt Elizabeth was greedy, but Jude Veilleux had been no better.

"Papa said a man's role on this earth was to serve God and a woman's role was to serve her husband and family. He said a man should not tolerate willfulness in any form and told me the weakness was far greater in a woman than a man."

"Well," Aunt Elizabeth said dryly, "by your father's standard, one might assume all men went to heaven and all women, flawed from birth, went straight to hell after working themselves into an early grave doing their husbands' righteous bidding."

Angelique's heartbeat quickened. Her mother had died in childbirth when Angelique was seven. She'd never considered her having gone to hell, but her father had never spoken of her being in heaven either. In fact, he'd rarely spoken of her at all.

"I don't think my mother was happy."

Aunt Elizabeth coughed softly. "Even as a little girl, Mary Foster never laughed or even dared smile. Her father was a mean, repressive tyrant who married her off to someone he could mold into his own form, much as the god he created in his hateful mind molded him."

Angelique held her breath at the sacrilege.

"I often thought," Aunt Elizabeth continued, "the father was more pleased with the son-in-law than his own daughter and the son-in-law more pleased with his father-in-law than his wife. The poor girl could have pleased neither if she'd sprouted golden wings."

How different things appeared from her aunt's point of view—and probably her poor dead mother's.

"Fear not, child. I can assure you, as quickly as any man of God might dissuade, as many women as men will make it to heaven, if such a place exists, and a man will be cast into hell's fires as quickly as any woman.

"Think for yourself and let no one and nothing stand between you and your god. And," she said, leaning toward Angelique and continuing softly, "be attentive to your life here on earth. It is the one thing truly guaranteed. Make the most of it."

Blasphemy for certain, but reassuring thoughts nonetheless, and Angelique wondered if Natchez were her Garden of Eden, this house the Tree of Knowledge, and her aunt the snake.

"And make the most of your marriage when the time comes. There are few other options for a young woman. Think of it as a contract. I had three husbands. The first I married for security, the second for love, and the third"—she winked at Angelique— "was a business arrangement that left me very wealthy.

"But in each case, I paid my dues as a woman, for my womanhood was my bargaining chip, my investment, if you will, to the partnership. The trick is to marry well, and you, my dear niece, have the advantage of a wise grandaunt who knows, after a lifetime, how to do that."

"To a rich, old—"

Aunt Elizabeth gurgled up another laugh. "We'll try to find you a young one, but rest assured, if he's too young, you may be stuck with him for a lifetime."

"But if I like—"

"What?" her aunt cried in mock surprise. "You have to like him, too? You ask much of me."

Angelique's mouth dropped open.

"Shut your mouth, child. I did come up here for a reason."

Her heart quickened anew with the hope the long-absent Mathias wanted to see her.

"You have visitors," Aunt Elizabeth said. "I didn't know if you felt well enough to see them, so I've left them drinking sherry in the parlor."

"Who are they?"

"A Mrs. Scruggs and her son Paul."

Angelique, her mouth suddenly dry as chalk, tried to swallow. The bright, immaculate room with its pristine walls, cherry furniture, and ruffled bed linens flaunted its purity and mocked her tainted innocence. Not since her first day home, when Baby covered her mouth to stifle a cry in the face of Angelique's ripped clothing and battered body, had the degradation of that awful day touched her. She started to tremble.

Aunt Elizabeth looked down at Angelique's lap where her hand still covered Angelique's. Slowly, the woman lifted her gaze.

"Mrs. Scruggs said she journeyed with you on the Trace and has come to check your welfare." She squeezed Angelique's fingers. "You do not wish to see them?"

Angelique shook her head till she was dizzy.

"Be still," her aunt said. "Their presence reminds you of the incident?"

Angelique closed her eyes. "They are horrible people, Aunt Elizabeth. They should not be in your house, and they shouldn't be drinking your sherry."

"What did they do to you?"

36

Angelique could feel her chin quivering and, for a moment, she didn't dare speak.

"Tell me."

"Mr. Tucker tried to help me w-when those men wanted to take me. William Hossman shot him. Mrs. Scruggs screamed that too many had died for me already. She told them I was a whore and I knew what those men would do to me. She said I would welcome it."

Angelique was drawing rapid little breaths now, and her stomach burned with the memory.

"She didn't know me well. She, her son, and two others had joined our group two days before. I believe her son was interested in me, so at every opportunity she prodded me with questions about my family and my background. I foolishly told her I was an orphan. But for making friends with Mary and Tom, I was traveling alone."

Angelique bowed her head. "Mrs. Scruggs thought I was after her son. I believe she intends for him to marry a rich wife. She knew nothing of me. I was penniless on the Trace, and she considered me unsuitable."

Aunt Elizabeth's silence prompted Angelique to look up.

"Are there women who like what those men were going to do, Aunt Elizabeth? I cannot believe anyone would like being beaten and forced."

Downstairs, the front door closed loudly, and Sarah Douglas said something to her daughter before one or both started up the stairs.

Aunt Elizabeth glanced to the slightly open bedroom door, then focused on Angelique. "Many women like men and the pleasure men provide. What those men were going to do had nothing to do with your pleasure. Mrs. Scruggs is a fool. Stay here—"

The stairs creaked in consonance with slippered footfalls and the whisper of satin skirts.

"I know what your interest in him is," Sarah said clearly. "You think I don't know what you young women whisper in the dark. He is an outcast and a whoremonger, and you find the danger exciting. His being forbidden entices you. You children—"

"I am not a child," Jane said.

"Do not interrupt me. Even mature women talk of him. God only knows how many he's lain with. But you have no idea what sort of life you would have married to a man such as him."

Aunt Elizabeth glanced at Angelique, then at the door and reached for the knob.

"He offers you nothing," Sarah continued.

They were right outside the room now.

"But he'd gain much by marrying you. Be advised your father will disown you."

Before Aunt Elizabeth could close the door, it flew open, and Jane rushed in. She stopped short and stared in obvious surprise at her grandmother. Jane's gaze moved to Angelique, and her eyes narrowed. Angelique had sensed Jane's dislike from their first meeting.

Sarah followed her daughter into the room. "Oh, Mother Boswell, I apologize. I thought certainly you and Angelique were in the parlor with Angelique's visitors."

"No, we were indulging in a discussion of marriage and were drawn inadvertently to rumors of devils and designing men."

Sarah's face reddened.

Elizabeth turned to Angelique. "I've lived through hard times, sweet girl. You, of course, already know there are advantages to having a ruthless demon champion your cause."

Her aunt alluded to Mathias on the Trace, of Hossman's death...and his bloody liver. Angelique managed a tremulous smile.

Aunt Elizabeth gave her a last, reassuring pat on the hand. "You will never have to deal with either Scruggs again."

With those words, the dowager rose, but before leaving the room, she took Jane's chin in one hand and forced the young woman to face her. "Do not concern yourself with Mathias' motives, my dear. He does not need you or White Oak Glen." She looked knowingly at Sarah. "He has his Grandmama. And I will remind you, Sarah, and my son if necessary, until I die, White Oak Glen belongs to me."

＊＊

$\mathcal{F}$rom his discreet vantage point in the adjacent dining room, Mathias watched the horse-faced man he recalled from the Trace rise when Old Bess entered the parlor.

"Mrs. Scruggs, Mr. Scruggs," his grandmother began with a formal nod. "I regret my niece is not available to you today, or any other day."

Defiance washed over the bull of a woman's face. "What did the girl say to you, Mrs. Boswell? There was much confusion that day. Perhaps Angelique misconstrued my comments."

"I think not, Mrs. Scruggs. A young woman who is about to be used by seven sordid men could hardly misunderstand when the only people standing between her and degradation and death state without remorse that she will enjoy herself."

Mrs. Scruggs surged from her seat. "That's a damnable lie!"

"No, it is not." Old Bess turned to the man standing in front of her. "The fact your son still lives, unharmed, is testimony to your cowardice and your lie. I must say, you have nerve stepping into my house today and enjoying my hospitality."

Mrs. Scruggs didn't falter. "I came to see Angelique. My son and I are concerned for her welfare, as we were during the journey and still are today. Paul"—she gestured to her son—"has an interest in the girl and hopes his suit will be considered."

Old Bess sucked in a breath, then narrowed her eyes. "Get out of my house."

Mrs. Scruggs fisted her hands and took a step. "Now you listen to me, Mrs. High-and-Mighty Boswell. Everyone knows what happened to that girl on the Trace. She's shamed, and most men ain't gonna want 'er, not to marry. My son still does, and it'd be in 'er best interest to take him seriously."

"Your son wants what you tell him he wants, and you decided you wanted my niece after you found out who I was, after you sacrificed her to those animals. Men, I add, who as bad as they might have been, were still better than you. The interests you and your son wish to further are your own. Angelique will not have him, and she will marry well."

39

"She'll end up Under-the-Hill."

Mathias noted Mrs. Scruggs' prudent movement toward the door and out of his grandmother's range, but the hateful old fish-wife turned suddenly and sneered at Old Bess.

"Another degenerate, like your bastard grandson. There's plenty said of your family, Mrs. Boswell. Born of the devil, it's said, not fit for polite society, and from what I know of 'is butchery on the Trace, I believe it and so do them that live here."

"Do not tell me what Natchez knows of Mathias. Natchez and I have grown rich and powerful together, and I do not care what people think. They do, however, care what I think."

The harridan smirked.

"Mrs. Scruggs."

The woman stopped at the calm order implicit in Bess' tone. Her son almost ran into her.

Bess stepped toward them. "If you've listened to the stories, you know the demon serves me."

Mathias tensed.

"It rid me of an unwanted stepfather and later a troublesome half brother. In return for its service, I provided my virgin sister and later my virgin daughter for its sexual pleasure. For those precious sacrifices, it provided me a special grandson."

Despite the sordid tale, Mathias was calming. He leaned against the doorjamb. The sow saw him, and her eyes widened.

"Mathias is my instrument," Bess continued. "A gift from a devil through whom I wreak havoc and death upon my enemies. I now count you, madam, and your pitiful son, among those."

The woman continued to stare at him, and Bess noticed because she looked his way, then back to the Scruggses.

"My influence in Natchez is remarkable," she said, "and it extends south, all the way to New Orleans. If you wish to improve your prospects, I would advise you to leave the Spanish frontier altogether."

Mrs. Scruggs tore her gaze from Mathias and glared briefly at her nemesis before making her way to the door.

"And, Mrs. Scruggs," Bess said softly, "if you spread any vicious lies that Angelique was violated by those men on the trail, I will see that little pieces of you and dear Paul are spread through the swamp—alligator bait never to be found, missed, or remembered."

When the door closed behind Paul Scruggs, Bess pivoted in Mathias' direction.

"So much for letting old tales die," Mathias said, stepping through the doorway from the dining room. "We've been slaughtering hogs at De Leau, I brought Baby lard. She wants to make soap. What was that about?"

"How much did you hear?"

"Everything since you came in the room."

She walked to the console and poured herself a brandy.

"Angelique was not violated, Grandmother," Mathias reassured.

"What about before you got there?"

"I saw everything while we set up for the attack. I had to be careful. There were only three of us, but I wasn't going to let one of them take her."

Old Bess waved her arm, acknowledging the truth in his words.

"I know. I think she would have told me by now anyway. Still, there's such shame involved for a young girl. But it won't matter if that woman has started rumors."

"Since she was planning on her son marrying Angelique, odds are she hasn't spread any lies yet."

André's insinuations were spreading, though; but Mathias didn't point that out to his grandmother. His older cousin set his own course and had reasons for it, and Mathias would deal with those in his own time. He stepped to the narrow console and poured himself whiskey.

"*Conquistador* sets sail out of New Orleans for Cuba in five days." He nodded to the door through which the Scruggses had departed. "Shall I arrange passage for your new friends?"

Her lips curled. "Could you possibly arrange for them to fall overboard?"

Chapter Four

"Be still, girl, or I'll never get this hem even."

"I'm sorry, Mrs. Henderson." Angelique looked down at Natchez' finest seamstress. "I fear the bodice is still cut too low." Mrs. Henderson frowned, and Angelique's stomach sank with dismay. She'd offended the poor woman, and that had not been her purpose.

"The dress is perfect," Mrs. Henderson retorted firmly, "and if I'm to have it ready by tonight, you must quit fidgeting."

Angelique stared at her image in the mirror. Aunt Elizabeth had picked the purple lutestring, saying the color complemented her hair and skin. She'd picked the high-waist, Empire style, also, with short, gathered sleeves. The bodice covered Angelique's shoulders, but to her dismay there was no tippet to fill the square décolletage. Her aunt already had Mrs. Henderson change it once, but the dress still displayed too much cleavage.

The skirt fell to the floor from a velvet sash and gently draped her hips and thighs. A soft train formed in the back. The dress was rich and, Mrs. Henderson told her, in fashion...and, Angelique feared, blatantly seductive. It was so unlike the modest, long-sleeved, low-necked dresses she wore over a tailored chemise or with a fichu.

Her aunt stepped into the parlor and studied the two of them. "Angelique," she said finally, "you are beautiful."

Angelique feared some might think she was trying to be.

"The men will hover around her like bees over a flower, Elizabeth."

With Mrs. Henderson's words, Angelique turned on her aunt.

"The color is too bright, the neckline too low. Papa would not approve."

"I do not know if my niece is in the market for bees, Edwina. Perhaps some fat old drone would do."

"What I don't want is to lose my nectar."

Aunt Elizabeth's eyes widened, then she laughed. Obviously she considered Angelique's concerns humorous, but Angelique didn't regard them as such. Her aunt stepped close and squeezed her wrist.

"You are fine, my dear. Your dress is in good taste, no one will fault you."

"The men will cater to your whims, and the women will burn with envy," Edwina Henderson said, then giggled as she rose from the floor. "In the market or not, it is good to keep masculine attention."

"Edwina...."

Angelique watched the woman's reflection turn to her aunt, then nod, subtly admonished.

No wonder her father had left. Given his attitude about propriety, Jude Veilleux must have found his aunt's house almost painful.

"I've had all the male attention I want for a while," she said, smoothing the dress over her belly. "I have no desire to tempt more."

"Your father's words," Elizabeth said, taking Angelique's shoulders and turning her. "If a woman must hide herself from a man because he cannot control himself, she is not the one to blame."

"But it seems pointless to beautify myself if I am not looking—"

"You are looking," Elizabeth snapped. "You are looking to eat well, make new friends, and impress potential suitors. You are alive, and you have as much right to enjoy yourself tonight as anyone there."

She had displeased her aunt, though she hadn't intended to, but she felt as if she were a trollop about to be put on display.

"I don't think women wear dresses like this in Baltimore."

"Oh, Angelique," her aunt said, throwing her hands up in obvious frustration and making Angelique wince, "of course they do. You have not been exposed to life, but that is over." Aunt Elizabeth shook her head, then mercifully turned away and fingered the cloth draped over a high-backed chair.

"This burnt orange silk is lovely," she said. "It will be perfect for All Hallows' Eve."

Halloween, a pagan festival her father reviled. Angelique glanced at the lovely material, then to her reflection, toying with the décolletage of the new dress. Aunt Elizabeth referred to Miss Abbey's party. Jane and Cora had been jabbering about it for days.

"You will be there, I assume?"

In the mirror, Angelique found André's reflection peeking in from where he stood in the foyer. Darn him, he'd sneaked up on them; she prayed, given the nature of the feminine discussion, not too long before. Adding to her embarrassment was this dress. But it was too late to hide, his eyes were already sweeping her likeness and now lingered on the inappropriately exposed swell of her breasts. Angelique longed to curse her grandaunt for trussing her up like this.

Given there was little else she could do, she straightened confidently and looked over her shoulder at him.

She wasn't comfortable with the man. He was thirty, wealthy, handsome, overly confident, and engaged to the daughter of an influential New Orleans businessman and landowner. Over the last several weeks he'd increasingly shown her what she considered excessive attention.

"Of course she'll be there," Aunt Elizabeth said.

Mrs. Henderson flounced Angelique's train. "You are done, my dear."

"An exquisite beauty to grace Governor Gayoso's table tonight if ever there were one," André said, stepping fully into the room and taking Angelique's hands when she pivoted.

She managed what she hoped was a heartfelt smile. There

45

was nothing physically offensive about her cousin, but despite his growing attention, she believed he considered her beneath him. "Thank you, sir." She curtsied, then met his eyes. He grinned, and she was sure he'd looked down the front of her dress.

"Color in your cheeks becomes you, Angelique."

Immediately she tried to free her hands, but he didn't let her go. How could she be expected to enjoy herself tonight?

André turned to his grandmother. "Has Mathias arrived?"

"No."

"Perhaps he is with the lovely Kate."

Angelique's heart jumped.

"He could be," her aunt said dryly. "But wherever he is, he has yet to make his way here."

"Is Kate his intended?" Angelique asked with all the nonchalance she could muster.

A wicked grin stole across André's face. "Not exactly."

He was sure he'd brought about the response from her he intended, trying to belittle Mathias in her eyes. He needn't try. Mathias saved her life. He was and always would be her golden angel.

"Kate Mallory is a widow, Angelique, who enjoys Mathias' company from time to time." Aunt Elizabeth cast André a stern look. "And this need not be discussed in my parlor or in Angelique's presence."

Despite her resolve, Angelique's stomach burned. Another conquest whose bed he enjoyed, and though to her Mathias might be an angel, he was, *despite popular opinion...but a man.*

André took her cape and handed it to a servant. She felt naked, but the mode of dress of the other women present indicated her gown was not conspicuous. Still, the many glances in her direction made her uncomfortable, and she couldn't help wondering if the guests' interest was curiosity about her personage or speculation over the events on the Trace.

Possessively, André led her to a distinguished couple in conversation with Aunt Elizabeth. The latter turned at their approach.

"Ah, there you are. Governor, my grandniece, Angelique Veilleux recently arrived from Baltimore."

"Ah, yes, my dear," Governor Manuel Gayoso de Lemos began, smoothly advancing the reception line. "I was sorry to hear your journey to Natchez proved such a hazardous one. It was most fortunate your cousins"—he nodded to André behind her—"came to your aid and, in so doing, did me the outstanding service of ridding Natchez of that despicable group." He bowed slightly. The Spanish governor of Natchez was handsome and charming and his English was impeccable, and Angelique had no idea what to say in response.

"Ha, Manuel, not what you'd call a longhaired, bearded frontiersman, is she?"

Angelique turned, thankful for the distraction.

Again the governor politely dipped his head. "Miss Veilleux, may I present Josephus Willingham and his lovely wife Penelope."

Angelique took Mrs. Willingham's proffered hand and quaked at the woman's pitying smile.

"And no, Josephus, she is not, nor had I expected her to be. French, I believe?" he said, turning to Elizabeth for confirmation.

"Pure French on her father's side. English on her mother's."

Governor Gayoso chuckled. "Ah! Mayhap a drop of Spanish with the French, Elizabeth?

"I am certain there is not. Perhaps with the English."

Gayoso laughed heartily. "I would consider that possibility even less likely, though I myself"—he looked to the woman standing beside him—"have found the Anglo female to be particularly charming."

They were partaking in political banter...and the governor perhaps of something more...and Angelique decided discretion to be her safest course. She hoped her stiff smile didn't look foolish.

"She's American, you Spanish tyrant," Willingham bellowed good-naturedly. "You've let another in to bring about your downfall."

Angelique furrowed her brow at the governor, who took her hand.

"We welcome Americans, Miss Veilleux."

"Thinks he's going to make Spaniards of us, Angelique," Willingham added amicably, "but I've given him fair warning it won't work."

Instinctively Angelique squeezed the governor's hand. "I thank you for my welcome, sir, and I have no intention of becoming embroiled in politics."

The governor laughed softly and, leaning forward, kissed her knuckles. "Welcome to my home, Angelique."

"Well said, my beauty," André whispered in her ear when he led her away. She sensed her cousin was telling her the truth. Governor Gayoso appeared pleased with her response, and Margaret, the woman at his side and an "Anglo," she assumed, held her hand warmly and lavished her with a sincere smile once the governor passed her on.

She drew unsought attention the moment she emerged from the reception line. Men hovered around her. Others stood back, but she feared their eyes watched and wondered about her also. Self-conscious, she lifted a trembling hand to her chest and smiled in agreement at some inane comment a middle-aged admirer made. She wished she were taller. She was surrounded by tall men, and given the décolletage of her dress, she wondered at the view these men enjoyed.

Her mouth was dry, and she was suddenly terrified, lest André, engaged in conversation with one of the fort's Spanish officers, a Major Carriere, would abandon her in this pit of strangers. She drew in a shaky breath. From the way they talked on and on and prodded one another, her admirers appeared to expect little from her, and the confidence she'd gained in the reception line faded. Witty conversation was not something she was adept at, and now she couldn't even hear these men for the hum growing in her ears. She nodded politely at something a young officer said, then discreetly brushed a wayward curl off her clammy forehead.

Another man joined the circle, blocking her view of the room entirely, and Angelique raised her hand to massage her aching temple. Given the race it was running, her heart seemed likely to burst.

Their words were making no sense, and moments later, she couldn't hear words at all—the hum in her head had become a roar. Someone offered her a glass of wine. She stared at it.

Her heart was in her throat. Unable to breathe, she turned away, raising her arms to push....

A hand, strong and warm, familiar in its touch, circled her bare upper arm and stayed her movement. Suddenly she could breathe, and did. The scent of sweet tobacco and sandalwood invaded her nostrils. Knowing without seeing, she turned her head and found Mathias' green eyes.

"Take the wine," he said softly.

With a quick nip at her bottom lip, she reached for the crystal glass half-filled with rich, dark liquid.

"Aunt Elizabeth sent me to find you," Mathias said loudly and drew the group's attention.

"Thank you," she said to the man who had offered the refreshment. The wine sloshed in the glass, but she didn't spill it. Mathias took it from her, and she stepped toward him. He started to say something else to her, but she caught his gist and turned to her admirers. André had been watching Mathias. Now he glanced at her.

"Gentlemen, if you will excuse me, please," she said with what she hoped passed for a brilliant smile.

Several bowed politely, and Angelique stepped quickly to Mathias.

"I want to go home," she said when they were away from the group .

"Shh." He extended her the wine, but she shook her head. "Take it," he said gently, "and then take a sip."

"I'm going to be sick."

"No, you will not."

She took the wine, but she wasn't about to drink any of it, not yet. "I'm going to humiliate myself, Mathias, and the family. Please take me home."

"You're not going to humiliate anyone, and neither of us can leave. Good God, that would cause a stir, me leaving alone with you."

They stopped, and she faced him. Guests buzzed around them, but he didn't seem to notice, and she didn't want to concentrate on anything but regaining her composure. Tilting her head back, she swallowed a major portion of the wine, coughed, then wiped her mouth with the back of her hand. When she looked up, she found him watching her, an amused glint in his eyes and a smirk on his handsome mouth.

"Public drunkenness would cause a stir also, Angelique."

Without thinking, she passed him the almost empty glass, and he took it without question.

"I never drank wine until I came here. Papa considered it sinful." Waving her hands over her breasts, she blinked back tears. "I've never worn a dress so revealing, either." The tears overflowed and Mathias pulled her into an uninhabited corner of the dimly lit room.

"Oh, Mathias, the women look at me with pity, and I have no idea what the men must think of me, but I'm sure they consider me someone of easy virtue."

He handed her a handkerchief, and she dabbed her eyes with it. At her side, he moved, and she heard him offer a greeting to someone. When she glanced up, she saw a person she did not know moving away. People milled about. Thank goodness, no one else approached them.

"Better?" he asked.

"Yes."

He took a step back and spoke briefly to someone near them. She didn't care to look.

"These people think nothing of the sort," he admonished when he returned his attention to her. "You are self-conscious. You and I know there is no reason for anyone to pity you."

"My papa would not agree. The perception that some might think I was touched by even one of those men would be enough in his eyes to shame me."

His fingers bit into her arm, and he forced her to face him.

"Then your father was a self-righteous, self-centered hypocrite, who cared more for appearance than he did his own daughter."

He felt her stiffen beneath his hold, and he focused on those brown eyes, which had now narrowed on him. Damn, she had spirit despite her short lifetime of that bastard's trying to stifle it. Spirit and strength.

"My father has been dead only months."

Pity he hadn't died years ago. Still, it was not wrong for her to defend her daddy, and he had been insensitive to malign the man.

"I apologize for stating my words in your presence."

Her mouth dropped open, and he braced.

"For saying the words in front of me, but not for the words themselves?"

Her self-consciousness was over, at least, and he would take credit for that. He couldn't have provoked her resurgence better if he'd tried.

"I can recall things about your father from when I was a child. Things he said, things he did. The strife he caused Bess without remorse. His intent became clearer as I grew older. No, I do not apologize for the words."

Her jaw set—he saw it—and she raised herself to her full height. Possibly he had traded one embarrassing scene for another. Warily, he tilted his head away from her. "This is not the time or place to rebuke me, Angelique. Let me take you to Grandmother." He reached out to take her arm, but she avoided his grasp.

"Thank you, so much," she said testily, "but I will—"

"What are you doing with Angelique, Cousin?"

If Angelique had not stood in front of him, Mathias would have cursed. Instead, he calmly turned and looked at André. What the hell did the man think he was doing with the girl?

Angelique stepped between them.

"Mathias and I are having an enlightening conversation," she said.

51

André studied her, glanced at Mathias, then looked back to Angelique. "I believe you were to join Grandmama and the ladies in the parlor?"

For a moment, Mathias thought André was about to bear the brunt of the wrath he'd engendered, but Angelique's countenance suddenly calmed. She turned to Mathias, at the same time placing her back to André.

"And I believe you were sent to escort me, sir."

Whether she acted by design or if she didn't realize her tactic would annoy André, Mathias didn't know, but he suspected that she knew. He reached to take her arm.

"Oh, there's Aunt Elizabeth. It appears she's given up on you, Mathias, and come searching for me on her own."

His grandmother had indeed entered the room, whether in search of Angelique or not, Mathias didn't know. Bess hadn't really sent him to find her.

A hand touched his, and he found Angelique watching him. She gave him a dazzling smile, false by any intelligent man's reckoning, and that assessment was strongly supported by the challenge in her eyes. She bobbed that head of flaxen curls, then glanced over her shoulder at André. "If you and André will excuse me."

She took two steps, then stopped and looked back at him. "Mathias?"

André shifted his weight, obviously chafed. Mathias tilted his head.

"Thank you."

"You are welcome."

She bit her bottom lip, then moved away. The "thank you" had been hard to say. He watched the soft train of her skirt sway as she retreated with Bess. He had managed to offend her greatly, but that was all right. Her preoccupation with being angry at him had possibly saved her tonight.

"What happened?" André asked.

Inwardly, Mathias cursed the bastard. "I got her out of that circle of lustful males before she started screaming."

André cocked his head, inviting him to continue.

"She was back on the Trace. You'd have realized that if you'd looked at her. She was pale as a ghost, her skin damp to my touch."

"I see no reason for you to spirit her to a dark corner."

"She needed a dark corner to compose herself."

"This corner was not dark enough. Too many curious eyes watched the two of you."

"I'm aware of what went on around us. The only concerned eyes were yours. But next time, I will find a more secluded spot in which to comfort Angelique."

André's nostrils flared. "She didn't appear comforted when I arrived."

"I"—Mathias furrowed his brow—"distracted her would be a good way of saying it."

"How?"

This was becoming tiresome. "The conversations I have with Angelique are not your concern." Mathias started around him, but André moved and blocked his way.

"You will do the girl no good."

"What makes you think I mean her good?"

Half a head taller, André stood like a wall blocking his advance. Mathias waited, and André flexed his jaw. "What does Grandmama have planned for her?"

"Ask Bess."

"Does she intend to send her to De Leau?"

Mathias resisted the urge to make fists with his sweating hands. "Another virgin sacrifice to sate the *démon's* sexual appetite, you mean?"

"You took a great risk rescuing her from Hoss' men. She could have been killed."

Mathias narrowed his eyes in suspicion. They'd had this conversation before. "You guessed my purpose, Cousin. Certainly the demon would have been displeased with a tainted offering."

André looked over Mathias' shoulder. "Ah, Angelique…"

Mathias spun. She stood there, contemplating him, the look in her eyes undecipherable. He fought to keep his features equally unmoved, but he knew she'd heard too much. Silently, he cursed André's black soul.

"Dinner is served, I assume?" André continued blithely.

She didn't respond or drop her unwavering gaze until André stepped around him and took her arm.

"Except for the early incident, Angelique did well, don't you think?"

"Yes," Mathias said. He didn't mention André's success in duping him in front of the young beauty. "I don't believe anyone noticed her discomfort. All the roosters had gathered around her, but were too busy trying to out-crow one another to notice how upset she became."

His grandmother took her place behind the desk. "I didn't consider her becoming frightened. Nervous, yes. I knew she was dreading tonight. She'd never been to a formal dinner." Bess fidgeted. "Never wore a dress in fashion, much less one that made her feel appealing. Damn Jude and his poisoned, sanctimonious mind.

"Rumors are spreading she was raped," she continued, keeping her eyes on him as he settled into the upholstered chair in front of her. "Not by one, but by several of the gang."

Bile swelled Mathias' chest. André fanned the lie. He and Angelique's fellow travelers, the gutless wonders who'd.... "I know, but she was not. She is a charming child—"

"She's a beautiful, fallen woman and fair game."

The odds were good his grandmother's assessment of the gossip was right. Thank God he intervened tonight before she collapsed in a hysterical fit. He considered that might have been André's intent, but doubted the man had enough feeling in his selfish soul to realize the girl could be disturbed as she had been.

"She needs to hold her head high," he said, "and make a place for herself in society. No matter how she balks, you cannot allow her to hide inside this house."

"I understand that, Grandson, but I have many enemies. People will attempt to hurt me through her." Bess sighed. "The sad part is they cannot hurt me, and they will be tearing Angelique apart for no reason. Did you note the way Carriere sniffed after her?"

"She doesn't like him. That was obvious to anyone watching them."

His grandmother cast him a sly look. "I've been told the major is taken with a number of women, including the widow Mallory."

"Kate is an independent woman. Our relationship is one of mutual gratification."

"Do you not have a jealous bone in your body, Mathias?"

Did she refer to something other than the primordial rage that pressed him to rip out Major Carriere's throat? And that urge did not begin to compare with what he wanted to do to André. Neither impulse had to do with Kate Mallory.

"Kate would not appreciate that fault in me. She lives her life as she wishes and wants no ties to anyone."

"Good for her," she said dryly.

Mathias kept steady eyes on her. "Carriere is not the only man with unsuitable designs on Angelique."

"I know."

"He has been by often?"

"I have seen more of him in the past month than I have in the past year."

Mathias said nothing, but hoped his grandmother would elaborate further on André's visits.

"Charles came over to meet Angelique last week," she said after a pause. "Louise has been here twice. Charles told me Louise is worried over André's interest in the girl. Louise is concerned about the engagement to Clarice Delacroix, but Charles told me there was no reason for either of us to be."

Mathias' head started to pound. If André had gone so far as to confide his desires to his father, he was not looking at Angelique as someone to seduce and sleep with for a brief amusement.

"André wants Angelique for his mistress?"

"Yes, a true New Orleans townhouse mistress, Damn them! She will not turn seventeen for another month. I had to muster a great deal of fortitude not to throw my firstborn out of this house. He is a fool if he thinks I will stand by and see my sister's grand-daughter put in that position, soiled reputation or not."

"The decision will ultimately be Angelique's."

Bess slammed her palms to the desk top. "The hell it will." She eyed him sternly. "I've more important plans for Angelique."

Mathias stared at his grandmother. "And those are?"

She rose with a flurry. "Suffice it to say she will not forfeit her destiny to become André's whore."

"'Destiny,' Grandmother?" A weighty word when used in ref-erence to a sixteen-year-old female.

"I owe Véronique that much," she said, staring out the win-dow into the dark.

"What do you have—"

She waved her hand in obvious vexation. "Enough," she said. He could see her reflection watching him in the dark glass. "I have no plans, but I know what I will *not* allow, and that is André's absconding with her."

Her words soothed him somewhat, if not entirely. He was sure if she did have plans for Angelique, she had no intention of divulging them to him tonight.

All of a sudden, she laughed and moved back to her desk where she picked up a pamphlet, open and lying face down. "One of William's treatises on tobacco planting. It's twenty years old if a day." She graced him with a wry twist of her lips. "Angelique is reading it. She's devoured everything in this library. She prob-ably knows more about indigo and tobacco planting than I do, and sugarcane is a particular favorite of hers."

Mathias grinned.

"Jude would allow her to read nothing but the Bible, and he chose the passages. Normally, she told me, he read it to her. Nightly. For hours on end, Mathias. Angelique wouldn't be liter-ate today, and her skills are still limited, except the poor little tit-mouse, forced to marry her father, fought him on that issue and actually won."

"I'm surprised Foster taught his daughter to read."

"Foster was a hypocrite. He was no more God-fearing than I am, but he preached the points that served him well. A woman's role included housekeeping, as well as childrearing and husband-serving, and he believed she required a minimum exposure to reading and numbers to accomplish the former. The bastard's fawning son-in-law had to agree. Therefore, our little Angelique is so starved for literary entertainment she finds delight in agricultural treatises." She tossed the thin document on top of the desk and sat. "Good Lord, she is not what André needs. She lacks sophistication and sexual experience. What in God's name does he mean with taking this tactic?"

"Angelique credits me with saving her on the Trace. Her admiration chafes André."

Old Bess closed her eyes, then briefly laid her head against the back of her chair. Again she rose, cursed without looking his way, and walked to the console where she poured them each a whiskey.

"Speaking of the incident on the Trace, tell me of the discussion after dinner?" She handed him his drink.

"The governor offered his heartfelt thanks."

"He offered you no recompense?"

"No."

"André?"

"An endorsement to Carondelet for the post in New Orleans."

She pursed her lips. "André thinks too much before he acts. Carondelet doesn't think at all. He will not be happy with him."

"Perhaps he won't, but Gayoso wasn't passing out land grants tonight, and André has wanted that posting for the past two years. It's common knowledge."

"Who led the attack against Hossman?"

The night was growing old. Weary, he sat forward. "There were only three of us—"

"Who led the attack, Mathias?"

"André is the oldest. He's landed and holds status. It stands to reason he should receive credit."

"That is no reason at all."

"I was not going to contradict André in front of the governor. To claim for oneself what is presumed for another is demeaning."

"Did André say anything regarding your conduct that day?"

"He did not," she answered herself when he said nothing. "He took the credit, the posting, and he wants Angelique, for no other reason than he thinks you might get her.

"He is ambitious, ruthless, and politically savvy, but when it comes to any form of military initiative, André is merely adequate at best. You orchestrated the rescue of Angelique, and you led the attack."

"You don't know that."

She whipped around in front of him, her satin skirts rustling. "I would know even if I had not already talked to Indigo."

"Indigo is loyal to me. His credibility is tainted."

Her eyes widened. "Indigo's first loyalty is to me.

"Damn," she said, sitting hard in the chair behind the desk. "I was hoping for a land grant adjacent to De Leau to increase the farm."

"De Leau is yours, Grandmother."

She found his eyes. "Yes," she said, "it is."

And she would hold it close. She always had. Mathias scowled in self-derision. Of all her properties it was of the least value, but it had been the first. The other holdings, White Oak Glen's acres and acres of cleared pasture and William Boswell's thriving mercantile business, headquartered now in New Orleans, she would cede to her second- and third-born sons. That was arranged. But De Leau was hers. Her heart was there, perhaps even her soul. She had been born there, and Mathias believed that in the end, she would die there. For sure she would be laid to rest in its family plot with her parents and siblings, two of her husbands, and her children. From the French, through the British, and now under the Spanish, Elizabeth Deschesne held the modest farm. People whispered she'd bartered for it, killed for it, even sold her soul to ensure it remained hers. Mathias wanted De Leau so badly he could taste the rich, black soil on his tongue.

"There's plenty of free land for squatting, Grandson."

"You know I could not leave De Leau any more than you could give it up."

She tightened her lips and looked away. An assurance from her would have been enough to relieve the ache in his chest. She did not give it. Once again he steeled himself to her cool exterior. She had given him a home, her name, even his life.

He set down his glass and rose.

"You will stay here tonight?"

He could tell by her voice she did not expect him to.

"No."

"The wicked widow may not be alone."

"She knows I'm in town. She will be."

"You're very confident."

"About some things, Bess."

Chapter Five

"I did not mean to offend—"

Angelique would have argued the point, but when she looked at Lydia Arcourt's half-closed eyelids and the smug smile on the woman's lips, she knew there would be nothing gained.

With a shaking hand, Angelique set her empty wine glass on an abandoned tray and moved into the near-deserted dining room of Abbey Falwell's single-story house. The brightly lit table was now a jumble of decimated platters, which two hours ago had overflowed with meats, breads, and assorted delicacies.

"Mrs. Arcourt is a most unpleasant person," Jane whispered in her ear. "She is extremely jealous of Grandmother's position in society here, wishing to supersede it." Jane positioned herself in front of Angelique. "I hope you didn't say anything to her that would embarrass the family."

Angelique's chest tightened. She had said nothing tonight to embarrass her grandaunt. The embarrassment had occurred with Hossman's men on the Trace. Hold your head up high, her grandaunt repeatedly told her, paraphrasing Mathias' words at the governor's dinner. Don't acknowledge their words or accept their sympathy or fall prey to their censure.

Angelique lifted an eyebrow. "And what could I have told her that would hurt Aunt Elizabeth?"

Timothy Dobbins snuck up behind Jane and nuzzled her behind her ear. With a soft yelp, Jane turned, and he kissed her.

"Tim, stop it," Jane gasped, "Mama might see."

"And force me to honor you?"

60

"Or have Daddy shoot you." Jane sucked in a breath at another caress.

They were not betrothed, and Angelique doubted such public display appropriate if they had been. Jane caught her watching, and her eyes narrowed.

"Must you stare?"

"I was certain you were putting on a public performance."

Jane straightened, but Tim's hand circled her upper arm. "Angelique is right. Come." And he determinedly pulled her toward a door at the rear of the dining room.

Angelique gritted her teeth and, lifting the skirt of the burnt orange gown, stepped quickly across Abbey Falwell's dining room and down the breezeway to the cookhouse. There, she went out the back door.

The cold October night cooled her flushed body. She pulled the door shut behind her and, in the darkness, swiped at a tear. The calming breath she sought deteriorated into a sob, and she descended three steps into thick grass, from where she started running toward her aunt's house.

On the narrow street, she slowed, oblivious of the cold and the dust she kicked up with her slippers. The sob became tears, but as long as no one saw, no harm was done. Her father despised tears, but Aunt Elizabeth said tears were good for the soul. Her aunt's and father's ideas about what was good for the soul were so different.

At the lane leading home, she stopped. Her tears had stopped, as well, and except for the fact that she was bitterly cold, she felt better. Perhaps her aunt was right in this particular case. She wrapped her bare arms around her shivering body. She didn't have her cape, and no one knew she'd left. She'd have to go back...eventually, after her tears dried. For now, she'd go home.

Rubbing her arms, she started down the dirt road, picking her way to avoid mud-filled ruts she couldn't see.

A sound whispered to her, and she stopped dead still. She and her aunt and cousins had walked to Abbey's house with a lantern. Only now, with a shadow several paces ahead looming against the backdrop of the night and the hair at the back of her neck on end, did she realize her folly.

She swallowed and tasted terror.

"Angelique?"

"Mathias?" she croaked.

"Yes." He stayed completely still.

Again, she breathed out his name. "You frightened me."

He walked to her. "I feared I had."

The scent of sandalwood filled her nostrils and, inexplicably, she reached for him. For reassurance, she guessed. She hadn't seen him since Governor Gayoso's dinner, and she'd yet to forgive his slander against her papa. But overhearing André's comments about De Leau and Mathias' subsequent reference to virgin sacrifices, mocking though his words might have been, had made her need for an apology seem silly.

He took her outstretched hand and pulled her closer. "I'm sorry I scared you."

Her racing heart didn't slow, and when she resisted his pull, he stopped. She could barely make out his features.

"Can you see in the dark, Mathias?"

"I sensed you, Angelique," he said softly.

How could he "sense" her?

"I can smell your scent."

A shiver, neither fear- nor cold-induced, moved through her. "I can smell you, too, but only when you stand close."

She felt his thumb against her cheek. "And do I smell as good as you?"

"You smell of sandalwood."

"That's not what I smell on you."

She freed her hand and stepped back.

Apparently undiscouraged, he said, "Why are you crying?"

"I'm not." Her teeth chattered, and she bit her tongue.

"You were."

"I was not enjoying myself."

He snorted softly. "You have no idea what a good time is, so I doubt you'd know you weren't having one."

Another veiled criticism of her father. "Well," she said haugh-tily, "your doubts carry no weight with me." She would not re-hash her concerns to him. He felt she should have no worries regarding the incident on the Trace, and from his point of view, perhaps he was right. She started around him, but he caught hold of her naked arm.

"You're freezing." Abruptly he let her go, and his shadowed form pulled off his coat. A black silhouette fanned over her head, and she jumped. Then the woolen coat, the scents of sandalwood and tobacco stronger than ever, covered her shoulders. His hands held it in place.

"Did I frighten you again?"

Her heart clamored against her ribs, and she admitted to her-self she had considered the possibility the coat was being thrown over her head.

"What did you mean at the governor's dinner party when you and André were talking of my going to De Leau?"

His fingers, still on her shoulders, tightened.

"To slake the demon's lust, you mean?"

"Yes."

He dropped his hands. "Did you think I meant to steal you away in the dark?"

"What were you and he talking about?"

"I still could, you know."

"Answer me."

Up the road, the front door of Miss Abbey's house opened, and Mathias threw an arm over her shoulder and drew her in the direction of the Boswell house.

"You've heard the stories, Angelique?"

She rolled her head against his shoulder, trying to see his face. "Well?"

"Papa rarely spoke to me of Natchez. All he said was that Aunt Elizabeth was a wicked person who had stolen his birth-right. But I heard him talking to my mother once when I was small. He was angry at her about something. I think she wanted Papa to write Aunt Elizabeth. She rarely ever argued with him, but this time she did. I can remember him yelling at her, telling her De Leau was haunted."

"By what?"

She tightened her lips as Mathias hurried them down the footpath to the house.

He squeezed her shoulders. "Did he say?"

"By the devil who is your father."

"I thought you knew. Figured you did when you realized who I was on the Trace." He all but dragged her up the porch steps. She could see him better now in the lantern light shining through the window glass. At the door, he stopped and faced her. "André knew you were behind me, Angelique. He wanted me to say what I did to frighten you away from me. Fool that I am, I did."

"But how did he—"

"The story goes Bess offered her virgin daughter in recompense for the demon's service in helping her secure De Leau. Older tales about my grandmother say the thing helped her get rid of her two husbands, her stepfather, and her brother. No one has thought to include William Boswell as one of the personages she wished to divest herself of." He shrugged. "Perhaps she'd become too well respected by the time he died."

"André believes this story?"

"No. André wished to turn you against me. He didn't know I had already done that with my words against your father."

Mathias' dislike of her papa seemed insignificant now. "Does anyone really believe this tale?"

"Your father did."

She opened her mouth to protest.

"You did."

"I did not. My memory of Papa's words is confused. I hadn't thought about what he said for years until I saw you on the Trace. That day you seemed"—she hesitated—"more than a man."

His lips, compellingly handsome in the gentle glow of lantern light, smiled at her. "And do you still believe me more than a man?"

She tensed. He'd twisted her compliment into an insult, and she detested it. "Do you?"

His smile disappeared, and his countenance darkened. Abruptly, he opened the front door and ushered her inside. "I don't know who or what my father is," he said to her back.

She spun around, reassuring herself with his appearance.

He noticed, and his look hardened. "You were expecting me to be different? Horns perhaps?" He raised a booted foot and flexed it in front of her. "Cloven feet?"

He closed the door with a deceptively ominous click.

She looked at the door, then to him in front of it. He had her trapped if that were his intent. She drew her hand to her quaking stomach.

"Are you comforted by what you see, Miss?"

She narrowed her eyes, and was thankful for his ensuing grin. Still, she wasn't sure if he were angry or amusing himself by teasing her. As for her, she was becoming angry.

"It's an illusion," he said.

"And what do you mean by that?"

"The monster lies beneath the exterior."

Angelique drew in a long breath, studying him all the while and wondering if such a thing were possible.

"Are you trying to see beneath my skin, Angelique?"

"I'm trying to understand why someone who looks like you would say such a thing?"

His eyes widened in what was, she was sure, mock surprise. "Someone who looks like me?"

Her cheeks heated, and he laughed and stepped from the door. For certain, he thought her a silly chit.

"Where is your cape?" His voice had lost its teasing lilt, and when he reached for the coat covering her shoulders, she shrugged out of it. His gaze moved slowly over her, head to foot, and her heartbeat quickened anew.

"I left it at Miss Abbey's."

"Ah, that's where everyone is, Miss Abbey's Halloween *soirée*."

"I was told Miss Abbey has one every year. I expected you there."

"I'd forgotten the date."

"You of all people forgot All Hallows' Eve?" She caught the glint in his eye and could have kicked herself for purposely provoking him again.

"Does anyone know you left?"

She blinked at him. "I fear not. I was.... I wanted to get out quickly and get some air."

"You mean you didn't want anyone to see you cry?"

"I must go back," she said and started toward the door. "Aunt Elizabeth will be worried."

He stepped in front of her. "I'll go," he said, placing a fisted hand beneath her chin and gently tipping her face to his. His gaze faltered, fell, then lingered on her mouth before returning to her eyes. Her knees weakened.

"You are not dressed the part tonight, sweet Angelique." His breath whispered warmly on her lips. "The object of Halloween is to frighten demons back into hell, not to tempt them."

His gaze locked on hers, and a delicious tremble swept her body, quickly displaced by shame. She splayed a hand over the swell of her breasts.

"Papa would agree. I told Aunt—"

"Hush," he said, opening his fist and feathering his fingers over her throat. "My words mean something very different from your papa's."

"No, Papa was a—"

"Self-serving, puritanical tyrant."

Satan take him. Stiff-armed, she tried to push away, but his palm exerted increasing pressure on the back of her neck, countering her resistance, and he drew her face to his. Knowing she was about to lose the struggle, she opened her mouth to protest and his firm lips touched, then covered hers. His hand cupped her jaw, holding her, while she twisted her fingers into his shirt. His mouth moved over hers in a demanding caress while his free arm circled her waist and drew her against him. He was hard and strong, secure and warm. In the space of a heartbeat, her body, still chilled from the cold outside, sought his warmth rather than resisted it. He must have felt the change in her, because in the next instant, heat seared her soul when his tongue invaded her mouth, then tangled with hers.

Her fear and anger gave way to something she could not identify, and she melted against him with an unbidden moan. He moved his hand along her jaw, gently stroking with his thumb before releasing her lips and raising his face from hers. He retained the arm around her waist.

"Your first kiss, Angelique?"

His question jolted her. How she wished it had been, but it wasn't.

"Hoss," she whispered hoarsely. "He yanked my hair back and—" She felt him stiffen, and his hold weakened. She thought she would die.

"I'm sorry. I didn't mean to conjure bad memories."

She crushed herself against him, desperate he not let her go. "You did not. You drowned them, Mathias. Until you asked, I had forgotten. Kiss me again, one more time, I promise I'll ask no more."

And he had, providing her the assurance she needed, while careful to keep his passions in check. No easy matter considering the innocent young woman didn't recognize her own.

What had he been thinking to initiate a kiss to begin with?

Truth was he hadn't been thinking at all, he'd used pure instinct. His body warmed, remembering her response and then her second kiss. He cursed himself.

Mathias knocked firmly before pushing Miss Abbey's door open. A servant intercepted him, then nodded at his grandmother. Bess had donned her cape and held another, which he assumed to be Angelique's. She was in harried conversation with his Aunt Sarah.

"Mathias," Abbey squealed, coming up to him and gracing him with a hug, "how nice you came."

Abbey liked him, and Mathias considered that was because

she hoped he was a monster beneath his human exterior.

Bess had turned at the sound of his name, and now a scowl contorted her features. "What are you doing in Natchez?"

He leaned over to kiss her cheek. "I've come up from Hawlin's."

She frowned at him, and he smiled.

"For a pint with Josiah Weber. He had an Opelousa mare he wanted me to see."

"How was she?"

"Looked like a mule."

"You should talk to Gayoso."

"He's not selling."

Out of the corner of his eye, he watched a lithe body float gracefully across the crowded room. "Hello, Mathias. You're late." Jane's lilting voice was soft and seductive, and neither he nor anyone else in the room, including Jane's mother, could have missed its suggestion. Jane's provocative manner gave him grim satisfaction, for Aunt Sarah saw and heard everything. He bowed stiffly in salute.

"Cousin, you look lovely."

"Thank you," she answered, breathing in, then exhaling a provocative sigh.

Her pouting lips were red and swollen. Bruised from Tim Dobbins' kisses, Mathias thought, watching Tim move up to take a place possessively behind her. Given the flush of Jane's skin and Tim's victory smile, more had occurred between the two than innocent kisses. Mathias caught Tim's eye and acknowledged his conquest with a curt nod.

His grandmother cast Jane a disapproving glance before turning to him. "I seem to have lost Angelique, and I'm beginning to worry."

He dipped his head to Jane and his Aunt Sarah, then took his grandmother's elbow and steered her out of their hearing. "She's home."

"Why?"

"Something happened—"

"Elizabeth, darling..." The plump and effervescent Abbey blundered into their conversation, a distinctive trait of Abigail Halloran Falwell's. Abbey was such a sweetheart most forgave her minor infractions.

"...she was seen talking to Lydia Arcourt a half hour past." Abbey's round face displayed a smile. She was enjoying her party, but the quick nod of her head and simultaneous rise of her brows, conveyed understanding between the two women.

"Thank you, Abbey. Mathias tells me she became ill rather quickly and went home. She still has bouts from her injuries on the Trace."

"She asked me to pass on her apologies and thank you for a lovely time," Mathias added.

Forming her lips into a sympathetic "O", Abbey winced. "I am sorry she doesn't feel well. I shall call on you both tomorrow, Elizabeth. I am so happy you came."

Slyly Abbey took Mathias' hand, then covered it with her other. "Will you not stay, dear boy?" She snickered at his grandmother. "I am certain Jane would love it, and it would annoy Sarah so."

"That is not the reaction I wish to provoke when seeking female attention, Miss Abbey."

As he suspected she would, Miss Abbey tittered like a girl.

"Thank heaven for that," Elizabeth said. "It is I who will have to endure Thomas and Sarah's complaint, and I have no desire to become embroiled in such prattle."

"Until next Halloween, then."

"You're coming to see me tomorrow, Abbey," Elizabeth chided, leaning over to kiss her friend's cheek. "It was a wonderful party as always."

Someone had, without a doubt, made reference to Angelique's supposedly lost virtue, he explained to his grandmother while escorting her home.

Mathias stopped at the door and handed her Angelique's cloak. He didn't want to see the petite beauty again tonight. She

69

was too vulnerable and too far removed from him. He would do her harm, in that André was correct.

"The rumors disturb her greatly," Bess said.

"I think part of what worries her is disgracing you."

"If the poor child only knew."

"She knows the stories. What she doesn't know is you."

"She will learn in time I live by my own convictions."

"And the ones you profess are more wicked than those you actually live by."

He saw her smirk in the lantern light, and he licked his bottom lip. "Rachel asked me to speak to you regarding Ethan."

Bess closed her eyes.

"He brought five steer to the fort for me this morning. He works like a pair of oxen. He's more than paid for himself."

"And if I free him, do you think he'll stay at De Leau?"

"Is that what you fear, that he'll leave?"

"I fear he'll leave and take Rachel."

Of course, he should have realized that before. "Even if he did leave De Leau proper, he'd not go far. There's nothing on the Loosa Chitto for him now, and yes, he could follow his old master back to New Jersey. By all accounts Dickson was a good man, but if that's what Ethan wanted, he'd have told Rachel so before you bought him."

"Have you talked to him?"

"Not about his leaving. The thought never occurred to me, but I will. He wants his freedom."

Bess sighed. "Being wed to a free woman makes him feel less than a man in her eyes."

"And she suffers his frustration."

"I don't want him taking Rachel away."

Mathias smiled in understanding. "You can't keep everyone here with you forever, Bess."

"A fact I learned before you were born, but I can try to hold to what's still here."

He started toward the steps. "I'll talk to him about his plans."

"The moon is rising, Mathias," she said, then teased him with

70

a growl. "Do you enter the swamp this Halloween night in search of victims?"

He'd already tasted the prey he wanted. "I have a willing victim waiting at the end of town."

"A redhead, I trust?"

"Most assuredly red." He looked down at the toe of his boot on the next to top step. "Jane does not appeal to me, Bess. She's a snobbishness about her that reminds me of her mother."

"She does not share her mother's prejudice of you."

He grinned in the darkness. "Aunt Sarah's concern deals with social stature. Jane's interest lies between my legs."

"You are fresh tonight, Grandson."

"She's developed a reputation for flirtatiousness, you know?"

"Being kind to your enamored cousin? I fear she has developed a reputation for more than that."

Little happened within this family, or in Natchez, that Elizabeth Boswell wasn't aware of. Mathias stifled a yawn and started down the steps. "Have no fear for her from me, Grandmother."

"Should I fear for another?"

His stomach contracted, and he stopped on the bottom step to look up at her. "Not yet."

Chapter Six

"What do you know about a man called Derussy Lee?"

Baby, startled, dropped three pieces from the stack of wood she was bringing inside. Angelique hurried around the table to help her.

Before Angelique's arrival, her Aunt Elizabeth had lived alone, but for Baby and Ben. Wee Ben, everyone called him, though he was anything but "wee." Ben and Indigo, the man who had been with Mathias and André on the Trace, were Baby's brothers. Angelique initially thought they were slaves, but they weren't. Their father Benjamin, whom Angelique assumed to be the "big" Ben contrasting the younger Ben's "wee," had been a slave years ago in the days of Aunt Elizabeth's second husband, Robert Douglas. Ben's children, however, were freeborn, their mother the offspring of a Choctaw woman and a French trapper. Indigo, his father Benjamin, and the rest of their extended family lived at De Leau with Mathias.

Angelique tossed one of the logs onto the pile. The hour was late, but she couldn't sleep, her body still throbbing with lust, her conscience with shame over the kisses she'd shared with Mathias.

The second time he'd kissed her, she'd tightened her arms around his neck and drawn him to her. And he'd taken what she offered. Her father said a weak man was easily led into sin by any woman. Her erect nipples tingled from being crushed against his hard chest, and liquid heat still pooled between her legs each time she thought of his tongue caressing hers. What must he think of her?

"What you doin' up, missy?"

72

"I couldn't sleep."

Baby giggled. "Them rich foods they give you bad dreams that's fo' sure."

Angelique did have nightmares, but not tonight. "I've yet to sleep, Baby. Now, do you know about this person called Derussy Lee?"

Baby stacked the wood in the bin, straightened, then wiped her hands on her apron.

"Yes'm I know that bad man you be askin' 'bout."

"Mathias killed him?"

Baby started to speak, then turned from her as if searching for something else to do...anything else.

"Tell me."

Baby glanced quickly over her shoulder. "Long time ago." Again she averted her gaze and stepped toward the breakfront.

"Who was he?"

Baby opened a cabinet door.

"Baby, please. I'll help you finish your chores for the night, but talk to me now."

The young woman looked at her.

The fire was long out, the kitchen cold. Angelique pulled her wool shawl tighter around her nightgown.

"Chores all done. I'd of finished earlier, but I sneaked over to Miss Abbey's to see her free man Luke."

"And did you see your Luke?"

Baby laughed. Angelique sat at the rough worktable and patted the surface with her open palm, bidding Baby do the same.

"Tell me about Derussy Lee."

With a twist of her mouth and a heavy sigh, Baby sat. "He was a trapper, from Georgia we learned later. New to these parts. He come to De Leau with a man named Homer Coupée. Mr. Coupée passed through De Leau regular, trading skins for goods or working for trade in kind. This time I'm tellin' you 'bout was the first time he brought Derussy Lee with him. They had beaver pelt and wanted to trade.

"The women was there. All the men, 'cept Wee Ben, him bein'

too little, and Mathias, was at White Oak Glen bringing in Master Boswell's tobacco crop. Rachel was fourteen. Mathias was a few months behind her. Them two growed up together like brother and sister.

"Mathias had went off in the woods that mornin' roundin' up cattle. One of the new Spanish officers at the fort told him he'd give top dollar for three head." Baby smiled at her. "I was a little bitty thing, but I r'member he was so excited to earn money for De Leau and make his grandmama proud."

"So there were no men at De Leau when these two trappers came?"

"No, but nobody thought nothin' about Homer Coupée comin'. We knew 'im." Baby nodded knowingly at Angelique. "Didn't know Derussy Lee, though. Don't know how well Homer Coupée knew him either, but I reckon not very.

"Anyways, Rachel took a likin' to some beads that man Lee had, and he took a shine to her. Turned out he weren't going to take no for an answer. While Mama was bartering with Mr. Coupée in the cookhouse, Derussy Lee took what he wanted from Rachel out behind the corn crib. Mama didn't find her till after those two left. He'd beat her.

"Mathias come home with his steers soon after. He tracked them men. Found 'em and killed 'em."

"How?"

"Shot poor Homer Coupeé for sure, but there be one story say he killed Derussy Lee with a knife." Baby shook her head. "But Daddy and Indigo say Mathias shot 'em both. Mathias was only a boy. He couldn't have won a knife fight with a growed man."

"Why did he kill Homer Coupée?"

"Cause he knew what happened. Mr. Coupée went to find Derussy Lee after he was done barterin' with Mama. He found his partner with Rachel, but instead of rightin' the wrong, he gathered him up and they run from De Leau. Daddy say Mathias couldn't forgive that."

Angelique thought back to that day on the Trace and swallowed. "Tell me about Rachel."

Baby yawned, then fidgeted with her skirt. She was ready to go to bed, no doubt. "She's married," she said. "Miss Bessy bought one of Mr. Dickson's slaves up on the Loosa Chitto Rachel went and fell in love with. They live out at De Leau."

"There are no children?"

"Not yet."

And no further elaboration. Angelique drew in a breath and looked around the kitchen. "Are you sure there's nothing I can help you with?"

"Not before mornin'. Tomorrow's bakin' day. Got to get up real early."

Angelique nodded and started to push herself up. "Thank you for talking to me."

"Miss Angelique?"

She sat back down, and Baby leaned across the table.

"No matter what my brother and daddy say, there's them that believe Mathias used a knife on Derussy Lee. Say he cut off Lee's cock, then stuffed it down his throat."

"You mean his manhood?"

"Sure, his manhood." Baby motioned her closer, and when their noses almost touched, she whispered, "While he was still alive."

Angelique sat back. Baby straightened more slowly.

"But my mama says ain't no truth to that. Says it ain't nothin' but a scary tale Yo tells so people will fear Mathias."

I gave her Yo's brew from the Choctaw Lily. She told me she has blood in her urine. The drug will stem the bleeding. The liver is for Yo. Angelique shuddered at the memory of those words. "Tell me about Yo."

"Old slave out at De Leau. Been there longer'n anyone livin'. Miss Elizabeth's daddy bought her when she was a girl. Your great-grandmother was carryin' Miss Elizabeth in her belly then. Yo and Miss Elizabeth, they hates each other."

"Do you know why?"

Baby shook her head. "Goes way back. I've heard Miss Bessy fussing at Mathias. She say Yo ain't nothin' but a black witch.

75

But"—Baby waved an index finger under Angelique's nose—
"when I was a little girl out at De Leau, I heard Yo say same such
'bout Miss Elizabeth."

Chapter Seven

"Mama received this land in 1765 in a land grant from the British for the service my father provided the Crown between 1741 and 1760 when he died."

Angelique looked over the fields pointed out by her cousin, Thomas Douglas. The morning was chilly, the sky clear blue, but there was no frost. She sank a bit in the soft dirt outside the barn, but managed to miss the areas still muddy from the rain two days ago. This was the third and final day of her first visit to White Oak Glen.

Thomas smiled. "For the most part, 'service' meant stirring up hate and discontent between the Chickasaw and the French allied with the Choctaw. I always thought it fitting he fell in love with a young French widow trying to survive alone with a newborn babe and a younger brother and sister." He turned to Angelique. "And let no one fool you, girl, your great-uncle, Robert Douglas, loved my mama.

"I was thirteen when Daddy was killed. Charles was sixteen. But even while Daddy was alive, things were hard at De Leau. French colonization all but ended with the massacre at Rosalie. You could count the families out here on three fingers. We lived off the land. There was some trade with the soldiers in Natchez, but most trade was done with trappers or the Indians, who themselves traded with whites farther north and east. When I was sixteen, the British drove the French out. The British encouraged colonization and trade." He nodded to some small, low-standing buildings. "Drying houses. Tobacco was good for a long time. So was rice and indigo, but the British are gone and Spanish trade laws are unwieldy and out of date. There's no more market for our tobacco in Spain, and the Spanish Crown won't let us trade with other nations, not legally. Gayoso is a godsend. He treats his citizens well and does his best to encourage growth and settlement."

Thomas shook his head. "Americans have come here bringing their ideas of free trade with them. Every day we hear rumors of invasion from Kentucky. Gayoso is hard-pressed to stand against that bunch of renegades and keep Carondelet in check at the same time. Madrid's policies hamper his efforts, too. It's my opinion that in a few years, the Spanish will be driven from this district altogether."

"If tobacco is no—"

"People and land change, Angelique. Some folk are speculating cotton as a cash crop. The invention of the power loom in England is promising, and there's rumor of a good machine for removing seeds from the cotton."

Pursing his lips, Thomas looked over his fields. "We know it grows well here. I'm thinking late winter I might risk a few more acres in it, but not many. Corn is safer."

She pointed to the left where rows of green crops shone in the early morning sun. "Collards, Sarah told me. The growing season here is long."

He nodded. "Our season is long. Greens like cooler weather." Taking her by the arm, he moved her along. "We also grow rice and sugarcane."

"And the indigo?"

"Unhealthy to process, Angelique."

She whipped around in search of the man whose voice nightly charmed her dreams and chased away restless spirits of dead ravishers. Even now, in the light of day, the sight of Mathias sent her heart racing.

"And the recent blight about wiped us out," Thomas added, then extended a hand to him. "You still move like an Indian, boy. I'd say it was a skill taught by your grandfather if you'd known him."

Mathias shook Thomas' hand, then looked at Angelique. "I didn't mean to startle you."

She hadn't seen him since Halloween when he'd kissed her...and she him. Now, under his scrutiny, she turned away to hide the shame heating her face.

He took her chin in his calloused hand and forced her to face him. "Is that a flush?" he asked with a grin. "I didn't mean to cause you embarrassment either...at any time."

As discreetly as her temperament would allow, she twisted from his grasp.

"I am flushed from the cold, thank you, sir."

"She followed me out at the break of dawn. Been after me the last three days to show her White Oak Glen," Thomas said.

She watched Mathias' turn toward the broad expanse of field. Lord, he was a handsome man.

"A lot to see on foot," he responded casually.

"If she's seen one field, she's seen them all. I was taking her to see what's left of the indigo vats."

The tone of Thomas' discourse had stiffened, and he turned away. Angelique followed, and Mathias fell into step beside her. Even now his footfalls were quiet.

"You are here early, Mathias," Thomas said. "Did you come from De Leau?"

"I spent the night in Natchez. I wanted to talk to you, Uncle."

Thomas stopped abruptly and turned with a wary look.

At her side, Angelique heard Mathias release a soft sigh. "Not to worry. I've come on business."

Uneasy, Angelique reached out and touched the cuff of Thomas' coat. "I'll return to the house. I have —"

"My business can wait, Angelique."

"I'm cold, Mathias, and I've worked up an appetite. Thank you for the walk, Thomas." Tentatively, she turned to Mathias. "Will you be at the dance tonight?"

His brow furrowed.

"Santa Maria's," Thomas said. "Christmas is coming, or have you given it no thought?"

"No thought. I'd forgotten the dance and the season."

She held out her hand, and Mathias took it, his touch heating her down to her toes. Goodness knows what her expression told him, because she swore he smirked. Chagrined, Angelique tried to free her hand, then sought his gaze when he refused to let go.

"Aunt Elizabeth has forced Jane and Dora to teach me to dance," she ground out. "If I must be there, I think you should suffer as well."

"Are you implying to dance with you would cause me distress?"

She gave him, she hoped, a haughty smile. "I was referring to mingling with society. As far as dancing is concerned, my cousins have taught me well. I won't step on your feet."

He laughed. "I don't know that dancing with the devil will stand you in good stead, Angelique."

Her stomach tensed. Thomas stood to the side, listening. What must the man be thinking?

"Hold my head up high is what you said." She swallowed. He wouldn't come despite her challenge. "I do that best when you are there."

His gaze held hers. Gently he ran his thumb over her knuckles, warming her entire hand. Then he let her go.

"I'm a fine dancer, sweet angel. Save a dance for me."

She was able to hold a giddy laugh in check and turned with what she was sure must be a silly-looking grin to nod at Thomas.

"Angelique," Mathias called when she started toward the house. She turned to see him fishing something from inside his coat. He handed her a booklet and kept one for himself. "Bess says such things interest you."

A treatise on cotton planting. She laughed happily, which had nothing to do with the booklet on cotton, and thanked him.

𝒜athias watched her go. He hadn't wanted her to leave, but he sensed, rather than knew, the subtle antagonism between his uncle and him had driven her away.

"That girl has a lot of interest in farming," Thomas said when she was out of earshot. "I've seen it here at White Oak Glen, and Mama told me also."

Mathias nodded. "I hear she's about to worry Baby to death. Spends more time in the cookhouse than she does inside."

"She shows understanding of profits and loss. Seems to have a business sense about her. Reminds me of Mama in that. 'Course, Mama had little choice but to learn." Thomas started them toward the collard patch. "Angelique will make a good farmer's wife."

Yes, throw Angelique to the devil and ensure the safety of your own daughter — and good name.

"Jane and Dora have spent the last two days teaching her quadrilles and minuets."

"And a reel?"

Thomas shrugged. "Probably. She's never been to a dance. Sarah says she's excited, but I'm not sure. She seemed pleased you said you'd be there."

Mathias stepped carefully over the furrowed ground. "She can do better than an unlanded man with no name."

"You belittle yourself."

Easily said, considering the source. "Do I?"

Thomas stopped and Mathias stopped with him. "I want you to keep away from Jane, Mathias. She's willful, and your reputation with women is well known."

"I make a point of staying away from Jane." Mathias started walking again. Thomas joined him. "And I have no reputation for deflowering virgins, but you and Aunt Sarah know that. What you fear from me is a proper offer."

His uncle glanced away.

"Jane will never be anything but a cousin to me."

"Your mind works by instinct, Mathias, like a wild animal. That frightens me for my daughter."

Good instinct, Mathias thought, but not wild. In these parts, men lived by instinct or they died. "Lack of social position bothers you and Aunt Sarah, but not nearly as much as your doubts about my sire."

81

He heard his uncle's quick intake of breath.

"It is of no matter," Mathias said. "I didn't come to talk of monsters, wives, and death." He handed Uncle Thomas the treatise he held in his hand. "Cotton or cattle do you think?"

"*Y*ou will be the scandal of Natchez tomorrow, Angelique." André's eyes glittered while he led her through their third minuet.

But not their third dance.

"Why is that, sir?"

He leaned over her and whispered in her ear. "Look around. All eyes are on you and me. Every tattling mother in the district is watching us."

Angelique's dismissive laugh didn't match her nervous mood. André was speaking of attention she was sure she was better off without.

"We are cousins. I see nothing wrong with our dancing." But her heart was beating faster, and she wondered if her words were true. Surely Aunt Elizabeth would have intervened before now if, through her own ignorance, she were behaving in an inappropriate manner.

"Yes," he said, "and I'm betrothed to another. They all know you have bewitched me. There will be the devil to pay with my future in-laws."

Angelique watched his pretentious skimming of the crowd. Goodness knows he was correct in that they stood out on this dance floor, him a towering pine in an immaculate green woolen coat and her some sort of squatty rose bush in red satin. They made an appallingly awkward couple, and him thinking they were an attractive pair. Something had bewitched the man, but she was confident it wasn't her.

She studied his strong nose and chin. Neither matched what she suspected to be a weak character. Beneath his coat, he wore a matching waistcoat and a crisp linen shirt, ruffled at the neck and sleeves. Woolen knee breeches, light brown, covered his trim belly and muscular thighs, English riding boots his calves. His hair, so black it was blue, he'd pulled into a queue. He resembled his father, Aunt Elizabeth's eldest son, Charles Richard. André was a handsome man, and he knew it. And he was so much older than she was. Why he would be attracted to her, she could not imagine.

"This is all a game to you, is it not?" she said, her mouth dry.

He grinned and held her gaze.

"Where is your intended tonight?"

His grip on her arm tightened, and she fought the urge to disentangle herself from his hold and leave the dance floor.

"She is at her father's house down river."

"Why did she not—"

"Because I did not want her here."

The Spanish post had emptied one of the military storehouses on the new landing to host this dance in honor of Saint Mary and the Christmas season. All of Natchez' polite society had been invited, and was expected, to attend. André had wronged Clarice Delacroix by not attending with her.

He moved with the music, taking Angelique with him. "If she were here," he said patiently, "tongues would wag all the more if I spent the entire evening dancing with you. And I want to dance with you. You hold my attention in Natchez."

"You flatter me, André. I hear she is beautiful."

"She does not compare to you, nor," he said, again glancing around the crowded building, "does any other maiden, or woman, in this room. And they know it. They are envious, and they'll be eager to inform the Delacroix of my interest in you."

The man obviously considered Natchez had nothing better to talk about but him or—her stomach quaked—about her.

"You may have some ulterior motive for making your future wife jealous, but I find your lack of consideration for her distasteful."

He sighed. "You hurt me, Angelique. My interest is in you, not in distressing Clarice."

"Why are your parents not here?"

He leaned over again to whisper in her ear. Another provocative gesture. She pulled away. He pulled her back.

"Too many Anglos my mother says, and Papa would prefer no social engagements at all."

"Surely Gabrielle would have enjoyed the dance?"

"Gabby's betrothed is in New Orleans. He would not approve of her attending without him."

"Not even if escorted by her brother?"

André smiled. "I fear my sister will find her husband generous with his wealth, but stingy with her person."

Not unlike you, Angelique wagered. "And the Delacroix?"

He shrugged. "Clarice's papa is in New Orleans, and I do not enjoy the company of my prospective mother-in-law. I have a lifetime to spend with the Delacroix."

"Perhaps not if you anger them and they refuse you their daughter."

"My betrothal is safe. My father's possessions are extensive, on both sides of the river, thanks to my mother's father. My mother was an only child and inherited everything, which, of course, is now my father's. Our lands to the south adjoin the Delacroix's. It is a good match. No one will cast it aside."

"For your frivolous flirtations, you mean?"

"For anything, frivolous or not."

Her confidence wavered as the music faded. The minuet was over. She would not dance with him again tonight. She freed her hand, but he seized her arm and turned them in the direction of her seat beside Carla Douglas, her cousin recently arrived from New Orleans. Carla, her sister Rose, and their mother Elaina would stay with Aunt Elizabeth through Epiphany. Michael Douglas, their father and husband, in addition to being Aunt Elizabeth's youngest son, would join his family Christmas Eve.

"I am wealthy," André continued, keeping step with her, "more so than Grandmama. When I wed Clarice Delacroix, I shall be wealthier still. She, too, is an only child. I shall have influence and political power."

At her seat, Angelique turned to him. He bowed and took her hand. The musicians had taken a break and the dancing had stopped. She needed this intermission, and she wanted André to go away. His eyes met hers when he lifted her hand. His fingers were soft, and she resisted the urge to cringe.

"I can have anything I want," he said. His lips caressed her palm, and she tensed at the barely perceptible tickle. Irritated, she withdrew her hand. She longed to tell him to find what he sought elsewhere, but did not.

A hum hung in the air with the cessation of the music. Feigning interest in the disjointed splashes of color moving around her, Angelique turned from him and scanned the crowd.

"You are a touch indiscreet tonight."

Whether Jane's comment expressed disapproval of André's behavior on the dance floor or of her appearance, Angelique wasn't sure. She smoothed her red satin skirt. Aunt Elizabeth had picked the style and color of the dress, which again Angelique considered too provocative. But if her bustline was too low, so was most every woman's in this room. She perused her cousin, dressed in a low-cut French gown of purple satin. Including Jane.

"Do you think so?" Angelique asked, meeting her cousin's smug smile with a haughty tilt of her chin. "And all evening I thought my popularity the result of the excellent manner in which you and Dora taught me to dance."

To Angelique's left, Carla stood and looked over her head. "Mathias is here, Jane."

"Is he?" Jane said and strained to see where Carla pointed. Stomach qivering, Angelique looked, too.

"He's near the door, talking to Tim Dobbins. He's been watching Angelique and André dance."

Angelique felt her skin prickle, and she sat back in her chair and twisted her fingers together. Of course, Carla was probably only teasing Jane at her expense. These two older cousins didn't appear to like each other any more than Mathias and André did.

"I need some wine," Jane said.

"I'm sure Tim will provide you succor, should you need it." Carla frowned at Jane. "And you do look pale. Does your stomach still bother you?"

Jane appeared to ignore the gibe. Moving past Angelique, she made her way toward Tim and Mathias.

Carla reached down and squeezed Angelique's fingers. "I'm sorry, cousin dear. I could not resist."

Angelique cast her cousin a sheepish smile, but Lieutenant Gerard moved in front of Carla with a flashing smile and a quick click of his polished boots, depriving Angelique the opportunity to ask if Mathias really had been watching. Carla and Rose were raven-haired beauties and had danced their share of sets with a number of the officers, many of whom they knew. Michael Douglas' branch of the family may have made its home in New Orleans, but they were well known in Natchez.

Mr. Higgins took the platform and pulled out his fiddle. His two sons followed. They were going to play a reel. Of the dances she'd learned the past three days, the reel was her favorite, and she looked around for a potential partner.

Not spying one, Angelique leaned back, disappointed. Carla took the handsome lieutenant's hand, then spoke to someone whose body she shielded. After a moment, she leaned forward for an apparent kiss before stepping aside and revealing Mathias. He held out his hand to Angelique, and she reached to take...

Fingers closed around her bicep, and she jerked her gaze to find André holding her possessively. Heart in her throat, she calmly pulled on her arm.

"I am sorry," she said and placed her hand in Mathias', "but I promised this dance to Mathias."

André's gaze passed to Mathias and hardened to a glare, but he dropped his restraint. Angelique stepped between them and tugged Mathias to the floor.

"Your hand is sweating," he said, as they lined up.

Jane and Timothy Dobbins lined up on the other side of Carla and Lieutenant Gerard.

"Do I make you nervous, Angelique?"

You make me quake. But she shook her curls off her shoulders, smiled, and looked him in the eye. "No," she said, "the dance excites me."

"Always the ingénue."

She frowned.

"Let your partner think he makes you nervous, even if he doesn't."

"Very well, you make me terribly nervous, but not when we are dancing."

His hand touched her waist, and he drew her closer. "Does André make you nervous when you are dancing?"

She narrowed her eyes in what she hoped was a stern rebuke. "André never makes me nervous, Mathias. André makes me anxious."

*A*ngelique's face haunted Mathias even as he searched for Kate's lips in the dark.

"André Richard warned Carriere away from your young cousin tonight, did you know?"

His heartbeat quickened. "Angelique?" he asked, but he knew of whom she spoke.

"Yes. He told Miguel neither he nor your Grandmama would tolerate his attention toward the girl any longer."

"Good," Mathias said.

Kate giggled.

He sat up in the bed, then brought his legs over the edge of the mattress and reached for the flint.

"You don't think he'll comply?"

"I do not think he would have acquiesced on Richard's say. He believes André's warning was for his own benefit, not the girl's."

Most assuredly.

"But you, my handsome devil, are another matter entirely."

Mathias snorted in the dark at the same time the flint sparked to light. He leaned away and lit the candle. A golden glow illuminated a small area of the room around them, and he turned to Kate. He'd tied her arms securely to the headboard, above her head. She looked at the candle in anticipation and in its light, it seemed, her dark eyes began to glow. He smiled. Her response was more than fancy, and he would happily quench his need for Angelique in Kate's lust.

"Grandmama has spoken with Stephen Minor regarding Carriere's attention," he said, trying to appear uninterested.

He reached beneath the covers and found Kate's naked breast. He squeezed it, and she whimpered.

"The colonel's speaking to Miguel will no longer be necessary," she breathed out, but he could tell by the anticipation in her voice, her interest in Carriere and Angelique waned. "Perhaps the colonel should speak to André?"

Mathias' lips twitched. "And when did Carriere tell you he believed André had designs on Angelique?" He turned to the candle beside the bed and lifted it, letting the hot wax drip into the holder. To his left, he heard the slight catch of Kate's breath.

"He escorted me home after you left with your womenfolk."

"How long did he stay?" He returned the taper to the socket.

Watching his movements, she licked her lips. "He didn't. I left the dance when you did in anticipation of your coming."

He yanked down the covers and exposed her naked body. Her legs were spread, bound to the foot posts. "Are you sure?" he murmured.

For what must have been the thousandth time over the last four years, he watched her eyes widen in faux fear. "See for yourself..."

His fingers feathered over her pubic hair, then spread her vaginal lips. He inserted a forefinger inside her. She arched at his touch and thrust her hips, forcing his finger deeper.

"Ah, sweet Kate, you whore. You've been with another."

It was a lie. No man had entered her yet tonight. "I fear I shall have to punish you."

She swallowed and watched him reach for the candle. "Gag me," she forced out between two ragged breaths. He stopped and set the candle down, then reached for the silk scarf next to it. Always prepared was Kate.

Taking the scarf, he leaned over and kissed her passionately before covering her mouth with the cloth.

Chapter Eight

"André has fallen in love with her."

Eyes fixed on the cracked parlor door, Angelique hesitated on the bottom step and let Dora's words soak in.

"He wants her," Jane said. "Love has naught to do with it."

Angelique's fingers tightened on the stair rail.

"And you think he means to seduce her, then cast her aside?" Dora asked.

"I think his plans go deeper than that, little sister," Jane said dryly.

"You think he intends to break his engagement to Clarice and marry her?" Dora squealed.

"Really, Dora, you are so silly."

That was Rose. In her time spent with her cousins, Angelique had noted the others' frequent scorn of Dora. Before Angelique arrived, Dora had been the youngest in the group, and they regarded her, somewhat cruelly, as a foolish child. Angelique felt sorry for the girl, although her sympathies were diminishing.

"Rose," Carla admonished, "there is no need to belittle Dora."

Carla felt no compunction at putting any of them in their place, including Jane. Angelique liked Carla.

"No, Dora," Jane said, her voice softer. Angelique glided silently down the stairs to get closer. "Gabrielle told me Aunt Louise has been raising a fuss with Uncle Charles about the attention André shows Angelique. Uncle Charles talked to André, and they've come up with a suggested 'arrangement'."

Angelique stopped outside the door. Two months ago, the prospect of Dora and Jane's companionship had filled her with

89

wondrous anticipation. Except for the brief friendship she'd developed with Mary Ivers on the Trace, Angelique had never had a female friend, or any friend for that matter. Now, having gotten to know her cousins, she no longer desired to be so much as in the same room with them. Unfortunately, Jane and Dora were at their grandmother's house too often.

"And we know what the arrangement is," Rose said.

Angelique leaned her forehead against the door molding and closed her eyes.

"Angelique will not agree to it. She doesn't like André."

Carla was the one talking now, and she was correct. Her discomfort with the domineering André had soured into dislike.

"Hmmph, what does Grandmama say?" Jane asked.

"Apparently, she's not saying much. André argues Angelique's prospects are dim with the multiple rapes on..."

"It's impolite to eavesdrop."

Angelique's heart caught in her throat, and Mathias grinned when she pivoted on him. She closed her eyes tight and released a breath. Gracious, he'd frightened her. Touching his arm, she scurried around him and entered the dining room from where, she assumed, he'd come.

"Polite was not my purpose," she rattled out quickly and quietly, "they were talking about me, and I chose to listen."

"What they say is of no account."

"They're my family."

"Mine, also, and you know the things they say of me."

"Is the tale told of you as big a lie as the one repeated about me?" Her eyes had found his, but she couldn't determine his thoughts.

"That depends on which tale is being told," he said.

A tremor moved over her body. Tales of murder and lust and demons....

"Angelique?"

She blinked. He was waiting, and she swallowed hard, not sure if she should pursue this conversation. But she steeled herself. "Did Aunt Elizabeth's demon kill my mother's father?"

Something flickered in Mathias' eyes, and she considered she'd caught him off guard. "Your father told you that?"

"He said my grandfather was trying to wrest De Leau from Aunt Elizabeth for him. Papa said he was De Leau's rightful heir and Aunt Elizabeth had promised him the farm. But when time came for him to claim his right, she changed her mind."

Mathias pulled out a dining room chair and motioned her into it. He sat in the one next to her.

"I'll tell you the story as I heard it. There's no question Bess planned to leave De Leau to your father. That would have pleased your grandmother, and pleasing Véronique was important to Bess. But I don't believe she promised your father De Leau before she died. De Leau is her home, it's precious to her. She'll not give it up while she lives."

"So she expected him to work De Leau, without title to it, until she died?"

"As I am doing."

"And you will inherit when she's gone?"

"She's made no promises to me."

Angelique studied him. His expression had not changed, nor his tone, but something scarcely noticeable had crossed the space between them. He wanted De Leau.

"Your mother's father became De Leau's neighbor on the east during British times. He was a veteran of the war in Europe. Initially, there was some conflict over his claim, awarded for his service, and lands belonging to De Leau. Those were resolved in Bess' favor. That didn't please Foster. He was an English Protestant with a good eye for business, farming, and politics and had no qualms in using religion to sway matters to his benefit. He also had a meek, fifteen-year-old daughter he was willing to barter."

Angelique grimaced. Not unlike her father's regard for her when he'd been alive.

"By the time Tobias Foster arrived, De Leau was a fine working farm. Acres and acres of it were cleared, there was a substantial house on it, and still today it has the best source of water in the area, a spring-fed creek, the source of which is in the farm's northwest quadrant. The site was a *vieux village*, an old fallow Indian field. The water is the reason our great-grandfather picked the site when he joined the Mississippi Company. De Leau was well east of the safety of Fort Rosalie, but out of flood range of the Mississippi as well.

"Your father had...a kind of craziness...about him." She opened her mouth to protest Mathias' words, but he held up a hand. "Don't say you didn't see it, Angelique. You've told me too much about him that assures me you did."

She shut her mouth.

"Bess blamed his often irrational behavior on the malaria that almost killed him. He claimed there was deviltry at De Leau, and when he was a child, he said he saw a creature, unnatural, come out of the swamp during the night, then return to it before sunup. He was also constantly exposed to the squabbling between Bess and Yo."

"The slave at De Leau?"

"If one could call her a slave."

"Baby says Aunt Elizabeth calls her a witch."

"And vice versa. Something happened between those two women, and it cut deeply. I've seen them express no affection toward one another in my lifetime, and I am told the ill-will goes back long before I was born. But something links them."

Mathias rubbed the back of his neck. "As time went by, Foster befriended your father. By then, Robert Douglas was long dead. Jude was young and impressionable, and the man easily converted Jude's zeal and fear of the demon into a passion for the Good Book and Christ Almighty. To this day, Old Bess despises any organized church and people who believe God has given them the right to think for others. She had no use for Tobias Foster, but Jude considered himself a kindred spirit. Foster gave Jude his daughter, your mother, in marriage. What Foster really wanted was not a convert or a son-in-law, but De Leau.

"Needless to say, Bess fought them and their accusations of witchcraft and deviltry. Your grandfather reportedly disappeared while crossing the swamp. He was on his way to a magistrate's court in Pensacola. No trace of him was ever found. Your father took his wife and left the Natchez District shortly thereafter, sure the demon would destroy him next."

"But do you know what really happened to my grandfather?"

"My guess is Indians, but I don't know. All I can say for certain is I didn't kill him. I was six years old when he disappeared. Little hellion I might have been, but I didn't kill a man at that tender age."

"You were thirteen when you first killed..."

His discerning gaze silenced her. She bit her lip, but didn't avert her eyes. Finally, he flexed his jaw.

"That's right, I was thirteen. This conversation did begin in reference to 'gossip,' didn't it? Are there any other tidbits you'd like confirmed?"

"Or denied," she snapped. "I didn't ask you to confirm anything."

"I can't deny it, nor will I."

She balled her hands into fists. "You think I wanted you to lie to me?"

"I'm not ashamed of killing the men I have."

"I've seen you kill," she said, standing. "I know what you're capable of and..."

He furrowed his brow, grabbed her hand, and yanked. She sat down hard, then leaned forward.

"...I'm thankful for it," she said more quietly, not wanting to draw the attention of the four girls in the room next to them. "All I was trying to say was I will never think ill of you no matter what you've done, and I hate to think you forfeited your soul for me."

He leaned closer to her, too. "Rest easy. Now you know Will Hossman wasn't the first I killed, and he probably won't be the last. I may have forfeited my soul, Angelique, but I did so long before I found you on the Trace. And if the God you believe in would damn me for killing a raping, murdering bastard, be assured I'll feel no regret in casting my lot with the devil and taking whatever he offers."

Chapter Nine

"Your aunt is home?" Tim Dobbins, his face pinched from the cold, stared at her across the threshold, and Angelique wondered at the uncharacteristic gruffness in his voice and the cause that brought him to this house at such an early hour on Christmas Eve.

"She's in her study. I will call her—"

"No," he said, removing his hat before entering the front door. He didn't take off his coat. "I'll go with you. You announce me please."

"Baby," Aunt Elizabeth called from the door of her study.

Angelique had returned to the parlor where she sat reading her book. Her aunt called for Baby once more, and Angelique started to rise and help find the young woman.

"Yes'm," Baby responded from the dining room.

"Tell Wee Ben to fetch Mathias here."

"He be at De Leau, Miss Bessy?"

"He's at the widow Mallory's."

Alone, unseen in the parlor, Angelique sighed heavily, then from where she sat, she saw Tim Dobbins step into the foyer. He disappeared from view. Her aunt followed him. She heard the front door open, and Aunt Elizabeth said, "You will hear from Thomas soon."

Tim mumbled something unintelligible, and the door closed. Once again her aunt crossed the open doorway. A moment later the study door clicked shut.

❧

$\mathcal{M}$athias raised his fist to knock on the door of his grand-mother's study. Down the hall, the front door burst open. Uncle Thomas stepped in and then aside, allowing Aunt Sarah and Jane to enter behind him. He was here, Mathias realized, because they were here. The study opened, and his grandmother looked at him, then down the hall to the others.

"I was hoping to talk to you before they arrived," she said.

"What's wrong?"

Approaching quickly down the hall, Thomas, his nostrils flar-ing, glared at Mathias. "You will not get away with this, damn your hellish, fatherless hide that took my sister's life."

Mathias' chest tightened, but his grandmother moved in front of him and faced Thomas. "How dare you say such a thing to him and under my roof."

His uncle's red face blanched. Aunt Sarah, her arm locked through Jane's, looked up nervously before sidestepping Uncle Thomas and entering the study, Jane in tow. Jane held her head up and looked Mathias in the eye when she passed.

"How could you?" Sarah spat at her daughter. Mathias' mouth went dry.

Thomas followed his wife and daughter in.

From where he stood, Mathias watched Angelique peek her head out of the parlor, her beautiful brown eyes full of questions. He made no move to greet her, but turned and almost collided with his grandmother.

"I assume," he said, "you want me in here."

"$\mathcal{T}$homas, your name calling and accusations serve no pur-pose but to estrange the family," his grandmother said.

"He is not—"

"Don't say it, Sarah," Bess warned. "Your daughter claims the child she carries is his. If that is true, the baby will be your grandchild, and you will live with it"—Bess smiled—"as I did."

Mathias' gut twisted, and he wondered if his grandmother ever gave thought to the things she said in front of him.

"Oh Jane," Sarah whined, "after the trouble we went to..."

Mathias stood by the fireplace, his shoulder propped against the mantel, staring at Jane. She briefly held his gaze, before dropping hers.

"Jane," his grandmother began.

She looked up.

"You claim to be with child?"

"Yes, Mother, she is." Aunt Sarah burst into tears. "She didn't tell me. I guessed it. She's had the morning sickness straight for the past two weeks. Dora says she was sick while with you."

"Yes, I recall." His grandmother refocused on Jane. "Answer me."

"I am, Grandmother."

"And who is the father?"

"Mathias," Jane said, without hesitation.

Old Bess moved around the desk. "Mathias," she said slowly, "have you had carnal knowledge of Jane?"

"I have not."

Aunt Sarah turned and looked at him in astonishment. A pity, Mathias thought, she didn't choke on her surprise. He did, after all, want White Oak Glen and a fine wife to grace his bed.

"He's lying, and he's not going—"

"Hush, Thomas," Sarah admonished.

Ah, the more practical father who wants his daughter honored and out of his house. Who cares if he weds her off to the devil himself?

"He's lying, Grandmother," Jane said quickly. "He is the father of my child. He toyed with my affections and now wishes to abandon me."

Bess cocked her head at Jane. "When and where did this toying take place?"

"Halloween."

Again no hesitation on her part. The lovely, deceitful Jane had thought her lie through to completion.

"Halloween?"

"Yes, Halloween." Jane started to cry.

"A fitting night for a demon to take a virgin, would you not

96

say so, Thomas?" Old Bess' tone dripped with sarcasm. She reached out and took the girl's hand, patting it gently. "There now, do not cry, Jane, I believe you..."

Mathias' heart lurched.

"About Halloween, that is." His grandmother looked beyond Jane to her mother. "Would you ask Angelique to step in here, please?"

Sweet Jesus. He did not want the girl privy to this.

"Why must she be brought in here?" Jane asked.

His grandmother frowned. "Because she may shed light on the facts."

"How?" Jane cried. Behind them, Angelique stepped hesitantly into the room, and Aunt Sarah closed the door behind her.

The petite beauty looked immediately to him. He thought she would, and he forced his expression blank.

"Angelique?"

She faced Bess.

"Jane is with child. She claims Mathias is the father."

The girl paled, and he sickened.

Bess released a long sigh. "We are discussing Halloween night. I want you to listen."

Mathias saw Angelique's lip quiver, and she nodded. Wide-eyed, she looked back at him. He wasn't sure what he saw in those eyes—disbelief, disappointment...devastation?

"Mathias was with me after I left Miss Abbey's," Bess began, directing her statement to Jane. "I know also your mother, sister, and you returned to White Oak Glen together shortly thereafter. Mathias had been at Hawlin's earlier. When did you meet him?"

"I met him out back," she said quickly. "In the dark, shortly before he arrived at the party."

"How long were you together?"

"Certainly long enough to—"

"How long, girl?" Bess demanded. "Did you rush outside, raise your skirts for him and, when he was done, rush back inside before you were missed?"

"Oh, Mother," Aunt Sarah groaned.

Uncle Thomas glared at Mathias.

"Around half an hour." Jane's voice shook. "We went to the larder behind the cookhouse."

Bess snorted. "Fitting one with so little couth would shag a young woman in such a place. Still more shocking is that a lady would allow it. Your needs must have been great."

Uncle Thomas turned toward him, and Mathias brought himself to full height ready to meet the challenge.

"For pity's sake, Thomas, stop your intimidation," Old Bess said. "I am—"

From the corner of his eye, Mathias saw Angelique step forward. "You are lying, Jane."

Her soft words stayed everyone, and Jane turned on her.

"You were with Tim Dobbins. I was with Mathias."

He sucked in his breath at the way she said it, her words sounding as if she were in the dark, cold larder with him.

"You?" Jane said at the same time her mother held her hands to her cheeks and exhaled Tim Dobbins' name.

"It was innocent," Mathias said, moving from the fireplace toward Angelique. "She'd become ill at Abbey Falwell's party. I found her on the street and escorted her home."

Thomas was looking at him in utter confusion. No one else, except for the enraged Jane, cared what he had been doing with Angelique.

Jane took a step toward the girl, but Bess moved in front of her.

"You are found out, Granddaughter."

Jane bowed her head and began to cry softly. After a moment, Bess raised Jane's chin and searched the young woman's face. "Tim Dobbins has already been to see me this morning."

Jane's eyes opened wide.

"He said you had a disagreement, and he feared you intended to do something rash to get even with him. You and I know that was never true. You've intended to trap Mathias to your will for years. Unfortunately, or fortunately as the case may be, a different young man entirely has beaten you at your own game."

"Dobbins?" Thomas asked.

"Yes," Sarah said, relief evident in her voice, in her smile, in the glow of her skin, "Timothy Dobbins. That good-looking Kentucky boy who has been visiting the house for the past two months." Sarah threw a smile over her shoulder before wrapping her arm around her daughter's. "How nice, dear. We have a grand wedding to plan."

Mathias watched his grandmother's eyes roll. "And I would advise you to be quick," she said to Sarah.

"We will," Sarah said and kissed her daughter, who smiled wanly at her through a veil of tears. Sarah turned Jane toward the door, talking to her of wedding preparations, and exited without a backward glance.

Uncle Thomas looked at his mother, his eyes narrowing. "Dobbins?"

"You will love him, Thomas," she said. "A dirt poor Kentucky boy who has managed to fornicate his way into one of the wealthiest and most powerful families in Natchez. He hasn't a drop of demon blood."

Thomas drew in a breath and turned to Mathias. "It wasn't that. It was simply that I thought you had broken your word to me."

Mathias didn't bother to respond, and after a moment, Thomas left. He watched his uncle go, then glanced at Angelique, quietly watching him.

"Thank you, Angelique," Bess said.

She dropped her gaze and left.

Thomas' harsh words to Mathias dominated her thoughts, making it impossible for Angelique to concentrate on her book—Thomas' words and Sarah's giddy relief at discovering Tim Dobbins, not Mathias, was the father of Jane's unborn child. They had talked to and in front of him with no regard for his feelings. Days ago, she, too, had, inadvertently, hurt him.

For a long while, she stared into the fire, and when she heard the study door open, she jumped to her feet and intercepted him leaving by the back door.

"Mathias?"

He hesitated as if the sound of her voice irritated him, and she immediately regretted stopping him.

He turned, his eyes cold, jaw tense.

"I-I—"

"Thank you for your help today."

Her lips quivered. "You're welcome."

He started through the open door.

"You will be here tomorrow?"

He stopped and turned, his expression quizzical. "You mean for Christmas?" The harshness of his accompanying laugh humiliated her. "Can you think of one reason why I would want to be?"

Her face heated, and he must have seen her embarrassment, because, for an instant, his gaze softened. Then he quickly moved around the dining room table to stand in front of her. Her erratic heartbeat accelerated to a pounding pace, but she didn't back up or push away when he wrapped his arms around her in a hold so tight it was almost brutal. The inherent sense of safety she felt in his arms struggled against instinctive fear.

"Do you understand what you heard in that room?" he asked roughly.

"A lie made up by Jane to force you—"

"What you heard and what you saw," he said, twisting his mouth into a hateful sneer, "are what people see when they look at me. An abomination that none in polite society wish to associate with, and I don't want to associate with them."

"I don't either."

His arms tightened, and she found it hard to breathe. "You are part of that society."

"You know I don't—"

"My father was a monster."

"I don't believe that," she forced out, then struggled against his hold. "Let me go!"

He did, partly, freeing one hand to place two fingers over her lips, shushing her. He tapped her lips with deceptive gentleness. "A monster, Angelique. Whether or not he was flesh and blood, he was still a monster, and he sired me. And I am a monster. I cannot escape that."

"That's not true."

"Listen to what I'm saying to you," he said, shaking her when she squirmed. His hard gaze moved over her face, studying her nose, her lips, then settled on her eyes. "I kill without remorse, I make love without caring. I am not a good person, and you are wise to fear me."

"I do not fear you."

He shifted her body slightly, then placed his hand against the small of her back so her breasts pressed against his chest. "You lie. I feel you trembling."

Her eyes found his and, steeling herself to his tactics, she said, "You think it is fear that makes me tremble?"

A strange look, brief and unreadable passed over his stern visage. Cradling her buttocks with one hand, he pushed his manhood against her pelvis. He was hard and hurt her, but she realized more than subtle pain. Shame heated her face.

"Do you feel me, Angelique?"

"I feel you," she said, determined not to let her voice quiver.

His eyes narrowed. Ah, she wasn't responding the way he wanted, and that pleased her.

Abandoning her derrière, he moved his free hand to her breast. Her bravado wavered, and she wiggled.

"Stop," he commanded, "I'm not trying to hurt you. Not yet." She gave up the struggle, wondering what cruelty he resorted to now.

He placed his hand over her racing heart.

"There's a woman at the end of town."

Her vision blurred, and she cursed her helpless tears.

"She is beautiful, experienced, and makes no claim on me. No ties. I come to and leave from her bed at my leisure. She satisfies me completely. I want nothing else. Do you understand?"

A shudder moved over her, and she knew he felt it. She swallowed those unbidden tears.

"Yes."

"Find a man who wants you. One who can give you everything you desire. Marry well and let me be."

She nodded, and he relaxed his hold.

"Mathias?"

"Yes?"

"You saved my life. Might we not at least be friends?"

Without warning, he yanked her back to him and crushed her lips beneath his, plundering the recesses of her mouth with his tongue. He freed her lips, then pressed his face to her neck, momentarily breathing in before placing his mouth against her ear and whispering, "No."

He pushed her back to arm's length. "I will protect you as I would any member of this family, but I don't wish to be your friend. I have no friends. I will use you, and I will hurt you, and in the end, I will not care. That is how I am. I've warned you, and that is as good a friend as I will ever be." He turned and left through the door without looking back.

With a leaden heart, she pressed the back of her hand against her bruised lips and watched him go.

Aunt Elizabeth stepped into the dining room as the back door closed. Slowly the woman walked toward her, stopping close and following Angelique's gaze to where she'd last seen Mathias.

"They hurt him, Aunt Elizabeth."

"He's been hurt all his life. He disguises pain well."

Sometimes perhaps. "But there was no reason—"

"There's always a reason."

"For his own family to torment and reject him?"

"The torment has given him strength."

"It could easily have destroyed him."

"A lesser man, yes. But for Mathias, his ordeal has done much to make him who he is today."

Yes, he would have been different if not for the battle he'd waged all his life.

"Don't worry for him, Angelique. He can take care of himself."

Aching with grief, Angelique looked into the cool, gray eyes of her dowager aunt.

"And what he cannot, or will not, do for himself," her aunt continued, "I do for him."

Chapter Ten

A soft knock drew Angelique's attention to her bedroom door.

"I brought you tea."

"Thank you, Baby," she said and returned to her reflection in the mirror. "Do you think my hair appears unkempt around my face?"

Baby set the service on the table near the bed. "Them girls tell you that?"

"Dora said it looked like a wig of sheep's wool."

"They jealous. Pay them no mind. Your hair is the color of corn." Baby squeezed a handful of curls. "Soft like corn silk. Ain't no sheep in these parts. How would Miss Dora even know to say such a thing?"

"Baby," Angelique said suddenly when the girl turned to leave. "Tell me what you know of Mathias' father?"

Baby stopped and studied her. For a moment, Angelique doubted she would tell her anything, but Baby sat down at the foot of the bed.

"Yo says his daddy's a demon that carried his mama off into the swamp and got her with child." Baby nodded her head seriously. "Yo swears it's the truth."

"Do you know where it came from?"

"The demon?"

"Yes."

"Yo..." Baby blew out a breath. "Yo, she says Miss Bessy called it out of hell."

"For what purpose?"

Baby shrugged. "Never really heard Yo say why Miss Bessy done it, but she says what the demon wants is vengeance.

"But others, 'specially them don't like Miss Elizabeth, say she called the devil up to kill her stepfather 'cause he meant to take De Leau from her. Say years later it come back to kill that man's son, Miss Elizabeth's half brother, for the same reason. But my daddy says it ain't so. He says that boy run off.

"And," Baby whispered, her eyes wide and foreboding, "folks say Miss Bessy gave the demon her virgin daughter in payment, for him to have a son by, and the baby was to serve her and her godless ways."

"How does he serve her?"

"He gits rid of her enemies, those that threaten her family and them she cares about."

"Did you ever hear she gave my grandmother to the devil?"

"Oh, that be a very old tale, and they's a baby's grave at De Leau, born to Miss Véronique. The baby, it died at birth. The father's unknown."

Angelique's mouth dropped open. "Boy or girl?"

"Boy, I think. It was long, long time ago. Long before your daddy was born. Long before Miss Véronique ever even knew your granddaddy."

Her father had a brother, and she had not known.

"But my daddy," Baby continued with a light laugh, "he says the people who tell that bad story on Miss Elizabeth are them that don't like her, and if she did such things, there'd be no one to tell the tale, 'cause Mathias would've killed 'em all."

"You don't believe the tales, do you?"

The sound of Baby's gentle laughter reassured her.

"Mathias, he's a handsome devil, if he be one, but Yo says the demon changes to its true appearance when it's with a woman."

Angelique stared at Baby. The girl leaned closer, spoke softer.

"Can't control its body, Yo says. Too busy taking its pleasure. Demons lust for mortal women. They enjoy riding a woman more than a man do, and any woman they lays with enjoys them more than she do a man."

"What does it...he look like?" Angelique whispered in response.

Baby slowly shook her head. "I hear it be ugly and smells of death."

She was teasing her, Angelique just knew she was. "Has Mathias ever lusted after you or your sister?"

Baby chortled. "No," she said, the laughter still in her voice. "Like I said, Miss Elizabeth says pay Yo no mind." The girl rose and stepped to the door. "I got to go and git dinner."

Angelique refocused on herself in the mirror. There she found Baby's reflection watching her.

"Yo says it comes back sometimes." Amusement no longer laced Baby's ominous tone. "Says it sits out in the swamp, waiting...watching De Leau."

A chill ran down Angelique's spine. "Waiting for what?"

"Ain't nobody knows. Yo says Miss Elizabeth has no power over it now. Says it ain't finished with the hate. Says it won't be done till Miss Elizabeth is dead."

Chapter Eleven

If there had been more time between Mathias' disillusioning enlightenment and Christmas Day, Angelique would have enjoyed the holiday more. As it was, despite church, feasting, and celebration, she focused more on Mathias' rejection and, with mixed emotions, the absence of her father, than on the presence of a large and boisterous family basking in wealth, power, and good health.

Michael Douglas arrived from New Orleans late Christmas Eve, joining his wife and daughters at Aunt Elizabeth's. Thomas and his family arrived from White Oak Glen Christmas morning. Jane did not speak to Angelique, nor she to her, but her cousin appeared in happy spirits, clearly excited over her impending nuptials. No one asked after Mathias, and Angelique wondered if he was ever here at Christmas time.

Later in the afternoon, Tim Dobbins joined them for Christmas dinner. He doted on Jane, outwardly unperturbed by her having claimed another man sired his child.

"You have a question, Angelique?"

She turned from watching Jane and her intended and met her aunt's gaze.

"Something perplexes you about the happy couple?"

Briefly, Angelique questioned whether it was wise to put forth an observation to Jane's grandmother, then said, "I was wondering what type of marriage they will have."

"It's hard to tell, but my guess is it will be a lasting one. Tim Dobbins has achieved exactly what he set out to. He doesn't love Jane any more than she loves him, but they make a handsome couple, and they are well suited. Love will grow. And he will not inherit White Oak Glen unless he takes care of Jane and pleases Thomas. He's smart enough to know that."

"How could she do it?"

Her aunt raised a quizzical brow. "Do what?"

"Give herself to another if she loves Mathias?"

"Oh, that," her aunt acknowledged, watching Jane and Tim across the room. "Angelique, Jane loves only Jane. She set great store in herself, flaunting her wiles, sure the best man would snatch her up and keep her close. She was sure that man would be Mathias.

"But Mathias didn't want her, and that hurt her pride. When she found herself trapped by another, she put forth the ploy you witnessed yesterday morning and tried to get even with both Tim and Mathias. Her gambit served to wreak vengeance on them and mollify her ego. She underestimated Tim, however. It turns out the best man for Jane is Tim. She is far luckier than she realizes."

"Why did he come to you and not Thomas?"

"I told you earlier, he's smart."

Jane and Tim's wedding took place on New Year's Day. The couple settled into married life, and Natchez settled into winter. Waves of bitter cold swept down from the northwest, chilling the town with freezing rain. The clear days, which followed were even colder. But inevitably, the bitter cold would lessen, yielding to warm, spring-like temperatures. The warm spells ended when the cycle repeated. The periodic warm-weather reprieves allowed inhabitants to function beyond what could have been the drab confines of their homes. Winter was freer here in the South and less inclined to keep people under siege for endless months.

André scanned Angelique's cape and beaver bonnet. "You are going out?"

"Yes." And she was more thankful for that than ever since he had just arrived, unannounced. André closed the front door, muting the brilliant blue and tender rose colors of the hall carpet.

Despite the pall he shed over her spirits, she managed a smile, but did not offer him a kiss on the cheek. He bestowed one on her instead.

"Aunt Elizabeth made no mention of your coming this morning."

"She's not expecting me. I wanted to tell her Papa received word a flatboat from up the Ohio is to arrive this morning."

Angelique frowned. "In Natchez?"

He smirked. "Nearby."

Meaning it was loaded with contraband. Spanish custom authorities may or may not know of the boat, and Angelique did not care one way or the other. She glanced toward the dining room door. Where in the world was Baby?

"You came up from River's Bend this morning, then?" she asked to make polite conversation. She pulled on her remaining glove.

"Yes, my real reason for coming was to pick up an order of glass."

"And how was your ride?"

"Cold."

Angelique turned when Baby, a bonnet on her head and a dark blue woolen cape flowing behind her, finally entered the foyer from the dining room. Now, they could escape.

"Baby is accompanying you?"

"I am accompanying her to the market. Some fruit arrived from New Orleans this morning, Spanish cargo from Cuba." Angelique took André's arm and ushered him to the door of the parlor. "Do warm yourself by the fire. Afterwards, Aunt Elizabeth wants me to visit the clothier. Mrs. Henderson says he has some new silks and satin ribbon from England. I'll rather enjoy that."

And she would. She pushed a pang of guilt aside. Her papa abhorred such luxurious adornments for women. Though he always dressed in silk shirts and the finest wool because a man must look the part for the sake of business, a woman belonged in her home, sensibly dressed, not in pursuit of vanity, which led to desirability and lust, and finally to sin, damning a man to hell.

"Where is Grandmama?" André asked, stopping outside the doorway to the parlor. Again, he raked his eyes over her.

Desirability, it seemed to Angelique, came to some women, whether they pursued it or not. Papa would say it was their fault.

"She is in the study with Thomas," she answered. "They're talking about the pork market, I believe."

"Ah, beef is the staple and corn is the crop." He winked at Angelique, and begrudgingly she gave him a smile. "Too much upriver competition with pork."

Maybe there was pork on that Ohio flatboat André was ferreting out, and she'd give anything if he'd go right now and find out. "Are you going to tell them so?" Angelique asked, moving toward the front door.

André followed her. "No, they know as well as I. Corn and cattle." He stopped when he came alongside Baby and looked at her.

"Carla and Rose are not coming?"

"Carla and Rose have yet to rise."

He frowned thoughtfully. "I'll accompany you. I would enjoy perusing the Cuba shipment."

She didn't believe him. "And the clothier?"

He nodded.

"And what of your Ohio flatboat?"

He smiled. "It's a visit best put off until nightfall."

"It could be gone."

He shrugged. "It's a smuggler's paradise out there, my beauty. There will always be other treasures to smuggle in, or out, of Natchez."

In defeat, she watched him swing the front door open. She didn't want him to accompany her and Baby. Beyond being uncomfortable in his company, she would be at the mercy of his boredom, and he would shorten her time shopping. With a playful bow, he ushered her and Baby outside. The morning was crisp and cold. A gust of wind stung Angelique's cheeks, and she inhaled deeply, trying to curb her frustration. In the distant forest surrounding the town, green magnolia and golden cypress added color to a gray landscape.

Off the porch, she and Baby stopped and waited for André,

then they walked the short distance down the lane to intersect Second Street. Fortunately, the street was no longer muddy, only the deeper ruts still containing water from a rain two days before.

Another gust of wind attacked, and Baby pulled her cloak around her. Angelique threw her arms around the young woman and laughed. The two almost toppled.

"Baby hates the cold."

André smiled his politic smile. "And you do not?"

"I don't mind it." She squinted into the painful brightness of the clear sky. "Winter is milder here than in Baltimore. I like the change of seasons without the harshness."

André took her hand, and she gritted her teeth.

"You have yet to spend a full summer here," he said. "Then you will know harshness."

With a quick squeeze of his fingers, she removed her hand from his. "It can be quite hot in Baltimore."

"Yes," he said, his eyes acknowledging her challenge. "But does it stay hot forever?"

Angelique loved the market, the sights, the scents...the sound of Baby haggling with vendors in a myriad of ethnic tongues. Baby had trained her weeks ago to curb her curiosity about the origins and preparation of native melons and squashes, as well as the vegetables slaves had introduced from Africa. Angelique's friendly questions for the Negro and Indian traders undermined Baby's bartering, the servant told her. Hold your questions until the bargain is made. Though much of her curiosity had been quenched since that first visit, Angelique's interest had not. But she did wait until Baby had secured her purchases before querying a number of vendors with what André called irrelevant, implying silly, questions, and Baby admitted that shopping took twice as long with Angelique in tow.

Baby was particularly pleased with a purchase of oranges, a little soft, and promised orange cake tonight "if she got back in time." André signaled to a boy of around ten years and gave him coin.

111

"You take these and go on home, now," he told Baby matter-of-factly. "This young man will help you."

Baby glanced at Angelique, surprised by André's directive.

"Baby has work to finish at home," André said. "You've kept her at the market too long."

"I intended to help Baby in the kitchen after shopping."

"And I intend to accompany you to the clothier, then treat you to lunch at Baily's Tavern."

The thought of going to Baily's Tavern for lunch was almost enough to outweigh going to lunch with André Richard, and she wasn't sure if it were irritation, excitement, or the combination of both making her heart hammer so.

"Baby wishes to see the new fabrics."

"She does not. She wants to make orange cake in her kitchen. Alone." He looked at the dark-skinned girl. "Is that not so?"

Baby gave Angelique a furtive glance before gracing André with a stiff smile.

"There is nothing improper happening here. I shall explain to Miss Bess if you are concerned."

Angelique watched his blue eyes glint at Baby, silent warning not to challenge him further. Resigned, Angelique nodded to the girl to go home, but inwardly, she seethed. André had ruined their day, and he had no right. Three and a half months in Natchez, without having a man to wait on hand and foot, to tell her what to do and how to think, had spoiled her. She resented this one.

André sat close, his presence as cloying as the ale he'd coaxed her to drink.

"What does Grandmama have in mind for all those ribbons you purchased?"

Angelique reached for her package on the bench beside her and laid it on the table. Carefully, she unwrapped the tissue. "She plans dresses for her granddaughters and daughters-in-law."

"A grandniece?"

"And a granddaughter-in-law as well."

André licked his bottom lip. "There is much I need to say to you."

She was not interested in anything he had to say. She didn't like being here with him, either, and hoped her silence conveyed both.

He looked at her a long moment, then took her loosely fisted hand and opened it. He would have kissed her palm, but she pulled her hand away. His expression hardened, and she steeled herself to his anger.

"I care for you," he said.

"We are in a public place, André. I am without proper escort, and you are betrothed to another. I understand I lack the world-liness of the women with whom you usually associate, but I understand propriety. I don't want you kissing my palm or touch-ing me at all, nor do I want to listen to your false allegations of caring. I want to go home."

"You would benefit greatly from my affection and my...tute-lage."

"I would prefer Baby teach me to make orange cake."

He smirked. "There is all manner of sophistication. Why do you resist my protection as well as my affection?"

"I do not need your protection, and I do not return your affec-tion."

"You most assuredly do need my protection, and I do not believe you do not reciprocate my feelings for you." He laughed. "You are being coy, my beauty."

Her gut tensed. She didn't like him, but was reluctant to tell him so. And how could he possibly believe she returned his affec-tion when she believed his to be false. Truly, he considered her a ninny, easily enamored with his wealth and good looks, in addi-tion to his lavish flattery and attention. "I want you to take me home now."

He rose to tower over her. "Come, Angelique," he said, and extended her a hand. "I shall take you home."

Chapter Twelve

"They ate at Baily's. The innkeeper said they left during the mid-afternoon."

"What was her condition?" his grandmother asked.

Mathias shook his head. If Old Bess didn't quit winding that damn timepiece, she was going to break it. As for himself, he felt he'd swallowed a brick.

"Put the watch away, Grandmother. She was fine. André purchased ale, but Angelique drank little of hers."

She squeezed the watch until her knuckles whitened, but at least she'd stopped fidgeting with it.

"Why in God's name did she go with him?" she said.

Mathias sat heavily on the settee and rubbed his eyes with his thumbs. "You have to consider the possibility she has left freely with him."

Bess turned, with a swish of her satin skirt. "Do you believe that?"

No, he didn't. "If she did not, Bess, then I may kill your first-born grandson."

She blew out a tired breath. "Any killing done would be on my say so, and if you think I am about to kill Charles' only son, you are wrong."

"And condoning the rape of your sister's granddaughter?"

She cursed and turned her back on him. "We must find them quickly. His plan has always been to take her to New Orleans, and in his blind selfishness, he was sure I would agree to the arrangement."

Mathias pressed the heel of his hand to his forehead. "When

114

you thwarted him, he decided to take his offer to Angelique. You should have warned her of him."

"I saw no reason to warn her, Mathias. She doesn't like him. I know that. I've seen how nervous she is in his presence."

"She has been dominated by a tyrant of a man her whole life. André's arrogant approach would appear normal to her."

"Dominated she may have been, Grandson, but I've seen her spirit since she's come to Natchez. You've seen it, too..."

Yes he had, and that spirit was growing stronger every day.

"...and that is why I didn't concern myself with André. He's the last thing she wants. She smells freedom, and she will never find it with him."

"And you didn't consider his taking her by force?"

"Of course not! I have never given any thought to one of my children or grandchildren defying me in this way."

A knock sounded on the doorframe leading into the dining room. Indigo stood there, and behind him, twisting his hat in his hands, stood Hector, a River's Bend darky who often accompanied André.

Old Bess took two quick steps toward the portal. Indigo grinned. "Found him in the cookhouse waiting on Baby."

"I'm sorry, Miss 'Lizabeth. I snuck up from the riverfront to visit. Mister André says we wasn't gonna leave till midnight, and he done went off to find us a flatboat captain."

"Where is Angelique?" Bess said quickly. Mathias moved up behind her.

Hector furrowed his brow.

"The girl André had with him," Mathias said.

"Ain't seen no girl, Mathias," Hector answered, wadding his hat beneath a tightly clenched fist. "Might be one though. Mister André done sent me home to tell his daddy he was leavin' for New Orleans tonight."

"Where were you?"

"Townsend's, gettin' glass Master Charles ordered. Mister André and me come up from River's Bend this mornin' to pick it up."

"You took the glass to River's Bend by wagon?"

"No, sir. Turned out to be heavier than he thought, and Mister André feared it might break." Hector glanced nervously to Bess. "Plan is to store it in Miss Elizabeth's warehouse number two at the landing."

Mathias caught Indigo's eye, then turned to find his coat.

"Gonna rent ourselves a flat boat to take it down river next week. Mister André, he talked to Townsend, then told me —"

"She's at the warehouse," Mathias said to Bess, then motioned Indigo to the back door. He stopped there and looked at Hector, clearly perplexed. "Hector, you probably need to keep out of Baby's sight now. The fewer people who know you were here today, the better it may be for you."

*A*ndré had stowed her away hours ago in one of Aunt Elizabeth's warehouses on the river. The area was safe, he told her, up a piece from Under-the-Hill. Judging by the surrounding quiet, that much was true. The windowless building was spacious, its cold air heavy with the stale scents of hay and aged wood. It was mostly empty, but she had managed to make herself somewhat comfortable on a bag of cotton seed. André apologized for the lack of creature comforts, but said his plans had changed abruptly and he hadn't had time to prepare for her better. Then he'd left her in the keeping of a burly, somewhat dirty, easy-mannered "river rat" he called himself. She hadn't bothered him, and he hadn't bothered her.

André hadn't tied or gagged her, and told her he wouldn't unless she tried to escape. She'd agreed to his terms, then waited patiently for such an opportunity to occur. It hadn't. Dusk had fallen, followed by evening. Her keeper had lit a tin lantern, which was sitting on a crate near her. Her stomach ached, and she needed to empty her bladder.

The wide door swung open, and André's silhouette stood outlined against the shimmering backdrop of the river. He moved inside, taking form in the faint light, and motioned his man outside.

"I've had enough of this," she said when the door closed. "I'm cold, and I want to go home."

He did not acknowledge her immediately, but lit another candle. "I apologize for the discomfort," he said after he hung the tin lantern from a hook above his head. "We leave for your new home at midnight."

Not comprehending, she stared at his handsome face shrouded in the dim light. Folding his arms across his chest, he said, "I'm taking you to New Orleans with me."

"I want to go home to Aunt Elizabeth this very moment."

"Trust that in the time to come you will be safer, and happier, with me."

Angelique thought she would be sick. "I need protection from you, not with you, and if you think you can make me happy by forcing me against my will, you are a fool."

André snagged her wrist in a pincer-like grip and yanked her clumsily from the sack of feed. His mouth covered hers, and she clamped her lips tight. "You'll not resist long," he said, when he let her go.

Wrapping her arms around her body, she pulled her cape tighter. "I'll resist you until you let me go or kill me."

"I shall remind you of those fighting words when you tell me you love me."

She tamped down the urge to wipe his contamination from her lips. And, yes, he would. He was the kind of man who would throw a conquest back into the face of any twit silly enough to surrender to him. The man was an arrogant fool. She glanced around the dark expanse of the building. She would soil herself if not allowed privacy soon.

His gaze moved over her. "God, you are beautiful. Your body new, so young and tender. Exactly what the demon wants. I shall make certain he never knows you."

"What are you talking about?" she said, backing away from him.

"Grandmama. You cannot trust her, Angelique. I fear her plans for you."

"You are the one I don't trust. Your intentions toward me are dishonorable and deceitful. Take me home! I'll take my chances with Aunt Elizabeth."

"As my mistress, you will live like a queen," he said softly, "and I shall make love to you like no man has ever loved a woman."

She shook her head. "I want more than a man's bed, André. I want to share his life. Your life will be with Clarice, I will be nothing but your town whore."

He smiled. "And a fine town whore you'll be. You are the one who will scream out my name in passion. You are the one who will provide me pleasure. There is no more important role for a woman than to please her man."

"You are drunk on your own vanity." She swallowed, no longer willing to take her eyes off him. She couldn't reason with this. He was obsessed with her, and she couldn't understand why. Everything he told her about the relationship he expected between them was in opposition to what she'd been taught. And though what she'd been taught was no longer what she wanted, she was certain she did not want what André proposed and certainly not with André. She moved quickly away from him, and put the crate between them.

"You will have to destroy me. I will never make you happy. I won't even try. I'm going home."

"Boyd is right outside, if you even get that far."

She heard him move behind her, and she quickened her pace, grasping the door lever at the moment his arm circled her waist.

He pulled her hard against him. "Which you will not," he whispered against her ear.

She struggled, clawing his arm, but she inflicted no damage beneath his wool jacket, and he laughed.

"Your fight excites me, Angelique." He kissed her ear, forcing his tongue inside, and she strained away from him. His grip tightened, hurting her ribs. She screamed for him to let her go.

"You're going with me, my love. In a week, I shall have tamed your stubborn heart, and you will see that I am right."

118

She kicked back, bringing her heel in contact with his knee. He grunted and turned her in his arms. His mouth found hers, and with a snarl, she clamped his bottom lip between her teeth. He grabbed her hair and yanked, but she held firm until she tasted his blood on her tongue, then she let him go. In morbid fascination and no small degree of satisfaction, she watched him wipe his mouth, then stare at the blood on the back of his hand. His face, barely visible in the dim light, assumed a dangerous appearance. Angry eyes found hers, and with no warning, he grasped her arm and twisted it behind her back, hurting her.

"You like to play rough, my sweet?" he said, slurring his words, "I can be rough, too, so be certain that's what you want."

"I want nothing from you but my freedom," she said, her voice catching in her throat.

His eyes narrowed, and he pushed her pinned arm higher. Liquid fire seared her shoulder, and an unbidden cry tore from her lips.

She saw him smile, then his head jerked away from her face, and she heard the lever lift on the warehouse door behind her.

"Go away," he called, "I'm not done here yet."

Angelique heard the door creak, and as if she were something foul, André shoved her away. The wall kept her from falling. Immediately, she reached for her aching shoulder and whirled toward the open door.

Indigo stood there, a smile on his face, and Angelique's knees weakened from relief. She took a wobbly step toward him, at the same time covering her mouth to stifle a sob. André reached out with the bloody hand he'd used to wipe his mouth and roughly stayed her.

"Evenin', Master André," Indigo said, "Miss Elizabeth done sent me to fetch Miss Angelique home. She's missed supper."

"You have no authority here. Go home."

"I got all the authority I need." Indigo stretched his hand to Angelique. "I got Miss Elizabeth's say so."

Angelique put her hand in Indigo's. He tugged her his way, and André's grip on her bicep tightened. Indigo's gaze moved from André's restricting hand to his face. "Even if I didn't have Mathias with me."

In the door, a shadow moved against the backdrop of the moonlit river, and the brutal pressure on her upper arm ceased.

André sucked in a breath. "Your hero, Angelique — Mathias Douglas, the devil's bastard."

In the dim light, Mathias' gaze found hers, then his features hardening, he stared menacingly at his older cousin.

"He's the one you think you want," André ranted. "He has no name, no bloodlines, no heritage, yet he aspires to be everything I am. He wants everything I have, that I earned by right of birth. He means to have you, and his grandmother will let him."

Mathias started to move. Indigo's large hand stayed him. "Remember what your grandmama said."

Angelique turned from Indigo to Mathias, and finally to André, glaring at her in the ominous light. *Mathias.* Of course. It all made sense. André didn't want her for her. He wanted her because he thought she wanted Mathias, and because he thought Mathias wanted her. On this horrible day, which was not over, her potential violation and disgrace was because André was jealous of Mathias. She was nothing more to André than something he would deny to his younger cousin. She closed her eyes and tried to calm herself.

"Call off your man here, Cousin."

She looked with Mathias' words and saw he watched Boyd over his shoulder.

André turned away, pulling a handkerchief out of his coat. "Call him off yourself."

Mathias turned his back to Angelique. He was poised and dangerous, the way he'd been that day on the Trace.

"Indigo..." The man's name from her lips sounded like a plea.

Indigo looked around to Mathias. "Careful," he warned. "Don't forget the girl here."

The only reason Indigo cared if Mathias killed the man was her seeing it. She whipped around to André. "Call Boyd off. Mathias will kill him for no purpose."

"Or Boyd will kill Mathias," he said before turning his back to her.

Dear God. She grabbed the long rifle Indigo held relaxed at his side. Indigo reached for the weapon, but Angelique pulled away, determined he would not thwart her. Welding the barrel like a club, she raised the rifle over her head and brought the stock across André's shoulders. "You selfish pig," she screamed, drowning his grunt. "You would cause men to die for your pride." André stumbled, and she hit him again. Indigo grabbed hold of her as André fell to his knees. "Mathias doesn't want me, you fool."

Her entire body surged with life and strength and fire. She jerked herself from Indigo's gentle grasp and, still holding the rifle, turned her back on him and André, who was struggling to get off his knees. She charged through the door, past Mathias. He moved, she thought, to stop her, and she whirled on him.

"Stop it," she spat at him, and he froze. "Just stop this." She heaved in a breath, exhausted suddenly, her head still pounding, her bladder still full. She blinked at Mathias, then turned to Boyd, roughly ten paces in front of them. "Get out of here, Boyd. *Monsieur* Richard has been stopped. You have no purpose now. Go away before Mathias kills you."

Boyd looked her over, glanced warily at Mathias, then back to her. He tipped his hat and turned away, meandering down the riverfront in the direction of the brothels and taverns of Under-the-Hill.

Spent, Angelique lowered the rifle. The thing felt lighter, and she looked at it. The stock was gone. Somber, she handed the barrel to Mathias, who took it without a word.

"I broke it," she said, turning to find Indigo, who held the stock in his hand. "I'm sorry."

She started to shake, and Mathias stepped toward her. She turned instead to Indigo, and he put his arm around her shoulder. "I don't feel good," she said. "I want to go home."

Chapter Thirteen

Old Bess turned from where she stood near the parlor fire-place.

"She's all right," Mathias said, stopping at the door. "And the only damage done to André is what your grandniece inflicted on him. Other than preliminary abuse, she was untouched. I distanced myself from him as quickly as I could."

"She wasn't leaving with him of her own accord?"

"He was taking her by force."

Bess sighed and stepped to the settee. "Where is she?"

"Visiting the privy." He stepped full into the room. "Did you want to talk to her?"

"I wish to talk to you both," she said, taking a seat.

"She's cold and tired."

"Where's André?"

"I left Indigo to see he got home to River's Bend. Angelique broke the stock of my best rifle across the back of his head."

"Did she now? Was he conscious?"

"He was." Making his way to the console, Mathias poured himself a whiskey. "It's good she's no bigger than she is. He might have slept a fortnight."

He sat in the upholstered chair before the fire and stretched his legs. He was cold to the marrow, but the room was warm and bright. God, he was relieved the ordeal was over and Angelique was home relatively unscathed, at least physically.

Mathias heard the door between the breezeway and dining room open, then Angelique's soft cough, followed by the closing of the door. Bess rose and stuck her head into the dining room.

"Angelique, are you all right?"

If the girl responded, he didn't hear and whatever signal she passed to Bess, he didn't see, but a moment later, Bess stepped back from the portal and a pale Angelique, still in her blue woolen cape, stepped into the parlor. She glanced at him, barely acknowledging his presence, then looked away as Bess guided her to the settee.

"Are you hungry?"

"I have no appetite."

Well, he could eat an entire boar now that they had her back. Perhaps when Bess was done talking to her, he could coax her to eat. If she wouldn't eat for him, maybe Bess. He knew for a fact Baby had black-eyed peas and rice still warm in the cookhouse, and he'd learned she favored both.

"Take this."

Angelique shook her head violently at the liqueur Bess held out to her.

"Peach brandy, made here in the District. It will warm you."

"I cannot drink that, Aunt Elizabeth. The smell alone makes me ill."

Bess passed the glass to him, and he felt Angelique's eyes on him as he downed it. The cordial was too sweet for his liking.

"Did André tell you his plan?" Bess asked, taking a seat beside the girl.

"He wanted me to go with him to New Orleans and live with him in a townhouse there." Mathias watched her chin pucker, but then she turned to face Bess, and he could no longer see.

"You told him you did not wish to be his mistress?"

"Yes, repeatedly. Aunt Elizabeth, I didn't want to go to lunch with him, but I feared for Baby. She refused to go home."

Bess draped an arm around Angelique and pulled her head to her shoulder. "Let this be a lesson. No one abuses my servants. André and Baby know it. I should have warned you of André's intent some time ago, but I didn't want to burden you with his designs after your ordeal on the Trace. I had already told Charles that André's proposal was unacceptable."

Angelique lifted her head and started to search inside her cape. Bess handed her a handkerchief, and Angelique swiped at her nose. "I thought he was using me to make Clarice jealous. I had no idea how twisted his mind really is."

Mathias' heart beat faster.

Bess rose. "André is spoiled and can be difficult. His political power grows stronger every day. Carondelet likes him. Mathias' wresting you from his clutches will prick his pride, but your outright rejection has made him, simply put, dangerous."

Mathias studied Angelique, watching Bess pace back and forth in front of her. "What are you saying?" the girl asked.

Bess stopped and looked at her. "I'm saying André is a threat to you."

Cautiously, Mathias leaned forward, wondering where his grandmother was leading this conversation. At the same time, Angelique waved her hands in front of her.

"Surely not now," she said. "His plan has been exposed."

"Most assuredly now. In André's mind, you kicked him squarely in his manhood."

"Then I left with Mathias," Angelique said and averted her eyes.

Bess nodded, but the fair-haired beauty didn't see. The girl seemed stronger, yet more vulnerable, smarter, but knowingly confused. She rose with a weary sigh.

"I shall avoid him."

"Avoid him?" Bess echoed.

"Yes."

"Avoiding him will be impossible here."

Mathias watched doubt and apprehension cloud Angelique's eyes. He was beginning to feel a bit worried himself.

"You wish me to leave Natchez?"

"I wish you safely wed..."

Fire licked Mathias' gut.

"...and safely ensconced in a man's home."

"To whom, Aunt Elizabeth? No man wants me. I am shamed, defiled."

"Nonsense." Bess turned to him. She wanted his validation, and though she was right in her assessment of what Angelique needed to do, he didn't know if he could muster the heart to agree with his grandmother this time.

"I want you to marry Angelique, Mathias."

She might as well have whacked him across the chest with the fireplace poker. But despite his bewilderment, he maintained his outward composure and simply stared at her. Bess raised a brow and waited. Breathing in, he glanced at Angelique who was watching him in unconcealed disbelief. Refocusing on his lunatic grandmother, he rose on rubbery knees.

"No," Angelique said, her voice a loud whisper.

Bess tightened her lips, never taking her eyes off him. "I'll give you De Leau as her dowry."

That damn poker pierced his chest, then ripped his heart out. He turned to Angelique, who was watching him, and she raised her chin.

"De Leau, Mathias?"

Quickly, Bess turned to Angelique. "Yes, De Leau. You agree, my sweet?"

The nefarious witch was running roughshod over them. He took a step toward the girl whose bottom lip had begun to tremble. "Angelique?"

"Yes," she said, "I am agreed, if this is what Mathias wants."

Her voice cracked, and with a swirl of her cape, she pivoted, putting her back to them. For a moment, she searched frantically inside her cape. Then she stopped, bent her head, and rubbed her temple.

He wanted to go to her, to hold her. She suffered from a misery only human contact could assuage. Still, he doubted she'd accept his comfort.

"What are you looking for, Angelique?" his grandmother asked gently.

Her head twisted toward Bess' voice, but Angelique didn't turn around. Ashamed of her tears, he suspected.

"I'm sorry, Aunt Elizabeth. I fear I've lost our ribbons."

Chapter Fourteen

"Why in God's name did you do that?" Mathias asked when his grandmother returned from escorting Angelique upstairs.

Bess poured a brandy, then downed it. "You are displeased, Grandson?"

"You could have discussed this with me in private and let me approach Angelique."

"There is no time for you to court her. I want you wed tomorrow and back at De Leau."

"I have not agreed to this."

"No," she said and took his abandoned seat by the fire, "you have not."

"When do you intend to tell her you want us wed tomorrow?"

"As soon as you tell me you agree to the union."

He swallowed.

"What bothers you, Mathias? I've seen the way you look at her, and I've given you De Leau as sauce on the pudding."

"I never considered your bargaining De Leau." He studied her, and she returned his gaze. "What are you up to, Bess?"

"I want her at De Leau. From the first moment I laid eyes on her, I knew that's where she belonged."

"Why?"

She looked at him pointedly. "I have a debt to pay."

"To the living or the dead?"

"Or to good or evil?" she snapped. "Whatever, the debt is mine and is of no concern to you. Suffice it to say I am growing old and out of time to pay it. Why do you hesitate taking her?"

"I'm damned if I do and damned if I don't."

"Yes?"

"I set her away from me."

"Ahhh," she breathed out. "Christmas Eve, wasn't it? I wondered what happened to upset Angelique so. But why?"

"She cared for me."

Bess' eyes widened. "Oh, I see. To protect her from the devil's bastard." Suddenly she laughed. "How noble of you. You would deny yourself the purity and love you seek rather than risk tainting it. Do yourself and Angelique a favor and tell me you will marry the girl."

"She'll think I'm marrying her for De Leau."

"That's the reason I put it on the table, to tempt you and to ensure her acquiescence. She knows you want it. You'll have the rest of your life to convince her of your true feelings. I want her out of Natchez and away from André. I want you away from him, as well. I didn't realize until today how dangerous his obsession has become."

"I'm not afraid of André, Grandmama."

"I am. Afraid of him and for him. He could kill you or you him. The survivor will hang, I'll see to it. No matter which, I'll lose my grandsons."

He doubted her threat, but then with her, he was never certain. "I want Ethan."

She nodded.

"Yo?"

She drew in a deep breath. "No."

Her refusal of Yo didn't surprise him, and he wasn't about to argue. He was making out better than he'd ever imagined. He had Rachel's Ethan, he had De Leau, and he had Angelique.

He stood. "I'll free him."

"I've already talked to the magistrate." She rose and poured them each a glass of brandy. "You agree then?"

He took the glass, wished it was whiskey, then raised it in salute. "I agree."

"Good," she said and sipped her brandy. Setting her glass

down, she pulled a rolled parchment out of a deep pocket in her dress and handed it to him.

"What is this?"

She reached for his glass. "A wedding gift. One you earned by rights, on your own, and which I made sure you received."

He unrolled the document and perused it, his heart pumping faster. It was a land grant of twelve hundred arpents, roughly one thousand acres, given for service to the Spanish Crown in the eradication of the Hossman gang. Though without a doubt drafted here in Natchez under the guidance of Stephen Minor— Bess herself probably provided him the land description—and approved by Gayoso, it had been Hector, Baron de Carondelet, the Governor of Louisiana, who had signed it. Impressive. Old Bess had been working on this for a while.

"The land abuts De Leau on the east," she said. "It's forested, but once it all was."

He rolled up the document. "Thank you, Grandmother."

She nodded, and he started for the door. There he stopped and looked back at her, standing at the hearth and watching the fire while she rubbed her thumb over the enameled surface of that damned watch.

"I would have taken her without De Leau, you know."

Bess stilled, then looked over her shoulder at him. "Yes, but would she have taken you?"

Chapter Fifteen

er head ached, but the nausea had passed. She felt Mathias' hand close over hers.

"Angelique?" he said, his voice low. No one else could possibly hear him.

She kept her eyes fixed on the jovial Irish priest, fat-cheeked and red-nosed, who stood patiently watching her. She swallowed, and again the reflex hurt her throat. Goodness, she was hot despite the unheated log church with its rough benches and high-pitched roof. Overhead, a non-existent ceiling exposed the massive cypress beams used to create the vaulted cathedral overlooking Natchez' plaza.

A Catholic priest, a Catholic church, but other than the Irishman's use of the French language, the ceremony had been an English Protestant one. There had been no banns, no confession, and no Eucharist. Early this morning, Governor Gayoso himself had, at Aunt Elizabeth's request, provided written permission for the marriage.

Angelique dropped the good father's gaze and leaned toward Mathias, kneeling beside her. Their shoulders touched.

"I heard our cousins talking this morning."

He glanced at her and waited.

"They think I'm pregnant with André's child."

He put his mouth to her ear. Behind her, someone in the sparsely occupied pews shuffled their feet. Only family was here.

"I know you are not."

"Does it not bother you?"

"No."

Of course it wouldn't. He might not care if she *were* pregnant with André's child. Cold settled over her, but as with the impatient silence behind her, she didn't care. She breathed out and saw her breath, then looked at the priest. "Where are the Scruggses?" she asked Mathias.

Beside her, she felt him fidget. "I put them, admittedly under duress, on a Spanish ship out of New Orleans for Cuba. They're alive."

"She tried to hide, so I wouldn't see, but I know Aunt Elizabeth cried when she saw me in this dress."

He squeezed the hand he'd covered. "It's your grandmother's dress. Véronique was married in it."

She had thought it must be something like that. "Mathias?" she asked, cocking her head at the priest.

"Yes?"

"I haven't understood most of what the man's said. What does he want from me now?"

"He wants you to say yes."

She frowned, still watching the Catholic father's bemused expression. "And what do you want from me, Mathias?"

"I want you to say yes, too."

❧

You are a sacrifice. A debt Grandmother must repay for a service rendered years ago. Innocent virtue, Angelique, in exchange for vengeful purpose. I guessed her design from the beginning. Ask Yo at De Beau the tale of the devil's bastard, and tonight, when you whore your soul and an unimaginable horror devours your beautiful body, remember whose arms should have held you.

André.

The knock was so soft, she barely heard it above her pounding heart. Hands trembling, she folded the thick stationery and put it in the pocket of her dress. She would burn it, but there was no fire in the grate.

She bid Mathias enter, she knew it was him, and reached for the cape draped over the bed. His gaze traveled over her.

"I am ready," she said.

"We'll stay here tonight."

"No."

He frowned at her, no doubt surprised by her response.

"I heard you and Indigo earlier. The weather is worsening and you've a farm to run. I know if there is too much rain we might not get across the swamp for days."

"That doesn't matter."

She swung the heavy cape over her shoulders, and he came the rest of the way into the room.

"You're ill, Angelique. All day yesterday in that freezing warehouse and this morning in the church. Exposure is taking its toll on you. We may not beat the rain home, and it will be icy."

Raising her chin, she tied her cape. He stepped forward and reached for the bow, but she caught his hand.

"Please, Mathias. I have no place here now. I want to go..." — she almost said 'home' — "to De Leau."

"There will always be a place for you here, Angelique," Aunt Elizabeth said, pushing the door wide and stepping next to Mathias.

Angelique closed her eyes. Another *faux pas*. She felt something brush her fingers. "Drink this," her aunt said.

Angelique took the small glass, half filled with an amber liquid.

"Yo concocted it," Aunt Elizabeth said. "Whiskey and the juice of the Choctaw Lily and God knows what else. She'll tell you the Indians taught her how to make it, but Bounty will, in her own taciturn way, tell you that is nonsense. Whatever the truth, there's something in the witch's brew that will cure what ails you, if it doesn't kill you first."

Angelique glanced at Mathias, and he nodded. "It's what I gave you on the Trace, but less of it. It will not hurt you. Drink it."

131

She tilted her head up and drank the shot, immediately recalling the terrible taste from months before. The brew warmed her inside out. Nausea chased the heat, but she fought it back and sucked in a breath.

Aunt Elizabeth held up her watch for Mathias to see. "It's almost noon, go if she is determined. She knows you want to."

Her aunt was being kind, helping appease her husband in the wake of her defiance.

"I'll find a wool scarf and another pair of mittens. Make sure she gets another dose of brew once you reach De Leau."

Chapter Sixteen

ngelique felt her horse shudder. In front of her, Mathias reined his stallion in and dismounted.

"Something is spooking Dan," he called to Indigo, then started walking back to her.

A shiver stroked her spine, and Angelique wished he'd provided a more concrete description of the apparent threat. Her head ached horribly, and she was sleepy, but Mathias had told her the drowsiness was from the brew.

"They all nervous. Wonder what's got 'em stirred up?"

For more than three hours, they'd crossed a mostly forested landscape cut by bluffs, which fell steeply into sandy creek beds. Angelique looked up. Far above, good daylight shone through the crowns of towering hardwoods surrounding them. They'd come now to a low area. On either side, black water and slime-covered sloughs spread amid giant cypress and ancient stumps as far as she could see. The trail reminded her of the Trace, and she trembled. Mathias grasped her around the waist. Instantly, his gaze sought hers, and she knew he'd felt her quivering.

"An animal is my guess," Mathias called back, swinging her from the saddle of the mulish-looking little horse. "We'll walk for now. I don't want Queen Anna bolting with Angelique."

"Don't need to be dawdling long, Mathias, that storm's movin' in." Indigo's saddle creaked with his dismount. He looked behind him, another disconcerting action, which increased Angelique's foreboding. "Dusk still comes early, and we don't want to get caught in the storm."

"You are cold?" Mathias asked her softly.

Without a doubt, he thought his touch had made her shudder. "Yes," she answered, "that and this place."

Mathias draped his woolen cloak over hers. It was heavy and dragged the ground. "That should help the cold. All I can do about this place is to get you out of it."

Shortly before sunset, the dense forest thinned to more sparsely spaced oak and walnut. Soon after, they emerged on to cleared land. Their farm, Mathias told her. A bitter wind stung her face, and Mathias turned to her and pointed in front of him. "Your home, Angelique," he called over the wind, "De Leau."

In the distance, she could make out the house in the darkening sky. Built well off the ground, it was broad across the front. A large porch appeared to wrap around it, and the roof was pitched high.

"It's grown over the years," he continued, dropping back now that he no longer had to keep to a narrow path. "When Pierre Deschesne built it for our great-grandmother almost seventy-five years ago, it was a one-room cabin. Now it has four rooms, and the wide opening has been enclosed to make an entry."

She noticed the rows of sterile fields went almost to the bottom step, little of the land set aside for a yard. In time, perhaps she could change that. She glanced at the handsome man at her side. How much concern would he give to her desires? She had brought him De Leau, but now she was only a wife.

The temperature, struggling in the face of a strengthening north wind, dropped perceptibly by the time they drew the horses up at the dark house. Mathias handed his reins to the waiting Indigo, then helped her dismount. She was stiff from cold and from the ride. Dampness hung in the air.

"The sky looks like snow," Angelique said.

"Doubtful." Mathias pulled her meager bag from the pack animal. "We'll get a freezing rain for sure. I'm thankful we're here."

"When you find Bounty," he said to Indigo, gathering the last of the horses' leads, "send her to the house with the brew."

Mathias took Angelique's arm and guided her up the steep steps. "Let's get a fire started."

The door, centered on the front wall, creaked on its iron hinges when he pushed it. Inside was dark...and cold. It smelled of cypress, soaked with a thousand scents of tobacco and food, people and passions. Angelique hesitated when Mathias moved out of the windowless entry into an adjacent room, dim in dusk's waning light. She lost sight of him, but heard him moving around, then heard the scrape of flint and saw light. Her teeth started to chatter.

Moments later a door on the far end of the hall opened and a large woman, briefly silhouetted against the leaden sky, lumbered into the house and down the hall toward her. She appeared not to notice Angelique in the darkness by the door, but turned into the room where Mathias had disappeared. Angelique took a step after her. The woman kneeled in front of the hearth and there set to work on the fire, all the while admonishing Mathias for returning so late. Bounty. She had to be. Baby, Wee Ben, and Indigo's mama, a woman of mixed blood, her mother Choctaw, her father a French fur trapper. She'd become Benjamin's squaw when he'd been, nominally, a young captive of that tribe. The Scots-Irish trapper and British agent, Robert Douglas, had freed him, or recaptured him, during a Chickasaw raid on the more peaceable Choctaw. After Robert Douglas wed Elizabeth Boswell and settled at De Leau, he'd recovered Ben's woman from the neighboring tribe. Ben and his family had been a part of De Leau for over forty years.

All this she'd learned from Baby, Wee Ben, her aunt, and cousins during her more than three month stay in Natchez.

Mathias called her name. Angelique stepped fully into the room and answered him. The woman twisted on bent legs and stared.

"This is Angelique," Mathias said, stepping through a door from a back room.

A shy smile shaped the woman's lips. "I knew it. I knew the instant I saw her she was Miss Angelique come to visit De Leau. Indigo said you brought home a surprise."

"She's my wife."

135

The woman's eyes widened slightly, the only sign his words surprised her. She rose from her squat, then spread her arms and hugged Angelique, as if she were a daughter and not a stranger. The woman was soft and warm and deceptively strong. She smelled of sweat and cornbread and the cold outside. She pushed Angelique to arm's length, then looked again to Mathias. "It's good your grandmama put an end to that foolishness with the Mallory woman."

Angelique doubted any foolishness would end unless Mathias wanted it to, and from what he'd told her three weeks ago, that was unlikely.

"Angelique, this is —"

"Bounty," Angelique finished for him and managed a smile. "Baby and Ben have told me all about their family."

The woman nodded. "I am Bounty." Angelique knew from Baby that Bounty was a woman of few words. The father, Benjamin, was the opposite.

"You 'bout froze," Bounty said, "come." She stepped aside and guided Angelique into a Windsor chair in front of the fire. "Your daddy and grandmama before him born in this house. Oh, Miss Véronique, she be so proud to see you sittin' here today. Comin' to Natchez ain't nothin'. You at De Leau now, all the way home."

Angelique had been about to speak, but Bounty's words took the breath from her. She averted her gaze and stared into the fire. This morning, she'd almost referred to De Leau as home. Her father had spoken of this place with mixed feelings. It was first and foremost his, but stolen from him. Second, it was an evil place he had no desire for. Now it was hers...or did she belong to it? She glanced over Bounty's shoulder at Mathias who studied her with an unreadable expression.

For as long as her husband kept her.

The fire brightened the room, and Angelique noted some fine furnishings, mahogany and cherry, many professionally turned. Her aunt would have collected those during the British era. The expensive pieces mixed favorably with more rustic furniture that included a rough-hewn trundle bed and a spinning wheel. She'd never learned to spin, but now she thought she would, living here on the frontier.

Bounty briefly fed the fire, then dusted off her hands. "I'll get you food. My Baby girl say you partial to black-eyed peas." She looked at Mathias. "Cookhouse warm. Bring her before the rain comes."

Angelique watched the woman disappear into the entry. When she heard the back door click, she turned to Mathias. "She acts like your mother."

Mathias picked up her cloth bag. "She was my wet nurse when I was an infant. I've been one of her own from the day I was born."

He started toward the back room.

"Does she live in the house?" she called. She rose and with cold hands searched clumsily inside her cape for André's note. Holding it with numb fingers, she knelt in front of the fire.

"She lives"—Angelique jumped at his voice immediately behind her—"with Ben in a cabin a ways behind the cookhouse." Mathias' hand covered hers in a firm grip.

"No, Mathias!" She tried to hold the missive in the flames, but he twisted her away. Seizing the note, he blew out the flame that had caught at one corner and dropped her hand. She jumped for the paper. "Give it to me," she said when she missed. "You have no right."

He held her at bay, and his eyes found hers. "I have every right. You are my wife."

She slapped once at his arm, then pushed him away. "And you are my husband. What rights does that bring me?"

Unmoved, he read the note, and she collapsed, exhausted, into the chair.

Face expressionless, he crushed the paper in his fist and tossed it into the flaming fireplace. "I disdain André, Angelique." He looked down at her. "I won't tolerate secrets between us."

"If they are mine, you mean?"

He stared at her, the flames from the fire reflecting off his hair and body, shimmering in the golden light as if he were its source and not the fire.

"Defiant for a young woman who has crossed a haunted swamp and finds herself ensconced with a man who might 'devour' her tonight."

She looked away. "André wrote those words, not I."

"Why didn't you tell me about his note?"

"Because it would cause more bad feelings between the two of you."

He turned from her and stoked the fire. Shortly, she felt his hand touch hers.

"Come," he said, "let's go to the cookhouse and meet the rest and get you something to eat."

𝒜 violent wind billowed her skirt and tore at her hair. Taking her hand, Mathias moved down the porch steps, then ran, her in tow, to the brightly lit cookhouse a good fifty paces behind the cabin. The kitchen wasn't raised like the main house, but sat on the ground. Hard-packed dirt formed its floor. The single room was warm and inviting.

The rest of Bounty's family, every one of them, was inside preparing a meal for the travelers. Rachel and her husband Ethan, the slave Aunt Elizabeth purchased to marry Benjamin's oldest daughter, were closest to the door. Hence, Mathias introduced them first, then informed Ethan he was now a free man. While Ethan beamed, Benjamin, the large graying father in whom Angelique noted prominent features inherited by Indigo, grasped the young man's shoulder. "I told you so. Yes, I did. Told you she'd free you. Know Miss Elizabeth real good, I do."

Charlotte was a Negress, another freed slave and Indigo's wife. She and Indigo had two young sons, Jacob and Hank, who were, judging from their enthusiasm, totally enamored with the new mistress of De Leau. For a few moments, Angelique forgot her headache and hunger and squatted at their feet and returned their interest.

138

Her stomach growled—the kitchen smelled so good—and Jacob laughed. "Oh, Aunt Rachel, Miss Angel dun' swallowed a bear. You best be gettin' her and Daddy some suppa' 'fore he jumps out'n gobbles all us up."

Angelique's mouth opened slightly in surprise. Rachel, an amused look on her face, motioned Angelique to a bench at the table and placed a wooden bowl filled with black-eyed peas atop rice in front of her.

"We should feed Mathias, too, don't you think, Jacob?"

"Oh yes'm," he said in his little high-pitched voice, and he climbed up beside Angelique on the bench. "Mathias gonna need him's stren'th."

Across the table, Indigo laughed, and Angelique felt her cheeks heat. Rachel was already pulling Jacob off the bench and Charlotte was coming around to shoo the boys outside.

"Says that each time we feed Mathias, Miss Angelique," Rachel said. "He don't know what he's sayin'."

But Ben was tickled at the far end of the rustic table.

"It's all right," Angelique said softly and picked up her spoon. She glanced across the table at Mathias, who was preparing to sit. He looked at her, but didn't say anything.

Rachel put a bowl in front of him, then gave him a nudge. "Baby says Miss Angelique eats all the time, but stays a little bitty thing."

Mathias' lips twitched. Obviously, Baby talked as much about her as she did the rest of the family.

"Miss Véronique was like that, ate and ate. She was a good eater," Ben said.

Angelique squared her shoulders and stuffed another spoonful of rice and peas in her mouth, then told Rachel this was the best meal she'd had all day. In truth, it was her only meal, but she didn't say that.

Mathias pulled the edge off a pan of cornbread and offered it to her. "The crust is the best part," he said when she took it. He then turned to Ben and the two started talking about a turnip crop and clearing the cotton field in preparation for planting once

139

the weather allowed. Angelique knew from the treatise Mathias had given her that cotton needed a long growing season. The real work, she suspected, would come in the spring, when corn planting began. Briefly, she glanced at husks of corn suspended from the rafters. When she looked back, she caught Mathias watching her. "Seed corn," he said.

The north wind's gusts rose, and rain pelted the closed shutters of the cookhouse. Mathias stood. "The horses are in?" he asked Indigo.

The man nodded. "They're good. You sit down."

Charlotte took Indigo's bowl. Rachel had already removed Angelique's and Mathias', and now she told Angelique to stay seated when she would have risen and helped clean up. A woman hadn't ought to be doing housework on her wedding day, Rachel said.

Mathias stretched. "I need to check the fire in the house."

He was going to leave, and Angelique wondered what he wanted her to do. She wanted to lie down and close her eyes. When he reached for his jacket, she stood and found her cloak.

The cookhouse door tore open, and all eyes turned toward it. Angelique thought the wind had blown the thing open, but a bent and shriveled black woman, ancient, if appearance were any indicator, stepped in from the darkness. Mathias shifted his weight, but the woman didn't acknowledge him. She'd fixed her gaze on Angelique at his side.

The withered body took several steps toward her, but stopped next to Mathias. Water rolled off her heavy coat and formed a muddy spot around her feet. Still staring, she said to Mathias, "*Vous a fait épouse la fille?*"

"*Oui,*" he responded.

Yes, he had married the girl.

The ancient woman drew up before her. Angelique glanced nervously at Mathias and found him watching the Negress. This must be the infamous Yo, who'd frightened her young papa with scary stories and the one person who routinely defied the indomitable Elizabeth Boswell without any visible retribution.

Angelique remained still. The old woman came toe to toe with her, then placed cold hands on either side of her face.

"Etes-vous retournée du mort, Véronique? Elizabeth saw it."

Have you come back from the dead, Véronique? Angelique would have shook her head had the old woman not held her so firmly.

Outside a dog barked, and the wind picked up, sending a violent spray of rain against the walls of the rugged building. Ben shut the door. The old woman turned at an angle and glanced to the ceiling, then to Mathias, and again to her.

"Et quels démons vous ont suivi à la maison?"

Angelique shuddered.

"I'm the only demon she's brought home," Mathias answered the old woman.

Another dog barked, then another. The wind slammed something against the side of the cookhouse. Rachel jumped, and the sporadic barks of hounds became a chorus of sharp yelps and vicious growls.

"What's wrong with those dogs, Ben?" Mathias said, his voice loud to compensate for the roar of the wind sweeping through the trees around the house site. He turned on his heel.

Yo frowned, not looking at the retreating men. "More than one ghost returns to De Leau this night, Mathias," she said loudly.

He stopped, as if he'd heard, then disappeared out the door.

Yo's rough fingers drifted over Angelique's face before she dropped her hands. "Elizabeth sent you here?"

"I married Mathias."

Lightning struck close, shaking the ground beneath their feet, and Angelique felt her hair stand on end. Yo snorted, apparently oblivious of the storm outside.

"She arranged the union?"

Yes, she arranged the marriage. Aunt Elizabeth arranged everything.

"She soothes her guilt." Yo tilted her head and listened. "But it rides the storm."

141

"Her guilt?"

"*Incarné*. De Leau's *démon*."

With a violent shudder, Angelique stepped around the woman. Outside, the frigid rain slapped her face, and the wind stung her wet skin. She sucked in a breath, then moved beyond the light cast by the open door. Above the wind, she called Mathias' name. The cookhouse door slammed shut, and she jerked her head around.

A lantern waved far to her right. Somewhere in the darkness, Indigo shouted, but not at her. She pulled the cape around her and drew the hood over her head. To her left were the inviting lights of the cabin, and she turned that direction, eager to get out of the weather. Dipping her head to protect her face from the rain, she started to run, only to plow into a hard body. Someone's fingers circled her bicep, steadying her. On her right, Indigo, his body illuminated by the light he carried, held up his lantern to reveal Mathias, his golden hair, out of its queue, streaming violently in the wind.

"Why didn't you wait in the cookhouse?" he cried above the wind.

"I'm tired, Mathias," she hollered in return. "I want to go to the house."

Mathias' arm circled her waist. "Come."

The heavy cloak, leaden with water, hindered her climb up the stairs, and before she reached the porch, she'd wearied of raising one foot before the other. She might have faltered if Mathias had not been there to coax her onward.

With his shoulder, he pushed the back door open and maneuvered her around him and inside. He entered behind her and slammed the door, shutting out the violence of the wind and rain, but not the eerie howling of the dogs. Angelique pushed the cape off her head and moved down the hall.

"Do your dogs always act like this in a storm?"

She heard him push away from the door and follow her into the front room. "No."

"They sound like hounds from hell."

"And how many hell hounds have you heard?"

She heard the sarcasm in his voice, and she turned on him. "Just yours."

He watched her keenly, and for a moment, she dared to search his eyes, looking for the anger she knew was there. If it was, he masked it well, and when she untied her cape, he reached for it and pulled it off her shoulders. Motioning her into the Windsor chair in front of the fire, he draped the soaked cape over a ladder-back chair and pulled it close to the hearth also.

"What is out there?" she asked.

"A predator, I imagine."

"You imagine?"

"Nothing more exciting than a wild beast. My imagination is not as good as yours." He touched her forehead. "You're hot."

"My head aches and I have chills from time to time, but going in and out of the cold—"

"Chills are different from a shiver, Angelique."

He took an earthen bottle from the mantel and poured liquid into a pewter cup, which he held out to her. She didn't take it.

"It's only the brew, the same as what Bess gave you before we left. I'm worried about you. You'll catch your death."

"And you with De Leau now."

Ah, there was the anger.

"Drink it, Angelique. I'm not trying to poison you, if that's what you think."

Still, she refused the potion. After a moment, he set the cup back on the mantel, then picked up another log and tossed it into the flames. Sparks splattered across the hearth. The fire crackled and burned more brightly than before, and he stared at it. He was so handsome in the flickering light. Her golden god. Tears filled her eyes, and her vision of him blurred.

"What am I to you?" she asked.

"You are my wife."

"An unwanted wife."

"That's not true."

"Why did she do this to you?"

143

"She didn't force me to marry you."

"She withheld De Leau from you until you married me."

"No, she offered me De Leau to take you. This farm was never promised to me."

Angelique briefly closed her eyes. "She forced you to take someone you didn't want to get something you did."

"Even if that were true, such bargains are not unusual."

"Both should have something to gain."

"Is having me so bad?"

Not so long ago, he was the one thing she did want. His rejection of not only her love, freely offered, but even her friendship imperiled that.

"My wants were never considered, Mathias. The other party in the agreement was Aunt Elizabeth. She wanted me at De Leau, and she gave you De Leau to bring me here."

"You agreed."

She rose on wobbly legs. "I agreed so you could have this farm, not to force myself on a man who does not want me."

Devil take her soul, her voice broke, and she reached for the pewter cup on the mantel, threw back her head, and downed the noxious dose. Beside her, Mathias moved and drew her attention.

He glowed in the firelight. Light against shadow, orange and gold. His dark eyes roamed over her forehead, her eyes, nose, and lingered on her lips. "You've not been forced on a man who does not want you," he said softly and turned to the fire.

Above them, the clouds burst open, and the volume of rain pounding the roof increased ten-fold. She tilted her face to the deafening roar. Mathias did the same.

"Why am I here?" she asked and stepped toward him. "What secrets are you and Aunt Elizabeth holding from me?"

His eyes found hers, and she thought for an instant she detected surprise, quickly masked—or simply dismissed?

"My secrets are as mysterious to me as they are to you."

"Does she have the answers?"

He pursed his lips and from the hearth, picked up the poker. She tensed, but all he did was stir the flames. "Perhaps."

"And what of her secrets?"

He stopped poking at the fire. "The demon, you mean?"

"Any of her secrets."

"She harbors many, and they are based on guilt."

"For something she did?"

He shrugged. "Or didn't do. She's never told me what drives her, and I doubt she ever will."

"Does she drive you?"

"She manipulates me when I let her."

"Like she manipulated you into marrying me?"

"And you me." Mathias looked down at his body, then at her. He removed his wet jacket and hung it on a peg beside the fireplace. "But we allowed ourselves to be."

Angelique retook her seat.

"You should rest." He nodded to the back room. "The linens on the bed in there are clean."

Her eyes burned. He didn't intend to consummate their marriage. Could fate be more cruel than to wed her to the man she loved and him not want her? Not want her for anything. Drawing her trembling lips tight, she stood.

"Where do you intend to sleep, husband?"

Chapter Seventeen

Outside, the wind howled, passing between the heavy wooden shutters to rattle the windowpanes. Angelique's gaze swept the room, and she hugged herself. "Or do you intend something else to share my bed tonight?" Her eyes settled on him, watching her, gauging her words.

"Angelique," he said, his voice gentle, "I thought you understood the demon André referred to was me."

"But you don't intend it to be you, do you, Mathias? You never did."

Outside, a scream, indecipherable and ominous, made her draw her arms tighter around herself. She watched him glance at the north wall of the house. Something was out there, he knew it as well as she.

"You might be André's demon," she said, "but what of Aunt Elizabeth's?" She widened her eyes. "What of hers, Mathias?"

"It's the wind."

"It is not the wind. It frightens even you, but you would give me to it."

"No," he said and reached for her. She backed away from his grasp.

"There is nothing out there," he said.

Another cry, far away. Angelique closed her eyes and rocked herself. A floorboard groaned, and she opened her eyes to find he'd come closer.

"I'm all right," she said. "Perhaps it is only your dogs."

He frowned and took another step toward her.

"Let me be, Mathias. I don't want your comfort."

146

"Do you really think I intend to give you to my grandmother's demon?"

She rubbed an aching temple.

"Look at me."

Her eyes stung, and she turned her back on him. She heard his sigh.

"I would never share you with another."

"Lie with me then," she said, looking at him over her shoulder. "Take my virtue and be done with me if that's what you want. At least whatever is out there will no longer want me."

"You think that's all I want from you?"

"I don't think you want even that. I want it done."

"But, Angelique," he said, "I might anger the demon if he desires your virginity."

She screwed up her face. "You think me a little fool, don't you, lacking in experience and desirability?"

He winced at her words.

"I don't care. I have my virtue. You did, by default, agree to take it when I brought you De Leau. Now I insist you do so, then you never have to touch me again. That will be agreeable to me."

She spun for the bedroom, but stopped abruptly and turned. "I never thought...."

So help her, she would not let him hear her voice crack again, and she held her chin high.

"With all my faults, I never thought I would have to beg a man to lie with me, certainly not my husband."

"Begging, you little wench? You are, in truth, demanding sex of me."

Oh dear God, perhaps she was. She sounded no better than Jane and the other women fascinated with rumors of his sexual prowess, and all he wanted was his widow Mallory. Tears filled the back of her throat, and she swallowed.

"I want this marriage annulled, Mathias."

His features hardened.

But he wanted De Leau. In defeat, she closed her eyes and turned away.

"Look at me," he said.

"Go back to hell."

"Look at me. Now."

Sucking in a breath, she turned. He had pulled the damp shirt over his head, and he stood before her, naked to the waist.

"I could have made this so much easier tomorrow."

He was strong and beautiful. If only he wanted her. "Do not force yourself, Mathias. All I'm doing is trading a demon who desires me for a man who does not."

"Maidenly jitters, Angelique?"

She clenched her jaw. "I simply prefer not to give myself to a man who doesn't want me."

He tossed his shirt aside and came closer. "You've decided on the demon, then?"

"You mock me still. There is no demon."

"What there is not," he said, pulling her into his arms, "is a man who doesn't want you. The demon now holds you in his arms. Unfortunately, or fortunately depending on your viewpoint, he will not take you once for your virtue. He will possess you over and over, and you will cry out in pleasure again and again until you beg for his mercy." He dipped his head. "And when it comes to possession of your body, Angelique, the demon will show no mercy."

She closed her eyes in anticipation of his kiss.

"Touch me," he whispered against her lips.

She placed her hands on his broad shoulders, then smoothed her palms over his biceps, his muscles rippling when he tightened his embrace and kissed her. Warming, she spread her hands on his naked chest and shuddered pleasantly at the feel of his skin, smooth and firm, beneath her fingertips. He coaxed her mouth open with the tip of his tongue. Emboldened, she moved her fingers over his breast. He groaned when she touched a nipple, and he plunged his tongue inside her mouth.

Mathias pulled back at her unbidden whimper and picked her up in his arms.

"Truly, I meant only to give you time before we consummated

148

our marriage. I did it for you, but now you've infected me with the fever devouring your body." He pivoted and entered the back room. Kicking the door shut behind him, he sat her on a bed, then covered her body with his.

*L*ightning struck, and thunder shook the foundation of the cabin. A wicked night beyond the walls, but inside Mathias basked in his young bride's beauty. He would seduce her with his touch, then feed his lust with her innocence. He would have her tonight after all.

Behind him, the shutters rattled in the violent wind, and outside, the hounds barked, far away. Yo's "evil" played at the periphery of his mind. Angelique watched his face. He no longer concerned himself with the doubts lingering behind those lovely eyes. His caution had served no purpose but to expand her fears and make this deed more difficult.

His body tingled at the thought of her naked flesh next to his. He moved his hand, and she caught it.

"Second thoughts?" he asked. Despite his outward concern, misgivings would do her no good now.

"I don't want this if you are angry?"

"I'm not angry." He bowed his head and kissed her neck, then suckled below her ear. Her breath stopped for a moment, and his heartbeat quickened.

The wind lulled. Far away an anguished cry, not identifiable, followed a dog's eerie howl.

"Do you hear it?" Angelique asked softly. He pulled away. "Are they hounds from hell, Mathias?"

"They are my hounds. Only a devil would have hell hounds," he whispered.

"You play with me still."

He licked her throat, and she raised her chin, giving him better access.

"Could there be something else out there?"

Simultaneously with the hair rising along the back of his neck, he traced her jaw with the tip of his tongue.

"Sound travels on the wind," he told her. "The storm alters the air as well as its scent. What you hear is something natural."

She touched his chest, and her fingers scorched him. "I fear it comes closer."

"No."

"Take my virtue, Mathias. I want you to have it, no matter what you think of me."

He kissed her deeply, then lay beside her supporting himself on one arm. His gaze lingered on the neckline of her dress before roaming over her hips and thighs to the hem of the woolen skirt. Her breath quickened at his perusal, and his eyes immediately sought hers.

"Do you wear a chemise beneath your dress?"

"A short corset." Her voice trembled, damn her. She wanted to please him, like the *woman at the end of town*, not respond to him like a timid little mouse.

"I hate corsets," he said and leaned close to kiss her yet again behind the ear. Oh, she liked that.

"I had to wear it."

Seizing the hem of her dress, he tugged it over her knees. "Sit up."

She did, then raised her hips at his coaxing, and he pulled the high-waisted dress up, then over her shoulders and head. She sat shivering in a corset and pantaloons.

"You're cold."

"I have a chemise."

"You won't need it," he said and pulled on the ribbon securing her pantaloons.

She averted her eyes, and though she didn't want to confess it, she said, "I'm nervous."

He shifted his weight and pushed her into the mattress. "There's naught to worry about. I prefer your chills from nerves," he said, removing his boots. "Nerves I can do something about."

He reached for her feet and began unbuckling her shoes. Periodically, his gaze returned to her breasts. Her head was pounding, and after a moment, her bravado failed. Crossing her arms over her chest, she covered her nearly naked body.

"Put your hands above your head."

She hesitated, then raised them.

"I enjoy looking at you," he said, pulling her pantaloons over her ankles. She blinked and swallowed hard, but his ensuing kiss calmed her. Stretching out along her side, he touched a nipple exposed above the corset.

A groan escaped her lips. Immediately, he rolled her to her side. His calloused fingers touched the skin on her back, then yanked on the laces securing the corset. The garment gave.

Her hair was still pinned atop her head, giving him access to the back of her neck, and she held her breath as his tongue followed the path of unlaced corset down her spine. Easing her onto her back, he pulled the corset free.

"Mathias —"

"Shh." He sat up and blew out the candle flickering on the bedside table. Darkness. "That should soothe your shyness," he said.

She felt his breath upon her skin, and he ran his hand over her ribcage.

Instinctively, she arched her back at the explosive sensation of his tongue on her nipple, and he grasped her wrists above her head and held them in place. His tongue traversed her chest to lick her other breast.

Far away, another eerie cry portended doom, and he stilled his wandering tongue. She sensed him raise his head.

Her body burned with fever and unfamiliar need. Unsure once again, she moved against him. "Don't stop."

His lips found hers, then his hand touched her thigh.

"You are feeling better?"

"Yes."

"Yo's brew. Thank God, because you'd have given me an impossible task tonight if you still felt as you did earlier."

"Nothing about me feels the same, and I do not believe the reason to be Yo's brew."

"Flattery, my angel?"

"Honesty, my devil."

With her words, he wove his fingers into her pubes and found her clitoris. She twisted with the sweet heat and would have reached for him, but he still held her hands in place.

"Always the ingénue, my sweet. Your honesty will get you in trouble." His voice had deepened.

"Tonight?"

She heard his chuckle in the dark, and suddenly, desperately, she wanted to see him. If not see, then....

"I want to touch you."

She felt his hesitation, and her anxiety swelled.

"What part of me would you like to touch?"

Your face, your chest, the skin on your back....

Holding one of her hands in place, he straddled her and guided the other to the hard bulge between his legs. "Touch me there, Angelique."

She opened her closed fist and did. He released her suddenly and sat back, his hands bumping hers in the darkness. He was tearing at the buttons on his britches. When he rolled away, she reached out and found a hard bicep.

"I'm almost done," he said, and she heard his britches hit the floor.

In the darkness, he pushed her down, his palm on her belly. "You are so innocent." His hand moved up her thighs. Heat and energy emanated from his touch, tensing her pelvis. She groaned, and he inserted a finger inside her vaginal opening. His thumb caressed her womanhood, and she writhed.

"Innocence lost," he said softly.

She opened her eyes, but could see nothing. She would have pushed back, but he tightened his hold and increased the pressure on her clitoris. Then she felt the delicious wetness of his tongue against her breast. She eased her head back, surrendering to the mounting pleasure, teetering now on pain, and spread her legs.

Sensation blotted everything but the dark form she reached

for. He crushed her to him, breast to breast, and she hid her face against his throat. His skin was smooth, his scent pleasant. Delicious shudders ravished her body, fulfilling a physical need she had never known existed.

She was helpless in the wake of the climax that tore through her body, and he held her through each subsiding wave. Never had pleasuring a woman been more important or so simple—sweet success given Angelique's purity and innocence, and all the richer in the face of her doubt. His swollen penis ached in anticipation of taking the last of her innocence and making her completely his. The demon had conquered the angel, now the angel seduced him.

Distracting her with kisses, he straddled her once more, then coaxed her calf across his back. She followed his lead, repeating the action with her other leg. He nestled in the apex of her thighs and pushed. Angelique whispered he was hurting her. He soothed her with soft words, but held her in place and waited. When he felt her relax, he thrust without warning.

Fire seared his shoulder. She'd bit him, and he howled in satisfaction. After a moment, his pain subsided, and he asked if hers had, too. He felt her nod, the hair on her head tickling his chin. "I fear I've brought blood," she said, "I did not mean to bite." He kissed her cheek. "I forgive you. I've brought blood, too." When she laid her head against his shoulder, he placed a hand beneath her firm buttocks, and pushed her down. He sensed her protest and before she could ask, he pinned her hands above her head. "I'm not done," he said, "but the worst is over."

He pulled out, then pushed back. She was tight and not immediately pliable. She struggled against his hold. "Relax," he told her.

"I want to hold you, too."

"Shh, in a moment." He moved, careful not to hurt her. She fell in with his rhythm. Dear heaven this was good. Sweet torture swelled with the growing friction along his cock.

The wind wailed.

Heat and sensation consumed him. Beyond the cabin walls, the storm raged, and on it rode a savage scream. With one last thrust, he stiffened and closed his eyes. Light exploded inside his head, and his cry of sweet agony drowned the condemnation of the night.

With the fading of the hideous cry, Mathias collapsed next to his bride. Rolling her onto her side, he pressed his spent manhood against her bare bottom and pulled the quilts over them.

Hesitantly, she took his hand and brought his fingers to her lips. "Did you hear it?" she asked.

His labored heart quickened. "Did I hear what?"

"The beast outside."

"The beast is inside, sated for now."

"It was not you."

"It was only the wind."

Chapter Eighteen

athias knelt on one knee near the carcass of the hound. A frigid wind buffeted him. Overhead the sky was clear. Bare branches rattled in the breeze, and he shivered, the first discomfort he'd felt in hours.

"Bear?" he asked Indigo, who stood beside him.

Indigo pulled the long rifle from his shoulder. "Or wolves...or cat."

Mathias stood and looked around. "I don't think the dog would have gone after wolves, do you?" He turned to Indigo, and the bitter wind hit him full in the face, causing his eyes to tear.

"Or cat either," Indigo said, "but Judy was a stupid dog."

Mathias focused on the man who had taught him to hunt and to track. Indigo was good, trained by Ben, who had learned from the Choctaw and from Robert Douglas. If Indigo had found no sign, there was none.

Yo's one-room cabin sat on the edge of the woods a short distance east of the swampy waters surrounding De Leau. A good quarter mile from the main house and the other servants' quarters, her home offered cherished isolation from the other human inhabitants on the farm. She had lived here for as long as Mathias could remember, and she feared nothing.

Hunkered down, she tended a fire outside the cabin. There was no hearth within. Some years ago, Mathias had wanted to build her one. She was growing old, and the winters had their bitter spells. But she'd told him to let her alone. She'd lived this way

155

for fifty years and had no desire to change at the close of her life.

"Lost old Judy last night," she called to him when he came within earshot.

Her knowing didn't surprise him. She'd probably been up and around since long before the sun. Mathias stooped and warmed his hands over her fire. "Yes, we're thinking bear, maybe cat."

"You think Old Judy chase after some bear in that weather last night?"

"You tell me what it was then."

"You know what I think, boy."

"Came close to you last night."

"Fears me," she whispered, "won't come near me."

"It came close last night."

She wrinkled her nose and poked at the fire. "Not close."

He grinned. "Tell me what it really is, Yo?"

She offered him a piece of the chewy cornbread she'd fried over her fire. She'd been feeding it to him all his life, the bread and her scary tales.

"Elizabeth sent the young beauty here, didn't she?"

Mathias frowned, and Yo raised an eyebrow.

"The demon is not sated, the debt not yet paid. I warned Elizabeth."

Mathias placed a chunk of the bread in his mouth and chewed. Where once he'd listened to Yo's ramblings to seek information about his lineage, in recent years, he listened for entertainment. Always he thought there had been a grain of truth threading through the tale. The one other person who knew for sure was his grandmother, and he feared she would take that knowledge to her grave.

He reached over and took another hunk of bread. "The only devil who will take Angelique has already done so." He tore off a bite-sized piece. "And will do so again. If your demon wanted her virtue, he's too late."

Yo's eyes narrowed on him. "It cares nothing for her virginity. It wishes to inflict pain. What watches De Leau and your young bride is something monstrous. It will come for her, and it will take her will to live as it did Julianna's. And it will do so to hurt Elizabeth. Hatred and vengeance drives the demon, rape and ravage are but its instruments."

𝒜 sickening sweet stench filled Angelique's nostrils, dragging her from the sleep demanded by Yo's brew. The quilts tugged. She pulled them back over her.

A floorboard groaned, and the door squeaked shut.

She rolled over in search of Mathias, his warmth and his touch. He was gone, his side of the bed cold.

But the unpleasant scent lingered. She sat up suddenly. The scent of death.

Sunshine highlighted the perimeters of the closed shutters, heralding early morning and a clear day.

The house creaked, and she called Mathias' name. Somewhere, a door closed, the front one, she thought.

The scent of death had faded.

She threw back the heavy quilts, and her breath caught in her throat. Vomit and air vied for dominance. A new stench overwhelmed what lingered of decay, and for Angelique, vomit almost won the battle. Human feces stained the white Holland sheets where Mathias' had slept. Tangled in the filth were coarse black hairs, long and wavy.

Holding her breath, she turned to her side of the bed and hastened out of it. She was naked, the room frigid, but the cold felt good on her damp skin. She squatted and bowed her head. Blood, her virgin blood, stained her upper thighs, but despite that final repulsive catalyst, she fought back the nausea.

She'd gotten sick was all, sometime after Mathias left this morning and before she'd forced herself awake. Perhaps diarrhea was a consequence of Yo's healing brew, and perhaps she'd confused that stench with that of death....

Head still bowed, she closed her eyes tight.

But what of the coarse, dark hair?

-≥·≤-

157

"Good morning," Mathias said with an appreciative glance. "You've bathed."

She turned to the lug pole on which she hung the steaming kettle over the fire.

"Yes." With hot water and lots of lye soap. She'd donned a clean shift moments before he'd walked in on her.

"You rose early," she said, looking at him now and searching his eyes.

He closed the door. "I slept till dawn. A luxury for me, but last night was my wedding night."

She averted her eyes, but heard him move closer.

"Did you miss my not being here when you woke?"

Yes, she'd missed him. How she wished he'd been here in the daylight. Now she racked her brain wondering what had been, if not him. "The bed was cold without you."

"Was it?"

Wringing her hands, she stepped toward him. "You might have woken me to rise with you."

He tossed his hat to the floor and started removing his jacket. "I wanted you to rest. How do you feel?"

Sick and scared. "My throat no longer hurts. My headache is gone." Or it had been when she woke.

He took her hands. "Do you have other pains this morning?"

She felt her cheeks heat, and she looked away. He squeezed her fingers.

"I only ask if you are all right this morning, Angelique?"

"Why?" She'd snapped at him, and she hadn't meant to. But why did he ask?

His brow furrowed. "Because..."

She closed her eyes and breathed him in. The clean scent of sandalwood engulfed her.

"...last night was your first time. I want to make sure I didn't hurt you."

She opened her eyes. "Did I please you?"

His mouth dropped open, then he grinned. "Yes, Angelique, you pleased me."

"Make love to me, Mathias. I know I told you you'd never have to again, but—"

His mouth swallowed her words. Warmth spread over her. He held her close against his strong body, hard and still cold from being outside. He was fresh and clean and once again her golden god in the light of day. "Hush," he said, when he pulled back. "I didn't take what you said to heart last night."

"You'll make love to me then?"

"Now?"

"Yes, please, Mathias."

He smiled gently, and wrapping his arm around her scantily-clad shoulder, he started them to the bedroom.

"On this bed," she said, quickly moving from his hold toward the smaller trundle bed in the corner of the main room.

He frowned. "No one has slept in this bed for—"

"I don't care. It's warm in here and I..."

With a bemused expression, he coaxed, "Yes, my sweet?"

"I soiled the other bed...my blood, you know, from last night."

He nodded knowingly, then took her hand and drew her toward the smaller bed.

"*Mathias!*"

Angelique stilled.

"*I hear you've a bride.*" The voice belonged to a man, and the man was outside

Mathias cursed softly, but when she looked up at him, he was grinning and focused on the window overlooking the front porch. He bent his head and kissed her quick.

"Our tryst will have to wait, my wanton beauty. It's Jack Summerfield, our neighbor. Hurry and dress, he wants to meet you."

*A*nd doubtless the man pitied poor Mathias for wedding a lazy woman. Mathias probably thought the same, but his faulting would be from her wanting to drag him back to bed when he had work to do.

"...I say it is bear. Sign all..."

The stranger facing the cookhouse door stopped talking when she walked in. Mathias and Indigo turned her way. Ben looked up from the table. Then Mathias, his eyes softening, extended a hand and drew her to him.

Jack Summerfield was a tall, broad-shouldered man, handsome despite the telltale gray streaked through his light hair. Angelique guessed him to be well into his forties.

"I'm English," he told her a short while later, joining her when she sat down to breakfast. "I came to this region with my pa and two brothers when I was a boy. Pa was the third son of a British army officer. He was well-educated, but he's what folks today would call a black sheep with a lot of roving in him. Personally, I think he was on the run from the Virginia constabulary, and Natchez was French then." Jack shrugged, looking up when Mathias poured amber brew into his steaming coffee. Mathias poured some in his own, then held up the jug for her.

"Whiskey?" she asked.

"Corn whiskey."

She shook her head.

"Anyway," Jack continued, "Pa squatted on a patch of land three miles to the northwest of De Leau. As much a tradin' post as a farm back then."

"None of us would have survived in the early days," Ben said, "but for the Indian trade." He nodded when Angelique looked at him. "You ask your Aunt Elizabeth. She knows better than any of us."

"'Cept Yo," Jack Summerfield said.

Ben nodded. "Yep, 'ceptin' Yo, you're right."

Mathias grinned and sat. "Who used to change Bess' diapers."

"Relations have always been good 'twixt our families," Jack said. "Mathias' granddaddy was British. Robert Douglas was a fur trader, employed by the Crown and not, Angelique, to gather furs. He came to stir up trouble for the French, using the Chickasaw as his allies. Old rumors have it he was directly responsible for the attack that took Charles Richard's life. Elizabeth's first husband. Two months later, he wed Elizabeth.

How much Elizabeth knew in advance of Charles' demise, no one knows. Folks hereabouts at the time said Charles was not good to her."

"Don't you believe them stories, Miss Angelique," Ben said. "Robert Douglas didn't get a whiff of Miss Elizabeth 'til his 'huntin' party' had kilt Richard. Was Robert kept the Chickasaw from massacrin' everybody here. Only ones left was women and children."

Mathias took a sip of his coffee and smiled at Angelique. "Granddaddy moved right in."

"He and Elizabeth lived together for sixteen years," Jack said, "and had three children before he was found murdered not far from here."

"Who killed him?"

"Choctaw we thought. Never knew for sure." Jack shrugged. "Yo's always said it was the demon for a blood debt. But could have been Indians for the same reason. Them Indians got long memories when it comes to vengeance. Living amongst the savages is a two-edged sword.

"After my father died, my brothers left. They saw no future here, but I did. The French were at war with Britain by then, and I hoped if we won, the Crown would see the potential of this place. We won.

"No sooner had the provisional government been set up in Pensacola than your great aunt, oh she had nerve, went before it, French accent and all, and asked for compensation in the name of her deceased husband who had served the Crown for over twenty years. Hence—"

"White Oak Glen," Angelique said.

Jack smiled. "One thousand acres of the world's richest land." He furrowed his brow at Mathias, then looked again to her. "But you know this story already?"

"Bits and pieces," Angelique said. "Please don't stop."

"The solicitor who represented her was the Englishman William Boswell, whom she married years later after he became a widower."

"Were they happy, do you think?" Angelique asked Mathias.

"They were content. Two compatible people who'd lost the real loves of their lives. He's buried in Natchez next to his first wife, Miranda. That was the real love match Grandmama said, and where he belonged. Bess and William Boswell's marriage was more a business partnership, but he was a good person, respected. She was twenty years his junior, and he had no children."

"Yep." Jack nodded. "A banker, lawyer, and the owner of a lucrative mercantile business that so far Michael Douglas has managed to keep thriving despite Spanish trade laws.

Jack slapped the table suddenly. "I've a new wife of my own. Not as new as you. Two years. She was newly widowed when I found her. Had two young'uns. Real young, six and four they are now. She gets lonely. We've few neighbors out here, and God knows Mathias offers her nothing in the way of feminine conversation. She's wanting to meet you. I'd have brought her with me, but she's well along with our first babe and not comfortable making the ride."

Angelique smiled. "This baby will be your first?"

"Noooo," he said, returning her smile, "Martha's not my first wife, but my third. Lost my first to yellow fever. My second marriage was short-lived. Janet was kicked in the head by my horse."

"I am sorry."

He shook his head as if he hadn't heard her. "Shot the thing afterwards, and horses in these parts were hard to come by. Good ones still are. But in answer to your question, I've two grown boys by my first wife."

"They're with you?"

"They are." He laughed. "And if I have my choosing, they'll stay. Finally got 'em old enough to earn back what I put into 'em."

*A*ngelique spent the morning learning how wash was done on the farm. A full day was set aside for this chore, and today was not the day. To make things worse, this day was cold, so even if it had been washday, Angelique got the feeling the resident women would have preferred to postpone it.

Ultimately, Bounty overruled Charlotte's efforts to talk Angelique into waiting, Charlotte's argument being that there were several sets of clean sheets in the house. The two women had then helped her draw and heat water, then boil the soiled sheets—which Angelique made sure no one touched but herself—in a cast-iron cauldron in the cookhouse.

"You find that agreeable?" Mathias asked.

Her mind tangled in those soiled sheets, Angelique blinked. "I'm sorry?"

"You find Jack's concern for his pregnant wife nice?"

The men had gone into the woods earlier, tracking the supposed bear. She'd hoped Jack would return with Mathias for the noon meal, but he'd gone home instead. His wife's time was growing close, and he didn't like to be away for long periods.

"It's sweet he worries over her."

"'Sweet.' That's a term I doubt is often used in reference to Jack Summerfield."

She looked at her plate. "I meant no offense."

He reached over and covered her hand. "I didn't mean to embarrass you."

"You didn't."

"I did."

"I simply meant it was nice he—"

"Displays concern for his wife."

"Yes."

"Men do, you know."

"Some, perhaps."

He frowned at her, and she considered he thought her comment a slight against him.

"I can't recall my father fussing over Mama is all I meant."

He nodded, then speared a piece of salt pork with his knife.

While stranded in the cookhouse with the wash, Angelique tried to make up for the inconvenience she caused the women by helping Rachel cut up pork and onion, which they cooked in left-

163

over pea juice for the noon meal. She and Mathias were eating their portion in front of the fireplace in the main room.

"Bounty said you washed the sheets."

Angelique frowned. "She's angry with me, isn't she?"

He laughed. "No, she says you were shy and ashamed and she knew there was no arguing with you."

"I'm sure they think I'm horrid." She took a sip of cider, an "import" from up the Ohio, he'd told her earlier. From the glint in his eye, Angelique figured it was smuggled into the District.

"They don't think that at all. Out here, much of what we need, we make and supply ourselves. A woman's work is particularly hard. They're glad to have you here."

She glanced at the ledgers stacked neatly on his desk and stood. "I was confused by the bookkeeping." She rose when he looked at her, and she walked to the desk. "You keep two sets?"

"I do," he answered. "One for business and one for bartering among neighbors."

"But why would bartering—"

"I don't know how it's done in the east," he said, "but out here bartering makes up a significant part of the economy."

"Oh." She ran a finger down the column of neatly entered entries. "So—"

"I don't expect you to keep the books."

She looked up. "But I kept Papa's books. I assumed..."

He was shaking his head, and she clamped her mouth shut, not certain why she took offense to his not letting her keep the books. Aunt Elizabeth kept her own books.

Of course, Aunt Elizabeth didn't have a husband to do it. She shut the ledger. "Will you hunt the bear?"

Mathias leaned back in his chair and sipped his coffee. "If bear it is. Predators, and Indians for that matter—we can't completely rule them out—wreak havoc out here. Whatever it is has gotten to my livestock over Jack's way. If a beast, we need to kill it before it hurts a person."

"Did you come back to the house this morning?" she asked, retaking her seat.

"You've forgotten already?"

"Before that. Between the time you left and the time you came in the house and found me in this room."

He set the cup down and stood. "I did not. Why?"

She stood, also. "I heard someone inside. I"—she looked away—"I thought for a moment whoever it was might have been in the bedroom."

"When was this?"

"I was still in bed. The sun's rays were filtering through the shutters."

"Rachel. I asked her to bring in the tub for you."

"I think whoever it was went out the front door." Angelique started gathering the dirty plates.

"Leave them," he said and took her free hand. "That should have been Rachel. She was probably stacking firewood inside the front door."

And she had heard Rachel finishing her task. That was possible...and the hair had been there all the time...and she'd become ill while she slept...and the stench had been—"

Mathias tugged on her hand. "Would you like to see your farm?"

"All this you see," he said, leaning toward her from atop Dan and pointing to a far tree line, "will be in corn come spring. Closer to the house, we'll put twenty acres into other crops. We've steer..."

She'd seen a number of them.

"...and hogs. They forage in the woods." Shifting in the saddle, he waved toward the northwest. The not too distant forest loomed dark and bleak in front of them. "Jack Summerfield's place is roughly three miles the other side of that forest. There is a road, rough, but well-worn."

Mathias turned Dan and beckoned to Angelique. The docile old mare she rode followed the stallion.

"Bess has always kept a family presence at De Leau. Squatters are quick to lay claim to an abandoned home site, and possession counts for more than who holds the deed. Then there's been the succession of crowns. The incident with your grandfather's claim highlights the threat. French, British, now the Spanish."

"Do you think the Kentuckians will invade?"

He smiled. "Those rumors have persisted for ten years. I don't worry about them anymore."

Mathias pulled up far beyond the house. Here lay a patch of untilled ground next to a small isthmus of trees that widened as it flowed into the forest. He dismounted and walked over to help her down. "Are you cold?" he asked, holding her close.

She shook her head. "Not very. I'm enjoying the ride."

"Good." He let her go, then took her hand and glanced behind her, to the west. "The sun will be going down soon. We'll have a hard freeze tonight."

Long rifle in hand, Mathias led her over dry grass. The thorns of dead blackberry caught at her skirts and gloved hands, pricking her before she realized what they were.

"They grow wild all over this place," he said, helping free her. "And have tasty berries come June."

She took a moment to study a stalk, but all she could make of the plant now was that it was a gangly bush, which viciously protected its fruit. Blackberries were known in Baltimore, but this was her first opportunity to see the plant in the wild. Letting go of the dead stem, she pulled her skirt from another prickly tendril and looked up to find him watching her.

"De Leau has a peach orchard." He pointed with his chin to the south. "Beyond and to the east of the house."

"Hickory pecan?"

"They're native. The trees in front of the house are hickory pecan."

"I like the nuts. Are any left?"

He tugged at her hand. "Bounty, Rachel, and Charlotte went over the yard in the fall. There'll be some in the larder."

He stopped abruptly and pointed to the ground. She saw the first marker before he spoke.

"This is the family plot."

She moved ahead of him and squatted, then pushed away the dried grass. *Pierre Deschesne 1690-1736.*

"Our great-granddaddy," he said. "Your grandmother and grandfather are over here."

She smoothed away the grass from where he indicated.

"Bess ordered the markers from New Orleans a number of years ago. The wooden ones were in a state of decay. I've sometimes wondered if we got the right markers on the right graves, but Old Bess assures me we did."

Angelique touched the marker of Véronique Veilleux. "Does Aunt Elizabeth know what a mess this place is in?"

"She and Yo have always done what keeping's been done. It grows up quickly. I'd hoped you'd spend time on it in the spring."

She looked up at him.

"This farm is our ancestors' monument, Angelique. They lived here, and they died here, and in between, they built De Leau. Now it's ours."

He reached for her. "I want to show you something else."

She took his hand, and he pulled her up and led her toward the barren forest. The sun was lowering behind them, and the tops of the trees were bright with sunshine. A breeze chilled her cheeks, and cold air stung her nostrils. With her free hand, she pulled the hood of her cape beneath her chin. He squeezed the hand he held.

"We'll go to the house after this. I'm cold, too."

Mathias stepped carefully into the woods, his booted feet rustling dried leaves and cracking twigs.

"What about the predator?"

He looked back, over her head. "See the horses?"

"Yes."

"They're calm. If anything dangerous were near by, they'd be nervous."

They had ventured a short distance into the sterile, winter forest, when Mathias stopped at the edge of a pool, sandy on the bottom, and crystal clear.

"*Ressort de l'eau,*" he said.

Spring water.

"De Leau. Our great grandmother Marie Deschesne gave the farm its name based on this spot."

"It's beautiful." She took her hand from his and removed her glove. Then cupping her palm, she dipped her hand and drank. "And sweet."

He squatted and thrust his hand in, again shattering the mirror-like surface. Angelique watched the sparkling ripples flow outward in repeating half circles. He did not drink.

"This pool is formed from a spring-fed creek," he said nodding to the north. "Can you see?"

She could and told him so.

"The water stays at a constant temperature inside the earth. It's cold now, and remains cold during summer's hottest days."

"How deep is it?"

"You could stand in it and have your head above water." He nodded across the pool where huge trees grew. "Roughly twelve feet across at its widest and fifteen feet long." He stood. "It makes a fine swimming hole in the summer. This spot is like a garden when everything is blooming." He picked up a twig and whipped it at a dead plant frond.

"Yo's Choctaw Lily," he said when she turned to see what he was doing.

"It flowers?"

"Bright red in the spring. She uses the bulbs for medicine."

"For which ailment?" Angelique pulled at a dead frond, placed an end in her mouth, and bit. Her tongue stung.

"Don't," Mathias said and pulled the plant from her lips and tossed it away. "The fronds are poisonous, but she uses the bulbs for every ailment known, I think."

To her right, Angelique heard an almost imperceptible murmuring. After a few steps, she saw that the pool water flowed over a natural spillway from where the creek continued merrily south. Kneeling, she took another drink, this time to wash the bitterness from her tongue.

Hushed steps echoed mutely in the silence. Her heart labored, and she rose. She sensed rather than heard him. Fingertips gently squeezed her shoulders. His soundlessness bordered on sinister. Mathias' pulled her against him. He kissed the lobe of her ear. His hand cupped a breast. His thumb stroked a nipple. Desire consumed her. The world teetered, and when she looked up, the darkening heavens whirled. She was falling. On the periphery of her vision, surrounding her like ominous fortress walls, the bare, clawing branches of trees reached for a frigid, purple sky. The chilled ground was damp beneath her spread thighs. She tried helplessly to move her weighted legs. Her arms were pinned above her head. Mathias' face loomed over her.

Her heart raced at frightening speed and her world dimmed. He was holding her down, not allowing her to move.

He was not who caressed her. Warmed her. Heated her. Unbearable need crushed her fear, and she spread her legs wider, then writhed on the ground and watched a dark being thrust against her. She arched and cried out, reaching for and seizing a blinding ecstasy that devoured her, then spat her out. Eyes closed, she floated back to the cold ground on subsiding waves of pleasure. Weak and trembling, she opened her eyes.

Her cape was open, her skirt bunched around her waist. Mathias lay on top of her, his eyes dark, his face strained. He held her hands above her head, and his body lay nestled between her bare thighs. His manhood filled her. The sky, dark blue, still held light. Little time had passed.

"My God, Angelique, what possessed you?" he said, freeing her hands and rolling off her.

She sat up and yanked her skirt over her legs. With a quick twist of her head, she looked around. No one else was here. She whimpered and looked at him again. No other "thing" was here for that matter. Scents of sandalwood and male musk invaded her nostrils. With a trembling hand, she reached out and touched his cheek.

Concern clouded his face. "What's wrong?" he asked.

She leaned away from him and threw up.

Behind her, she felt him nestle closer, and he rubbed her back.

"Mathias," she said, unable to keep the tremor out of her voice, "is this place bewitched?"

He wrapped his arms around her shoulders and pulled her close. "Yo has always said so," he whispered into her hair. "This is where my mother came the day she was taken."

Chapter Nineteen

"**W**hat are you doing in here?"

Angelique jumped at Mathias' gruff voice, and water from the bucket sloshed on the brick hearth. Dropping the pine shuck brush into the dirty liquid, she stood awkwardly and shook blood back into the foot that had fallen asleep on her.

"I'm cleaning this room." She saw her breath when she spoke, and her hand ached from contact with the cold water.

"Why?"

"It's filthy. From the looks of it, it hasn't been cleaned in years, and I was hoping we could sleep in here." She said those last words quickly, not sure she'd be able to get them out otherwise.

"You don't like our room?"

"I freeze in there. This one has a fireplace." Excited by her cause, she moved toward him. "It's bigger, and it seems a waste not to use it."

She'd been at De Leau a week and finally ventured into the two rooms on the other side of the house's broad foyer. Today was not her first time to see them. She'd peeked in the day after her arrival, but was so discouraged by the cleanup needed to make the rooms livable, she closed them off again. Four frigid nights later, she was ready to make a change.

More importantly, she was apprehensive. Mathias hadn't made love to her since that day at the pool, and though he told her he wanted her soreness to abate, she believed the real reason for his restraint was he sensed her anxiety. She hated herself. She needed more to take her mind off him than the quilt she and Charlotte were piecing.

171

He stood before her, dressed in buckskin trousers and jacket, so handsome despite his wind-flushed face. He smelled of the cold outside, and yes, she should have talked to him before coming in here, but she hadn't wanted to give him the chance to say no.

He stared sternly. Finally, she drew in a tired breath. "You're going back out?"

"I wasn't, but considering this going on in my house, I may."

She was cold and tired and needed a bath in this chilly place, and she would suffer to get one, shivering bitterly the entire time. She thrust out her chin.

"This is my house, too, Mathias Douglas, and as its mistress, I am responsible for its cleanliness and upkeep. You should have considered that having a wife would cause some disruption to your well-ordered, messy life, and you might have been so considerate to have done so before you brought me here and consummated our marriage, after I requested an annulment. I am more than something to keep your bed warm at night. If that's all you wanted, you should have brought one of the dogs in to sleep with."

He blinked. "But, Angelique, you do more for me than keep me warm."

Yes, she cooked and cleaned, and darned and mended and sewed...and washed, and had to struggle with the other women, their own roles secure within the farm organization, to even do that for him. She was his servant, his slave. She'd brought him De Leau. He'd consummated the marriage as she'd requested, and he'd given her...

"I'll sleep in here." Her voice caught, and she clenched her teeth. "You don't have to. Now let me be, so I can finish and get your supper."

His intimidating stare softened to a sheepish look. "I've said something to upset you."

She pivoted away from him. "It's cold in here, and I've much to do yet."

Behind her, he moved, and she tilted her head to make certain he didn't try to touch her, although his touch was her true wish.

And one not granted. He had, in fact, turned away from her and now studied the formidable, rough-hewn bed. Odd he'd not been using the huge piece of cedar all these years.

He sat on the mattress, his calves rubbing against the old footboard. "It's filled with moss. Heaven knows when it was last turned." He glanced up at her. "Your grandmother was born in this bed."

Solemn, she watched him.

"As was Bess and my mother, Julianna. Seventeen years later, Julianna died in it, shortly before giving birth to me."

Angelique touched her twitching belly. "Before giving birth to you?"

"Ben cut me from the womb with his hunting knife after my mother died."

Her chest felt suddenly weighted, and she feared she might cry. "I'm sorry. This place must have unhappy memories for you. I'll close it up."

She started around him, but he reached out and grabbed her hand. Holding it, he stood. "Actually, Angelique, I don't remember it at all."

He bent low, and she bowed her head to prevent him from seeing her eyes. He nudged her forehead with his chin, and she surrendered and looked up. He had a gleam in his eye and a gentle laugh in his throat. She smiled, and he kissed her.

"Are you done with the fireplace?"

"Yes."

"I'll help you build a fire and warm the room. Not only has this mattress not been turned in years, it needs re-stuffing. We'll trade the one on our bed. Rachel can help you do the rest."

"Are you sure?"

"I am. Every winter I think about moving in here, but truth is I haven't wanted to be bothered." He pulled her close and with his thumb rubbed at something on her chin. "You are a tarnished angel."

Their great-grandfather Pierre Deschesne, third son of a low-ranking French nobleman, had come to Natchez in 1720 with his fifteen-year-old bride, Marie, Mathias told her while he built the fire. Shortly thereafter, Pierre built a simple, one-room cabin, the main front room where he and Angelique had done most of their living until now. The Natchez Indians burned the original cabin in the uprising of 1729, but the floor and walls survived, the roof lost. Pierre and his family had escaped, thanks to a warning from a friend among the Choctaw.

The displaced family spent the next two years in safety with that same tribe while French troops wiped out the Natchez. Pierre then returned to the farm with his wife, their two young daughters, and their only remaining slave, fourteen-year-old Yo. Pierre repaired the cabin and added the room Mathias and Angelique now slept in. Jean Larocque, Marie's second husband, added the other two rooms, joined by a dogtrot, in the English style. Many years later, Angelique's grandfather, Etienne Veilleux, enclosed the dogtrot into a broad foyer and added the wrap-around porch.

That night, Mathias reached for her in the dark. Her body simmered before she could ask him to light a candle. His adept touch and wicked tongue assuaged her fears and dispelled her doubts. Breathing in the scents of sandalwood and clean linen, she clung to the hard body probing hers in heated passion. Later she lay in the crook of his arm and listened to him breathe. She touched his breast and licked his skin, and when she woke him, he loved her again. He kissed her awake when he rose with the sun, the room shrouded in cold, dim light, and neither filthy sheets nor foul air tainted the pleasures of the night.

The cherry table with its assorted blend of oak, walnut, and even two fine mahogany chairs gleamed in the dim light of the room. A week had come and gone since Angelique usurped the old master bedroom and made it her and Mathias' own. Today she completed cleaning the room next to it, the one in which Elizabeth Douglas's growing family had shared its meals.

A fine four-poster cherry bed sat against the south wall of this room, a huge rustic breakfront on the west. She, Charlotte, and Rachel had pulled the latter far enough from the wall to clean behind it. Angelique yanked on one of its drawers, the one that always caught, and retrieved a linen tablecloth. White originally, the fabric had yellowed with age. Faded embroidery graced its edges. She covered Mathias' dinner. Ethan had killed a deer this morning, and tonight she'd feasted alone on venison and corn.

On tiptoe, Angelique blew out the candles in the pewter chandelier Mathias bought in Natchez two days ago. The room was cold, as was his dinner. Early this morning he and Indigo had left with two steer to trade for pelts at an outpost a far piece to the north of them. He told her they might be late getting back. Night had fallen. He liked to be out of the woods before dark, and she'd begun to worry.

She picked up the tin lantern and entered the wide foyer. To her left was the ladder leading to the attic above her head. More than once, she'd thought of venturing up there, but Mathias told her the space was good for nothing but storage. Tomorrow she'd climb up anyway and see for herself. Tonight she longed for the wingback chair and a warm fire. She'd darning to do.

In the front room, the fire she'd left before dinner had faded to glowing embers, and the coveted warmth had diminished. She sighed in mild frustration. During the afternoon, she'd noted the waning wood supply and meant to bring some up from the pile beneath the porch, but a cold, steady rain falling on De Leau since late morning had discouraged her. She crossed the hall and checked the bin in their bedroom. That pile was low, too.

Stinging cold bit her nose and ears when she opened the cabin door, and she drew the hood of her cape over her head to shield her face against the freezing wet. The bleak night and shrouding hood impaired her vision, but she descended the steps unscathed.

She was familiar with the location of the woodpile, and feeling her way, Angelique gathered three pieces of wood. Upstairs, she dropped them unceremoniously inside the front door. She repeated the trip without incident, but on her third time down, she tripped on the bottom step. Catching herself on the handrail, she swore. From the depths of inky blackness beneath the house, a sound echoed her mild curse, and she stopped.

The steady drum of the rain lulled her. The sound did not repeat itself. Cautiously, she stepped from the stairs. The last load, she thought with growing unease. One log, two...but something...

Good God, something was with her.

The third log fell back into the pile with a thud. Her heartbeat quickened, and her hair pricked the back of her neck.

The stench of death filled her nostrils.

Fighting down the bile flooding her stomach, she clutched the remaining wood to her breast and twisted around, stumbling as she slammed into a foundation post. Pushing away from the support, she bolted from beneath the porch and scrambled up the steps.

Above her, the open door called out for her to hurry, and a hairsbreadth later, something caught her skirt. She tripped and had to catch herself to keep from falling on the stairs. The scent of death weighted the air. Under the steps, something moved, and darkness, black against black, filled the gaps made by the high risers.

Unbalanced, Angelique placed her free hand on the railing, straightened, and lurched blindly upward. Again something tugged at her foot. She cried out and yanked away. On the next step, it caught the other foot. She flailed and dropped the last two pieces of wood, then stumbled two more times, once hitting her shin.

The porch thumped with her footsteps. She fell through the door, then spun to face the inky abyss. She pushed at the door. It closed in slow motion. Beyond the edge of the porch, a step creaked, almost silent beneath the strumming rain. A violent shudder racked her body. Something, unseen, outside her line of vision, followed her. The door shut, and she slid the bolt in place. Dry mouthed, she swallowed, then listened. All she heard was her heartbeat in her ears.

Angelique laid her forehead against the heavy panel. The

door vibrated with a violent blow, and Angelique, her head echoing the clamor of her heart, jumped back. She stumbled, then righted herself and locked her wobbly knees. Twisting her head around, she found the door brace and set it in place.

Chapter Twenty

She scarcely breathed, fearful of disrupting the prevailing silence, of letting *it* know she was here.

"What are you doing?"

She shrieked and whirled. "Oh God, Mathias, you scared me!"

He glanced at the barred door. "From the looks of things, you were frightened before I got here."

Her lip quivered, and she bit down to make it stop. He placed a hand beneath her chin and made her look at him.

"What's wrong?"

"Were you out front?" She flexed her chapped hands. She'd been twisting her fingers together, and they stung now.

"No."

"You've only now arrived?"

"I've been in the cookhouse for a spell, talking to Ben."

"Have you eaten then?"

"I ate venison left out there."

She started around him, but he stopped her. "What happened, Angelique?"

She shook her head. "I-I don't know. I went out to get some wood," she said and pointed to the cut pieces scattered inside the door. "I couldn't see anything." She could hear the tremor in her voice, but the terror had abated with Mathias' presence. Untying her cape, she slipped it off. "Something was out there with me."

"What?"

She shrugged. "I'm cold."

Mathias took her arm, but she pulled away and reached for a stick of wood. He bent to help.

"Is this all you got?"

She nodded.

"It's not enough."

He reached for the door.

Her heart lurched into her throat. Stumbling around him, she placed herself between him and the door. "Don't!"

After a long silent stare, he took her arm and attempted to pull her out of his way.

"Stop it! You're not going out there."

He dropped his hand. "You get a lantern, I'll get my rifle. It's probably a wild animal."

Violently she shook her head.

Concern etched his face, and he pulled her into his embrace. "We must have more wood, Angelique, and we need to set your mind at ease."

She still held the cloak, and he took it and put it over her shoulders. "Get the lantern," he said softly, and he walked to the back door to retrieve his Kentucky rifle.

"But when I got into the house, I slammed the door shut. I no sooner had the bolt secure than something ran into it."

He frowned at her.

"It was not a coon."

"They're tricky things."

"And what grabbed my feet as I came up the steps?"

"There are rough edges on the footers. Your skirt caught them. By then you were too frightened to know what you were doing."

"I was never that frightened, Mathias."

"I showed you the raccoon, Angelique. You saw the thing with your own eyes."

"Yes," she said. "I saw the beast. It did not hit the door with such force, I'm telling you."

"Then the wind blew something against the door."

"And what of the smell?"

He turned away. "Something's dead near the house, no doubt. The scent was caught in the wind."

"In all that rain? No, Mathias, whatever I smelled was beneath our porch."

"*I* don't see how the fish is gonna make a dead flower grow, Miz Angel. That old fish is gonna die and rot and stink worse than now."

Ah, to be the five-year-old Jacob. "The fish is already dead," Angelique explained, "and when it rots, it will enrich the soil and the rose's roots will feed off it and make beautiful flowers. Despite its looks, the flower is not dead." She pushed the loose soil over the twisted nub of the French Rose and packed it with her foot, then moved to the next hole. Jacob followed with the bucket of brim Charlotte caught this morning in the creek, the ones Bounty dubbed too small to eat. Those she sent to Angelique to fertilize the roses Mathias brought from his trip last night.

Those roses, Mathias told her, came from up on the Loosa Chitto, south of Fort Nogales. A sizeable group of English settlers lived there, one of whom was a Mrs. Constance Bright, an elderly woman with a love of horticulture. She and her husband had come west from South Carolina back in the seventies. Bess, he elaborated, was an old acquaintance of Mrs. Bright. Mathias thought in time, given her interests, Angelique would enjoy a visit to the woman's farm.

Constance Bright was also the maker of the peach brandy.

"Me next, Jacob."

Hank was three and, goodness, he could be a handful.

"No—"

Worse yet was the two of them fighting. Quickly, Angelique moved between them. "Here, Jacob," she said, "let your little brother do this one. He wants to help. Besides"—she smiled at the older boy and leaned close—"as soon as you let him put a fish in, he'll want to do something else."

Jacob frowned, but gave her a conspiratorial nod before holding out the prized bucket of dead fish to his brother. Hank smiled, bright-eyed, and seized a fish. It slipped from his hand and fell back into the bucket. "Oh, Miz Angel," he said and wiped his hand on his coat. She grabbed his wrist. "Fish don't feel good."

Angelique wrinkled her nose. "They don't smell good either, and if you wipe your hands on your clothes, you'll smell like them."

"But I don't want that nasty stuff on me."

"The very reason why you shouldn't put it on you. No, Hank..." She grabbed him by the arm when he again tried to wipe his fingers on his coat. "Here, put a fish in the hole, then go wash your hands in the pan out back."

Hank glared at the bucket Jacob held. Then, with a look of disgust, he stalked off. "I don't want to do that. You do them all, Jacob."

"I will."

"See," Angelique said, "sometimes it's best to be nice, and problems will work themselves out."

"Yes ma'am, you right." Jacob tossed a little brim into the hole and continued, "Why is there a spring, Miz Angel?"

"Well," she said, packing the earth around another dormant plant, "the earth goes around the sun and tilts on its axis —"

He furrowed his brow. "On what?"

Angelique looked at the child. "I know a story you might like about why the seasons come and go."

"I luv' stories."

So did she, and while they planted, she told him the Greek myth of Hades and Persephone. Without a doubt, her father would have reviled her for repeating the story, but she was glad she was able. From the start of this planting endeavor, she'd been certain Jacob would tire of working and run off to play. That would leave her to put the stinky, slimy fish in the hole.

"You learned that story from a book, Miz Angel?"

"I read it in one of Miss Elizabeth's books."

"I wish I could read."

Their labor finished, Angelique placed her arm on Jacob's back and guided him toward the back of the house. Never once had she considered the literacy of the servants.

"Can your mama read?"

"No, ma'am. Daddy can some, though. Miss Julianna teached him when he was little. Says he'll teach me and Hank one day."

She stopped at the back steps. Julianna. Mathias' mother.

"I'll teach you to read, Jacob. You and Hank, if he wants, but we need to talk to your daddy first."

The boy jumped, then raised his hand to shield his eyes from the morning sun.

"I know he'll say yes. I know it."

"But you have to have patience and sit still for a long while, and you've got to learn to write at the same time."

"Write, too?"

"Yes."

"Ooh-wee!"

She took that cry and Jacob's accompanying smile as an approval and handed him the bucket of remaining fish. "Take those to your grandmother."

He nodded at the remaining six bushes. "What 'bout them?"

"I'm going to put them at the gravesite, but I want to clean it up first. Go on now."

He started off, then grinned over his shoulder at her. "I'll come on up in the mornin' 'bout sunup."

"No, you won't. We'll work after the morning chores are done."

With a laugh and a shake of his head, he was off. What had she done? He was so young and probably wouldn't sit still for long. She watched him stop and say something to Hank, struggling toward her with a large wooden box. She didn't hear what he told him, but she figured he was telling his little brother about the teaching, and she smiled. Regardless of the work, it would be a satisfying effort.

"Gonna set a trap, Miz Angel," Hank said, when he reached her. "Gonna catch that coon scared you last night."

She smiled her thanks at the little one. Bless him, he meant well. Mathias had gathered Ben and Indigo this morning, and they'd searched the area around the house. They found nothing to indicate anything more sinister than a coon had been near the place last night. The branch of a hickory pecan lay on the roof, and Mathias told her the limb probably accounted for the loud noise.

He could say whatever he might. What she heard had hit the door.

Chapter Twenty-one

"Mathias' papa haunts De Leau—no, not that way." Yo nudged her out of the chair. "Like this." Angelique watched her pull the cotton thread around the spindle. She should be concentrating harder, but Yo had brought up the dark tale, and Angelique found it more interesting than learning to spin.

"Did you ever see him?"

The woman stopped what she was doing. "I saw the demon."

"Where?"

The old woman raised a crooked finger. "He goes—"

"Back into the swampy waters of hell."

Angelique jumped and turned to the door, but Yo regarded Mathias calmly. "No water in hell, boy."

"And there's no devil in the swamp. What are you doing in here, Yo?"

"She's teaching me to spin cotton," Angelique said. She was happy to see him. He left yesterday morning and spent the night with his grandmother in Natchez. The procurement officer for Nogales was passing through on his return north following a trip to New Orleans, and Steven Minor had requested that Aunt Elizabeth deal with the man directly regarding the additional purchase of fresh beef for the fort. In turn, Aunt Elizabeth sent for Mathias to handle the details, since he would sell the meat. Besides, De Leau was his now.

"Spinning cotton or spinning tales?" His voice was gruff, and he was staring at Yo.

"I brought the story up," Angelique lied.

He glanced at her. "With very little coaxing, I'm sure."

184

"You're being unfair. I had a bad—"

"She doesn't need your protection, Angelique."

Yo rose from the chair. "The girl was frightened last night."

"Naturally she's afraid," he bellowed. "You're scaring her."

Angelique seethed. Why would she be more frightened by scary stories than anyone else?

"The children of De Leau grew up believing my tales, Mathias. You would deny your wife this amusement?"

"They're not an amusement to my wife. She foolishly believes them."

"I tell her nothing foolish," Yo said, stepping closer to him. "You put her in great danger bringing her to De Leau. Your Grandmama will pay the debt, and you will help her."

"I don't want Angelique hearing any more of your tales. I can't leave for a night without worrying about the rubbish you're putting in her silly head."

Queasy, Angelique placed her hand on her stomach.

Yo sidled past him on her way to the door. "You should worry more with what visits in the night than with my coming during the day."

"Let her be, Yo."

At the door, Yo turned and found Angelique. "Charlotte knows the wheel. She will teach you."

Did that mean Yo would no longer talk to her?

The old woman graced Mathias with a look of silent contempt before disappearing into the hall. Mathias didn't see it, but Angelique did. She faced him and found he watched her. Removing his wide-brimmed hat, he slapped it against his thigh.

"What did she say to you?"

"She speaks such foolish prattle you could hardly expect a simpleton such as myself to follow her tale."

He grimaced. "I was angry."

"Why should you be?"

"And I'm becoming so again."

"You never stopped."

His nostrils flared. "A point you should consider."

"Or you will do what, Mathias, cut out my liver?"

He stiffened, visibly, and she looked at his hands, fisted at his side. He was, she suspected, holding himself in check, but she still reeled from his thoughtless comment about her "silly head." She thought about the woodpile incident he so readily dismissed and the...

"It rained last night."

He blinked at her.

"Ethan found a dead steer this morning."

"I know," he said and relaxed his hands.

"What is out there?"

He stepped toward her, but she moved away, out of the reach of his hypnotic touch. He came no closer, but moved to the front of his desk instead.

"A bear, we think."

"A bear isn't making you act the way you are."

He snorted. "There is no devil out there."

"Your father?"

"My father. The demon. To Yo they are one and the same."

"Are they?"

His eyes found hers.

"She knows something. Something about Aunt Elizabeth—"

"Angelique...." His voice tensed with renewed warning, but she held out her hands in supplication.

"Don't you w-want to—"

"Don't you think I've asked?" He raked his fingers through his hair and dislodged his queue. "Whatever happened is in the past. Old Bess wishes to keep it there."

"Yo says the threat remains."

"Yo speaks in riddles."

"Does Aunt Elizabeth have the answers to those riddles?"

His handsome visage hardened, and he folded his arms across his chest. Leaning his buttocks against the desk, he crossed one dust-covered boot over the other and stared at her.

And continued to stare, as if he saw right through her, as if she weren't there, and his indifference sucked the soul from her and left her hollow. Steeling herself, she turned away, blinking at tears she didn't want him to see. She was frightened of Yo's phantom hiding in the swamp, but more and more, she was disheartened, wondering how much her aunt understood of Yo's ramblings, and terrified the woman had perpetrated a hideous betrayal. But the thing that gnawed her most, the one thing eating her alive, was the possibility that the angry man standing behind her, the one she'd fallen in love with, might be part of the plot, accepting De Leau in payment for delivering her to something evil.

"Do you have the answers, Mathias?" she said, not looking at him.

"What did Yo tell you?"

"That your father haunts this place. You heard everything meaningful."

"And what are you thinking?"

He scoffed at her fears, but she loved him too much to hurt him with her doubts. She started to the rear bedroom, but he caught her arm and jerked her around.

"Tell me what you think is happening?"

With a violent wrench, she tore her arm from his grasp. "The morning after our wedding night, I woke to find our sheets soiled."

"With virgin—"

"My side had blood," she said defiantly, "yours had human defecation."

He stared at her. "I did not—"

"I thought maybe I'd done it, that perhaps Yo's medicine made me ill, but there was hair in it. Long, dark, thick hair."

"I can't explain it, except to tell you I didn't leave it."

At least, he had the good grace not to openly sneer at her. She watched the movement of his throat as he swallowed hard. Perhaps her story had caught him off guard.

"What happened at the pool?" she asked.

"The day after you arrived?"

"Yes."

"We made love. You enjoyed it. You, in fact, initiated it."

Angelique tensed with his words. She could remember the passion and the pleasure, but she didn't remember doing anything to provoke their lovemaking. "Who else was there?"

He cocked his head slightly as if trying to understand what she asked.

"Who else was there?" She screamed the words this time.

"You were there," he said cautiously.

"I wasn't there. I *wasn't* there. Not the entire time. I was bewitched." She stepped away from him. "Who else was there, Mathias? Or what else?"

"No one."

"No one, but something?"

He was watching her now as if he thought her out of her mind. That or he was calculating.

"I saw it. You held my hands above my head."

He nodded slowly. "I did, to stop their roving." His voice was calm, quiet. "You were driving me wild, and I needed time."

An errant tear spilled over her lashes, and she swiped at it. She couldn't bring herself to believe him, not without some doubt. She would not have done...

"Do you believe I would share you with a monster for carnal pleasure?"

She hardened herself to the pain in his voice. He either thought her mad or was intent on making her so.

"I don't know what to believe," she said, moving around him to the desk where his immaculate ledgers lay. Picking up an open book, she raised it over her head and slammed it to the floor.

She looked down at the thing, not sure what she'd proven or why, but satisfied she'd done something. Then she raised her head and faced him.

"I have collards to wash in the cookhouse. And if it's your plan to keep me from talking to Yo, I advise you to keep close to home and sleep in your own bed."

"What do you mean by that?"

"Something was here last night. Something that set the dogs

to howling. I swear I heard whatever it was creeping around the porch—all the way around—peeking in the windows, searching for me. I was scared and alone. Where were you, husband?"

Chapter Twenty-two

"Finally got that gal away from De Leau?"

Mathias acknowledged Jack's statement with a nod, then glanced at Angelique, who wore a smile on her face. She hadn't smiled much these past two weeks, and Mathias was glad to see one on her now. She hadn't talked much either, at least not to him, but she had kept busy working the farm side by side with Rachel, Charlotte, and Bounty, as well as teaching Jacob to read.

Mathias had restricted the movements of the women and the children. The predator's aggression concerned him. The animal was smart, too, and there had been so much rain this winter they couldn't track it with the beast repeatedly disappearing into the safety of the swamp. He feared Angelique regarded De Leau more prison than home.

She alighted from the horse before he had a chance to help her and extended a hand to Jack. The latter turned to the house, but didn't need to call his wife. Martha Summerfield's very pregnant form filled the doorway, and Mathias noted, not for the first time, that Jack had found himself a handsome woman, and they actually liked each other.

"Oh, Mathias, thank you for the visit," Martha said, lumbering down the steps. Angelique moved around Jack to greet her.

"Come." Martha smiled, placing an arm around Angelique's small shoulders. "Jack bartered me English tea yesterday, and I was about to make some."

Mathias watched them climb the steps, chatting about Martha's pregnancy. He regretted Jack didn't live closer.

190

"Anything happen during that storm last night?" Jack asked when the women were out of earshot.

"We found the carcass of one of my steers on the way here."

"I've told Johnny and Peter to stay away from the woods. Those boys are going stir crazy, and it's hard on Martha."

Mathias grinned. "I hope this new one is a girl."

"I don't know which of us will be more disappointed if it's not. No doubt, she'll turn out be the biggest hellion of all the whelps." Jack eyed Mathias. "And how's married life suiting you?"

Mathias slapped the horse's reins against his palm. "Not as well as it suits you. Angelique grows more afraid each day."

"Yo's demon?"

"Partly. She has nightmares and imagines hearing and seeing and smelling strange things, usually when she's alone."

Jack reached for the reins. "Give me those."

He led the horses' to Indigo, who was talking to Jason, the younger of Jack's two sons by blood. Mathias waited, then Jack pointed the way into the fields.

"She'd heard too many of the tales before we wed. Yo started weaving her yarns the night I brought her home." Mathias stopped and looked down two rows of corn. "Nice and straight. Your fields look good."

"A new moldboard on my plough and fine oxen. Need to quit worrying about horses and get yourself a pair."

Mathias shook his head and started walking again. "I wish finding a good brood mare was all I did have to worry about. Yo talks to Angelique at every opportunity. I fear now she doubts my motives."

"You can't keep her away from Yo?"

"I can't keep her a prisoner. She's a feisty, stubborn little thing. I'd have to beat her, and I won't, even if I thought it would work short of beating her to death."

"Have you told her you love her?"

Mathias eyed Jack skeptically, and Jack grinned. "True or not, boy, those words work wonders on a woman."

The sky was clear, stamped occasionally with a high cloud, and the warm morning promised a hot day like the one before. Angelique pulled out a dead weed and tossed it aside. She yanked at another, and the long strands tore at her fingers. Quiet encompassed her, not even a bird sang. Strange. She looked to the woods, two stone's throws away and searched the budding forest. A far distance from where she worked the deep pool reposed in shade, but she couldn't see it for the looming darkness of the trees. Chill bumps crawled over her skin, and she forced herself to imagine what the spot looked like now, in full bloom. The half-formed image died with the inexplicable quickening of her heart.

Something was watching her.

She leaned forward to push herself up and watched a shadow pass over her grandmother's grave. Steadying herself on shaky arms, she twisted around.

The urge to spring away dissipated, and she closed her eyes.

"I walked right up on you," Mathias said softly.

He always did. He invaded her thoughts, her dreams, her nightmares.

Mathias stepped around her and, kneeling, tore out the lanky growth she'd been struggling with. "I frightened you?"

"I had a feeling I was being watched."

"I've been watching you."

"Were you over there?" She nodded to the vicinity of the spring-fed pool. She knew he hadn't been.

"No." He tore out more grass. "I was behind you."

Uneasy, she looked at the woods. "It wasn't you."

"Do you still have the feeling?"

"No."

He smiled. "It was me."

It hadn't been him. Tentatively, she returned to the weeds covering her grandmother's grave. Mathias' ardor had cooled since the day she threw his ledger on the floor almost a month ago. The day she'd hurt him. And she had hurt him, she knew she had. This past week, he'd been in Natchez three days, visiting the riverfront, he said, and buying tools and seed in preparation for the growing season. Despite his absence, she'd had no more "visits." She yanked hopelessly at a prickly plant. A needle pierced her finger, and she quickly brought it to her mouth. He reached once more to help her, and she sat back on the dry ground and watched him continue the work she'd started.

"Why are you out here alone?" he asked quietly.

She waited for his reprimand, and when it didn't come, she pointed with her chin to Ethan and Rachel hoeing the vegetable patch off to her left. "I'm not alone." Rising to her knees, she reached for the scraggly grass covering the stone plate that marked Etienne Veilleux's grave.

"I want to get the roses in. It's March, and if I don't plant them soon, I'll be too late.

"You've done a good job here."

Her eyes searched his, then she smiled. He stood, and she rose with him. Ethan and Rachel really were too far away, and she didn't want to remain here without him.

"I have Great-grandmother's done," she said. "I didn't realize she'd been buried with her child by Jean Larocque. Jean died on the fifth of June, three days before Great-grandmama. So many deaths. How horrible it must have been for the family."

He stepped closer to her. "She died in childbirth. That baby was her second with Larocque."

She knew a little about the first, her grandmother and Aunt Elizabeth's half brother, who disappeared at sixteen. "Where did the first boy go? Do you know?"

"Still searching for information?"

She ignored the taunt. "Do you think Aunt Elizabeth killed him?"

"I think she has the strength to do almost anything, but all I can tell you regarding what happened to him is it happened long before I was born." His gaze pierced hers. "I was not part of it."

"I never thought you were."

He sighed. "The consensus among the family is he simply left. He didn't get along with Grandmama or Robert Douglas, my grandfather. Some say he lived with the Choctaw for a while. Years

193

ago, Bess learned the Cherokee killed him." Mathias shrugged. "She doesn't doubt the story and doesn't appear to care one way or the other."

"There's another baby here," Angelique said, pointing next to Véronique Deschesne's grave. "My grandmother's."

"Your little uncle. He was born at seven months and lived but a few hours, I'm told. Your grandmother was fifteen."

Angelique drew in a steadying breath and asked, "Do you know who the father was?"

He shook his head. "Old Bess knows."

"Yo says —"

"I know what Yo *implies*," he said roughly. "The demon's own, the product of an earlier rape, payment for an earlier crime."

With his booted foot, Mathias smoothed weeds from another marker. Angelique read Julianna Douglas' name.

Tentatively she reached out and touched his fingers, and he clasped her hand in his. His was warm, and he made a half turn and pulled her into his embrace. Her arms circled his waist, and he dipped his —

"Mathias!" Bounty hollered.

Mathias raised his head, then, with barely veiled agitation, he eased Angelique to arm's length.

"You got a visitor," she called again.

"Who?" he asked, when she reached them.

Bounty glanced at Angelique, then to Mathias. "The widow Mallory."

Angelique's heart fell. Mathias cursed, dropped Angelique's hand, and started toward the house alone.

She stared at his back, then glanced at Bounty, stoically watching her. Angelique smiled, trying to display confidence she didn't feel.

"I should go greet my guest."

"Wants to see Mathias alone."

"Does she?" Angelique responded coolly, despite the heat washing over her. Hiking up her skirts, she strode off in search of her husband and the widow Kate.

194

Kate Mallory had dismounted, but her escort remained some distance away on a plump, ugly horse. As Angelique watched, the tall, handsomely dressed woman placed her palms on Mathias' chest. He took her hands and held them away from him, but he didn't put them down. Kate leaned closer, and Angelique heard her laugh, a throaty gurgle that promised pleasure. Then they saw her.

Kate slowly removed her hands from Mathias'. She smiled beautifully, but Angelique did not miss the impudence in the icy green eyes. Mathias made introductions.

"I congratulate you, my dear, on your marriage. I thought no one would ever catch him."

"It is Angelique who has been captured, Kate," he said, conveying, by the way the woman returned his gaze, some hidden meaning to the widow Mallory. Angelique bristled.

"Might I offer you and your servant refreshment, Mrs. Mallory?" Angelique asked.

"Good, Angelique," Mathias said, turning his attention to her. "Fetch a cup of water for Kate and Jim."

Angelique hoped he didn't see her blanch, but he couldn't have missed her eyes. Angry tears blurred her vision, but short of scurrying out of their view, she could do nothing to hide them. As she turned the corner to the back of the house, she again heard Kate's sensuous laugh. Not knowing the secrets the woman shared with Mathias wrenched her inside out.

Water-filled bucket, copper ladle, and two tin cups in hand, Angelique reemerged around the far side of the house and approached the servant Mathias referred to as Jim. With a smile full of bright teeth, the large man took the proffered drink, and Angelique started toward her husband.

"Has she seen the delights offered by your attic, Mathias? Will she ever?"

Angelique's body tightened with every step. The woman was making little effort to keep her voice low. Angelique quickened her pace. Mathias could see her coming, but to the best of her knowledge, Kate Mallory did not know she was there, or she didn't care.

"She is a sweet and pretty child, but that does not mean our relationship has to end."

Damn that woman's dark soul. Angelique moved faster, and Mathias' gaze locked on her. Kate turned. Thrusting the cup into Kate's hand, Angelique shot her a saucy smile. "Spring water, pure and cold...and sweet. Be careful you do not drown in it. And drink up fast. We fear there is a vicious bear in the swamp. Jim and I believe it is time for you to go."

Kate's eyes narrowed on Angelique, then she held out the cup. "I'm not thirsty," she said, "but I agree it is time I be on my way." She mounted the glossy horse she'd ridden from town and turned to Mathias. "Remember what I said."

She spoke the words so seductively Angelique considered yanking her from the saddle. Mathias must have sensed that, because he stepped close to her and grasped her around the waist. "I meant what I told you," he said to Kate.

Angelique wanted to scream. Once Kate and Jim moved away, Mathias relaxed his grip, and Angelique broke his grasp. She glared, barely resisting the urge to throw the cup of water at him, then collected Jim's cup and walked to the cookhouse. Mathias followed, and he was waiting outside when she emerged.

"I want to talk to you," he said.

She spun on him, and he feinted.

"You were rude to Kate. I don't think she'll be coming out here to see you anymore."

"More prattle for the foolish wife, Mathias?" She turned to the house. "It wasn't me she came to see."

He caught her arm, but she shook him off and lifted her skirt to climb the stairs.

"I'm going to talk to you."

She stopped at the porch and turned, which brought Mathias to an abrupt halt two steps below her. "Is she why you have not—" Angelique caught herself and, with a choked sob, spun and pushed open the back door. Mathias dogged her heels. In the foyer, she nodded her head to the rough ladder leading to the attic.

"What's in your *delightful* attic you do not care to show me? But"—she whirled on him again—"you do show her?"

He moved in front of her, blocking the door to the main room. She glowered at him. She was behaving horribly, but had no intention of calming, despite the glint in his eyes, which told her he was getting angry himself.

"Eavesdropping again, Angelique?"

She stretched her height as best she could. Never in her life could she remember being as angry with anyone as she was with him at this moment. "I heard what she said, yes, but you know I wasn't eavesdropping. You saw me coming. You didn't care if I overheard her."

"I do care," he retorted, "and you didn't hear all our conversation."

"No, I didn't. You conveniently sent me off to fetch her water while you continued your...your..."—she waved her hands in the air—"assignation."

"Assignation?" he repeated loudly, then cursed. "I needed to make something clear to her in private."

"Fine," Angelique responded with a brisk shake of her head. "You've had your conversation. No doubt you and she will share other 'delights' you have no intention of showing me." She tried to sidestep him, but he blocked her again and gave her a wicked grin.

"Do you want to see the attic, Angelique?"

Immediately the texture of their argument changed. She looked at him a long moment, trying to gauge his mood. Dangerous, and that excited her.

"I will take you up there," he said softly, leaning against the doorframe.

She stared at him, then started to move away.

"Afraid?"

"I'm not afraid of you."

He smiled wolfishly. "You don't trust me. That's the root of our problem."

"You're wrong."

197

"Go with me then."

She raised her chin. "You're trying to frighten me because you don't think I'll go." She narrowed her eyes, then poked him in the chest with two fingers. "You don't want me to go."

He straightened to tower above her. "Yes, I do, Angelique. More than anything in the world right now, I want to get you in that attic."

Chapter Twenty-three

The floor was solid, the cypress-shake roof high. Standing in the center of the room was easy, even for Mathias. Surreptitiously, Angelique watched him turn and set the candle on a dusty table. The quiet of the musty, secluded place melded with the eerie glow from the wax taper, creating an atmosphere both uncertain and darkly provocative.

He straightened and turned, and his eyes found hers. Her golden god once again gleamed in the ethereal glow of the flame, his predatory grace focused on her. Sweat tickled her cleavage, and she pressed a hand to her breast before tearing her gaze away.

Other than the small table, a few pieces of furniture, and an old trunk in one of its corners, the attic was empty. Angelique glanced around, then started at the invasion of her peripheral vision.

"Nothing to be afraid of, only one of the delights I intend to demonstrate for you here in my attic."

Double ropes hung a short distance below a cross brace and ended in slipknots a shoulder's width apart. Angelique drew a breath. Standing beneath them, she might barely be able to touch the knots. Mathias moved, and she turned and watched him pull his shirt over his head. The sheen of sweat covering his broad chest reflected the flickering glow of candlelight. He found her eyes and held her gaze.

The attic heat engulfed her, encumbering her ability to breathe. He took a menacing step.

Delicious fear chilled her, and burning need cried out for surrender.

But she didn't want to surrender.

He reached for her. Without thinking, she raised her hands to ward him off, but he seized an upper arm. She started to struggle, and his hold tightened. The knuckles on his hand inadvertently caressed the side of her breast, and her nipples tingled in reaction.

"Stop," he whispered in her ear.

Dizzy, she did.

His grip lessened. "Do you know what the ropes were used for?"

"To bind slaves while you beat them."

"We've never had many slaves at De Leau, and we have yet to beat the first one." He smiled knowingly. "I thought you'd guess wives."

She blinked at him.

He looked up and studied the hemp ropes. "Wives would be justifiable, but you're right in your thinking. Kate liked to pretend she was the slave and I the brutal master. She is the mastermind behind this little chamber of torture."

Angelique shuddered, but did not struggle against his grasp.

"I put these bonds up two years ago." With his free hand, Mathias pulled on one rope, then the next, testing for strength. He looked at her. "Then I put Kate in them."

Mathias circled the ropes, all the while keeping his hold on her. Apparently satisfied with the restraints, he pulled her with him to the wall from which he removed a coiled whip. She hadn't noticed it before, and now watched the frayed end slither to the floor. Gently, but firmly, he pushed her under the dangling ropes.

"How many times did you bring her up here?"

"I didn't keep count, but not many. Kate rarely visits De Leau."

Angelique licked her lips. He had stopped in front of the closest bond.

"I don't believe you'd abuse a woman."

He riveted his gaze on her. "There is abuse, and then there is abuse."

200

She swallowed.

"Kate, for example,"—he dropped the whip and gently brushed his fingers over the rope—"likes 'controlled' abuse."

"I see." She'd heard enough about his relationship with Kate Mallory and pulled out of his grasp. Instantly, Mathias seized her wrist and yanked her to him, then he pulled her hand toward the slipknot.

She tried to get away, but he braced himself and slipped her hand through, and when she yanked down to free herself, the knot tightened around her wrist. Desperate, she reached with her free hand, but she was off balance, forced to stand on tiptoe because of the height of the rope. Mathias reached for her other hand, but she turned on him and kicked out, losing her precarious footing. Her arm twisted painfully at the shoulder while the rope cut into her ensnared wrist.

"Careful, you'll hurt yourself," he said and, grasping her other hand, slipped it into the second noose. She tried not to repeat the mistake, but her body was stretched tight, and she couldn't maintain her balance long enough to untangle herself. She lost her balance and the noose tightened, hurting her. She sucked in a breath and glared at him.

"Let me go."

He stepped back, hands on hips, then lifted her skirts. "Hmm," he said, and dropped her hem. "I should have lowered the ropes. You could become a little uncomfortable before I'm through with you."

She yanked once more, then wrapped her fingers around the ropes in an effort to relieve the pressure. "Let me go, I said."

His eyes moved over her body. "No."

She was thirsty and hot, sweat drenched her now. She looked up at her wrists, then to him. "Please, Mathias, the ropes are burning me."

He took a step toward her. Her gaze roamed over his shoulders and biceps, his shimmering chest with its dark nipples, then downward to the cleft of his navel, and rested finally on the bulge in his pants.

Misgivings melted into desire.

"This is the reason we are here, sweet Angelique. Pain, coercion, submission."

Vaginal moisture dampened her upper thighs. *He knows, God take his soul. He knows exactly what I feel.*

"Those are the delights Kate referred to."

She yanked once more at the bonds, hopelessly frustrated by her body's betrayal.

Gently, he rubbed his knuckles along her jaw line. "Careful, my beauty."

She closed her eyes at his seductive touch. "Did you beat her?" she asked, her breath catching in her throat.

She felt his arm around her waist, and he lifted her, relieving the pressure on her wrists. "Sometimes," he answered, his breath kissing her skin.

Heart pounding, breath short, she felt his hand under her thin skirt and chemise, moving slowly up her bare thigh. He brought it to rest on a buttock, and she opened her eyes. With a feral smile, he gently pinched her.

"Right about here."

"Are you going to beat me?" Her voice faltered.

He brought his lips closer to hers. "I beat her, Angelique, because she wanted me to. Do you want me to beat you?"

She shook her head.

He studied her face, his eyes hovering on her lips, then blessedly, he kissed her, and with relief, she welcomed him. He pulled back far enough to sigh against her mouth.

"Why would I want her up here with me, when I have you?"

"Because you want to beat some —"

He silenced her with another kiss. "No, Angelique, that's not what I want to do." Still supporting her with one hand, he reached down with his other to pull her skirt around her waist. He spread her legs with his body. She struggled to pull back so she could close them, but he held her firm. Then he uncovered his free hand and reached for the bodice of her work dress. With one hand he unbuttoned it, taking his time with the small buttons.

Done, he pushed the chemise down, exposing her breasts. He looked into her eyes and kissed her again before dipping his head to suckle a nipple. The fingers of his free hand closed gently around the other, and he kneaded it. She wiggled, but could not get away.

"This is what I want, to touch you, feel you, and know you want me, too." He moved his mouth to her ear. "And you do. I can tell by the way you breathe." He cupped her left breast, and she pressed against him. "By the beat of your heart."

"Mathias..." She moaned.

"Shh," he whispered, "enjoy my touch. There is nothing you can do to stop me, so enjoy it." Holding her beneath the buttocks, he shifted her weight around his waist and unbuttoned his breeches.

His fingertips feathered along the inside of her thigh and she squirmed, not wanting him to feel the liquid heat between her legs, but powerless to prevent it.

His fingers stroked her vaginal lips and gently pinched her clitoris. Then his forefinger entered her, and with the hand holding her bottom he pushed her on to first one finger, then two. She struggled against surrender. Hopelessly, she knew.

He flicked her clitoris with his thumb, and pushed her back on his impaling fingers. "Why do you fight me?" he whispered in her ear. "Your body is wet with need."

She whimpered and twisted her head away from him.

His tongue burned a path from her ear to her collarbone. "Is it pride, Angelique? I have no pride when it comes to wanting you, and I will allow you none in wanting me."

She threw her head forward. "I've never displayed any pride when it comes to desiring you."

He kissed her again, and she responded shamelessly. Indeed, she'd always sought his caress. How could he accuse her of pride?

Sucking her tongue, he impaled her on those two invading fingers, then pulled away, over and over until she moaned with pleasure. "I make you want me," he whispered in her ear, "even though you don't want to."

"I do want you."

"Yes, when you have no choice. When I've forced your body to conquer your fear of me."

Delicious pressure was building in her thighs. She drew a desperate breath. "It's not you—"

"Hush. I will take you any way I can have you, and if I can give you pleasure when I do, that's even better."

His adept hand continued to work her body while he spoke. The pleasure built, warming her and weakening her resolve. She relaxed in surrender, but he stopped, denying her the climax promised with his touch, only to begin again, over and over until she nearly wept with frustration, strain, and exhaustion, her need so intense she could not stand it. There was no shame, no remorse, only sweet, demanding need.

"Please, Mathias, no more," she sobbed when he denied her fulfillment yet again.

"Wrong words," he said, easing off the relentless pressure before starting again. "I feel your warmth. I know you want me, and I want you to tell me so. Devil or not, tell me so."

Heart pounding, she lifted her eyes to his tense face. He suffered, too, damn his black soul.

"I want you, you...."

He grinned at her, watching her eyes as his fingers entered her again. "'You' what, Angelique? You devil? Or were you going to say 'bastard'?"

She shivered, not unpleasantly, and pushed away from him as best she could, but he pulled her back, thrusting those relentless fingers deep inside her. Again his thumb pressed against her clitoris. She closed her eyes against the exquisite torture.

His thumb stopped its movement, and on the verge of collapse, she opened her eyes. "I would never say such a thing to anyone, least of all you."

"Why?" he asked in mock shock, "because it's true?"

"In fact it may be true. Until this moment"—she gasped when his thumb moved again—"I never considered it true in the symbolic sense."

He removed his hand, and she cried out in protest. But he chuckled softly and positioned himself to enter her. "No matter what you may have called me, I intend to give you what you want."

She arched at his thrust. He pulled out, then plunged again. Sensation soared through her, and she almost wept at the veracity of his words. Yes, I want you! Fill me! Ride me!

And he did, slamming his pelvis against her spread thighs until the pressure he'd created with such sweet cruelty erupted in waves through her body. Seconds later, he grasped her to him when he reached his own climax.

He held her, their bodies slick with intermingling sweat. After several moments, he stirred and blew on her naked breasts. Good Lord, that felt so good. Raising her chin, she slowly rolled her head, and he continued the favor along her neck.

"God, you're beautiful," he said. Straightening suddenly, he told her to keep her legs around him while he freed her hands. When he did, she wrapped her arms around his neck, crushing him to her, her face against his throat.

"You've no cause to be jealous of Kate," he whispered to her. "You're the one I want. I told her so today. I haven't seen her since before we wed, and I told her there would be no more visits."

He stood her on her feet. Her knees buckled, and with a light laugh, he caught her, then steadied her as she melted, sated and exposed, to the floor. He sat in front of her, his gaze wandering over her naked breasts. And she, watching him lust for her still, hungered for him anew. She couldn't get enough of him, and she felt oddly perverse and insatiable.

Possessed.

"Does it not bother you?"

"What?"

"My response to you."

"No."

"Would I respond the same to any man?"

She did not miss the subtle tightening of his jaw. "You respond to me."

"Why?"

He flexed his jaw, then said, "You and I are sexually well matched."

"Are there women with whom you aren't well matched?"

"There are women with whom I have no desire to find out."

Her mouth was dry, and she swallowed. Sweat tickled her breasts. "Who are they?"

"Every woman, but you."

Every woman... Good Lord, he was weaving a web, ensnaring her to his will, and she didn't care.

"Can you feel it?"

He frowned at her.

"The passion. Can you feel it?"

The hint of a smile curled his lips, and she weakened more. She was suffocating, completely at his mercy. He could pass her to a hundred demons at this moment, and she would not fight them.

"Even now, exhausted"—and sick, she thought—"I want you again."

Dizziness conquered her. Above her, the rafters whirled. She felt his hands on her clothing, then her flesh, and he was lying on the floor pulling her, completely naked, astride him, impaling her on his shaft. His hands caressed her breasts, his fingers torturing her nipples with delicious friction. She groaned, and he sat up, taking a breast into his mouth, while he held her impaled with one hand and pressed his other against her back, forcing her breast against his insidious tongue.

The final waves of her climax coursed through her, and Mathias came, too, with a fierce tenderness that swelled against her womanhood and prolonged her own wondrously agonizing fulfillment.

Angelique collapsed on his chest. He kissed her lips, then rolled her off him, and she curled into a ball on the dusty floor, her back to him.

"My God, Angelique," he said, molding his body to hers and wrapping her in his arms, "you are driving me mad."

⇒·⇐

She was trembling, but certainly not from cold. She was hot as hell. They both were. Exhaustion, perhaps? He rolled away from her. Or doubt?

She moved and looked at him over her shoulder. "You are dressed."

Not really. His chest was bare, but he still wore his breeches, partway down and open, and his boots. Pulling his breeches over his hips, he pushed his spent member inside and buttoned the waistband. She raised her head, in search of her dress, he imagined, but he pushed her down and feasted on her nudity.

"Why am I naked and you are dressed?"

"I undressed you when you said you wanted me again. Don't you remember?"

"Vaguely," she said. He felt her relax, and she closed her eyes. "What consumes me, Mathias?"

Passion, lust.... With a finger, he traced the gentle swell of her belly, and his stomach contracted.

"When I'm with you like this," she said, "I'm unaware of anything but need." She opened her eyes. "And it's a painful need that will eat me alive if I don't slake it."

He cupped her breast. The changes taking place in her beautiful body would make her hunger in many ways.

She curled toward him. "I believe something was here again this morning before sunup. It was here yesterday morning, too. It came upon the porch."

"Something that smelled of death and decay?"

"I smelled it in my dreams. When I woke, I heard the boards creaking, then it was gone. It haunts me only when you're gone."

He removed his hand from her breast and rolled onto his back. Damn her doubts. He'd had a lifetime of whispers and furtive glances from curious women and dangerous men. Angelique's suspicions threatened everything he longed for, but he owed his grandmother too much to challenge the woman's purpose.

"I wish I felt more in control of this passion," Angelique said, "that I could remember...."

Remember what happened that winter day at the pool is what she'd been going to say. Silently, he cursed her hazy memories. Torn between duty and want, he pulled her unto his naked chest and luxuriated in the feel of her heavy breasts against his skin.

Angelique jerked and reached for Mathias. He wasn't there. She shouldn't have expected him to be. He'd not come to bed with her. Except for their sojourn to the attic, a brief respite from self-imposed celibacy, she supposed, he treated her with a gentle, but cool respect, as if he feared to make love to her.

The shutters were open and the window raised slightly out of respect for a warm night. A three-quarter moon cast ghostly shadows on the walls, and Angelique searched the room's dark corners. She bit the inside of her mouth to make sure she was truly awake. But for her pounding heart, there was silence.

Through the open window, the unpleasant smell of death wafted, followed by a guttural growl. Her fingers curled into the sheet. What made the sound was on the porch and lurked at her window.

Yanking open the bedroom door, she lunged across the foyer into the main room where she had left Mathias working on his books. His desk was empty. Somewhere distant from the house a dog barked, and Angelique whispered Mathias' name.

The backdoor opened, then closed with a click, followed by footsteps tracking down the hall. She turned to the open door.

Relief accompanied Mathias' entry. "Where were you?" she croaked.

He held up a bottle. "I went to the cookhouse for—"

"We need to brace the doors," she said, grasping his arm and sidestepping around him.

He set the bottle on a table, and she tugged him into the hall. Immediately, she let him go and rushed to the front door.

"Mathias, please." She dropped the brace in place, then ran back past him. He wasn't doing anything.

"What the devil is wrong?" he asked, following her more slowly to the back door.

208

He grabbed the heavy brace she bungled and put it in place. "What is it?" he asked, giving her a little shake.

"Wait," she got out, all the while struggling against his hold. "Mathias, the bedroom window is open."

He let her go, and she hurried up the hall, but at the door, he hooked her from behind and pulled her out of the room. Stepping in front of her, he entered. She followed, maintaining a tentative touch on his arm.

Shadows decorated the dark walls, but the room was light enough to maneuver in, thanks to the combination of moonlight and lamps across the hall.

Mathias went straight to the window and looked out. Then placing his fingers beneath the vented window, he pushed...

...no, God no. She grasped his shirttail and pulled him back.

"Stop!" she screamed. "It will get you." Moving in front of him, she grabbed his arm and tore one hand, then his other, away from the sash and slammed the window shut. Immediately, she stepped away from the ominous portal.

"There is nothing—"

"Brace it."

"Angelique—"

"Please, Mathias, hurry."

He did. Then holding her tight by his side, he walked through the house and secured all the windows.

"You're ashen," he said, pushing her hair from her face. "Tell me what happened?"

She drew in a shaky breath. "Something was outside."

"Where?"

"Outside the window, the bedroom window."

He looked at her a moment before taking hold of her upper arms. "Angelique," he started slowly, "I was outside. I went to the cookhouse to get some brandy."

"Do you stink?" Her heart plummeted at the confusion on his face, and clenching her fists, she hit his chest with her lower arms. "Do you?" She grabbed his clean white shirt, pulled him to her, and gave him an exaggerated sniff. "No, Mathias, you do not."

※

"I heard the screech owl last night late, Mathias."

"I heard that owl, too," Ben said in response to Yo's words. "Them things sure do sound like they come from another world. Your granddaddy used to tell his young'uns it was a *banshee,* the fairy of death'"—he growled—"calling 'em to the moldering grave."

Angelique heard a sudden movement inside the cookhouse, followed by Hank's shrill squeal. Ben laughed, and Bounty admonished him with sharp-sounding words composed of a strange mixture of her Choctaw tongue and frontier French. Ben laughed again. Angelique had no idea what Bounty said to the man, but she had never seen him overly concerned by his wife's fussing.

"Sweet Jesus, don't say that in front of Angelique."

"You don't have to tell me not to scare Miss Angelique, Mathias."

"Warn her is all I do," Yo said.

"You're scaring her senseless," Mathias said. "She has a lot on her mind. I was up half the night with her. She has bad dreams and hears things that aren't there."

Angelique studied the partly open cookhouse door, suspecting Mathias would be irritated if he found her eavesdropping again. They had been up late. She hadn't wanted to return to the bedroom, with or without him, so she'd sat by the fireplace and tried to read while he worked on his ledgers. The fear and the brandy he gave her conspired to make her throw up. Mathias waited patiently by her side, rubbing her back, while she heaved. She wouldn't even let him empty the slop jar, terrified for him to leave the house. Finally, he coaxed her to bed and cuddled her close through what remained of the night. Not long before dawn, she fell asleep.

She looked at the sky, then around her. How different things were by the light of day.

"Mornin', Miz Angel," Jacob hollered, running up from behind and throwing his arms around her waist.

Thus exposed, Angelique sighed. "Good morning, Jacob,"

she said, and squeezing his small body to her, she guided him through the door. "Have you had breakfast?"

"Way 'fore the sun come up. Been helpin' Mama collect them cattles' dungs."

"For the corn patch?"

"Yes'm."

As she expected, they were all facing the door, waiting, when she and Jacob entered.

"Grandmama made injun persimmon bread," Jacob said, freeing himself and running to Bounty.

Bounty handed her a pewter plate containing corn mush and a slice of fresh ham. "Mathias says you sick during the night. Better now?"

Angelique looked at Mathias. "I'm tired. The brandy made me sick."

Yo's shadow fell across the table. "You have bad dreams?"

Angelique's gaze traveled over the old black woman's shoulder to Mathias. "Last night wasn't a dream."

He stepped around Yo. "Depending how long you stood on the other side of that door, you also know I said you were hearing things in the night."

She raised her eyebrows. "'Hearing things that were not there,' if you want to be faithful."

He squeezed her shoulder. "I'm sorry I said that. I don't know what you heard."

"Or smelled."

"Or smelled. I checked on and under the porch this morning. I found nothing. I'll have Indigo check when he gets out of the fields. His eye for tracking is better than mine."

"Not good as mine was, though, Miss Angelique," Ben said. "Trouble with me is I can't see the track good 'nuff any more to identify it." Moving awkwardly, he sat on the bench across from her.

"Your back is hurting you again, Ben?" Angelique asked.

"It do. It sure do."

"Too much bendin'," Bounty said, her face expressionless.

"Woman's work. Git," she told him. "Let Missy eat her break-fast."

"You smelled the scent again?" Yo asked.

Angelique swallowed the mouthful of mush she chewed. "Yes, the smell of something dead." She glanced at Mathias, who was watching both of them attentively.

"It was not sulfur and brimstone she smelled, old one."

Yo turned and ambled slowly to the door. "You scoff, Mathias, even though he comes to your doorstep. Time grows short. Check your days."

"*M*artha's had her baby," Mathias said when he stepped into the dining room for the noon meal.

Angelique pivoted from where she stood in front of the break-front. "Was it a—"

"Katherine Suzanne." He smiled, and she smiled in return. They'd gotten their girl.

"Named her after his and Martha's mothers."

"How is Martha?"

Mathias shrugged. "Fine as can be, I reckon. Jack said the baby was big, but the birthing went fast."

"I need to get over there—"

"I asked if she needed help. The squaw of the old Tunica help-ing with the planting is there."

Mathias pulled out a chair, and Angelique handed him a pewter plate. Cold ham and fresh baked corn bread sat centered on the table as did a porcelain bowl of collards.

"You look pale." His voice softened. "Have you been sick again?"

"No, Mathias," she said, trying to hide her irritableness. "It was the brandy." She took the cut, crispy edge of the corn bread before he grabbed it, then grinned at the surprised look on his face. "Here," she said, tearing it in two. "I'll share with you, which is more than you would have done had you'd gotten it first."

He took the half she offered. "I introduced you to the crust. Now you're taking it all."

She sat her piece on her plate, then moved it to the other side, farther away from him, when she saw him eyeing it.

"There's plenty of bread, Mathias."

"Not an edge like that."

She smirked and took a piece of ham. "The planting is going well?"

"Yes," he responded. "And Jacob's lesson this morning?"

"Oh, the little whelp fell in the pool. He went fishing at sunup. He was still damp when he got to me, and he shivered so I sent him home to get dry. He hasn't returned."

Mathias gave her a knowing look. "He didn't want to go home to his mama is my guess. Charlotte probably blistered his backside. Indigo and I have told you all to keep out of the woods until the predator is killed."

"He shouldn't be down there alone, predator or not. He's too young. He could have drowned."

"Can't keep a boy like him away from a swimming hole like that one. Jacob's a good swimmer. I swam in that pool since I could walk, year around."

"That's nonsense, and you know it."

A smile formed on his lips, and her stomach fluttered. She enjoyed their rare, inconsequential small talk, and suddenly she wanted him to make love to her.

"Your rose sticks, as Jacob calls them, are budding."

"I know."

"In the plot."

"Oh?" She hadn't been there in days and feared her delay getting them in the ground might have doomed them. "All six?"

He nodded and stood. "I'll try to get a fence around the plot come winter."

"Stone?" she said, rising with him and wondering why he'd hurried through his meal.

"And where would I come by such? I'd like wrought iron from New Orleans."

"Won't that be expensive?"

"I'll discuss it with Uncle Michael." He reached for his hat in

213

an adjacent chair. Obviously he hadn't wolfed down dinner to make time for loving.

"You're returning to the fields so soon?"

By the way his eyes searched hers, he must have heard the disappointment in her voice.

"Indigo and I are going to Natchez this afternoon. Uncle Michael is up from New Orleans. In addition to the fence, I need to talk to him about the pork market. Do you need anything?"

So much for luring him into the bedroom.

"Ask Aunt Elizabeth to request a baby blanket from Mrs. Henshaw. She weaves such beautiful ones. "

"Rachel will stay here with you tonight."

She felt her skin blanch, and the light lunch she'd finished surely curdled in her stomach. Averting her eyes, she rubbed her tummy.

"Are you sick?"

Immediately she dropped her hand and began clattering serving plates on top of one another. "No."

He made a sibilant sound. "With Rachel in —"

"Don't concern yourself, Mathias," she said, slamming a wooden spoon against the table surface. "I'll be fine with Rachel, but being alone in this house tonight is not what concerns me."

"You've no cause to be jealous of Kate."

"You've not touched me in almost two weeks. What am I supposed to think?" There, it was out. She could have slapped herself, but it was as well she'd said it.

"You've been ill, physically and..."

"And what? Mentally? You think me mad, Mathias?"

"I was going to say 'spiritually'."

"For heaven's sake. You treat me like you think I'll break." She reached for his plate.

"You're frightened, and part of your fear has to do with me."

"I'm afraid of what's in that swamp," she railed. "Of dark secrets, of lies, of making no effort to —"

From outside, at the front of the house, Indigo bellowed Mathias' name, and Mathias cursed.

He reached out and grasped her hand, then gave her a quick kiss. "I'm supping and sleeping at Grandmama's, and yes, like it or not, I am being careful with you."

Chapter Twenty-four

"I can't get warm, Miz Angel. You was right. I shoulda changed my clothes."

Angelique had found the missing Jacob in the cookhouse when she took her and Mathias' dirty dishes to Bounty. The April day had grown warm and the area around the cookhouse fire was warmer still. The child's being unable to shake off his chill was worrisome at best. She rubbed his head, something she often did. Jacob's skin was light, but his brown eyes and tightly curled hair were those of the African.

She joined Charlotte and Rachel in the pea patch a short while later, determined to exhaust herself and her jealous worries over Mathias at the same time. They had cleared this patch, sown with corn the spring before, just last month. Alternating the corn with cowpeas, Mathias told her, replenished the soil depleted by corn. Even using that tactic, they had to clear additional land every few years to maintain their subsistence crops.

Angelique straightened and placed a hand on her lower back, which ached from bending. The afternoon was waning, but if sore muscles were an indicator, her ploy was working. If she weren't hurting too much by the time she climbed into bed, she'd sleep well.

"Your hands ain't used to this," Rachel said, looking at her. "You gonna have blisters."

"I've already got blisters, and I need to get used to this. Besides, I'm going to eat my share of these peas when they come in." She looked over the last row they'd completed. "And we're going to have lots of..." Angelique shielded her eyes from the sun and watched Bounty approach from the direction of the cook-house. The woman hailed Charlotte, who started toward her. The two met halfway. Moments later, Charlotte dropped her hoe and took off running in the direction of her cabin. Rachel stopped working and joined Angelique, and they headed toward the approaching Bounty.

"Jacob, he got a fever now," Bounty told them. For someone who mightn't know her, Bounty appeared matter-of-fact and completely calm, but Angelique had become familiar enough with the woman's reserved, often taciturn, countenance to know that strong emotions were working behind those black eyes. Bounty was scared, and, therefore, so was she.

"Moved him to his daddy's cabin. Got him covered with blankets, but the fever comes on quick. I fear for my grandson."

Pressure expanded behind Angelique's eyes. "Should we send for a doctor?"

Bounty shook her head. "Doctor's in Natchez. Too long. I'm goin' for Yo."

*A*ngelique held her fears in check until she saw him. Then she crumbled inside. His skin was hot to the touch, dry, his eyes closed, his breathing labored. A short time later, Angelique supported him in her arms while he threw up blood and phlegm into a wooden bucket. The retching stopped, and Charlotte bathed his small body with cool rags. On the narrow front porch, Rachel held Hank and tried to keep him out of the way.

Yo came. Bounty hadn't searched for Ben and Ethan. They were on the newly-acquired land girdling trees in preparation for clearing.

"Pneumonia," Yo said, confirming what they already knew.

Angelique watched Charlotte's shaking hands pull the quilts over her son. "What can we do?" Charlotte asked.

Yo touched the boy. "Had a cough, and his nose ran yesterday."

Charlotte started to cry. "And this mornin' he went fishin' and fell in the pool." She covered her face with her hands. "He stayed

217

in wet clothes, 'fraid I'd spank him." She covered her eyes. "I did, too. I told him and told him to stay out of the woods by hisself."

Bounty walked around and hugged her daughter by marriage.

"I'll make the Choctaw medicine," Yo said to Bounty, then turned to Angelique. "They taught me when I was young, when Pierre and Marie took me with them after the Natchez slaughtered Rosalie. Your Grandmama was a baby." She nodded to the flailing Jacob. "Elizabeth, was 'bout this boy's age here. I was maybe thirteen, fourteen." Her eyes focused on Angelique. "I learned much from the Choctaw. They taught me well and I"— she opened her eyes wide and tapped her head with an index finger—"remember well. Wanted to be useful to Master Pierre and Miss Marie. Slave traders brought me here from Africa. I didn't want Pierre Deschesne to sell me to someone else." Yo's bottom lip trembled, and she looked at Jacob. "He never did."

From what little Angelique knew of her great-grandfather, he never would have.

"I have much I need, but I must have the bulbs of the Choctaw Lily. It grows by the pool."

Bounty moved. "No, I need you to help prepare," Yo told her.

Charlotte started to get up.

"Stay here with Jacob, Charlotte," Angelique said. "Mathias showed it to me. I'll gather it."

"Two bulbs. It grows deep."

Spring was in full bloom, but Angelique took only cursory note of its beauty. Her thoughts remained with Jacob. Cautiously, she stepped into the woods, careful not to trip. She feared she might be unable to identify the plant, but that fear dissolved when she pushed through brush and entered the clearing. The plants, now two feet in height, grew profusely around the edge of the pool, their brilliant red flower a signal flag. Hot and winded from her run here, she took a moment to bathe her flushed face in the cold water, then cupped her hand and drank. Next to her, she spied a corncob float attached by twine to a cane pole, Jacob's discarded fishing effort from this morning.

The ground was damp and soft. Still, the job would have gone faster had one of the men been unearthing the plant.

She knelt and finished digging up the second bulb with her hands. Sitting on the back of her legs, she dusted the root.

New leaves rustled in the breeze. A gentle wind...a subtle smell. In the span of one erratic heartbeat, the scent of death overpowered that of freshly dug dirt. Squeezing the bulb, she twisted at the waist to look behind her.

The breeze died leaving an ominous stillness in its wake. With her free hand, she pushed herself up.

The stench of death coated her sweating skin and filled her nostrils and lungs. She salivated, then coughed and stepped toward the open field.

Chapter Twenty-five

"Angelique?"

Cold, black silence ignored his call.

"Rachel?"

Chest tight, Mathias reached for the tin lantern inside the dark front room. The flint sparked and with it, an eerie light illuminated the quiet house.

For the last several hours his single thought had been gauging the look on Angelique's face when he walked through the door. But he didn't find her on the other side.

She sat in a rocker holding Hank and listened to Charlotte hum Jacob a mournful tune. A tear slid down her cheek, and she held Hank tighter. For hours she'd watched Charlotte work tirelessly, doing everything a mother could do to make her baby more comfortable, touching him with love to last eternity.

Yo stood back. She had given Jacob a second dose of the medication she brewed this afternoon, mumbling to herself that the medicine had taken long to make and may have been given too late. Rachel sat in a chair, gazing into the fire crackling in the fireplace.

The door to the cabin opened, and Angelique looked up into Indigo's face. He turned, and when his eyes met Charlotte's shattered gaze, his expression changed from one of surprise to the haunted look of disbelief. With a sob, Charlotte rose and lurched for him. He took an ungainly step toward her.

"What's wrong?" he asked.

"Pneumonia," she said, the word muffled against his chest.

Mathias materialized behind Indigo, his countenance transforming from instant relief to anger, then to confusion when he saw Jacob in the rough-hewn bed.

Angelique rose and gave the sleeping Hank to Rachel. She put her hand in Mathias', and he pulled her outside the door of the crowded cabin.

"What happened?" he asked hoarsely.

"Jacob has pneumonia." She closed her eyes tight, fighting back tears. "I do not think...."

Yo followed them out, the light from the cabin briefly lighting her withered face before the door shut. "I will stay until it's over, one way or the other."

Mathias breathed in. "Sweet Jesus."

Yo opened the door and went back in. Angelique couldn't see Mathias well, but felt his possessive touch. "I'm staying," she said before he had a chance to speak.

He pulled her into his embrace and kissed her forehead. "I'll be close," he said. "There is naught to do now but wait."

The evening crawled to midnight, then into the wee hours of morning. During the night, she and Rachel took turns trading chairs and rocking Hank. Bounty shared duties with Charlotte, bathing Jacob's tortured body with cool compresses. Indigo sat on the other side of Jacob's bed holding his son's little hand. He stared silently at the boy and hardly moved at all.

Halfway between midnight and dawn, Yo sneaked quietly out the door. Angelique looked anxiously at Jacob, sure the wait was over. But he remained where he was, his parents on either side of him.

The interminable night waned and the untended fire languished to embers. Rachel and Bounty lay curled up close to each other on the floor, sleeping fitfully. Angelique heard soft whispers, then Charlotte crying. With heavy heart, she turned to see the woman's face close to her son's. Indigo leaned close, too. Charlotte was talking to the boy, and Angelique thought for a moment that, in her grief, Charlotte had lost her grip with sanity. Charlotte, her face illuminated with a bright smile, turned and looked at her. Then there was the sound of another voice, and tears filled Angelique's eyes. Jacob was talking to his mother.

"The fever's broke," Charlotte said to her.

Angelique stifled a sob, and tried to rise, but she'd forgotten Hank. Then Rachel was there, her hand covering her mouth as she fought to maintain her composure. Indigo looked up, weary, and Bounty sat down at her grandson's feet and wept silently.

The night air chilled Angelique as she ran to the cookhouse in search of Yo. She pushed at the door. It opened, and she stepped inside a warm room saturated with the scent of cooking food. Ben looked up anxiously from the table, and near the hearth, Mathias straightened and searched her eyes. She turned from him and focused on Yo, who calmly glanced at her, then resumed stirring the kettle over the fire. "The fever has broken," she said.

"How did you know?"

"He should have been dead three hours ago. When the child continued to live, I knew the medicine was working and he would survive."

Angelique fell against the door and drew in a long breath. Why had the woman not said so earlier?

"The danger is not past," Yo said, "though his chances are good. He must be nourished and watched until his strength returns."

"What are you three doing in here?"

"I make the boy a broth. It's almost done. He is awake?"

Angelique nodded.

"He will not want much, but we must get him to eat a little."

Angelique let out a tired little laugh. "He's thirsty."

"Let him drink as much as he can."

Angelique turned to go, but Mathias stopped her as Bounty walked through the door. "Bounty will take care of that, Yo. Angelique is going home."

"But I want to help."

He had her by the arm, pushing her out the door. "You've been up all night. You need rest."

She freed her arm and turned to look at his dark form beside her. It was still pitch black outside. "I'm not the only one who was up through the night. Everyone has been."

"Except for Charlotte and Indigo, everyone has gotten some sleep, but you." He took her hand in the dark. "It's too crowded in that little cabin. We all need to settle down."

Undressed to her undergarment, she watched Mathias pick up the torn, dirt- and blood-stained dress from yesterday afternoon and berated herself for not having hid it. But she'd been in too great a hurry to return to Jacob.

He tossed the dress on the bed then carefully pulled the chemise off her shoulder. "How did you do that?"

"I fell in the woods."

Turning to the mirror, she took her first good look at the injured shoulder. After she'd gotten the superficial bleeding stopped yesterday, she'd paid little attention to the wound or its intermittent throbbing. The bruise was indeed ugly. No wonder it hurt.

His reflection moved up behind her. "Why were you in the woods?"

She breathed deeply at the sight of him, his blond hair loose around his shoulders. Her eyes found his, watching her with growing perception. If she leaned back, her head would fall against his chest. Her stomach fluttered, and she parted her lips. He knew what was on her mind, and knowing he knew, she smiled at him. He grasped her arms and her stomach fluttered. He pulled her closer, but only enough to whisper in her ear.

"Why?"

"I went to get the bulbs of two Choctaw Lilies," she answered and turned to face him. Her gaze roamed from his eyes to his lips. "Yo needed them to make medicine for Jacob."

She inched forward. A smile touched his eyes, and he didn't back away. Finally, when her scantily-covered breasts touched his chest, he drew her into his arms for a passionate kiss. His hands did not roam. But his mouth did.

"How did you fall?" he asked, making a row of kisses across her cheek to her neck, behind the ear.

."I tripped on the spade," she whispered, twisting her head to ease his access.

"What did you hit?"

She hadn't stopped to find out. She'd scrambled back to her feet and charged out of those woods. "I don't know," she answered and, circling her arms around his neck, she breathed against his skin.

"Damn you, you little minx." He picked her up in his arms and turned to the bed.

Angelique jerked awake, her heart hammering and Mathias' name on her lips. She dreamed of him hovering over her, his eyes red and glowing. Then he'd entered her, and she'd wanted him. Even knowing that after he'd sated his need for her body, he would feast on her blood. She knew his intent, as one knows things in a dream one would not know when awake.

In search of the reassurance only he and the safety of his arms could provide, she reached out in the darkness and touched his thigh, warm and hard and bare. Desire replaced her fear, and her labored breath took on new meaning. Blatantly, she moved her hand up his leg. She had yet to openly explore his body, despite his sporadic indulgence in hers.

Brushing her fingers over the chamois-like softness of his testes, she touched his penis and found it hard. Scooting closer, she wrapped her fingers around it.

"Are you awake?" she asked.

"Very."

From the sound of his voice, he was not displeased with her, and she pulled the sheet away, uncovering his nakedness. Hand still holding his penis, she raised herself over him.

"I've never touched your most private parts. Do you like it?" It was still dark, but a late moon shone brightly enough to catch the gleam of his smile.

"Yes."

"Tell me what to do next."

This all seemed so simple, and suddenly, pleasing him was

very important to her. If she could make him as happy as Kate did—"

"Stroke it, up and down."

He groaned when she did. Without thinking, she bent and kissed the tip of his manhood. He sucked in a breath, and she licked it.

With a growl, he flipped her onto her back. She tensed at his reaction. The thoughtless act had been perverse. No doubt she'd offended him greatly.

Yanking the hem of her chemise up, he entered her and thrust only twice before his body stiffened. "Damn, Angelique," he whispered presently, "I had no time to get you ready."

Dawn was breaking, and she could make out his features. "I displeased you?"

His mouth fell open, then twitched at one corner. "No, sweetheart, you did not displease me." He validated his words with a passionate kiss, before drawing her into a sitting position and pulling the chemise over her head. "Now I'm going to pleasure you in kind."

$\mathcal{A}$ngelique stepped out of the bedroom, her hands behind her, tying her apron strings. The back door opened, and Mathias stepped inside. Her pelvis warmed. Never had she known pleasure such as he'd inflicted on her at dawn.

"Only now rising, wife? You should be whipped."

"Is it time for dinner?"

He laughed and took her arm, ushering her into the front room. "Have you not returned to earth yet? It's late, but still morning. I need to talk to you about yesterday in the woods."

Her stomach crashed into her gut.

He motioned her into the upholstered chair. "I talked to Ethan. He said you fell because you were running from something."

"I told you I tripped on the shovel."

"I fear you've left a great deal out."

"I had more important things to think about last night than why I fell."

"What frightened you?"

She didn't want to have this discussion, but there was no way around it. "Perhaps it could have been the predator. Something charged through the woods. I thought it was after me, and I bolted."

"You didn't see anything?"

She laughed, convincingly she hoped. "It was making a horrendous racket. I didn't wait for it to get to me."

"Was there anything else?"

Yes, but she didn't want to tell him so, and though she suspected bears smelled, she was relatively sure they did not smell like they were walking dead.

"Did you check around the pond?" she said instead.

"We found trampled bush, but no sign."

She breathed more freely. That, at least, was something.

"Is there any chance you are responsible for the trampling?"

If disappointment were edible, she could have feasted on it. "Do you think that would have been before or after I stabbed myself in the shoulder?"

"Don't get upset. I thought maybe something frightened you and you rushed through the underbrush trying to get away."

"Did I leave no sign for you, Mathias?" She tightened her lips. This was pointless. "I ran toward the open field. Ethan saw me coming. And so that you have the entire truth, you should know your *bear* reeks of death. The thing, whatever it really is, smells as if it died days ago."

He didn't believe her or he didn't want to believe her...or he knew she was telling the truth and didn't want her to know it. Immediately, she dropped her gaze and started around the chair. "I'm going to find some breakfast. How is Jacob?"

He straightened when she passed him. "Better."

"I'll go see him after I've eaten."

"Angelique?"

She stopped at the door.

"What was your nightmare about this morning?"

Damn him for asking. "You."

226

"I was what threatened you?"

"Yes." Her eyes burned, and she wasn't sure if it was anger or hurt she saw on his face. "But remember this, Mathias, you were who I reached for in the dark."

And she reached for him because she needed him. Yes, she wanted him, wanted him before he even put her to bed. But when she woke out of the nightmare, what she felt was more than want. She needed his touch, his strength, his protection.

Angelique tripped over a furrowed piece of ground and almost fell. Every day she loved him more, and each night her doubts grew. Sometimes she thought Mathias' did, too. She wanted all their doubts removed.

She speaks in riddles, he said of Yo. Well, if that was true, then she would try to make sense of Yo's words, not simply listen to them.

The beautiful day bordered on hot, but made for a pleasant walk across open field with no dark, disconcerting woods to worry her. The wind filled her skirt, and despite her mood, she laughed and turned in a full circle. Another gust blew her skirt up, and with a whoop, she pushed it down and started to run. This would be her first visit to Yo's cabin. The others had told her where it was. Now she could see the crude structure in the distance, and the old woman moving inside and out, then inside again.

She was outside by the time Angelique got there. Near where the woman sat on a rough stool, an iron pot hung over an open fire.

"More medicine for Jacob?"

Yo turned, her calm movement indicating no surprise, but her eyes told a different tale, and Angelique smiled. The old woman went inside and returned with another stool.

"The boy is doing well," she said. "Last afternoon, I did not think we'd have him today. Old Yo's medicine worked good, huh?"

Angelique sat. "You did wonderfully."

227

"Something was with you at the pool yesterday? That's why you've come to me?"

"Yes."

"Mathias does not believe you?"

"He believes I'm afraid, but he says there's nothing to be afraid of."

Yo leaned toward her. "He's wrong. Elizabeth's demon exacts payment through you as it did Julianna."

"If Julianna was payment way back then, why does it want me now?"

"Hatred runs deep. The demon will not rest while Elizabeth lives."

"Did she kill her brother for De Leau?"

"*De Leau was hers.*"

She clenched her fists and looked around. He stood there, long and tall, at the corner of the cabin, his gaze fixed on her. His green eyes held a subtle warning, which curbed her anger and increased her frustration.

"I saw you walking this way."

She raised her chin. "I wasn't trying to keep my visit secret."

"You should have. Better still, you shouldn't have come at all."

"I didn't know there were places on De Leau I wasn't allowed to go."

"Now you know," he said coolly, walking toward her. "Some things are best not talked about, Angelique."

"And what are those?" she said, rising to meet him.

"My sire and Bess' secrets."

"Those are only part of my concern. I—"

He didn't stop coming, and when his fingers bit into her upper arm, she blinked at him. He yanked her away from where she'd sat.

"And I'm the rest of it?" he snarled. "Let me fill you in, my lovely bride. Twenty-seven years ago someone kidnapped my mother and kept her in that swamp for eight weeks, raping her until he was sure she was pregnant with me.

"He brought her home in the middle of the night and left her naked, wrapped in a blanket, on the back porch of De Leau."

Mathias jerked her around so she faced the direction of the distant house. "Right there."

"Six months later my mother went into early labor, and I was born." He glanced at Yo, then dragged Angelique farther away. She tripped. His hand tightened around her bicep, and he held her steady, hurting her. With her free hand, she pried at his brutal fingers, but he shook her and wouldn't let go.

"You ask if Bess killed her half-brother? Do you really believe the demon ghost of Jean Larocque lurks around De Leau seeking vengeance for his son? Since Bess raised Jarrod from age five, and since her father, who was not related to Jarrod Larocque, received De Leau long before Jean Larocque ever floated down the Mississippi, it's doubtful she would have killed him for something that was already hers and her husband's.

"The truth is, Jarrod didn't like his sister, and he didn't like Robert Douglas. He had no claims to De Leau, so he left in search of his fortune.

"And as for the whoreson who raped my mother and sired me, I don't know who he is, and I never want to know."

He pushed her in the direction from whence she'd come, freeing her arm at the same time. She stumbled, but didn't take her eyes off him. Her arm hurt where he'd held her, and she rubbed the spot.

"I'm sorry, Mathias," she said, holding her quivering chin high, "for you and for me. I've been a fool to think you might have cared..." Shutting her eyes against his hateful glare, she turned and started home. She'd overrated her importance to him. Even if he were not part of some sinister plot to destroy her, the blind loyalty he gave his grandmother would.

Mathias set the hat on his head, the anger draining from him as he watched her go. He turned and stalked away from Yo.

"You lie to her," the Negress hollered after him. "You say there is nothing out there, and you know there is."

"I know no such thing."

229

"You do."

He headed to Dan, grazing near Yo's cabin. Yo followed. "She is afraid."

"She should have thought about that before she married me."

"She does not fear your blood, you fool," Yo said sternly.

He continued to walk.

"Mathias!"

He stopped at her command. Best to let her have her say and be done with it.

She shuffled closer to him. "The fear of your father's blood is yours alone."

He closed his eyes. He didn't want to talk about this.

"Angelique fears the thing that terrorizes her. You ignore it because you are afraid to learn the truth."

"Angelique's demons are in her head."

Yo narrowed her eyes on him. Ah, the old witch had thought of something else. "You hurt her just now," she said.

Yes he had, though he wasn't exactly sure how. He was feeling pretty damned hurt himself. He started again for Dan.

"And she hurt you," Yo called.

He kept going.

"Without love there would be no hurt, Mathias."

Dan shied at his approach.

"You and me, we both know Elizabeth gave her to you. The debt is your grandmama's."

Mathias sucked in a breath, the twisted prophecy echoing in his head. He was tired of it now, tired of Yo's diatribes against his grandmother, tired of Angelique's doubts. He put his foot in the stirrup and mounted Dan, turning the stallion in the direction of the house. In the distance, Angelique walked toward home.

Yo tugged on the bridle, forcing Dan's head down. Mathias met her eyes.

"Be careful your fear of the truth doesn't cost you the thing you love most," she said. "I have seen how Angelique looks at you. She doesn't care if you are man or demon. You are her life. She wants only to live it."

Mathias stared at her. In some ways, her perception matched his grandmother's.

Yo nodded. "And she is yours. Believe me, Mathias, Angelique is in danger."

Chapter Twenty-six

*H*ours had passed since Mathias left the house. In the days since their quarrel at Yo's cabin, he hadn't returned to the house for the noon meal, and she hadn't tried to see Yo. She'd wait until he went to Natchez. Then it would serve him right when she snuck off back there.

The house was cool despite the increasing temperature outside. Angelique opened the windows in the main room and listened to bird song. The hickory pecans, dressed in spring foliage, rustled in a cool breeze, then were still. Before her ran acre upon acre of plowed earth, sprouting forth corn. In another month, Mathias told her, the corn would be so high it would block the barren trail leading west into the swamp and on to Natchez.

She turned from the window, glancing first at the cold fireplace, then the rest of the room. The mantel needed dusting, so did the desk. Slamming Mathias' ledgers shut, she stacked them neatly in the center of his desk and hoped her straightening the books angered him. His yelling would be more bearable than his infernal sulking.

Hunger pangs tugged at her, and she decided to visit Bounty in the cookhouse. Eating had become a necessary evil, and she was noticing its ill effects.

But when she stepped into the wide hall dividing the house, the ladder leading to the attic beckoned her. Excitement goaded her, and she lit a candle and climbed into the uncharted darkness.

Emerging through the trap, she stood, holding the candle high until she made out the trunk she remembered from the day she and Mathias had come up here together. The heat from the enclosed space baked her body, and her queasiness increased. Stooping, she placed the candle on the floor, then pushed at the heavy lid before retrieving the taper. Inside the box, she found a once bright blanket, faded with age, the soft pelt of an animal, baby booties, a half-finished sampler, a woman's dress, old and out of fashion. Tentatively she reached in and fingered the cloth, then lifted the rough blanket to see what lay beneath. A necklace of polished stones and animal claws strung on sinew fell out. She held it up, then put it back and picked up a wooden doll at the bottom of the trunk. Sitting on the floor, she studied the doll's minimal features, worn, no doubt, from play, and she wondered whose doll...

"It was my mother's. Everything in that chest is a part of her."

Not a floorboard or a rung had groaned at his ascent. He was halfway through the trap, his green eyes, black in the dim light, watching her. Carefully, she replaced the doll, and he hauled himself on up into the attic and closed the lid to the trunk. When she felt his fingers brush her arm, she took his extended hand, and he pulled her to her feet.

"What are you going to do?" she asked.

His eyes watched her lips, then met her gaze. "Do you think I would beat you?"

"It's possible."

"I'm not angry." He nodded toward the trunk. "Not over this. There are no secrets in that box, only the memorabilia of a woman I never knew."

She touched his arm. "We could go through it together."

He smiled. "I know what's in there."

But she didn't, and she wanted him to tell her the history of each item. He tugged on her hand. "Come downstairs, this space is hot, and don't come back up here without me. I don't want you on the ladder."

Alighting from the bottom rung, she made a beeline to the back door.

"Where are you going?" he asked.

"To the cookhouse."

He nodded, but moved toward the front room. "Jack was here. He and Martha have invited us to see the baby tomorrow."

A pleasant respite. She'd be able to deliver the baby blanket, and for Martha she would take one of the rose bushes she planted at the gravesite.

A warm breeze blew across her bare arms. White clouds, billowing into towering peaks, encroached upon the blue sky. Mathias was hoping for rain. There had been none for a week.

With heavy heart, Angelique walked to the foot of Julianna Douglas' grave and drew a breath in dismay. Her beautiful roses, the ones she thought she had lost to sloth, and had rejoiced over with their renewal, had been ripped from their beds and shredded, then scattered like fodder across the family plot. Her gaze passed over the discolored headstones, some slightly askew. The legacy of De Leau. Life and death. Love..., she thought of her father, ...and hate. Why the hate? Why?

She reached down and picked up a shattered stem from the grave of Julianna Douglas. Accidentally, she pricked her finger on a thorn and cried quietly when it bled. Mathias had suffered growing up, spurned by not only his peers, but even by members of his family. He'd achieved much by gaining De Leau, only to be burdened now by a marauder attacking his stock and a feeble wife. Doubtless, he wished she were someone, or somewhere, else.

She dried her tears and looked beyond the graves to the dark woods shrouding the deep, spring-fed pool.

Still, in the presence of Ben and Bounty and their family, Mathias had known love and in Jack Summerfield, the respect and friendship of a neighbor.

Mathias had brought her to De Leau as part of his grandmother's design. Other than a few passionate nights...and days, he'd asked nothing from her his servants could not provide. If he expected her to be his soul's companion—she placed her palm over her sick and swollen belly—or bear his children, he hadn't said. She glanced at the graves and hated herself for believing he might have played a role in this spiteful act, not to desecrate the graves, but to shove her more quickly toward madness.

Perhaps he had orchestrated everything, feeding her fear of an unreal demon, hoping she'd take her own life so he could live with someone he loved as he loved Kate Mallory? Worse yet, and she glanced again in the direction of the dark and looming forest, what if there was something out there, something to which he owed fealty, and he intended to turn her over to it?

Angelique rolled onto her back. Lightning flashed, and she covered her ears against the ensuing thunder. The noise faded, and she reached for Mathias. Why, considering her doubts, she did not know.

But the security she sought was missing.

In the corner of her eye, lightning flickered, and something dark moved against the shimmering night. Her gaze darted to the window, and she waited.

She jumped with the anticipated light, but only sheets of sparkling water washed over the panes. Relieved, she sat up and rubbed the sleep from her eyes. Again lightning struck, and once more she looked. A massive silhouette reared against the window.

A half-drawn breath lodged in her throat, and she choked on it.

Chapter Twenty-seven

An icy chill erupted up Mathias' spine. Shattering thunder echoed Angelique's scream and scrambled what remained of his senses. He surged from his desk, overturning the chair, and ran across the front room and foyer to the bedroom door, which he slammed against the adjacent wall.

The light from across the hall illuminated Angelique sitting on the bed, the sheet drawn over her as if she were a ghost. He breathed heavily and looked around the shadowed room. But for the woman whimpering softly in the middle of the bed, nothing appeared out of the ordinary.

"Angelique," he whispered, sitting gently on the bed so as not to frighten her further. She stiffened, and he circled his arm around her. Carefully, he pulled the sheet from her head.

Immediately, her wide-eyed gaze jerked to the window. He looked, too, but saw only darkness.

"What happened?" he asked.

She shook her head, not taking her eyes off the window, and he took her by the shoulders. "Look at me," he said.

She obeyed, grasping his arms to steady herself.

"What?" he asked.

"It's at the window." Her gaze returned to the window. Again, his followed.

Lightning flashed, and he felt her jump and curl her fingers into his biceps.

Rivulets of water were reflected in the glare of the ephemeral light, nothing more.

A sob escaped her lips. She pushed him away and threw back

the covers. He reached for her, but missed, and she bounded from the bed.

In the foyer, she grabbed a piece of wood from the depleted woodpile and yanked at the door.

He seized her arm. "What's wrong with you?"

She turned on him in a frenzy, striking out with the log she'd taken. He released her to avoid the blow, and she turned to the door. Again he took hold of her arm.

"It's storming out there."

In a fury of arms and legs, she attacked his grip. "Let me go," she shrieked, and he did.

"I'm going after it. This time, I'm going to make you see it."

His heart and head were pounding. She'd lost her mind, but he no longer tried to stop her. She pulled up the latch, and the wind caught the door, blowing it open. It hit her in the shoulder, staggering her, but she didn't seem to care. Waving the log, she stepped into the chilled darkness, the wind buffeting her body, the rain drenching her chemise.

"Wait," he cried, grabbing the tin lantern inside the front room. He rushed to catch her and studied the porch outside the bedroom window where she lingered briefly. Rain-soaked boards shimmered in the candlelight before the wind blew out the lantern. Angelique started to run, disappearing around the corner of the house. He heard her snarl angrily, but didn't interfere with her, allowing her to finish what she'd started. Back at the front door, she dropped the log.

Raising her hand, she brushed the dripping curls out of her face. The wind and rain continued to pound her, but now a dark calm seemed to possess her, and she looked at him beside her.

"You see, Mathias," she said loudly over the rain. "There is nothing there. There is *never* anything there."

She entered the house like a whirlwind, every muscle moving, her mind, if her physical motion was any indicator, working toward complete collapse. He secured the door behind them and watched her go through the house, methodically checking every-where. When she started up the ladder to the attic he tried to stop her, telling her he would go, but she yanked out of his restraining hold and went anyway. He let her go alone. The house was secure, and nothing sinister, with the possible exception of his beautiful Angelique, harbored within.

She was shivering in front of the cold fireplace when he returned from the back room with a blanket, which he spread over her. He stacked the few remaining logs in the fireplace, and once the flames erupted, she emerged from her trance-like state to watch the fire. He dried himself off and changed. He needed to get her out of her sodden chemise and get her warm, but he feared touching her, afraid she would explode like a rocket. Water dripped from her hair. The blanket he'd given her was now wet. He handed her a glass of brandy, and she took it, staring at him when she did. Her eyes filled with tears.

"You look like a god," she said slowly, her voice steady, cold. "The first moment I saw you, I thought you were a golden angel sent to rescue me. The one thing I remember clearly about that terrible day is you. I love you so much." Her eyes brimmed, and he took a step toward her.

"No! Do not touch me! Let me be, Mathias."

"Angelique," he said, moved beyond action by the nightmare that possessed her, "I want to help you." He wanted to hold her, to make her warm.

"I don't want your help."

For a moment, she paid him no heed, but stared into the fire. Then she asked plaintively, "Did you destroy the roses at the plot?"

What in God's name was she talking about?

When he didn't answer, she rested her gaze on him. "The bushes have been ripped up and torn apart."

"I would not do such a thing."

"Do you know who did?"

He clenched his fists, unable to fathom how deeply embedded her distrust of him had become.

"I don't."

She stared at him, undaunted and, he believed, unconvinced.

"Why would I have destroyed your efforts?" he asked.

"To drive me mad."

A tremble moved through him, but he fought the urge to reach for her. "I care for you, Angelique. Why would I want you mad?"

She closed her eyes, and he saw her shudder.

"You need to get out of that chemise."

Her eyes flew open, and she glared at him, daring him, it seemed, to touch her.

"You are going to get sick. Do you want to end up like Jacob?"

"Would it make a difference?"

He breathed in quickly through his nostrils. "Hell, yes."

Her eyes squinted as if she were in some terrible pain, and the sound of her ensuing words conveyed the same agony. "I'm going to have a child, Mathias."

He had been wondering when she'd tell him, but he'd hoped for a more joyful telling of it.

"I know."

Her lips curled slightly, and she blew out a contemptuous breath. "For certain you do. You probably knew before I did." She turned back to the fire. "Are you the father?"

His body numbed, or perhaps it was his soul. "I am the father."

She closed her eyes tight and covered her face with her hands, but not before he saw a tear slid down her cheek. He swallowed hard, not knowing what to do or what he felt. Anger, remorse, grief? Grief and hurt. And he was frustrated, because he wasn't completely sure what she was feeling. Betrayed, no doubt, and that thought hurt him all the more. She was unhappy she carried the child, his only consolation being she feared the baby was not his, but had, through deception, been forced upon her.

But which doubt boded worse for them?

Chapter Twenty-eight

ngelique studied the beautiful Katherine Suzanne, sleeping to the rhythmic clump of the rocking chair against the porch, and cursed her doubts about the baby growing in her womb.

"She's sleeping now, but when she's awake, she cries or eats, and a mother has little time for anything else." Martha was so obviously proud of the baby girl. "I'm lucky. Jack is helpful and so are his two boys. You'll have help at De Leau when your time comes."

Angelique bowed her face toward the baby's and blinked, hiding her eyes from Martha's.

The baby stirred. Angelique tensed. Moments before Katherine Suzanne let out a wail, Martha rose awkwardly and took her daughter. The birth had been difficult, Martha told Angelique earlier, and she had torn badly on delivery. She was still miserable.

"Let me help you to bed, Martha," Angelique said, rising. "You've been up too long with us here."

"Come inside and sit with me awhile."

"Martha, we have to go," Mathias called from the other end of the porch. "I want us home by dusk."

Angelique drew in a calming breath, "I'll help with the baby while Martha gets comfortable."

Mathias nodded and rose. He had disappeared with Jack shortly after they arrived, and for an hour Angelique's ears had burned, sure Mathias was talking about her. Martha would probably never let her hold Katherine Suzanne again.

He'd told her on the trip over that he, Indigo, Ethan, and Ben searched for hours this morning looking for anything to indicate someone, or something, had trespassed on De Leau the night before. There was nothing, and any evidence that might have existed was washed away by the rain. He did acknowledge the butchered roses, but offered no explanation as to who destroyed them or why. If Mathias hadn't been responsible, he probably thought she'd done it herself.

She closed her eyes and sucked in deep, steadying breaths in the wake of the inexplicable fear that had come upon her when they entered the swampy woods. Indigo rode in front of her. She concentrated on his back and fought the urge to turn in the saddle and tell Mathias they must go back. She'd not experienced this panic when they came.

Queen Anna knew the trail by heart and needed no guidance. Mathias, on Dan, was talking to Indigo, their conversation an annoying distraction that heightened her irritability and her growing fear. She peered into the foliage closing in on her. Mathias was speaking to her now, but she didn't comprehend his words. Her racing heart pounded faster in her chest. She swallowed and swung her head to one side, looking...

A shudder ran through Queen Anna at the same moment Indigo cried out to his mount and pulled up the suddenly skittish work horse. Again he jerked the reins. Behind her, Angelique heard Dan's hoofs hit the ground in quick succession before Mathias issued him a firm command. Dan reared again, and Mathias shouted. Queen Anna shied to one side of the trail, then bolted. Angelique yelped and pulled on the reins, trying to control the animal, but Queen Anna didn't respond, and in rapid sequence left the trail and tore through thick undergrowth, which slapped Angelique's face and body.

Initially, she saw oncoming branches and ducked. Then her ankle caught on a bush, and she threw up an arm to shield herself from a low-lying limb. Her arm smashed into her face, and she fell to the soft ground, landing on her back. The blow forced the air from her lungs, and her chest ignited in pain, leaving her helpless. She closed her eyes, and her head spun. Somewhere, the sound growing fainter with distance, she registered Queen Anna charging on alone.

An eerie quiet replaced the violent pounding of hooves and thrashing plants. Able to breathe again, Angelique sat up and forced herself to unsteady feet. From within the enveloping forest she heard a snarl, its source unseen, but much too near. Whatever spooked the horses was here, in the darkening woods, and it watched her now. Whether by design or not, Mathias had delivered her to it.

She whispered his name.

Behind her the forest tore open. Covering her head with her arms, she whimpered and dropped to her knees, a last vain attempt to shield herself from the atrocity descending upon her.

"Angelique!"

Still on her knees, she twisted around and saw Mathias reining Dan in. She scrambled to her feet, and he motioned for her to raise her arms so he could pick her up. She reached for him, but Dan reared. With a curse, Mathias tugged at the reins and settled the horse. When he reached for her the second time, he grasped her around the waist and lifted her, settling her firmly in front of and facing him.

Immediately, she wrapped her arms around his waist and buried her face in his chest. She felt his hand on her back, then a reassuring squeeze. The scent of sandalwood permeated her senses, as did his warmth, his strength, and the beat of his heart.

Mathias didn't scare easily, but now he felt a subtle tingling along his spine, that instinctive, primordial warning of danger. He'd almost run Angelique over. Queen Anna was nowhere in sight, but he didn't care. He wanted to get Angelique out of here as quickly as possible. He wasn't sure what wild beast was in these woods, but didn't doubt the threat.

She was shivering, her arms wrapped around his torso so tight they almost hurt him. He wanted to hold her, but had to keep both hands on the reins. Dan needed his firm touch. So he sandwiched her between his arms and crooned to her everything was all right, while he watched the forest around them. Everything was not all right.

There was no one on the trail where they'd left it, and he shouted for Indigo, to no avail. Keeping his hand on Angelique's shoulder, he stood in the stirrups and searched the dark undergrowth for a movement, a scent, anything to tell them they weren't alone. Dan had calmed. Again, Mathias called for Indigo.

"*Ho.*"

Mathias saw him, still mounted, reenter the trail from the thick woods roughly sixty paces ahead of them. Relieved, he turned Dan and nudged him on.

"Did you see anything?"

Indigo shook his head. "Nothin', it got away."

"Animal?"

Indigo cast a cautious glance at Angelique before looking Mathias in the eye. "Our marauder maybe."

Mathias nodded. "Tracks?"

Indigo shook his head. "Hit the swamp water but my guess is it was curvin' back your direction."

Mathias looked up through the trees towering above them. He wanted to get Angelique home. Even if he didn't have her to worry about, waning daylight precluded tracking.

He carried her from the horse to their bed. An inconsequential scratch ran for about an inch along her jaw, and an ugly bruise graced her forehead. She'd hit a tree limb and hit it hard.

With a shaking hand, he took her chin and searched her eyes. "Are you hurt anywhere else?"

She stared at him, and her lips trembled. "My head hurts."

"I believe that. Are you bleeding?"

She continued to stare at him, her eyes locked on his.

"Are you bleeding, Angelique?"

Tentatively she reached out and touched his cheek. Then her chin quivered.

He braced himself. "What's wrong?"

"You came for me," she said softly. "I didn't think you were going to."

Her words slammed into him, eclipsing all his other concerns. He rose from where he knelt in front of her and sat beside her on the bed, then placed his hands on either side of her face. "Why—"

She turned her cheek against his hand and kissed his palm. "I thought you had turned me over to whatever is out there."

Sweet Jesus. His arrogance and deference to his own selfish fear had allowed this nightmare to flourish inside her beautiful head. Why had he failed to make her see she was his golden prize, his treasure, the woman he dreamed about, but never thought he'd have? When Bess offered her to him, he'd gobbled her up. He hadn't known if that was love or carnal lust, but he knew the answer now. Gently, he drew her into his arms.

"I would never leave you out there. I love you more than my life. I will always come for you." He kissed the top of her head, her cheek, and finally her lips. She kissed him back, then tugged on his arm. Finding his hand, she laid it on her belly.

She hesitated a moment. "Are you happy about the baby, Mathias?"

"I would be but for your doubts."

She laid her head on his chest. "Hold me."

He squeezed her tight, forcing a "poof" of air between her lips. "When you hold me like this, I have no doubts. Make love to me."

He wanted to laugh in relief, but feared it would not be appropriate. And no matter how much he wanted to make love to her, he wasn't going to. She was pregnant, and she'd taken a bad spill.

"I'm afraid to."

Quickly she looked up. "I've talked to Martha. There's no reason we cannot make love."

Running a finger along her jaw line, he turned her head and looked directly into her eyes. "Yes, but you just fell off a horse."

"I have no pain, but if the fall will cause me to lose the baby, it has already done so. Our making love will make no difference."

He wondered if, somewhere deep inside, her doubts about that January day at the pool made her want to lose this baby. The thought hurt, but it was assuaged by the reality that she needed him now. And really, which was more important?

Dusk's dimness cloistered the room. A late-afternoon thunderstorm raged, bringing a cool breeze through the open window. Mists of rain blew in and sprayed his steamed body, but he didn't want to move to push down the sash.

"Could we both have been bewitched?" she said softly.

Angelique faced away from him, her derriere against his hip. They were naked, and he was enjoying the touch of her flesh against his.

"At the pool you mean?" He knew what she referred to, but hated for that cold winter's day to infringe upon the sweet lethargy of their most recent lovemaking.

He rolled to his side and snuggled his pelvis against her bottom. "I remember everything that happened, Angelique. There are no gaps in *my* memory. The only being to touch your body was me."

She looked over her shoulder. "You're sure?"

He laughed to reassure her and for that reason alone, because he wasn't feeling particularly joyful. What the hell had happened to her that day three months ago? She'd turned on him with wantonly aggressive lust, and he'd accommodated her, and filled her, and loved her to a deliriously happy climax for them both. At least he'd thought so at the time.

He propped up on an elbow. "Let's try another tack. Are you sure you became pregnant that day? When is the baby due?"

She rolled over and shook her head.

"When was your last monthly flux?"

She grimaced. "I have had a flux since I was twelve, but not a monthly one. I've always been irregular. My last flux was before Christmas."

"Let's think about this. If you became pregnant in January,

the baby should arrive in October." A long time to wait with doubts, though a doctor or midwife might be able to narrow the dates as the pregnancy progressed.

"It doesn't matter," she said wrapping her arms around his naked chest and kissing his nipple. "I know now you did not betray me."

But she wasn't confident they both had not been duped by something monstrous, and the child growing in her womb was not his. His gut tightened painfully, and he wondered how Julianna Douglas had felt about her tortured body being forced to nourish the parasitic offspring of something she despised.

Chapter Twenty-nine

"She's been dead at least three days. Probably killed the day she bolted," Jack said. Mathias stepped back. Underneath the trees, the morning was cool, but the day was shaping into a hot one, like the day before and the day before that.

"What do you think?" Mathias called to Indigo, who stood thirty paces from the putrid carcass of Queen Anna.

"Cat."

"Could be a sound guess," Jack said, "but vermin has gotten to her, so it's hard to tell for sure."

"No guess about it."

Mathias' gaze slid back to Indigo, who smiled broadly, and Mathias' heart skipped a beat. Finally, thank God.

"You've found sign?"

At Mathias and Jack's approach, Indigo pointed to the ground. It wasn't clear, but Mathias could see it when Indigo outlined it for him. "Left hind paw of a swamp cat. Big," he said and looked up from where he studied the ground. "Hasn't been a big cat around here for sure since I was a boy."

Jacob sat at the dining room table struggling to write the alphabet. He recited the sound of each letter to her as he wrote it. His time was almost up, and she could tell he was glad. Working inside was one thing during cold winter days. Spring and summer were entirely different.

Booted feet sounded on the porch, and the back door opened. Angelique's eyes closed as delectable warmth bathed her body.

"I'm in the dining room," she called.

Her handsome husband stuck his head through the door. "A good day is being wasted outside, Jacob."

"Don't tell him that."

Mathias ignored her and stepped over to look at the boy's work. "You're doing well."

The dark little face looked up with a flash of white teeth. "I gots to the *m*, Miss Angel. I can finish the rest tomorrow."

"All right, you can go," she said, hoping Mathias was early from need of her.

Jacob picked up the slate. "I'll show Mama."

Mathias had pulled her into his arms before the door slammed shut. When he finished plundering her mouth, he set her unceremoniously aside and moved to the table.

In mock aggravation, Angelique stared at him. "I beg your pardon?"

He pulled out his chair and sat down, flexing his jaw. "Where's my meal, woman?"

"Probably not yet in the pot, husband." She caught the twinkle in his eye and the smile at the corner of his lips, and she sauntered over to settle in his lap. "Unless it is other nourishment you're wanting." She kissed him, but he stopped her hands before she could make much progress stroking his chest.

"It's getting harder and harder to tease you, my angel. You give as good as you get."

Gently, she ran the tip of her nose along his jaw from chin to ear. "Are you complaining?" She breathed against his ear, then started to trace its contour with the tip of her tongue. He jerked back.

"Damn you..." he whispered, turning his head to give his lips easy access to hers, "I'm going to have to take you to bed, and I don't have time for this."

"Oh," she said, pushing against his chest in an effort to rise, "if that is how —"

He pulled her to him and lowered his head to suckle a clothed breast.

She tried to get away, but he held her firmly, kissing her until she stilled and returned his kisses.

"Before I take you to the bedroom and ravish you, I did have a reason for coming to the house early."

She tapped his chin with an index finger. "A reason other than me?" He sobered before her eyes.

"Jack found Queen Anna."

"How is she?" she asked softly, but she knew.

"Dead."

"What happened?"

He shifted his weight, settling her on his lap. "Looks like what spooked her four days ago killed her. Angelique...?"

"Yes?"

"Indigo found sign."

Her heart skipped a beat.

"It's a big cat."

So, there was an animal. "It's not a bear, then?" She asked the question as much to get her bearings as for any other reason.

"Not this time."

She wanted to reconcile in her mind the scent of death and the black silhouette against the window pane that stormy night, the hands that tripped her on the stairs as she gathered wood in the dark, the soiled sheets, but if nothing else, the "sign" did explain many things, and wasn't that best?

"Do such predators normally attack farms with so many people?"

"Cows and hogs make easy prey, my love. Cats are not stupid. They like things easy, as do the rest of us."

"Are you going to hunt it?"

"We can't find enough sign—"

"But if you have Queen—"

"The kill is too old. That's why we have nothing to follow. We'll hold out and see what happens."

Chapter Thirty

And see what happens. And something would happen, but perhaps that something would be nothing more ominous than the killing of a large cat. Maybe her pregnancy altered unpleasant scents and produced the delusion of rotting flesh where only the scent of a kill existed. But no matter what, they had finally stumbled across a clue indicating the terror stalking De Leau, no matter how dangerous, belonged to the natural world.

Comforted by the thought, Angelique rubbed her hand over fine leather binding. Since she came to live in Elizabeth Boswell's house, she'd discovered a love of books, and she enjoyed their fine construction almost as much as the story within.

Hugging her gift to her bosom, she walked into the front room. Mathias sat behind his desk. Pleased that he didn't look up, she walked over and placed a hand on his shoulder, then set the book in front of him.

"Happy birthday."

His gaze swept the immaculate volume of *Don Quixote*, before coming to rest on her. Then with a smile, he opened the cover and thumbed the book's pages.

"Bounty told me you enjoyed reading." She cocked her head. "So I sent a message to Aunt Elizabeth by Indigo. As luck would have it, Cousin Michael had recently received three copies—an illegal consignment, apparently. It's an English translation. This will be the start of your library."

He tugged on her arm, and she bent toward him for a kiss. "Thank you," he said and stood to pull over a stool. "You have

250

convinced me it's time I went over these ledgers with you. If I'm to find time for pleasure reading, you'll have to do them."

*A*fter supper, they lit lamps in the cabin, and for a long time he sat by her side, watching her make entries to his ledger in a bold, decisive script he couldn't fault. She had a good head for numbers, and she understood bookkeeping, a skill her father had taught her. From time to time, she asked a question, but for the most part, she took right to the work.

"You'll trust me to keep your books?" she asked finally.

"Yes, but be assured I intend to audit them occasionally."

"Until then, I believe you're in my chair. Yours," she said, pointing to the wing-backed one in front of the hearth, "is there."

*F*rom under the porch out back, he heard the puppy's whine, followed by the rustle of leaves in the pecan trees.

"The wind is picking up."

Angelique looked up from the ledger. "I heard thunder a bit ago."

"Good, we need rain."

She rose and went to the back bedroom. "The cloud is coming in from the northeast," she called. "We should move the puppy. He'll get wet."

He closed his book and started to get up.

"I'll get him," she said, passing back through the room.

He rose anyway and waited for her. She wanted to hold the thing. Damn Jack Summerfield. Mathias could deal with a dog, puppy or not, but Angelique had never had a pet, and she was totally enthralled with the motley little mongrel. It would never be large, and he doubted its value as a hunter. She walked in, smiling broadly and hugging the wiggling, whining little beast against her breast. She put him on the floor.

"Angelique, the first thing that dog will do is squat and pee."

She scooped it up. "I think it's sweet, Jack bringing you a puppy every year on your birthday. No wonder you have so many dogs."

By tacit agreement, the dogs belonged to Ben and Indigo. "Only four...well, five now, and you have again recklessly used the word 'sweet' in reference to Jack Summerfield. He probably has the finest hunting dogs in the district, but what he brings me, birthday or not, are the ugly little mutts his bitches produce when they manage to get loose while in heat."

"He's not ugly." She held the thing in front of her and studied its face. "He's as precious as an animal could be."

Mathias stepped over and patted its fuzzy head. It snapped playfully at his hand. "I thought so, too, when I was a boy."

He started to tell her about the kitten Jack brought on this date fourteen years ago, but lightning struck close. Angelique jumped with the near simultaneous thunder and crushed the puppy close. Lord, she'd all but hunkered on the floor, and she must have realized it because she immediately loosened her hold on the struggling pup, and searched Mathias' eyes. "I'm sorry."

She had no need to be, and he embraced her. "That was close. Made my own hair stand on end."

She leaned into him in quiet acceptance of comfort, then pulled away. "I have to find a place to put our puppy tonight."

Our puppy? Inwardly, Mathias cursed. "Outside?"

Again lightning struck.

"No, Mathias. This is his first night without his mother." Then, excited, she held up her free hand. "I know what we can do."

He turned with her when she stepped around him and went in the back room. "We are not doing anything," he said, picking up the lamp and following her, "you are doing it."

He found Angelique struggling with the large wooden tub they used for bathing.

"I'll put a blanket in here."

Thunder rent the air again. In the distance, a dog barked, then another. "Why," he said, taking her arm and tugging her upright, "are you trying to move it?"

"I thought we could put him in the room with us."

"He will keep us up all night."

252

She petted the puppy, then placed it in the tub. It immediately leaped for the side, barked at her, fell, rolled over, and again found its feet. Mathias snorted.

Above them, the roof hummed, then roared as the rain reached them. Outside, the barking increased. His handful of dogs might not be hunters, but from time to time, they made good watchdogs. He frowned at the bouncing mutt in the tub. With one ear tuned to the yelping hounds, he took Angelique's hand. "Puppies are a lot of trouble, sweetheart."

She looked at him, smiled, and squeezed his hand in silent acknowledgement.

"We should give it to Jacob and Hank," he coaxed softly. A crestfallen look replaced her smile, and he regretted that, but this beast would already be at Indigo's cabin if Angelique had not been present when Jack brought it.

"They are better suited to give it the attention it needs," he continued, he hoped convincingly. "Soon you'll have a real baby to care for, and this puppy will turn into a flea-bitten mongrel that drags garbage under the porch."

Damn. She wasn't saying anything.

"They are not cute when grown." He hoped she wasn't hearing the growing desperation in his voice, but he wasn't about to have a dog in his house. It was going to be a hell of a lot easier to talk her out of it now than after she'd grown attached to it.

Biting her bottom lip, she watched the pup struggling to get out of the tub. "I suppose."

"He'll still be here," Mathias added quickly, "but you won't have to worry with him."

"But Charlotte will."

Charlotte had the sense to keep the thing in the yard.

Amid the wind, the dogs, and the pounding rain, he heard a horse neigh. Forgetting the puppy, Mathias turned to the window, its panes sparkling against the night. Lightning flashed and the meager, muddy yard and half-grown corn stalks flickered in an eerie, yellow light. He spun and bounded through the house to the back door. Booted feet were pounding up the steps before he touched the latch, and when he yanked the door open, Indigo stood there, drenched and wiping water from his eyes.

"Something's after the horses," he hollered at Mathias, then turned to go.

"Wait!" Mathias reached for the long rifle above the door and tossed it to Indigo, then pushing his pistol inside his pants waist, he reached for a second rifle and powder horn. He spun in search of Angelique. She stood, pale and bright-eyed, behind him, and he pecked her on the lips.

*A*gain the storm lit the sky, and she glimpsed Mathias on the muddy ground, running to catch Indigo.

Darkness and shuddering thunder followed. The wind-driven rain left her damp and cold, and she shut the door. For a long minute she stood against it, listening to the house dance in the wind. Shortly after, she went from room to room opening doors and lighting candles. If she had to make more candles she might not have enough tallow to last until the spring slaughter.

The storm lulled, and she calmed, then faltered at the disconcerting creak of a floorboard. Wiping her sweating palms on her skirt, she barred the front and back doors and braced the windows.

A rifle exploded in the night, the sound muffled by wind and rain. Then another. A man shouted. Mathias, perhaps, but maybe Indigo or even Ben, though she hoped the older man was not out in this.

A dog howled, another yelped. Elusive and lonely cries carried on the wind.

Stiff as death, she sat in the wing chair and strained to hold a nightmare at bay. In her lap, the snapping puppy attempted to play.

The rain lessened, and the thunder grew more distant. The dog curled in her lap and slept. Angelique tried to stroke it, but unable to prevent her fingers from shaking, she balled them into a tight fist and gave up. Mathias would be back soon. She didn't want him to find her like this.

Quiet reigned, and her breathing steadied. She should unbar the back door and blow out some candles. Mathias need never know how close she'd come to breaking down. Placing one hand under the puppy's chest, she grasped the chair arm with her other one and leaned forward to pull herself up.

An unearthly yowl tore through the strange quiet. Halfway up, she froze, her equilibrium shredded and her fingers clinging like claws to the upholstered arm of the chair. Angelique turned toward the horrific sound, and in front of her, the window exploded in a shower of splintering wood and glass. She smashed the frantic puppy against her breast and fell back in the chair.

A large limb stretched from the desk to the shattered window, where its bare branches disappeared beyond the glassless hole overlooking the front porch.

The ledger, covered with glass and wood, lay open on the desk, the end of the severed limb dripping water on its meticulous pages. Pressing her free hand over her hammering heart, Angelique rose, puppy in one hand, and took a step toward the wreckage strewn across Mathias' desk. An accident, nothing more.

The dog squirmed, and she set him on the floor. A cool, damp breeze sighed over her body, and she breathed in to savor the promise of rain-washed air.

The stench of death and decay filled her nostrils, and she backed away from the window. The puppy was barking shrilly, and she wanted to scream at it to be quiet.

But she didn't make a peep. Just beyond the light, something evil watched her.

Chapter Thirty-one

Angelique lunged for the back door. Outside, Mathias was shouting her name and pounding for entry. She placed her palms against the brace, then whimpered when her hands slipped and she scrapped her skin on the rough wood. On the next try, she planted her hands firmly on the underside of the crossbar and pushed up.

The door flew open, and she stumbled back, avoiding it. Mathias caught her arm and swung her around, checking her, it appeared, from head to foot. The fear in his eyes dissipated to relief, then transformed into anger.

"Why was the door—"

"It's in the front," she said.

"What?"

Good Lord, she wasn't going to start this cycle again. She threw herself against him and locked her arms around his waist, and he held her while the puppy bounced at their feet.

Indigo helped him drag the limb from the room, and they closed the protective outside shutters over the hole where the glass-paned window had been. Ben braced it on the inside.

"No sooner you get all these glass windows finished, Mathias, than you have to start again," he said. "Waste of money, I think."

"The work done in Bruinsburg is mighty fine...and cheap. I've been thinking about putting sash windows in your cabin."

Ben chuckled. "Not as cheap as leavin' be. Mosquito nets fine with me."

"They don't keep you warm in the winter."

"I close the shutters."

Mathias grinned. "Then you can't see out."

"If I'm wantin' to see out, I'll go out."

Angelique completed removing debris from the desk. She appeared perfectly calm, a far cry from the near hysteria that had greeted him when he'd finally gotten in the door. In the back room, the puppy, trapped in its washtub, yelped.

"The ledger is ruined," Angelique said, when Mathias stepped up close to her. "I'll need to recopy several pages."

"I'll look at them later and see."

Indigo headed for the door. The slower moving Ben followed. "I'll check for the horses one more time," Indigo said.

"No," Mathias responded, turning to him, "take one of the rifles and you and Ben go on home. I don't want anyone out in the dark with that rogue beast about. We'll find the horses tomorrow."

Indigo nodded and pulled the door shut behind him. After a moment, Mathias heard them leave through the back door.

"The horses are out?" Angelique asked.

"Dan broke down the stall." Mathias shook his head in agitation, and fear, which he didn't disclose to her. He prayed he'd get Dan back alive. Damn few good horses in these parts, and he had one of them, purchased from Gayoso himself.

"Something else to be fixed tomorrow." He nodded toward the window. "Won't be getting that done tomorrow, though. First I've got to order a new one. The entire window has to be replaced."

He sat and started removing his boots. They had some mud on them, but most had washed off in the rain. Angelique stepped over to help him, but he seized her and settled her in his lap. "I don't want you to help in your condition."

"I hardly think it would hurt me."

She didn't mention the baby. "I can do this. You've done enough today." He tugged her closer and said softly, "What happened here tonight?"

He felt her tense subtly and foiled her attempt to escape his lap.

"I need to check the puppy."

The hell she did, and he held her tight. "Tell me."

"The limb fell through the window and frightened me is all.

"What was after the horses?" she asked, changing the subject, and he decided to let her.

"The swamp cat. We thought it was gone until we heard the cry up here at the house."

She laid her head on his chest.

"You did hear its scream?" he asked softly.

"Oh yes, I heard the scream."

He sat quietly, rubbing her shoulders. He was tired, but comfortable, relaxed with her on his lap. Unfortunately, his thigh was going to sleep, and he wouldn't be able to leave her there much longer.

"Mathias?" she asked.

Her warm breath caressed the skin beneath his partly unlaced shirt, and he forced his heavy eyelids open. "Hmm?"

"What does a swamp cat smell like?"

"Mathias," Indigo said.

"I know. It didn't fall." He had examined the roof extending over the porch. There was no damage.

"This limb's from that oak tree yonder." Indigo pointed to the large tree fifty paces from the house. "Been a limb from it lying on the ground all winter. Thing's gone now."

Unless a freakish cyclone had picked it up and tossed the limb through the window, the deed had been deliberate. Such storms were known to do strange things, but in view of no other damage to the farm, he didn't believe that's what happened.

"Any sign of cat?"

Indigo shook his head. "Washed away."

Convenient. Always convenient.

Ben came around the side of the house, Jacob following. "Horses back," Ben said. "They all right."

Mathias gave silent thanks.

"But we're missin' three dogs this mornin'."

That was significant. "We need to find them, or what's left of them."

$\mathscr{M}$athias looked at Jack Summerfield, whose sun-weathered face displayed a concern Mathias only partially understood.

Jack again glanced over the remains of the dogs and shook his head. "Our big cat, maybe. The three might have attacked in a pack or in close succession, and it killed all three. I've got to agree with Ben, though, boy. One animal mutilated like this, yes, but three on the same night? Killing is one thing, this mess is another. I'm skeptical. There's something else at work here or we've got ourselves one big, bad cat."

Mathias caught his eye. "Yo was here earlier looking at the carcasses."

"Says it's the demon, don't she?"

"Back again and after Angelique." Mathias removed his hat from his head and slapped it against his thigh. "And something happened at the house last night," he said, turning to draw Indigo into the conversation, "something more than the limb and the howl."

"What?" Jack prodded.

Mathias opened his eyes wide. "She won't tell me."

"Why not?"

"She says nothing happened. She's afraid I won't believe her like before, and she doesn't want to face my damn indifference again."

"So you're thinking this...demon or ghost or whatever the hell it is, might really be back? The thing that begat you?"

"If one is to believe old tales," Mathias responded crisply.

Jack glanced at the thick forest surrounding them.

"I've never believed that."

"These are strange happenings going on here, Jack. I've got to believe something."

Jack drew in a long breath. "I'm with you, boy. There's truth in Yo's tale. Not the literal truth she implies, but some thread of truth."

"Her riddles."

"Hell yes, her riddles. Riddles only Elizabeth Boswell can decipher." Jack nodded toward the carcasses Indigo was burying. "There were mutilations back then, too."

Mathias stared at Jack for a moment, then he focused on Ben, who turned to him now with a furrowed brow.

"They sure was." The old man shook his head. "He's tellin' you true, boy, they sure was."

"Like this?" Mathias asked.

Ben frowned. "Steer mostly. One sow. Found her and her piglets slaughtered in the woods the mornin' of the same day that devil took off with your mama. But them killings was goin' on for weeks before that, then that was the end of it.

"Damn, damn, damn," Ben continued softly, almost to himself, "thought it was *cat*. All them years up till now, I thought it was cat. They was sign." Ben looked at Jack. "Sweet Jesus, they be somethin' else I done remember now."

"What?" Mathias asked.

"Most of them attacks, they happened in the rain, like now. Got so we know'd every time a storm blowed through we'd lose an animal. Then Young Miss was taken. We searched the swamp for weeks lookin' for her, but never found her, not till the thing was done with her and brought her home. Killin's had stopped, but by then no one noticed."

His own heart thumping, Mathias watched Ben's jaw clench.

"O Lawd, O Lawd. All them years ago, I 'sociated that beast with Satan hisself." Ben locked his gaze on Mathias. "Every time we found a print, it was the left hind paw of a big cat—big, even for a male, like this one now."

"You're thinking someone made it to look like a cat?"

"It makes sense," Jack said, "a ploy to throw us off track."

"Or a clue?"

Jack looked at him. "Or a clue. Yep, you could be right. A clue left for your grandmother. Damn it to hell. It all ties in." His gaze moved over Ben, then came back to rest on Mathias. "We thought whoever took your mama, took her north, maybe as far as the Chickasaw country. Nobody knows where he had her, but he brought her home to die and to make sure Elizabeth suffered, too."

"Why would it come for Angelique?"

Jack pursed his lips. "Yo says it's payment, an act of vengeance for some sin committed against Jean Larocque's son."

"That boy Jarrod," Ben interjected, "he was no good, and after Miss Elizabeth raised him like her own. Yo says Jarrod wanted De Leau as his birthright, but Miss Elizabeth weren't about to let nobody take De Leau from her. Her daddy, he built this place long before Larocque married Miss Elizabeth's mama." Ben nodded knowledgeably. "But the law might not agree, so s'posedly, Miss Elizabeth got rid of young Jarrod. He was no good anyway, Jack."

Jack's head bobbed in assent. "Yeah, and I've also heard Elizabeth conjured up that devil to kill Jarrod and offered the thing her virgin daughter in payment."

Mathias made a sibilant sound. "That's one of several versions told by her enemies. My grandmother loved Julianna."

"She did," Jack said, squeezing Mathias' shoulder. "Perhaps the thing exacted its own payment. But something happened that's left a lot of unanswered questions, and you without a mother or a father. Now whatever evil Elizabeth conjured up all those years ago is coming home to roost."

Angelique was sleeping when he returned to the house, and Charlotte, who he'd asked to keep close and check on her, told him she'd had a difficult morning. "The sickness is bad for her now, Mathias, but it will pass."

Briefly, he stood in the door to their bedroom and watched her sleep. She'd been right all along, and now she was so worried he'd think her mad, she wouldn't confide what terrified her last night.

Lit candle in hand, he climbed into the attic and walked to the trunk containing his mother's belongings. From it, he pulled an old English trading blanket adorned with Indian symbols.

Solemnly he rubbed his hand over it before uncovering the necklace. Four lion claws, pierced at one end and strung on sinew, each claw separated by a series of polished stones. He balled it tightly in his fist before slipping it inside the waist of his pants.

Chapter Thirty-two

"Damn Yo's soul," Bess whispered. She looked up from the claw necklace he'd laid on her desk. "It was around your mother's neck when he brought her back." Bess closed her hand around her treasured silver timepiece, its chain looping between her fingers so tightly it creased her skin, and Mathias grimaced. "She gave you the blanket, too?"

He nodded.

"I told her to destroy them the morning Julianna came home. I never wanted to see them again. I didn't want anyone else to see them either. They are symbols of Julianna's torture and death.

"The markings on the blanket are Chickasaw. That's why some believed he took her far to the north." With eyes of cold steel, Bess looked at him. "Why in God's name did Yo keep them? Did she tell you?"

"She gave them to me when you gave me charge of De Leau. She said you told her to destroy them, but she thought they might be of use someday, so she didn't."

"She told you not to confide in me?"

"No, Bess. She didn't care if you knew what she'd done. You know that. I saw no point in speaking of it. It would have only increased ill feelings between you. But now," he said, straightening before her, "I have to know."

"Why?"

"Because someone, or something, is haunting De Leau, and I believe Angelique is in danger."

No part of her visage changed, and Mathias bridled.

263

"I must know the truth. If you care anything for Angelique...or me, it's time to explain what's happening and why."

She relaxed her stranglehold on the watch, absently studying its enameled cover while she brushed her thumb over it. "Mathias," she said softly, "I have hardened myself to maudlin displays of emotion. My few moments of weakness have cost me dearly. Strength has always gained me much more. I will not be judged or coerced."

"I don't want to judge you. I simply want the truth."

"Yo judges me and does her best to make sure you do, too. The truth is that my alleged blood debt is her curse on me."

He sighed heavily. "Well, her 'curse' threatens Angelique."

"According to that hateful old witch, Julianna's death was the price twenty-seven years ago. Why should Angelique be in danger now?"

"Apparently your crime was a significant one."

"My crime was one of omission, Mathias. In Yo's mind, the curse will not end until either I am dead or the demon is dead." She shoved the timepiece away from her and rose. "The demon *is* dead, and Yo is obsessed with a non-existent ghost."

Bess' riddles were as frustrating as Yo's.

"Why have you tolerated her all these years? What does she have on you, Bess? She's only a slave."

She raised a brow. "Listen to yourself, Mathias. Only a slave? And I'm Joan of Arc. Whatever hoax Yo is creating at De Leau is designed to make me feel guilty."

'Hoax,' hell. He straightened before her. "Tell me this, *Grand-mère*, do you think pretending not to care will lessen the pain of loss when it comes? Do you know the answer already, or am I the first you refused to love...and is Angelique the second? If you don't know, you may know soon."

Her jaw tightened, but her eyes softened in quick succession. "What has happened?"

He breathed easier upon her response. He'd always known there were chinks in her armor.

"First, we can assume everything Angelique said that she

heard and saw since coming to De Leau, she really did see and hear. I've lost eleven head of cattle since we wed, maybe two of those were to Indians. Last night something spooked my horses and killed three of my dogs. They were mutilated. We've found sign, the left hind paw print of a cougar. I'm now told that twenty-eight years ago there was a similar problem with what everyone thought was a swamp cat, shortly before my mother was taken. Do you recall it?"

His grandmother stared through him. "Yes," she said slowly, "I do recall that."

"There was sign then, also."

She blinked, then met his eyes.

"The left hind paw of a cougar." He said the words slowly, waiting for them to sink in. "Ben remembers clearly, because at the time the cat had wreaked such havoc on the farm he associated that left print with the devil."

Bess turned and walked to the window overlooking her garden.

"There is significance to the necklace, Grandmother?"

"It was meant for me."

"What is it?"

She shook her head. "There is nothing to associate Angelique to that necklace, Mathias." Slowly she walked back to her desk and reached for the necklace, but Mathias picked it up. On impulse, he crushed it in his fist. He was angry, and he was scared. Scared for Angelique and, he realized, scared of the dark secrets his grandmother was hiding. In all his life, he had never been at odds with the woman who stood before him, never confronted her over anything of real import. Not until now, and that frightened him most of all.

"The claws on the necklace came from a cat's left hind paw didn't they?"

"That, Grandson, I can tell you in all honesty, I do not know, but I am sure they came from a cougar."

It didn't matter. He knew the answer to his question though he couldn't prove it. He swallowed the frustration and the bitterness. "I love Angelique. I'm not going to let anything happen to her. Not for anything...or anyone."

He caught remorse in his grandmother's eyes, but quickly she disguised it. "That is what I hoped for," she said, and retook her seat. "In spite of what you think, we are not at odds here. Some things are best left in the past, and I have to believe this is Yo's doing."

"Yo did not carry a forty pound oak limb fifty yards up on my front porch and crash it through a window in a storm, Bess." Carefully he held out his fist. She opened her palm, and he let the claw necklace fall into it. "And the past only stays in the past if it is truly dead. Are you sure this is the case?"

He turned on his heel to go.

"Mathias..."

His hand on the doorknob, he looked back at her.

"On the off chance anything should happen, and she is taken, follow De Leau's creek north to where the swamp begins. From there he will leave the bog and head due north. Catch him before he gets that far."

$\mathcal{I}$t was early evening when he got home, but still daylight. Angelique turned to him when he entered the parlor, and he saw the tension drain from her face. Charlotte, whom she'd been teaching to sew this past week, sat with her. Standing, Charlotte reached for the fabric pieces, but Angelique stayed her hand. "Leave it here. There's nothing more you can do until we've turned the collar. I'll show you how to do that tomorrow."

Charlotte rose and cast Mathias a smile as she started for the door. "First thing Jacob gonna do is rip a hole in that fancy shirt, just you wait."

"He'll be proud of it."

"Oh yes, he will," she said, disappearing into the hallway, "but won't keep him from tearin' it up."

"I napped the morning away," Angelique said, setting the half-finished shirt aside. "Charlotte told me you had gone to Natchez to see Aunt Elizabeth."

He nodded. She wanted him to elaborate, he knew, and when he didn't, she said, "I saved you dinner. It's in the dining room. I'm sorry I didn't wait, but I was getting hungry and that makes me ill."

He kissed her, silencing her nervous rambling. "I'll eat in a bit. Now I need you to tell me what else happened last night."

"Nothing, Mathias—"

Gently he put his index finger on her lips. "The storm didn't send a limb through the window, Angelique. Of that, I have no doubt. Something else did it. Tell me what happened."

She searched his eyes.

"I will not think you mad, I never did. I knew you were scared, and I resented your doubts. Now I know you had good reason. And please," he emphasized, "tell me everything. I'm having trouble today with both the women I love not trusting me."

Chapter Thirty-three

"The thing was on the front porch, outside the busted window. Angelique was on the other side. Indigo and I heard the yowl and started to the house. I couldn't get in because she barred the door when I left." Mathias shook his head and took a seat opposite Jack in the cookhouse. "It was so close it could have come through that window and taken her and left me standing stupidly at the back door."

Jack pursed his lips. "It—damn you, you've got me saying it, and *it* makes my skin crawl. *He* might not have wanted to take her then. Maybe he's trying to frighten her."

Indigo stepped over and poured corn mash in Mathias' and Jack's coffees before adding some to his own. Mathias coughed.

"I'm not so sure anymore it is a 'he,' Jack. She said whatever it was smelled like something dead. The stench was strong. She's been saying the same thing for months." Mathias took a swallow of the bitter coffee and marked the liquid's burning descent down his throat. "I thought it was in her head. What's he waiting for? Why this frightful game?"

"Because he's a sadistic bastard. We know whoever took your mother inflicted physical cruelty on her. We must assume this is the same person."

Mathias felt his gut tighten. Throughout his life, he'd experienced emotional bouts with the unknown entity reputed to be his sire, but for the most part, his life secure here at De Leau, he'd steeled himself to the whispers of outsiders and locked his mother's violator deep inside his mind. Now he had to come face to face with the truth.

268

"A short time back," he said to Jack, "Yo told me he was coming soon. She said to check my dates."

"Your mother was taken at the beginning of October."

It was late May. "That's a ways off."

"Your birthday was two days ago, when the dogs were killed."

Mathias nodded.

Jack shrugged. "Maybe he did intend on taking her that night, but your coming when you did resulted in failure."

"If it's a symbolic date, do you think he'll keep trying, or will he wait until next year?"

Jack shook his head, then finished his fortified coffee. "I couldn't begin to guess at that. Where is she now?"

"She's inside, dividing her time between throwing up and sewing with Charlotte."

"She knows there's a threat?"

Mathias sighed heavily. "She and Yo are the two people who have always known."

"Someone needs to be with her all the time."

"I need to take her to Natchez, but she refuses to go."

"That might work," Jack said, holding up his cup and nodding for Indigo to pour in straight whiskey, "and it might not. It all goes back to Elizabeth. Whoever is after Angelique will know to find her with your grandmother. What are you going to do, leave the district entirely?" Jack, mouth drawn in a tight line, leaned across the table toward him. "No, boy, I think it's time we ended this once and for all."

$\mathcal{B}$ad mornings gave way to good afternoons, but her nights varied. Consciously, Angelique rubbed her belly. Bounty told her the acid stomach, which more and more tortured her days, was the result of what she ate, but she associated her misery more with venomous hate than pregnancy.

For days, Mathias had not come in for the noon meal. Neither had Indigo, nor Ethan. Instead, they searched the woods for a phantom. She spent that time sleeping, rising for the second time each day in the early afternoon to conduct Jacob's lesson.

But Mathias was always home before dark. They ate alone in the dining room. She loved being mistress of their home, preparing a table where they could sit and talk. Their conversations had been subdued over the past several days, ever since the night the tree limb came through the window.

But despite his reluctance to discuss in detail the results of the fruitless search, Mathias seemed pleased to be lord of their humble manor. After supper he helped clear the table, and at the cookhouse he routinely took her hand, and they would walk over small portions of the fields in the waning afternoon sun. They did not venture far from the house, and Mathias had her safely inside, doors barred, before dark.

He stirred at her touch on his shoulder.

"You've had another dream?" he asked quietly, taking her hand and drawing her in front of him.

"No," she said and sat in his lap. "I woke and you weren't there."

He placed his arm around her waist and rested his head against the back of his chair. "I'm never far."

"I knew where you were. Like last night and the night before."

"I'm not sleeping well."

"I know. I'm sorry for your nightmares, too."

He snorted softly. "No nightmares. I worry for you."

She studied his face a moment. "I know you do, but that's not what steals you from my bed at night."

"And what does?"

She smiled sadly before kissing him on the cheek. "The whoreson who raped your mother and sired you."

His words, slightly altered.

"The one you never wanted to know but now, because of me, you must."

He squeezed her. "What is happening, he's bringing on us. Not you."

Angelique settled her head against his throat. "But the fact remains, an old wound has been reopened and it causes you pain."

Her silky curls tickled his chin, and he kissed her head. "No, Angelique, not reopened. It's an old, festering wound and, truth is, it's past time to clean it out."

She snuggled closer. "You are a wonderful man, Mathias, and no matter what we find out, I love you, and I always will."

"*He*'s not around here, I'm telling you. He comes and he goes—probably a great distance. He covers his tracks with rain and with the swamp, and he stays away for days, even weeks, so we can't track him." Jack sat back on his heels and cursed.

Mathias threw a clump of dirt to the ground. "I wonder if that thought you had about my birthday was correct. He might not return for a year."

"Where does he go, Mathias? Where has the bastard been for the past twenty-seven years?"

"He'd keep a safe distance from De Leau, I reckon," Indigo broke in, "but sometimes he comes back to check on things."

Jack looked up at him. "Do you know that for a fact?"

"No, I don't, but it makes sense. Times over the years when stock disappears and no sign left tellin' what wild beast or injun done it. Dogs barkin' in the night." Indigo looked tentatively around the thick forest. "Owls hooting, warning of danger."

"The sense of being watched when no one is there," Mathias joined in. "I think Indigo is probably right. Whoever this person is, he's familiar with De Leau."

"I'll not disagree with either of you on that count." Jack said. "I've always said that."

"Trouble is..." Indigo continued, "all them it could be, they be dead."

Chapter Thirty-four

The sun was up, and so was Mathias. He'd been up for over two hours with Angelique. She'd been sick so often he was getting scared. A soft knock sounded on the back door, and he opened it to find Yo. She handed him a warm cup containing a dark liquid. "Tea, for Angelique."

Mathias motioned her in. She refused, but he insisted. Yo's eyes widened. "Old Yo is no longer forbidden?"

Forbidden? Damn him. How had he dared keep her out of the home that in reality had been hers through four generations? "Never 'forbidden.' I apologize, you old witch. I didn't want you frightening her. Now we're all scared."

She straightened her crooked back and held her head high. "It was not I who frightened you, Mathias."

"No, you were right. The truth frightens me."

Angelique was on the bedroom floor, stretched awkwardly on her side and supported by her hands. Her head was over the slop jar. Mathias knelt beside her.

"You have a visitor," he said softly.

She looked at him, her face pale, and he pushed her hair out of her eyes. She looked as if she were going to cry. "No, Mathias, send whoever it is away."

"She's here," he said, helping her sit up and handing her a linen rag to wipe her mouth. Yo squatted near Angelique and handed her the tea.

"It will help to settle your stomach. Later you must eat."

"I fear I'll throw it up."

"Try. I left more tea with Bounty. It will work for you."

272

"I think I'm going to die," Angelique managed to get out.

"Your body wants this child. It tells you so with the sickness." Mathias reached for Angelique's arm.

"No. If I stand, I'll get sick again." She gave Yo a wan smile. "Tea leaves of the Choctaw Lily?"

Yo snorted and rose. "Chamomile tea. Fronds of the Choctaw Lily will make you mad."

"Kill her, you mean?"

Yo graced Mathias with a rare smile. "No, 'mad.' Generation after generation, I tell the children here at De Leau it will kill them"—she tapped a bony finger against her temple—"because I know children. If I tell them it is poison, they will let it be. But if I tell them it will give them frightening visions and transport them to strange places, they will eat it just to see, and it will kill them anyway."

Mathias stared at Yo, then glanced at Angelique, who was studying him with eyes wide. She choked down a sob.

"A-at the pool...." Suddenly she covered her mouth with her hand, and for a moment, he was certain she was going to be sick again.

"You put a frond in your mouth," he finished for her.

"And you pulled it out."

"I thought I got it out before you bit into it."

"No, it was bitter." She laughed giddily before breaking down into tears. Without a doubt, Yo thought the two of them really were mad.

Angelique lovingly stroked her belly and smiled while tears ran down her face. "It was the plant."

Well, he'd always known the only demon there that day had been him, unless one were to count the beautiful Angelique. She threw her arms around his shoulders, and he almost toppled over. Steadying himself, he kissed her cheek.

"The tea, then food, remember."

He looked up at the somber Yo.

Angelique sat back and wiped her tears. "Yes, Yo, thank you."

--·--

Mathias followed Yo onto the back porch. When the door shut behind them, she turned. "You have talked to Elizabeth?"

He nodded.

"She told you nothing?"

"She said the past should remain in the past. She doesn't believe Angelique is in danger."

"You know that she is, don't you?"

"I believe she's in danger."

Yo studied him. "Many years ago, I told Elizabeth to end it, and if she did not, the blood price would be exacted."

"Tell me what it is?"

"I cannot."

He wanted to shake her, but didn't. With the exception of his and Rachel's sibling-like spats when they'd been small, he'd never laid a hand in anger on any slave or servant, and he never would.

"Why do you protect her, hating her as you do?"

"I do not hate her." Yo held her head up proudly. "And I protect her because it is my duty."

"Your duty?"

A second rare smile, and for the life of him, Yo looked younger than he ever remembered seeing her. An honest smile, though fleeting, that came from the heart.

"I loved Pierre and Marie Deschesne. The French brought me to Louisiana from Africa. Senegal, Master Pierre told me later. Told me I should always remember where I came from. I think I was in my eighth year.

"I was the property of the Mississippi Company. The master, he come to New Orleans to buy two men to help him in the fields. He didn't have coin to buy a third. I'll never forget the day he come. He touched my head and spoke to me so soft. I didn't understand what he said, but I could tell by his voice and the way he talked to the dealer that he was concerned for me. Few children were brung here. I came with my mother. She died of fever days after we come up the river.

"Master Pierre, he give up one of his hands so as not to leave me behind, and he brought me to De Leau to help Miss Marie. She was heavy with Elizabeth when I came. Miss Marie she was so pleased when she saw me." Yo laughed. "I didn't understand a word she said either, but I knew by her smile she was glad I come.

"Life was hard at De Leau, but good we were far from the fort. Master Pierre was a kind man, and he had friends among the Choctaw. One warned him when Rosalie was attacked. That one hand run off, but the Choctaw took the rest of us in until the French destroyed the Natchez."

Mathias watched her bottom lip tremble.

"Master and Miss Marie treat me like I am part of them. Elizabeth was my little sister, same with Véronique."

"And grandmother didn't—"

"That is not what divides us, Mathias. Elizabeth failed to do what she had to, and she wouldn't let me. She and those she loved paid the price." Yo's old lips tightened. "And those I loved."

A sinewy tenseness invaded his arms and legs, and he swallowed in a hopeless attempt to wet his dry throat. He was on the brink of discovering the secret that had hung over him like a cloud his entire life.

"What did she not do, Yo?"

She shook her head, and his hopes dissipated like cold water flicked on a hot griddle. "No one but Elizabeth can make things right. The demon will not rest until one or the other is dead."

"And what if she doesn't?" he asked, seething with anger he didn't try to conceal.

As if she could see something out there he could not, Yo gazed over De Leau, finally resting her eyes on the woods harboring the deep-water pool. "He comes now," she whispered to herself, then straightened and turned to Mathias. "But she will. This time I will see to it!"

Chapter Thirty-five

The tea, she said, made her better, and she actually was able to keep breakfast down. But Mathias believed nothing had done more to improve Angelique's spirits than the clarification of that cold January day. She'd suffer hell on earth, she told him later, for his baby growing in her womb. But though Yo's words had done much to relieve Angelique's anxiety, the black witch's words to him on the back porch had increased his, and he chose to work in the recently girdled woods close to the house instead of venturing into the swamp for another futile search.

At noon he found Angelique, Rachel, and Charlotte on the shaded western end of the porch with an unfinished quilt. Seeing them sitting together, the quilt draped over their legs, he felt twice as hot despite the fact he'd dunked his head into a bucket of spring water. The first week of June was half gone and unofficial summer had swathed the Natchez District in a blanket of insufferable misery.

He rested inside during the hottest part of the day, content listening to Angelique give Jacob his lessons. In the afternoon, he asked Ethan to relieve him near the house and returned to the newground with Ben and Indigo. He came in at suppertime to find food on the table and his young wife glowing and in the best of spirits, vastly improved from this morning.

They retired early, the day passing without a hitch. Yo's ominous warning at the start of the day had proved another aggravating riddle.

"$\mathcal{K}$illed twelve piglets with her. No reason but meanness." Bounty turned to block Jacob's access to the slaughtered farrow. "Git, boy, and don't you come back."

Mathias pulled his booted foot from where it had sunk into the muddy ground. It was first light, and he'd seen enough of the carnage to know what he had to do. "Get Jack over here for me," he said to Ben. His eyes turned to Ethan and finally came to rest on Indigo. "The bastard's here, and this time we're going to find him. Ethan," he said, "I want you to stay at the house with the women. Don't worry about the fields." He caught Ben's eye once again. "Indigo and I will head up the creek. You and Jack join us as soon as you can."

$\mathcal{H}$er nausea returned this morning, but nothing like the day before. She heard Mathias enter the back door and anticipated every footfall until he stuck his head into their bedroom. Anxiety hovered around his eyes and tensed his mouth. She was glad to be up and dressed, not wanting to add to his worry.

"You're up early."

"I heard Indigo come for you before sunup. What's wrong?"

"Someone killed a sow and her new litter during the night." She held her breath.

"He's back, Angelique. We're going to look for him. Ethan will stay at the house. Ben and Indigo are excellent trackers. I want them with me."

"And Jack?"

"Ben's already left to get him." He took a step into the room. "I want you to stay inside until I get back."

She took a step toward him, and quickly he closed the distance between them to take her in his arms and crush her to him. "I love you."

"I love—"

He silenced her with a deep kiss. "I'll be back."

He was gone, disappearing out the door while she fought the urge to call him back. With a shaky hand, she wiped sweat off her forehead and sat heavily on the bed.

***

$\mathcal{D}$e Leau basked in the golden hue of early morning sun when Jack Summerfield and Ben rode back through. Jack stopped in the house to check her, assuring her he would meet up with Mathias within the hour. He was taking his four best hunting dogs with him, as well as his older son. "With a relatively fresh track, Angelique, we'll catch this thing by nightfall."

$\mathcal{E}$lizabeth rose before dawn, and was glad to be dressed—the assertive knock this early on her front door meant an emergency best not met in nightclothes. Steeling herself, she pulled the door open.

Yo stood before her, wizened, stooped...short. She looked none the worse for wear, though Elizabeth knew without asking she'd walked all night.

"What has happened?"

"He will come for Angelique today."

Relaxing, Elizabeth laughed. "He hadn't come before you left?" she quipped, stepping aside to allow Yo's entrance. "You made a long trip for a far-fetched guess."

"I know him well, Elizabeth. I do not guess."

"That's right." With a swirl of skirts, Elizabeth turned from Yo. "You create fiction from fact."

She stepped to the dining room door and called for Baby. When the young woman responded, she instructed her to bring Yo coffee, then prepare breakfast.

"Come in here and sit down, damn you. You're too old for this foolishness."

Yo narrowed her eyes, but did as Elizabeth said. "What else is an old woman to do? Sit and die?"

"She certainly doesn't need to make dangerous treks through swamp and forest in the dead of night."

"I could make the trip blind."

"Obviously," Elizabeth said dryly. She pulled out a chair for herself. "Now what is this about my *démon* coming for Angelique today? I've certainly given him no such instructions."

"Don't mock me. You surrendered control and freed him to take his endless vengeance."

Elizabeth glared at Yo. "Yes, I forfeited control, and I paid for my mistake—double I paid for it. But I made things right. He is dead."

Yo leaned forward, bringing her face close to Elizabeth's. "*S'il est mort, alors les portes de l'enfer ne pourraient pas le tenir, petite soeur.*" (If he is dead, then the gates of hell cannot hold him, little sister).

"There is no ghost, demonic or other."

"He is alive, and he haunts you still."

"The only thing haunting me is you."

Yo stood as Baby placed her coffee in front of her, and she pointed a crooked finger at Elizabeth. "You never saw his body. He stalks Angelique while we talk here at your table. He will take her as he took Julianna, and he will do so to hurt you and Veronique."

"Baby, go!" Elizabeth watched the girl leave the room, then said bitterly, "Why do you think he comes for Angelique today?"

"Look at the date, *soeur.*"

"It is the fifth of June."

"What date did your mother die?"

Elizabeth frowned. "On the eighth."

Yo stared, then raised her eyebrows, silently coaxing Elizabeth to continue. And Elizabeth thought.

Suddenly her heart slammed against her chest, and inside her dress pocket, her hand grasped the timepiece. "Three days after...."

With a harsh curse, she rose and marched to the door leading to the breezeway connecting the house to the kitchen. Baby fell through when she opened it.

"Find Wee Ben," Elizabeth said, unperturbed by the girl's eavesdropping. "Tell him we need three horses from the livery. He'll go with Yo and me to De Leau. We leave as soon as he gets back."

"Yes'm."

"Hurry!"

Chapter Thirty-six

Charlotte brought her breakfast and returned later for the dirty dishes. Ethan sat on the back porch, sharpening hoes. The house was cool and quiet. Angelique dusted the dining room, then sat in the wing chair and read *Don Quixote*. She couldn't keep her mind on the book.

Occasionally, she would hear Rachel out back with Ethan, or a shout between Ethan and someone at the cookhouse. They remained close this morning, and that comforted her.

There was a quiet time, not long, when she dozed. The front room was relatively dark with the window shutters still closed. She woke disoriented and headachy and, giving up on reading, she leaned over and blew out the lamp. Everything was still, an eerie prelude to a movement on the front porch. As she eased out of the chair, she heard the back door open.

"Miss Angelique?" Apprehension tinged Ethan's voice.

Holding her growing alarm in check, she moved into the entry. "What's wrong?"

He closed the door behind him and looked around. "I don't know. I smelled something outside. It smelled like something...."

Dead. She smelled it too. Immediately she spun around. The front door was secured. "Ethan," she whispered, "bar the back door." But he was already in the dining room, checking the house. She covered the distance to the rear exit and barred it herself.

"I heard something out front," she told him quietly, all the while staying close to his side. She was afraid and, she realized, so was he.

He nodded and walked down the hall to the front bedroom,

brightly lit by sunshine. The room, with its neat bed covered by a colorful quilt and pillows, had a calming effect. Ethan looked out the front window onto the porch, then turned calmly to the side window next to the fireplace. Angelique watched him squat to look under the bed. Only an instant passed.

A shadow blocked out the sunlight. Angelique's gaze jerked to the window, and she choked out a garbled warning to Ethan as the window caved in and a hideous creature threw itself on top of the unsuspecting man on the floor.

The smell of dead flesh engulfed the room. Nausea assailed her. Terrified, she turned to run, but tripped over the empty slop jar. Pushing herself up, she looked across the bed to see the foul thing rise, dragging Ethan to his feet at the same time. With a fierce thrust and accompanying grunt, it slammed Ethan against the wall. Ethan groaned from the impact, then slid down the wall to the floor. Angelique scrambled to her feet and the monstrous being cocked its head at the sound she made. Shadowed by a crude cape of dark fur extending from the top of its head to its feet, the unseen face turned to her.

"Run, Miss Angelique!" Ethan cried, and then she was in the foyer, running toward the barred back door. Behind her, she heard heavy breathing and a lumbering gait, then scurrying followed by the thud of a falling body. Sweet Jesus, she would never get the door unbarred in time. Something grabbed her foot, unbalancing her, and she tumbled to the floor.

Pain pierced her shoulder when she hit, and she sucked in a compensating breath. Looking back, she saw Ethan had managed to knock the creature to the ground. It had, however, snagged her foot. She kicked out and freed herself. Ethan struggled clumsily to his feet and lunged on top of the monster. At the same time, Angelique scrambled to the door. Behind her the fight continued.

She had the bar lifted and was pushing up the latch when she heard Ethan's scream. Her fingers curling around the edge of the door to pull it open, Angelique twisted her head in time to see him stumble back. His hand, blood seeping between his fingers, covered his lower abdomen. Waving a knife, the creature closed in on him.

Outside, she could hear the shouts of the other women. Help was on its way, and that gave her courage. Driven by desperation and renewed hope, Angelique all but fell into the dining room and grabbed a half-filled bottle of wine. Thus armed, she launched herself down the wide-open hall and, reaching high, brought the bludgeon down as hard and as close as she could to what she thought was the creature's head. The monster turned with a roar, and the stench of death enveloped her as she stared at a formless shadow beneath the cape.

She stepped back. In the yard, Rachel cried Ethan's name, and Bounty screamed for Charlotte to hurry. Their feet were pounding up the steps. Dry-mouthed, Angelique started turning...

Her head exploded with bright light.

With mounting alarm, Mathias watched the dogs.

"The trail doubles back," Mark Summerfield said.

Dry-mouthed, Mathias nodded. The fact they had a trail at all told the tale. Why had he not realized it from the start? "He planned this carefully," he called to Jack.

"Yep, he laid this out last night or this morning."

Mathias made a beeline for his mount. "Forget the trail," he hollered to Indigo, still with the dogs. "We need to get back to De Leau, fast!"

Horses stood at the back of the house. Mathias arrived ahead of the others, despite Jack's distant cries for him to wait. He hit the ground running, and Jason Summerfield, Jack's younger son, met him on the porch before he could get inside.

"It took her about two hours ago," the eighteen-year-old said, following Mathias through the door.

He refused to believe the boy's words and, heart pounding, picked up his pace, walking with long, hurried strides down the wide hall to their bedroom. Outside the door, Charlotte stood, holding Katherine Suzanne. Giving her shaken visage but a cursory glance, Mathias entered the room.

His heart stopped. Ethan lay on the bed with a blood-soaked

cloth next to him and a gaping hole in his torso above the waist. Rachel sat beside him, her eyes red and swollen. Martha Summerfield was rising from a chair next to the bed, a bowl of bloody water in her hands and worry in her eyes.

Jack rushed in behind him.

"Thank God you're here," Martha said, "I was about to send Jason looking for you."

Sucking air into his aching chest, Mathias assessed the room, the smashed window, the broken furniture—his missing wife.

"It come 'bout an hour after Mister Jack and Ben rode back through," Bounty said.

"He was waiting." Jack stepped next to Martha and looked at Ethan's wound. "Knife," he stated.

"Rachel and me at the cookhouse," Bounty said. "Rachel'd just left Ethan. They was sittin' on the back porch, talkin'. Nothin' wrong, Mathias, nothin'."

"Short while after Rachel come back in, we heard a scream. We come as fast as we could, hollerin' for Charlotte. She was in the pea patch. Miss Angelique, she got the door open. The thing was in the house, already hurt Ethan." Stone-faced, Bounty blinked. "I come in, Miss Angelique had a wine bottle in her hand." She pointed to it on the floor in the hall, then shook her head. "Hit the thing in the back. Did no good 'cept maybe to save Ethan. It turned on her and hit her. Knocked her out. Slammed me against the wall."

"I think Bounty's arm is broken," Martha put in.

"Threw Miss Angelique over its shoulder. Knocked Rachel down the steps. Went north into the woods."

Jack looked at Martha. "What are you doing here?"

"After you left this morning, I decided I'd bring the children and we'd stay here with Angelique. I thought there'd be safety in numbers. We've only just gotten here."

Mathias raked a hand through his hair. "God," he said aloud. Everyone looked to him. Gulping in a deep breath, he stepped closer to Ethan. A deep, six-inch-long gap reached from his navel to his right side. His intestines were visible. There had been bleeding, which now appeared to be under control. Mathias assumed he was asleep or unconscious.

"Jason," Mathias said, struggling to hold on to his sanity, "get to Natchez and bring the doctor." The boy nodded.

"Mathias?" Ethan whispered.

Mathias looked down at the wounded man. His eyes were open. "She'd have gotten out the door, but she come back to help me. It woulda killed me sure."

He squeezed Ethan's shoulder. "Thank you."

Numb, Mathias turned and gave Bounty a silent hug on his way out of the room. He had to find this thing before it hurt Angelique. Two hours. He could already be too late.

"She'd have never gotten away even if she'd made it out the door," Jack said running up behind him. "He'd have killed every person on this place and taken her anyway."

"I know." He caught Dan's reins and mounted.

Indigo emerged from around the corner of the house. "The dogs are confused, Mathias. There are several trails."

Beside him, Jack climbed into the saddle. "Every step pre-planned."

Mathias calmed himself. He had to start thinking clearly if he were to outsmart this thing and get Angelique back. "Old Bess said if anything happened, we should head up the creek until the big swamp began, then cut due north."

"That's the way we came, boy. We'd have passed them."

Mathias looked quickly north, then to Indigo. "See if you can find a trail across Jack's land. One that would intersect the creek farther north?"

Indigo nodded. Mathias watched Jack dismount and follow, taking charge of his dogs.

Moments later, Ben exited the house and mounted his own horse.

"How is Bounty?" Mathias asked.

"They all more upset 'bout Miss Angelique and Ethan than anythin'. All else can be made right."

Mathias stood in the stirrups and looked over the fields in the direction of Yo's cabin. He wondered why she wasn't here. He heard a shout and turned to see Jack beckoning to him from the edge of the woods. The dogs had a scent. With shaking hands, he reached down and grasped the reins of Jack's horse.

"Give me Indigo's mount, Ben. You and Mark stay with the women." He kicked Dan into a lope. Moments later the three mounted men headed into thick, virgin forest.

Chapter Thirty-seven

She was upside down, sick, and aching. Good Lord, she *ached* all over. Worst was her head.

Beneath her, the ground passed away at a dizzying pace. Her abductor was carrying her over his shoulder and he was moving fast.

The putrid scent of decay seeped through her skin and poisoned her insides. She gagged and clutched at his furred cape in a vain attempt to steady herself against his rough gait. Her efforts proved to no avail, and finally she vomited. He stopped, and she felt her body slip to one side, then continue to fall until she slammed into the ground. Pain ripped through her already injured shoulder, and for a moment she lay curled, eyes closed, in stunned silence.

A booted foot slipped under her ribcage and rolled her over. Cool, damp earth caressed her back, then nausea attacked in a violent wave, and she scrambled to all fours and wretched again. Eyes open now, she stared down at the sickening remains of her breakfast, the pungent smell of vomit drowning the stench of rotting flesh.

She raised a trembling fist to wipe puke and phlegm from her lips. Her captor seized the back of her dress, yanking her upright, then he gripped an arm and twisted it behind her. When she struggled, he grabbed her other arm, forced her to her stomach, and placed a hard knee in the small of her back.

She stopped her fight, and he lifted his knee and rolled her over, forcing her arms in front of her. She pushed with her feet, trying to see what lurked beneath the dark cape. He caught her

286

wrists in one of his hands and slapped her. She whimpered with the stinging blow. He struck her again, and she surrendered to oblivion.

Cold water splashed her face followed by not so gentle slaps. She had no idea how long she'd been unconscious or how far he'd brought her from home. When she tried to breathe, water stung her nostrils, and she twisted away from the water's source.

She swayed with the movement, and her aching wrists burned. A rough hand seized her chin and forced her mouth open. Whiskey scorched her throat. Spontaneously she jerked her head away, but was unable to break his grasp. Still she managed to spit out most of the liquid, then clamp her mouth shut. He inserted his thumb, prying her mouth open, and growled, "I want you drunk. I like 'em very drunk."

Angelique bit down on his intruding thumb. He howled, removed the injured digit, then calmly pushed her away.

She swung freely, and the pain shredding her wrists doubled. Forcing her eyes open, she saw that she hung from a single rope tied around a tree limb. The limb was not high, though still some distance above her head. She kicked out, trying to find support, but her feet didn't touch the ground. He pushed again, and again, she swung, the rope grinding her wrists together and flaying her skin. She wailed.

"Hurts, don't it?" he said in a guttural voice. "Once you're drunk, I'll cut you down." He moved toward her. She kicked out at him, and with a curse, he stepped around her, yanking at her hair. She tried to pull away, but his hold tightened, searing her scalp.

"Open your mouth, you stupid bitch, and I'll let go."

She kept her mouth shut. He pulled harder, and she hissed through clamped teeth. Harder still, and she succumbed to the blinding pain, opening her mouth and allowing him to pour in the liquid. Only when she started choking, did he stop and drop his canteen. He lessened, but didn't release, his hold on her hair, and she closed her eyes tight in refuge from the pain.

His hand moved over her breast. She twisted to no avail, and he reached inside the bodice and fondled her breast. She struck out with her foot, but he laughed, easily avoiding her kick.

"Not much more, you simple chit. Won't take much to sodden a slip of a girl like you."

"Who are you?" she whispered, her eyes still closed.

With a grunt, he removed the hand from her breast. "Time for your next drink."

She opened her eyes. Again she clamped her mouth shut, determined not to surrender. She couldn't let him get her drunk, though she wasn't sure what difference it would make. Before he increased his grip on her hair, she twisted violently and swung sideways. Bending her legs at the knees, she kicked out with both feet and hit him hard in the stomach.

He stumbled back with a grunt, releasing her hair. With a quick movement, he threw off the fur cape that shrouded him and revealed a hulk of a man, tall. Taller than Mathias or even André. A gray and ragged beard extended to his navel and his hair fell in tangled, greasy locks to his waist. He smiled malevolently, revealing a mouth full of yellowed teeth interspersed with gaping holes. His eyes, a bright blue, glared at her with what she believed to be pure hatred.

"Have it your way then, girl. I'll take you while you hang there. It's easy to do, I've done it before. I'll take you until you carry my child just like Julianna." He snickered. "Mathias can raise his brother."

Angelique's mind calmed. She already carried Mathias' child, and she almost told him so. But quick enough, she realized that would be a mistake. She had to protect her baby from this grisly being, and if, at some point in the future, his believing the baby was his would secure that protection, so be it.

He stepped toward her. Only then did she notice the heads of small animals, in varying degrees of decay, hung from a leather sling around his waist. He took another step. Recalling the filthy hand that had touched her breast, she recoiled in disgust. Nausea sat like a cannonball on her chest, and she started to shake. She could not endure this person touching her, much less entering her. Wriggling, she screamed hysterically and kicked out. Her movement jerked the rope. Pain drowned her terror, her scream the roar in her ears.

The smile of triumph disappeared from his ugly face, and he stopped his approach. She sucked in a breath at the reprieve and watched him cock his head to one side. Then she heard what he heard, the chorus of hunting dogs closing on their prey. Garnering all her strength, she threw her head back and screamed Mathias' name.

The man whirled like a trapped animal, then drew his blood-stained knife. Angelique cringed as he lunged for her. Whether he intended to cut her down and run with her or kill her out of meanness she didn't know, but she desired neither.

Heart pounding, but spirit heady with the prospect of rescue, she wrapped her fingers around the rope for support and kicked out stronger than before. Her foot hit him between the legs, forcing him back and down on one knee. He grasped his crotch before raising his strained visage and glaring at her. Whatever his initial intent might have been, she was sure now he meant to kill her. With a loud bellow, he surged to his feet.

Chapter Thirty-eight

The monster charged.

Her life was about to end and so was that of the baby she'd so recently begun to love and want. The one she saw in her mind's eye growing up inside De Leau's old walls. A little blond-haired boy with green.... *Mathias.* Sweet Jesus, she was never going to see him again. The shadow of her captor fell over her, and she clenched her jaw.

The man raised the knife—then twisted and stumbled away from her, knocked back by two dogs leaping for his throat.

He snarled before throwing one of the animals aside. Two more dogs tore through the brush, barking and howling, signaling their master they'd found their quarry. Horses' hooves pounded, and from behind her, an arm circled beneath her breasts and lifted her into a saddle. The scent of sandalwood drowned the stench of her abductor, and she felt Mathias reach above her to cut the rope that held her suspended. For a moment, he held her to him, and she turned as best she could and pressed her cheek against his chest.

Indigo entered the clearing, Jack Summerfield behind him. Pistol raised, Jack pointed it at the man struggling on the ground with the three remaining hounds. A dog yelped, cast aside by the repulsive giant who now struggled to his feet, bringing the remaining dogs with him. Still fighting the dogs, he slung his body around and lunged at Jack's mount. Jack fired, scattering the dogs and hitting the man in the shoulder, but doing little to slow the progress of the monster's attack.

Mathias freed Angelique's wrists, then slid her down the side of the horse to the ground, and he dismounted. She collapsed at Dan's feet and held her breath while Mathias tried to pull her kidnapper off Jack, now on foot. Finally, Mathias doubled his arms and bludgeoned the greasy head. At the same time, Jack kneed the man in the groin, forcing him to his knees.

Growling, the downed man placed his hand under Jack's chin and, with a heave, pushed him back and to the side, then twisted around to reach for the dropped knife. Angelique tensed, and the euphoria she'd experienced since her rescue evaporated when he seized the weapon and thrust awkwardly behind him. Angelique cried out, but Mathias, adeptly evading the flailing blade, slipped the rope he'd removed from her wrists around the bear-like neck and yanked back with a violent jerk.

His teeth clenched in a painful-looking grimace, Mathias tightened the rope, twisting and pulling in an obvious effort to strangle the life from the hated man. Angelique sat, transfixed, her body shaking. The monster pulled, almost tearing himself from Mathias' grasp. He failed, but managed to propel Mathias forward, almost toppling him. Mathias' hold lax, the man started up. With a shout, Mathias regained his grip on the rope at the same moment Jack charged, violently throwing his body atop the foul hulk to control the huge hands wielding the knife.

Beside them, Indigo raised a pistol butt and brought it down with brutal force on the monster's head.

"Mathias!" Jack yelled in his face. "Mathias!" Jack was trying to tear Mathias' hands away. "He's out. Stop, dammit, you're going to kill him."

Mathias wouldn't let go, grunting at the strain of pulling the rope and trying to fight off Jack.

"Indigo!" Jack cried, "get his hands."

Shakily, Angelique rose from the ground and took a step toward her frenzied husband. Of course they couldn't let Mathias kill him now.

Indigo wrapped his arms around Mathias's torso and with some difficulty pulled him away. Furiously, Mathias shook him off and straightened. He faced Jack head on. Jack didn't back down, but met Mathias toe to toe. "I want him dead even more than you, but there's still questions to be answered." Jack placed his hands on Mathias' biceps and pushed. "Back away."

"And what if I don't want those questions answered?"

Jack turned to his mount. "I don't care," he answered bitterly, "I do."

Before Mathias could follow, Indigo clamped a large hand on his shoulder. "You do, too, Mathias. Ain't no boy ever loved a woman more'n I loved Julianna Douglas. You can't ever know how bad I wanted to put shot through this bastard's brain instead of knockin' him in the head, but Jack is right."

Mathias drew in a long breath. Indigo's fingers squeezed his shoulder. Then he let go and turned away. Angelique watched her husband release that breath, resigned, it appeared. Deflated. She stepped closer and touched his arm. He whirled, and his gaze locked on her. Instantly, love and tenderness melted the hatred and anger in his eyes, and he reached out and clasped her to him.

"Are you all right?" he said, pushing her to arms' length. "What did he do to you?"

She felt her chin quiver, and he must have noticed because he stroked her cheek. "It's all right," he said, his voice strained, "no matter what happened, everything is all right."

Trying not to cry, she forced her trembling lips into a smile. "Nothing happened, you got here in time. You always come in time." She circled her arms around his waist and tilted her face up to his. "Everything is going to be all right, Mathias. That thing is not your father."

"He told you so?"

"No, but I know."

"Let's get this bastard home," Jack said, leading the horses to them. He handed Mathias Dan's lead.

Home. Angelique pushed away. "Mathias, did he kill Ethan?"

In the distance, De Leau stood shimmering in the afternoon sun. A shout sounded from the house, and Jacob bounded down the back steps, running across the fields as fast as his short legs would let him. "Miss Angel, Miss Angel," he cried over and over as he came, adeptly weaving through the rows of half-grown corn.

On the porch, a crowd gathered to welcome them home. Charlotte started walking toward them, but stopped and waited.

Angelique sat forward, twisting her head to look at Mathias. "Aunt Elizabeth is here."

"I see her."

She noted his apprehension by the set of his mouth. He dreaded what the next minutes would reveal. For her, she thought she'd guessed the truth, at least part of it. One person knew for sure, so Angelique opted to keep silent and listen to what her Aunt Elizabeth had to say.

Mathias caught her watching him, and he kissed her before returning his attention to De Leau. He was nervous, distracted, and scared, but only for a short while longer. For her wonderful, handsome husband, a lifetime of doubt was about to end, and his world would finally fall into place. And she held a place in that world.

She bid him stop so she could dismount and hug Jacob, who hugged her back with hungry arms and sweet kisses. After a moment the boy skipped on to his father, and Mathias bent down to lift her up once more in front of him. He kicked Dan into a lope. Jack and Indigo, leading the horse carrying their now conscious captive, followed on foot at a slower pace. The three surviving dogs limped alongside.

Moments later, Mathias helped her from the horse and set her down in front of Aunt Elizabeth. The dowager, looking old and tired, stepped close and hugged her. "Are you all right?"

Angelique nodded her head against the woman's shoulder. "Yes, Mathias came in time."

Elizabeth pushed her gently, and Angelique stepped back and watched her aunt transform into her former self. The woman looked at Mathias. "You have him?"

"Yes, Grandmother, we have him."

"He lives?"

"Yes."

"Has he told you anything?"

"No."

Elizabeth Boswell moved around in front of them and waited in strained silence for the others.

Chapter Thirty-nine

Jack stepped toward their prisoner, but Indigo proved faster, pulling the bound man unceremoniously from where he lay across the back of the horse and letting him fall to his back on the ground. Mathias stepped around Dan and, her heart pounding, Angelique moved up to be next to him. She took his hand, and he held to her, pulling her with him to Jack's side.

The grotesque prisoner twisted on the ground, struggling against his bonds, his labored breath interrupted with growls and curses. Jack started forward.

"Stay back, Jack," Elizabeth ordered, "I will deal with this." With that, she dismissed Jack and took another step toward the man on the ground. "Do you have your bindings free, Jarrod?"

Angelique felt movement beside her and turned to see Ben had moved up close. "Oh, my Lord," he said under his breath.

"Do you feel my hands on your throat yet, Elizabeth?"

"I never feared you, you hulking coward. You prey on those who are weaker and kinder. Those who cared for you. My mother no doubt rolls in her grave at this moment, knowing she gave birth to you."

"You took everything—"

"Robert and I gave you everything. We raised you as our own. You were hateful and spoiled and used the loss of the pig that sired you as your excuse to hurt those who would have loved you."

He snarled. "You did—"

"I did what had to be done. As young as you were, you still

295

knew what he was doing was wrong. Like him, you believed it was all right to hurt others if you were strong enough to do so. He was a bully and so are you."

"This place—"

"Was built by my father—"

"And *my* mother."

"Yes," she hissed, "and one day you would have gotten De Leau had you been the least bit interested in it. It took more effort to get work out of you than it did for Robert to do it himself."

"You drove me out," he spat at her.

"An error in judgment. I should have never let you leave here alive."

He smiled wickedly, continuing to work on his bindings. Nervous, Angelique watched him, terrified he'd free himself any moment. She glanced at her aunt, who stood steady, calmly observing the struggling man.

Still pulling at the ropes, Jarrod looked long and hard at Mathias. "But my seed got De Leau anyway, ain't that so, Elizabeth? And the only work I had to do was spend two months raping Julianna. Pleasurable work and so satisfying considering how you felt on that subject."

Angelique felt Mathias tense. Next to him, Jack moved.

"No, Jack Summerfield!" Elizabeth admonished, "she was *my* daughter." Her voice caught. "Robert's little darling."

Mathias reached out and placed a steadying hand on Jack's shoulder, and Angelique looked around Mathias to view the other man's hardened features. When she glanced up, she caught Mathias watching her with a confused look on his face.

Playing with something in her pocket, Elizabeth stepped closer to the man. "That is the one reason I am so glad you're not dead, Jarrod. For a long time, I thought you were. But since you aren't, I have the even greater pleasure of denying you that triumph as you enter hell."

Jarrod stilled and stared at her.

"The day you took her down at the pool, she'd gone to meet her lover, a young man I disapproved of, someone I thought would leave her once he knew she carried his child." Elizabeth smiled grimly. "Julianna was already pregnant before you ever placed a hand on her. Mathias is not your son. Now I'm going to send you to hell, where I should have sent you forty years ago."

With a sub-human growl, Jarrod freed the last of his bonds and lunged at Elizabeth. Indigo seized him around the throat, but Jarrod had torn himself away before Elizabeth's cries to let him go registered. From the pocket of her skirt she had pulled a pistol, which she fired the moment Jarrod turned to her. The pistol ball pierced his left eye. He stood staring at her a moment with one bright, blue eye. Then he fell face down with a thud.

For a moment, no one said, or did, anything, then Yo emerged from the crowd and walked to the fallen man. Elizabeth moved up close to her.

"Well," she said clearly to Yo, "are we in agreement he is finally dead?"

Yo didn't look at Elizabeth, but nudged the man with her foot. Then she leaned her ancient body forward and spat on the corpse.

"They'd be alive had I done what you wished," Elizabeth said.

Yo staightened. "Robert perhaps..." Then the old black woman turned with a perplexed expression and stared at Mathias. His hand tightened around Angelique's fingers.

"But I told you," Yo continued slowly, "Julianna's hips were too narrow. No matter who the father, she would have died in childbirth."

Aunt Elizabeth looked over her shoulder, following Yo's gaze. "If not for the abuse, she would have survived a caesarean."

"If we'd had the courage to risk it before she died. So many 'if's'." Yo dropped her scrutiny of Mathias and studied Elizabeth. "You always held yourself from him, despite his features. I thought you did so because he was Larocque's seed."

Despite the distance, Angelique saw her aunt's chin quiver.

"Now I know the reason was his very visage, not Larocque blood," Yo said.

"The one secret I managed to keep from you all these years, old witch."

*L*egs weak and his chest tight, Mathias watched his grandmother pocket the pistol and start his way. She stopped in front of him, then nodded toward the dead man.

"Your Granduncle Jarrod, Mathias. A filthy excuse for a human being, yes, a demon, no." Bess looked at Jack, and Mathias did, too. Tension strained between them, his grandmother and his friend, and for an instant he considered Jack might throttle her. Guarded, Bess turned back to Mathias, and he saw the subtle movement of her throat when she swallowed.

"Neither demon nor your sire," she said softly. "Your father stands beside you."

The first thing Mathias was aware of after that was his eyes stinging, and then he breathed. His grandmother's words had sucked the breath right out of him. *Jack. All the time it had been Jack.* His gaze darted to Jack, who was watching him now with an expression of awe and relief and hope all scrambled together so that Mathias wasn't sure what the man was thinking. Mathias couldn't think at all.

Bess laid her hand on his arm, and Mathias jerked his gaze back to her.

"He always has," she said, squeezing his arm. "Once, I didn't think he would. I was wrong, and I am sorry."

"Why didn't you tell me?" Jack asked with barely disguised harshness.

Bess, her face calm, looked at him. "I realized later you knew. But if I had confirmed it to you, you would have taken him from me and perhaps wandered away as frontiersmen often do. I wanted him. I promised Julianna I would take care of her babe."

"Damn you, Elizabeth," Jack forced out. He paused, and with a shake of his head, he looked away before swatting at a tear on his cheek. "You wouldn't even let me see her."

"I begged her to let me send for you. She'd lost her will to live. I thought having you would give her a reason to go on where

even your child could not. Each time you visited, I told her."
Bess choked back tears of her own, then moved over to stand in
front of the man she had spurned for her daughter. "She was
never well after he brought her back. She suffered from exposure
and vermin-bred disease and fever. I was terrified she wouldn't
survive until the baby came, but she was so determined her child,
your child, would live. Half the time she didn't even know who or
where she was. She didn't want you to see her like that."

His grandmother, looking haggard and tired, briefly closed
her eyes. "He had defiled and degraded her so badly she told me
she never wanted another man to touch her as long as she lived.
Under the circumstances, she didn't think you would believe the
baby was yours, so she made me promise not to burden you with
it. I broke that promise today, but I know she would agree it was
the right thing to do."

Jack opened his mouth to speak. No words came out, and he
turned his face to heaven. Mathias wanted to go to him, and he
had started to raise his hand, when Jack said, "I always suspected, but I didn't know for sure Mathias was mine." He looked
at Bess. "You thought I would have denied Julianna when she
told me about the baby?"

"At the time I did, but she was determined to tell you anyway.
Immediately after her disappearance, I suspected you'd killed
her, but I soon realized you were too distraught."

"I would have welcomed the child and my father would have
welcomed Julianna as a dau...." His voice gave way to a sob.
"She was so beautiful and had so much to live for, and I loved
her so. To have a thing like that"—he motioned toward Jarrod
Larocque's body—"intervene in our life together, sickens my
heart to this day."

Old Bess released a stuttered breath. "I know."

This time Mathias did reach out and touch Jack's arm, and
Jack turned to him. For a moment, neither did anything. Despite
his having known Jack his entire life, it was as if he'd just found
him, and perhaps this familiar, and loved man, was feeling the
same awkwardness. Then his father wrapped him in his arms and

hugged him, and Mathias hugged him back until he thought they would crack each other's bones.

Jack yielded first. His old bones must be more brittle, Mathias mused, almost giddy with his grandmother's revelation. He caught Bess' eye, and she gave him a sad smile, and he wondered what her thoughts were.

With his past resolved, he remembered his future and looked over his shoulder in search of Angelique. She was close behind him, her eyes glistening and a big smile on her face.

"I knew it was Jack," she whispered as he pulled her to him.

Bess stepped away from them and looked at the others gathered around her. "Jarrod killed Robert," she said to them all. "I knew he'd committed both crimes when Julianna was returned wearing her father's necklace."

Mathias felt Angelique's arm circle his waist and he draped his arm over her shoulder. "The lion's claws?" he asked.

Bess nodded. "Robert wore it before I ever met him. A gift from a Chickasaw chief whose son Robert saved from the original owner of those claws. The Chickasaw regarded that necklace as a badge of honor. Jarrod took it from his neck when he murdered him. The blanket had been part of Robert's tack also. Jarrod would have never gone near the Chickasaw, they'd have killed him for certain."

Quietly, Martha Summerfield walked up and joined her husband, and Jack drew her close.

Old Bess turned to Jarrod's body and with a weary sigh looked to the heavens. Appearing more tired than usual, Ben stepped forward.

"I'll take care of him, Miss Bessy. Tomorrow we'll put him in the family plot."

"Away from Mother, Ben. Put him next to his father. Someone else will have to read words over him, though. This time I simply cannot do it."

Yo ambled up to Bess and held out her hand. Without any indication of thought, his grandmother reached into her pocket and pulled out the enameled-cased timepiece. Holding it by its chain, she dropped it into Yo's palm. "Ben," she said, not taking her eyes off Yo, "put this with him."

Ben took the watch from Yo. "I will, and I'll speak the Christian words. Don't need no more demons here at De Leau."

Chapter Forty

"Why did he do it, Grandmother?"

It was late, the house empty but for him and his two women. They'd even returned Ethan to his own cabin at his request. The laceration had not damaged his internal organs, and after the doctor stitched up the gaping hole to prevent the intestines from falling out, he told Mathias he expected Ethan to fully recover.

The doctor also wrapped Bounty's arm, declaring it badly sprained, but not broken. He'd finished his day at De Leau by giving Angelique a thorough examination. Despite the abuse and the associated scrapes and bruises, she and the baby were fine.

Mathias turned his attention from his grandmother when Angelique walked into the room, bathed and fresh. Even with the bruise on her cheek and her wrists wrapped in dressings, she was still the most beautiful thing in the world. He motioned her to him, while his grandmother watched.

"God, Angelique," Bess said, "how you favor Véronique." Then, she focused on him. "And you, Grandson? Once you asked me who I saw when I looked at you." She gave him a tremulous smile. "You may be Jack Summerfield's son, but you are the image of your grandfather, Robert Douglas—the love of my life." She stepped back and sat heavily in the wing chair. "I loved him and Véronique so much." She took a sip of the sherry Mathias had poured her and looked around the room. "There's so much history in this house. So many loved ghosts"—she raised an eyebrow—"and some not so loved.

"De Leau will always be home to me." She rested her gaze on

302

them, together by the fireplace. "I'm pleased with my arrangement of you two for each other, and I am happier still you have this farm. The best for the best." She chuckled softly. "And the rest of my children do not even realize what I've done."

She coughed and looked away. "You ask why Jarrod did what he did, Mathias?"

"Yes."

"Fifty-one years ago today I walked with Yo from my first husband Charles' cabin two miles from here." She dismissed the place with a wave of her hand. "The house there is gone, and the land is now part of De Leau. But then Charles' farm neighbored my father's.

"I was seventeen and pregnant with my first. Yo had come for me. Mama was sick. Her pregnancy had been difficult, and she was having contractions. She wasn't due for another month." Bess looked away and speaking softly said, "I had a pistol in my right pocket, like today. I carried it for protection.

"When I entered the house, Mama was sleeping in the front bedroom, but I heard Véronique crying in the back...crying loud enough to be heard above the telltale sound of a man taking his pleasure from a woman.

"I walked into the room. The grunting bastard had not even bothered to close the door. Raping my little sister while our mother lay dying, trying to give birth to his child." Bess' face twisted. "He was a bear of a man, Jean Larocque. I always hated the fact mother married him, but she needed help with this place and raising her young daughters after Papa died. It was that or return to France and De Leau had meant so much to Papa." She shook her head. "Larocque was very different from him.

"He touched me once, long before, but I was not as shy and passive as Véronique. She was just fourteen, small like Angelique." Bess grimaced. "I pulled the pistol out of my pocket and shot him in the back of the head. Seven months later, Véronique gave birth to his still-born son.

"I would have never given Jean Larocque's murder a second thought, but when I turned, Jarrod was standing in the corner.

303

He'd seen everything, the rape and the murder. He was five years old. Three days later our mother died in childbirth, and I became his mother, but he never forgave me. That or he used what I had done as a reason to hate me. I don't know which, and I stopped caring years ago.

"By the time he was sixteen, he was so like his father in appearance and person I wished he'd leave. One day, Robert left to conduct business at a trading post north of here. He took Ben with him. They were to be gone a fortnight. Robert told Jarrod before he left to start laying up the tobacco in the drying house. After they left, Jarrod refused, and when I argued with him, he became violent. He hit me, more than once. I believe he would have killed me but for Yo's intervening. She shot him with Papa's old blunderbuss, glared at him a moment, cursed him, then took the spare long rifle from the wall and started loading. She said in front of him she was ending Jean Larocque's line. Evil devils she called them. She despised Jean for what he did to Véronique and Jarrod for what he'd almost done to me. She was, and still is, pragmatic when it comes to strength and survival.

"But he was my brother and my mother's only son. I couldn't do it, and I certainly couldn't leave Yo to do the dreadful deed. I also knew if Jarrod didn't leave, Robert would kill him when he got home. He was bleeding and could hardly move, and I was little better thanks to his beating, but I managed to stop Yo's killing him. My interference infuriated her."

Bess chuckled softly and looked him in the eye. "You think *I* possess the strength to do what has to be done? Let me tell you this, Grandson, every ounce of conviction I wield, she forged in me. She was much stronger than Mama. Sometimes, I think, even Papa, too, and when I failed to kill Jarrod that day, I failed the entire family."

Briefly, she shut her eyes. "So Yo and I patched him up and ran the bastard off."

"And he became Yo's vengeful demon."

Bess released a mirthless laugh. "Literally, it seems." After a moment, she frowned. "We pay for our mistakes, one way or

304

another. God knows I've paid for mine on earth. Yo has never forgiven me for not letting her kill him, and she has always maintained he was alive out there, watching and waiting. She would not let it rest. And she was right."

Mathias furrowed his brow. "And the watch?"

"It was Jean's. I gave it to Jarrod when he was twelve. He was never without it. It was on him when he left at sixteen. The bounty hunters I'd sent to find him after he brought Julianna back found it on a decomposed body south of the Cumberland River at the northern end of the Trace. The skull had been split open, probably by a Cherokee tomahawk they said, the body scalped. I have no doubt the men found a body, and they were honest with me by their estimates. That's why I was so certain he was dead. The hunters had dogged his heels for months. It is obvious now he planted the evidence on a dead man to mislead them. I was convinced he wouldn't willingly part with the watch, but Yo was not so easily fooled. She said he loved nothing and no one, including his father." Bess' lips twitched. "She also argued Indians would have taken the watch. I maintained they had no use for such things, but she was right. They would have used it to barter."

Without warning, his grandmother rose and folded Mathias in a warm embrace. He closed his eyes against threatening tears, but could do nothing to still the trembling in the arms, with which he returned her hug.

"From the moment I first held you in my arms, I have loved you, Grandson, more than you could ever know. The pain of loss hurts no less with the denial of love, though once I thought it might." She turned and hugged Angelique.

"You thought I sent you here to appease a ghost, child? Well, in that you were right. But the ghost you perceived was my sister, Véronique. I failed her miserably with Jude. He would have inherited De Leau upon my death. I promised Véronique on her deathbed. Instead, he ran from me. I wanted to make that failure up to her through you." She smiled and held Angelique at arm's length.

"I have fulfilled all my obligations now. The ghosts are gone, my confession made to the ones I most wanted never to know."

*T*hey lay naked in each other's arms. He'd have forgone the exquisite pleasure of their lovemaking given the day she'd endured, but she'd been too persistent. Cuddled close, spoon fashion, she snuggled her bottom to his manhood, and he groaned.

"Are you pleased with your papa?"

Mathias rolled his head and smiled in the darkness. "I'm almost as pleased with him as with my wife." He was silent a moment. "When did you realize Jack was my father?"

"When he stopped you from killing Jarrod today and told you he wanted answers. I knew then he loved your mother."

And lost her. An anvil settled over Mathias' heart, and he swallowed hard. "I need to make love to you again."

With a giggle, she rolled over. "Why?"

"To forget."

She reached out and touched him in the dark. "I'm sorry," she said, wrapping her arm around his neck when he sat up and drawing him over her.

"I don't think I could go on if I lost you," he said against her lips.

"I love you, Mathias." She brought his hand to her belly. "I know when the baby is due."

"How?"

"The doctor told me."

"When?" he asked, his tongue trailing down her neck to a breast.

She arched her back. "Christmas."

And he forgot everything but her.

If you enjoyed *The Devil's Bastard*, don't miss

Wolf Dawson

Ten years after the Confederate Army reported him killed in action, dirt-poor Jeff Dawson returns to Natchez, Mississippi, a wealthy man and purchases White Oak Glen, the once opulent home of the now impoverished Seatons, the aristocratic family that years ago shattered his own.

Burdened with her drunken brother Tucker and besieged by greedy relatives, Juliet Seaton struggles to hold on to what remains of her farm. Now she finds her family faced with a new menace in the form of a marauding wolf, which slaughters valuable stock and assails the mind of her alcoholic brother. Tucker Seaton warns his sister that the man occupying White Oak Glen is a ghost, who in the form of that vicious wolf seeks to destroy what is left of the Seatons.

An infant when events occurred setting her family against the Dawsons, Juliet appears pitted against a neighbor hell-bent on avenging his sister, who died in childbirth after being violated by a Seaton male. Jeff's grandfather was part Creek Indian. Local legend states he terrorized unfriendly neighbors with tales of his ability to shape-shift into a deadly wolf. Persons unknown lynched the colorful old man following the savage killing, apparently by a wolf, of the Seaton who raped Jeff Dawson's sister.

But Juliet finds the handsome Jeff every inch a living, breathing man. Hot-blooded to boot. His seductive touch weakens her resolve and blinds her to the danger he poses. Jeff, however, is no longer compelled to destroy the Seatons, if he ever was; they've destroyed themselves and left the vulnerable Juliet to his mercy—mercy he's quite willing to give, though he's not ready to let the feisty beauty know that.

Into this explosive mix of fear and distrust comes a sadistic killer, and what this fiend kills is not Seaton livestock.

With the countryside ablaze with suspicion directed toward Jeff, he and Juliet overcome mutual distrust and strip away a lost generation's hatred as quickly as the clothes covering their bodies. Old lies give way to new truths, lust to love, and together, the lovers set out to uncover not only a killer, but the identity of the spectral beast haunting the countryside.

You can find *Wolf Dawson* in bookstores or online at Amazon.com after 15 January 2007.

About the Author

Charlsie Russell is a retired United States Navy Commander turned author. She loves reading, she loves history, and she loves the South. She focuses her writing on historical romance set in her home state of Mississippi.

After seven years of rejection, she woke up one morning and decided she did not have enough years left on this planet to sit back and hope a New York publisher would one day take a risk on her novels. Thus resolved, she expanded her horizons into the publishing realm with the creation of Loblolly Writer's House.

In addition to writing and publishing, Ms. Russell is the mother and homemaker to five children and their father.

To learn more about Charlsie Russell and Loblolly Writer's House, visit www.loblollywritershouse.com.